Edward Marston was born and brought up in South Wales. A full-time writer for over forty years, he has worked in radio, film, television and theatre and is a former chairman of the Crime Writers' Association. Prolific and highly successful, he is equally at home writing children's books or literary criticism, plays or biographies.

edwardmarston.com

By Edward Marston

THE BOW STREET RIVALS SERIES

Shadow of the Hangman • Steps to the Gallows

THE RAILWAY DETECTIVE SERIES

The Railway Detective • The Excursion Train

The Railway Viaduct • The Iron Horse

Murder on the Brighton Express • The Silver Locomotive Mystery

Railway to the Grave • Blood on the Line

The Stationmaster's Farewell • Peril on the Royal Train

A Ticket to Oblivion • Timetable of Death • Signal for Vengeance

Inspector Colbeck's Casebook:

Thirteen Tales from the Railway Detective

The Railway Detective Omnibus:

The Railway Detective, The Excursion Train, The Railway Viaduct

THE CAPTAIN RAWSON SERIES

Soldier of Fortune • Drums of War • Fire and Sword

Under Siege • A Very Murdering Battle

THE RESTORATION SERIES

The King's Evil • The Amorous Nightingale • The Repentant Rake

The Frost Fair • The Parliament House • The Painted Lady

THE BRACEWELL MYSTERIES

The Queen's Head • The Merry Devils • The Trip to Jerusalem

The Nine Giants • The Mad Courtesan • The Silent Woman

The Roaring Boy • The Laughing Hangman • The Fair Maid of Bohemia

The Wanton Angel • The Devil's Apprentice • The Bawdy Basket

The Vagabond Clown • The Counterfeit Crank • The Malevolent Comedy

The Princess of Denmark

THE HOME FRONT DETECTIVE SERIES

A Bespoke Murder • Instrument of Slaughter

Five Dead Canaries • Deeds of Darkness • Dance of Death

Shadow of the Hangman

EDWARD MARSTON

SW 2/16				

Allison & Busby Limited
12 Fitzroy Mews
London W1T 6DW
allisonandbusby.com

First published in Great Britain by Allison & Busby in 2015.
This paperback edition published by Allison & Busby in 2016.

A CIP catalogue record for this book is available from
the British Library.

10 9 8 7 6 5 4 3 2 1

ISBN 978-0-7490-1686-9

Typeset in 11/16 pt Adobe Garamond Pro by
Allison & Busby Ltd.

The paper used for this Allison & Busby publication
has been produced from trees that have been legally sourced
from well-managed and credibly certified forests.

Printed and bound by
CPI Group (UK) Ltd, Croydon, CR0 4YY

With love and thanks
to my literary agent, Jane Conway-Gordon,
who liked the idea behind this book when I first pitched it to her
and who encouraged me to develop it with all guns blazing

CHAPTER ONE

1815

Ned Greet was a short, slight, wiry man with long, straggly hair and the face of a startled rabbit. He was also one of the most prolific and successful burglars in London. Confident that it would never be claimed, he'd watched with amusement as the reward for his capture increased steadily in value. Most criminals in his position would have decided to lie low for a while but Greet was not going to let anything interfere with his lucrative occupation. Risk excited him. It made his blood race. As he set off into the cloying darkness of the capital that night, therefore, he was tingling with anticipatory joy. His target was a warehouse, piled high with exotic spices. Even small quantities of them would fetch a high price. Before he tried to break into the building, he walked furtively around it to make sure that no night watchmen were on patrol. When he felt that it was safe to continue, Greet used a jemmy to prise open the window at the rear of the warehouse. Climbing in was the work of seconds. Once he was there, he lifted the shutter on his lantern and let its light spill out. Temptation was all around him.

Taking a deep breath, he inhaled a dizzying compound of aromas.

What he could smell was pure profit.

Opening the large leather bag slung over his shoulder, he took out a handful of small canvas ones and began to fill each of them in turn from a different sack. Peppercorn, cassia, cinnamon, turmeric, cardamom and other spices were carefully gathered then placed into the leather bag. Absorbed in his work, Greet moved swiftly and deftly, assessing the value of his haul as he went along. He was in his element. Greet was only aware that he had company when he heard a voice behind him.

'You won't need those in prison, Ned.'

The burglar swung round to face a tall, lean, well-dressed man in his thirties whose handsome features were illumined by the lantern. Apparently unarmed, the newcomer seemed completely at ease.

'Who're *you*?' demanded Greet.

'I'm the person who will have the supreme pleasure of collecting the reward money for your arrest,' said the other, raising his hat in a mock greeting. 'I could have apprehended you earlier, of course, but I'm a patient fellow so I waited until there was an appreciable sum on offer. Your career as a thief is decisively over, I'm afraid. You were too greedy, Ned, and that brought you to *my* attention.'

Greet was shocked. 'You've been *following* me?'

'Let's just say that I've been keeping a friendly eye on you.'

'But I always cover my tracks.'

'Watching you doing it has been a rare entertainment.'

Greet was cornered. He was shaken by the news that his escapades had been under scrutiny by someone else. He peered intently at the man. The stranger looked bigger and stronger than him so Greet judged that he would come off worse in a fight. Instead, therefore, he snatched the dagger from his belt and lunged. But the man was far too quick for him, shooting out a hand and squeezing Greet's wrist so hard that he let out a cry of pain and dropped the weapon on the floor. The man kicked it out of reach. Releasing his hold, he clicked his tongue disapprovingly.

'That was ill-advised, Ned. Try anything like that again,' he warned, 'and I'll be obliged to kill you, albeit with regret.'

Cowering before him and rubbing his wrist, Greet changed tack.

'There's enough here for both of us, sir,' he said, with an obsequious grin. 'You can take your pick. I'll help you fill the bags. Choose wisely and we can both get away with a small fortune. Spices are rich pickings.' He added with a gesture that took in the whole warehouse. 'I know where to get the very best price for them.'

'That's of no consequence,' said the man.

'Don't you *like* money?'

'Why, yes, I love it as much as anyone – but what I'd like even more is the satisfaction of seeing you behind bars in Newgate. You'll enjoy different odours there, I warrant – some of the most pungent engendered by your own miserable body.'

Greet was indignant. 'I don't belong in prison.'

'Then you shouldn't have taken up thievery.'

'I've a wife and family to support.'

'They must look elsewhere for sustenance.'

'Look,' said the other, panic setting in, 'I'll strike a bargain with you, sir. I'll steal nothing. I leave it all for you.'

'That's uncommonly generous of you,' said the man, laughing, 'but I spy a problem. These spices are not yours to give away so freely. Morally and legally, they belong to someone else.'

'They're yours for the taking.'

'The same is equally true of you.'

'No, no,' said Greet, holding up both palms as his companion took a step towards him. 'Consider this, sir. I can see by your appearance that you have an excellent tailor. Seize the spoils on offer here and you can buy a dozen new suits from him in the latest fashion.'

'I have apparel enough to content me.'

Greet was dismayed. 'Is there *nothing* that'll tempt you?'

'I seek only your arrest.'

'Then we must part as enemies.'

The burglar was like lightning this time. Thrusting a hand into an open sack, he grabbed a fistful of pepper and threw it straight into the man's eyes, blinding him momentarily. Greet took to his heels, darting off into the gloom in search of escape. When he came to a staircase, he ran up it as fast as he could. The sound of the burglar's feet clacking on the wooden steps told the stranger exactly where his quarry had gone. With the lantern in his hand, he set off in pursuit. Finding the staircase, he began to ascend it but he got only halfway up before he had a glimpse of a blurred figure ahead of him. Greet had a sack of flour over his shoulder and he hurled it directly at the man, catching him in the chest, knocking the lantern from his grasp and sending him tumbling backwards down the steps.

Having disabled his attacker, Greet elected to cut his losses and get out of the warehouse altogether. He blundered along the upper floor. When he reached the door through which goods were winched up from below, he flung it wide open and jumped into the darkness, landing with cat-like ease on the ground below. To his utter amazement, he heard a metallic click as the shutter of a lantern was lifted and a pool of light was created. Greet found himself staring at the person he thought he'd just knocked down the stairs.

'That's impossible!' he howled. 'You can't be in two places at once.'

The man beamed at him. 'It appears that I can, Ned.'

CHAPTER TWO

Gully Ackford handed over the money then recorded the amount in his ledger. He was a big, well-built man in his fifties with the weathered look of a veteran soldier. His craggy face wore its customary smile.

'That's your share of the reward, Peter,' he said. 'By right, you should have had more because you actually arrested Ned Greet.'

'It was my brother who flushed him out of the warehouse. If anyone deserves a larger slice, it ought to be Paul. He still has bruises from the encounter. But let's not haggle over the takings,' said Peter Skillen, pocketing his money. 'Greet's arrest was the work of a team. *You* found out where the wretch lived, Jem trailed him for us, then Paul and I stepped in to catch him in the act.'

'I've watched Greet for a long time. He's like so many of his breed – a Tyburn blossom, who was always going to end up as a gallows-bird. He'll be dancing a jig for the hangman before too long.'

Peter was sympathetic. 'I'd sooner the fellow were

transported, Gully. No man should have his neck stretched for stealing a piece of ginger and a few cloves.'

'I disagree,' said Ackford, firmly. 'You're too soft-hearted, Peter. Thieves are vermin. If they're not exterminated, they'll steal the clothes off our backs. Besides,' he went on, 'Greet was not there for tiny samples. According to Paul, the villain grabbed enough in his grasping hands to set himself up as a spice merchant.'

'His punishment will still be too great for the crime.'

'Robbing the warehouse was only the latest of his offences. Ned Greet has been the busiest thief in London. We'll be applauded for netting the rogue at last and a lot of his victims will be there to cheer at his execution.'

'Instead of blaming the burglar,' said Peter, wryly, 'they should instead chide themselves for failing to protect their property with sufficient care. If people wish to keep thievery at bay, vigilance must be constant.'

Peter Skillen was a mirror image of his twin brother, Paul. They were not simply identical in outward appearances, their facial expressions and habitual gestures were also interchangeable. Their voices were so similar in timbre and pitch that even Gully Ackford – who'd known them for many years – sometimes had difficulty telling one from the other. What set them apart were profound differences of character.

'What comes next?' asked Peter.

'Need you ask? What comes next is the joy of spending that money I've just given you. If you're short of ideas on how to do so, I daresay that Charlotte will provide some suggestions.'

Peter grinned. 'My wife has a gift for shopping tirelessly – even if it's to buy things of which we have no need whatsoever.'

'Then give her free rein. When that bounty is fully spent, there'll be plenty more to make our purses bulge. As our fame spreads, commissions will begin to flood in. Banks are always in search of our talents and there is unlimited work guarding the more fearful members of the aristocracy. We'll never starve, Peter.'

They were in one of the rooms at the rear of the shooting gallery owned by Ackford. Used by a variety of clients, it offered instruction in shooting, archery, fencing and boxing. Ackford was an expert in all four disciplines. Among his most regular customers were the twin brothers, who liked to keep their fighting skills in good repair in case they were needed. As a young soldier, Ackford had tasted defeat at the hands of American rebels at Yorktown. Against Napoleon's armies, by contrast, he'd savoured victory in a British uniform. Peter and Paul Skillen valued his experience. He was a demanding tutor and a man with a rasping authority when it was necessary to impose his will.

'What will your brother do with his share?' asked Ackford.

'I daresay that Paul will spend every penny at some gambling haunt.'

'What if he *wins* at cards for a change?'

'That's as likely as his finding the woman of his dreams.'

'But he already *has* found her. The trouble is that she married *you* instead.'

'Oh, I think he's outgrown that disappointment,' said Peter with a smile. 'When Charlotte was no longer available, he quickly discovered willing substitutes and has been working his way through them ever since. They change so fast that I can never remember their names.'

'Paul needs to settle down.'

'He has done so frequently, Gully – but never for very long.' They shared a laugh. 'Don't try to change my brother. That's beyond the capability of any man. It would be like telling the moon not to shine or stopping the flow of the Thames. Paul is a force of nature. He'll go his own way regardless.'

Paul Skillen looked through the front window in time to see a figure hurtling towards the house. He identified Jem Huckvale by his speed rather than by any physical features. Short, compact and holding on to his hat with one hand, Huckvale was known for his prowess as an athlete and his skill at weaving through a crowd at full pelt. He would never walk if he could trot, and he would never do that if he could run flat out. When he reached the house, he paused to catch his breath then rang the bell. A servant admitted him then showed him into the drawing room.

'Come in, Jem,' said Paul, embracing him warmly. 'I hope that you've brought what I am expecting.'

'I have, indeed,' replied the other, taking a fat purse from his coat pocket. 'Gully has divided the reward and I'm delivering your share.'

'Then you are doubly welcome.'

'He sends his regards.'

Receiving the purse from him, Paul tipped its contents onto a table and spread out the banknotes and sovereigns. He lifted a handful of coins and feasted his gaze on them before letting them cascade back down on to the pile. Huckvale, meanwhile, had removed his hat and stood waiting politely. As well as being Ackford's assistant at the shooting gallery, he was a trusted messenger with wings on his heels. Though he looked to be no more than fifteen, Huckvale was ten years older but the freshness of his face and his small physique disguised his true age.

'This will help me to pay off my debts,' said Paul, counting the money.' He looked up. 'Has Gully given you your share?'

'Yes, and it's far more than I deserve.'

'No modesty, Jem – you played your part as well as any of us. Once we'd found out where Ned Greet lived, you shadowed him for weeks. That was dangerous work and should be recognised with payment.'

'It's a privilege to serve you and Peter,' said Huckvale, admiringly. 'My needs are limited and my wages at the shooting gallery are more than enough for me. Being able to work alongside you and your brother is the real recompense.'

'Thank you.'

'There's always so much excitement.'

'Is that what you call it?' asked Paul with a hollow laugh. 'There's no excitement in being knocked down a flight of stairs by a bag of flour, I do assure you. It was a miracle that I came off with nothing worse than bruises.'

'We caught him, that's the main thing.'

'No, Jem, we made good money for doing so. That's what is really important.'

'Peter says that we're helping to cleanse the city of crime.'

Paul shrugged. 'If my brother wants to view it as a moral crusade, so be it. I take a more practical view. Every time we deliver a villain to the magistrates, we get paid for our efforts and that enables us to indulge ourselves. Peter, of course, has turned his back on the multiple pleasures of the capital but I intend to enjoy them to the full – and that costs money. Unbeknownst to him, Ned Greet has both cleared my debts and supplied me with the requisite funds for gambling anew.'

'Greet has other thing on his mind at the moment, Paul.'

'Yes, he's having nightmares about Tyburn!'

His harsh laughter echoed around the room. Like most people, Huckvale couldn't tell the twins apart simply by looking at them. It was only when they began to express a point of view that he saw how dissimilar they really were. Peter was calm, reasonable and compassionate. His brother, on the other hand, was a man of trenchant opinions, reckless, irresponsible and wayward in his private life. Huckvale was devoted to both of them but – without really understanding why – the one he really idolised was Paul Skillen.

'News of the arrest is in the newspapers,' he said.

Paul curled a lip. 'I make a point of not reading them.'

'It's a way of building our reputation.'

'That will please Gully.'

'It pleases everyone who wishes to uphold the law.'

'I can think of a notable exception, Jem.'

'Oh – who might that be, pray?'

'I'm talking about the man who's been hunting Ned Greet as long as we have.'

'Micah Yeomans?'

'He'll have seen the fellow as his legitimate prize. After all, Micah is a Bow Street Runner. He thinks that gives him a monopoly on justice. Our success will make him seethe,' said Paul with wicked satisfaction. 'Micah Yeomans will be livid when he realises that we are the best thief-catchers in England.'

* * *

'The scheming devils!' roared Yeomans, holding the newspaper with trembling hands. 'The Skillen brothers have had the gall to do our job for us. They've caught Ned Greet.' Scrunching up the newspaper, he flung it aside. 'Why didn't we get to him first?'

'We were too slow,' said Alfred Hale.

'I blame you for that.'

'I did my best.'

'Patently, it was woefully inadequate,' said Yeomans with withering scorn. 'We keep a whole army of informers. Why could none of them earn their money and tell us where Greet was hiding?'

'They *did* earn their money,' suggested Hale. 'Ned paid them more to keep their mouths shut than we paid them to keep their eyes open.'

'Then how did those loathsome twins manage to track him down?'

'That's a secret I'd love to know, Micah.'

'You failed me again, Alfred. You've no right to call yourself a Runner.'

'I strive to please.'

'Ha! There are times when your incompetence *disgusts* me.'

Hale was about to point out that Yeomans had been equally incompetent when he remembered what happened when he last challenged the senior man. It was safer to accept the rebuke and lower his head to his chest.

Nature had been unkind to Yeomans, giving him a face of unsurpassable ugliness with a misshapen nose competing for dominance against a pair of huge, angry green eyes, two monstrous bushy eyebrows and a long slit of a mouth from which a row of yellow teeth protruded. Even in repose he looked grotesque. When roused, as he was now, Yeomans was positively fearsome. A former blacksmith, he was a big, hulking man with powerful fists that were well known in the criminal fraternity. Hale was a solid man of medium height but he looked puny beside his companion. Both were in their forties with long, distinguished records as Principal Officers of Bow Street. They hated rivals.

'The Skillen brothers live off blood money,' said Yeomans, contemptuously.

'We've had our share of that in the past,' Hale reminded him.

'Hold your tongue!'

'It's true, Micah.'

'We have legal authority. They are floundering amateurs.'

'Then why do they always show us up by harvesting our crop?'

'They've trespassed on our land far too long,' said Yeomans through gritted teeth. 'It's time to teach them a lesson, Alfred. Nobody can steal from us with impunity, least of all that pair of popinjays.' His eyes blazed. 'I want revenge.'

CHAPTER THREE

'O'Gara is behind this,' said Shortland, bitterly.

'We don't even know if he's still in the prison, sir.'

'He's here, Lieutenant. I *feel* it.'

'Then why have we never seen him?'

'They're hiding him somewhere. O'Gara's been a confounded nuisance since he first arrived. He's always trying to stir them up to mutiny and it looks as if he's finally succeeded. We should have locked him in the Black Hole and left him to rot.'

'The men did have a legitimate grievance,' argued Reed. 'The food contractor delivered a consignment of damaged hard tack that was almost inedible.'

'That problem was solved yesterday,' said Shortland, curtly. 'Fresh bread was brought in. Unfortunately, it didn't satisfy this rabble. They're determined to cause trouble and it's being orchestrated by Tom O'Gara.'

'He's only one of thousands of prisoners, sir, so it's wrong to single him out. They all want the same thing. The war against the United States has ended. They're demanding release.'

'*We* run this prison, Lieutenant – not a mob of American sailors.'

They were viewing the situation with increasing disquiet. Hundreds of prisoners were milling around the yard. The sense of resentment was tangible. Voices were raised, fists were bunched, and more and more prisoners joined the melee. Captain Thomas Shortland of the Royal Navy had been governor of Dartmoor for less than two years and he hated the bleak, unforgiving, isolated prison. He was determined to exert control but the strict discipline he imposed had only served to create anger and vocal resistance. It seemed now as if a full-scale riot was about to break out.

A soldier came running breathlessly towards the governor.

'They're hacking a hole through to the barrack yard, sir!' he yelled.

'I was right,' decided Shortland. 'It *is* a plot.' He swung round to face Reed. 'Ring the alarm bell, Lieutenant. Rouse the whole garrison.'

'There's more to report,' gabbled the soldier as Reed rushed off. 'Someone has smashed a gate chain with an iron bar. Prisoners are flooding into the market square. They're ignoring all commands.'

'Then they'll have to be taught a lesson.'

Events moved swiftly. The alarm bell clanged and the soldiers grabbed their muskets before running out of the barrack yard. Bayonets fixed and lines formed, they faced the horde of jeering prisoners. Shortland first tried to persuade the crowd to return to their quarters but his voice went unheard in the pandemonium. He resorted instead to coercion and ordered a charge. Though hopelessly outnumbered, the soldiers surged across the yard, their gleaming bayonets driving many of the prisoners back. Those near the gate continued to taunt their guards who responded by firing a volley over their heads. Enraged by the tactic, the prisoners fought back with ferocity, throwing stones, lumps of turf and anything else they could lay their hands on.

Battle had been joined.

The next volley was aimed directly at the seething mass of prisoners, killing some outright and wounding many others. Retreating in panic, the men bumped into each other in a wild bid to escape. Muskets continued to fire and more victims fell to the ground. It was a massacre. The yard was soon covered with bodies and stained with blood. Eventually, the shooting stopped and the hospital surgeon was able to rush forwards to examine the wounded. There were over sixty of them, some with serious injuries. Seven prisoners were already dead. Forced and frightened back into their quarters, the rest of the men were howling in protest. The tumult was deafening and the sense of outrage was palpable.

Horrified by what he'd seen, Lieutenant Reed sought out the governor.

'There was no need to fire directly at them, sir,' he complained.

'They asked for it,' said Shortland, unrepentantly.

'We'll have even more trouble from them now.'

'They had to be reminded who was in charge, Lieutenant. We were up against an insurrection. Only force would quell it.'

'We killed unarmed prisoners.'

'It was done under severe provocation. This was an

organised revolt. It had to be stopped in its tracks. And – God willing – there might be a bonus for us.' Shortland smiled hopefully. 'One of the dead men may turn out to be Tom O'Gara.'

Henry Addington, 1st Viscount Sidmouth, studied the report with unease. As Home Secretary, he did not have direct control over prisons but, since he was responsible for public safety and was the ultimate authority on the regulation of foreigners, an account of the Dartmoor riot had been sent to him. When he finished reading the document, he summoned Bernard Grocott, one of his undersecretaries.

'There's been a mutiny at Dartmoor,' he said.

'Has it been suppressed?'

'Yes it has, but with dire consequences.' He handed the report over. 'See for yourself. It's dispiriting.'

Grocott nodded then read the document with a searching eye. The elegant calligraphy yielded up a grim story and he clicked his tongue in disapproval. He was a short, fleshy man in his forties with a mask of permanent anxiety etched into his face. His eyebrows raised in consternation.

'This is disturbing intelligence, my lord.'

'I'd like to know more detail.'

'There's detail enough for us to form a judgement.'

'That's my concern,' said Sidmouth. 'Any judgement would be premature. At the moment, we only have one side of the argument. Far be it for me to take up cudgels on behalf of American prisoners of war, but they must have had cause to rebel in the way that they apparently did.'

An image of George Washington popped up in the undersecretary's mind.

'Americans are seasoned in rebellion, as we know to our cost.'

'That's a valid point.'

'I'm tempted to say that it's in the nature of the beast.'

'There'll have to be a full investigation.'

'It's not the first trouble we've had in Dartmoor,' said Grocott, putting the report back on the desk. 'When thousands of French prisoners were held there, they were always voicing complaints even though all kinds of concessions had been granted to them. They ran their own courts, meted out punishments, were allowed to buy food from a prison market and had both a theatre and a gambling house to while away the time.'

'Gambling was at the root of many of the disturbances there,' said Sidmouth, 'and doubtless it still is. If men bet and lose their entire food rations, they are bound to become desperate. Then, of course, there's the prevalence of disease in that Godforsaken place on the moors. The mortality rate is shameful. Prisoners have tried to escape simply to stay alive.'

'That doesn't make mutiny acceptable, my lord.'

'Quite so, Grocott, quite so – but we have to allow for the fact that the men held there are under duress. French prisoners have money to soften the impact of the harsh conditions. The Americans, by and large, have none. They *suffer*.'

Now in his later fifties, Sidmouth was a tall, slim, dignified man worn down by the constant pressure of affairs of state. Three years as Prime Minister had been especially burdensome, winning him few friends and a legion of detractors. Yet he was a kind, tolerant, unfailingly courteous man with greater abilities than his enemies recognised. By instinct, he was also scrupulously fair and liked to weigh the evidence regarding a particular issue before reaching a conclusion.

'I'd like to know more about this business,' he said. 'The war with the United States is, blessedly, finally over. These men should not be fretting away their days behind prison walls. They should be sailing back home.'

'The Peace of Ghent has been ratified,' Grocott pointed out. 'What is holding them up is the lack of transport. The sooner they are shipped out, the sooner we shall stop having alarming reports from Dartmoor.'

'It's a place of unrelieved misery.'

His companion grimaced. 'It was ever thus, my lord.'

'What do you mean?'

'I mean that the Home Office is principally the recipient of unending bad news.' He struck a pose. 'After a long war, Britain is in a parlous state. We have a gigantic national debt, falling revenue, a disordered currency, chronic unemployment and whole sections of our population are on the brink of rebellion. Only yesterday, for instance, we heard of more violence in factories where new machinery has been installed and secret societies are being formed with the sole purpose of undermining the government. On whom are these problems dropped? It is always us.'

'You are right,' agreed Sidmouth, sadly. 'Almost all the troubles of the nation are dumped on us. I own that there are times when I feel that the Home Office is nothing but a glorified wastepaper basket into which every other department of government can throw its unwanted litter. We are truly beleaguered.' He sat back wearily, then remembered something.

'Talking of wastepaper baskets, I couldn't help noticing that mine has not been emptied today.'

'We've all suffered that inconvenience, my lord.'

'What happened to our necessary woman?'

'She appears to have been lax in her duties.'

'That's highly uncharacteristic of Horner. Someone must tax her. When one is the nation's largest wastepaper basket,' he went on with a rare attempt at humour, 'one does at least expect to be emptied on a daily basis.'

Tom O'Gara was still furious about what had happened at Dartmoor. When the soldiers had fired their first murderous volley, he'd seen defenceless comrades fall to the ground. Unlike most of the prisoners, O'Gara had not fled back to his quarters. He and his friend, Moses Dagg, had taken advantage of the confusion to climb a picket fence, find a hiding place behind the hospital and stay there until nightfall. Under cover of darkness, they'd made their way to the Military Walk – the gap between the high, concentric stone walls that encircled the prison – and bided their time until the sentries on the wooden platforms went past. They then clambered up the steps to the top of the perimeter wall. After dropping to the ground beyond, they'd run as if the hounds of hell were baying at their heels. The next couple of days were spent dodging the search parties who'd come out looking for them.

'They'll never get me back inside that place,' vowed O'Gara.

'Nor me,' said Dagg.

'It ought to be burnt to the ground – and Captain Shortland with it.'

'I'd enjoy dancing round the blaze.'

'So would I, Moses.'

O'Gara was a sturdy Irish-American in his late twenties with a mop of dark hair and a fringe beard. He'd rubbed his face, arms and hands liberally with dirt so that he could be concealed in the part of the prison where the black sailors had been segregated. One of them, Moses Dagg, had been his shipmate when their vessel was captured. Both had been kept in custody in Plymouth before being transferred to Dartmoor. Conditions had been so appalling there that O'Gara acted as a spokesman for the other prisoners, voicing his demands with such insistence that he aroused the ire of the governor. Instead of winning concessions, therefore, O'Gara was promptly sent off to the Black Hole, a punishment cell made entirely of stone blocks. There was no natural light and only a tiny grille for ventilation. O'Gara was forced to sleep on the bare floor. The sparse rations were poked in through an aperture in the reinforced metal door. Though the maximum sentence was ten days in the Black Hole, the vindictive governor kept him in there for a fortnight. Instead of breaking his spirit, however, all that Captain Shortland did was to strengthen O'Gara's will to resist.

'Someone should be told the truth,' said Dagg.

'They will be.'

'But who would listen to us?'

'We have to *make* them listen, Moses.'

'How do we do that?'

'First of all, we have to get well clear of Devon,' said O'Gara. 'We'll have to steal to eat here. The best place for food and protection is London. I've a cousin there who'll take us in.'

'He may take you in, Tom, but do *I* look like an Irishman?'

'Yes – I'll tell them you're a lad from Killarney who caught too much sun.'

Dagg shook with mirth and punched his friend playfully on the shoulder. Adversity had deepened the bonds between them. Dagg was a solid young man with bulging muscles and a ready grin. When O'Gara's persistent protests had aroused the governor's ire, he put himself in grave danger. He became Shortland's scapegoat and was blamed for every sign of unrest. Dagg had sheltered his friend in the segregated area and thereby saved his life.

'Well,' said Dagg, chuckling, 'if *you* can be a black man, then I can be an Irish leprechaun. How do we get to London, Tom?'

'We'll do what we know best.'

'And what's that?'

'We're sailors, aren't we?'

'Yes, we are.'

'Then let's get afloat. When we reach the coast, we'll steal a boat and plot a course to London. Once we have a refuge, we can tell the truth about Dartmoor.'

'Who will we speak to?'

'Well, it won't be the Transport Office,' said O'Gara, vehemently. 'They're supposed to look after prisoners of war but they answer to the British Admiralty and we've seen the way *they* treat us.'

'Yes, they put that monster, Shortland, in charge of Dartmoor.'

'We'd never get fair treatment from the Royal Navy so we'll have to go above their heads. We've got a tale to tell, Moses, and we must tell it loud and clear. The person who really needs to hear it is the Prime Minister himself.'

CHAPTER FOUR

After a busy morning teaching the noble art of self-defence to a couple of young blades, Gully Ackford adjourned to the room at the rear of the shooting gallery and sat down gratefully behind the desk. Within minutes there was a respectful tap on the door then it opened so that Jem Huckvale could usher a stranger into the room before slipping out again. The newcomer was a stout, pale-faced individual of middle years with an air of prosperity about him. He introduced himself as Everett Hobday.

'I need your help, Mr Ackford.'

'With respect, sir,' said Ackford, noting the man's paunch, 'you are not exactly built for the boxing ring. It would be folly on my part to attempt to persuade you otherwise. I take it, therefore, that you seek instruction of another kind.'

'I've come to engage the services of your detectives.'

'Ah, I see.'

'I read the newspaper report of their latest success and

decided that they are the men for me. I want the best and I'm prepared to pay accordingly.'

'How can we be of assistance to you?'

Hobday explained that he was leaving London the following day and was taking the servants to his country residence. The last time he did that, his town house in Mayfair had been burgled. He needed someone to look after it while he was away. His request was not unusual. Peter and Paul Skillen had acted as night watchmen before in some of the more opulent houses. The difference this time was that their payment would be unduly generous. Hobday was well spoken and plausible. As proof of his honesty, he offered an appreciable deposit.

'Then I gratefully accept it, sir,' said Ackford, taking the money. 'Though one question – I have to confess – does remain.'

'What is it?'

'Why not leave a servant at the house? It would be a much cheaper solution. A servant would know the property well, whereas my men do not.'

'I tried that once before,' said Hobday with a sigh, 'and it ended in disaster. The servant whom I left alone to guard the house was surprised by the burglars and given the beating of his life. I could never subject an employee of mine to that fate again. This is a task for experienced men like yours. Since they were trained by you, they will be proficient in the use of arms.'

'They are proficient in everything, I do assure you.'

'*That* is the very reason which brought me here.'

'How long will you be away, sir?'

'Four or five days – I'll send word of my return. Needless to say,' he added, 'if my home *is* broken into again, and if the rogues in question have a price on their heads, your detectives will be able to claim every penny of the reward.'

'You speak as if you *expect* a burglary.'

'Houses are watched carefully in Mayfair. Properties that are left empty and unprotected are fair game for thieves. What I am really paying for, you see, is peace of mind. I wish to be able to leave London without any tremors.'

'Then you shall, sir,' promised Ackford. 'All that we need is an address and a key to the property. As soon as you quit the house, my men will act as sentries.'

Hobday thanked him profusely. After handing over a latchkey and giving him the relevant details, he left the gallery with a smile of satisfaction.

Ackford immediately summoned Jem Huckvale.

'Follow the gentleman who just left,' he ordered.

'Where is he going?'

'He claims to have a house in Upper Brook Street.'

'Do you have doubts about that, Mr Ackford?'

'It's always wise to make certain that a client is telling the truth.'

'What's his name?'

'He says that it's Everett Hobday – find out if it really is.'

'I will.'

Turning on his heel, Jem Huckvale ran swiftly out into the street.

Viscount Sidmouth found the news so disturbing that he leapt up from his chair.

'Horner has *disappeared*?'

'Yes,' confirmed Grocott. 'The alarm was raised by her sister, a Mrs Esther Ricks. It seems that they were due to meet yesterday evening but Horner did not turn up. Her sister went straight to her house and was told by the landlady that she had not come back the previous night.'

'Well,' said Sidmouth, resuming his seat, 'that explains another day of rooms that were not cleaned and wastepaper baskets that were not emptied. It's all very mysterious. I cannot believe that Horner would desert her post without giving us prior warning. She's renowned for her dependability.'

'Might she have been taken ill, do you suppose?'

'That's idle speculation. The salient fact is that she is simply not here.' He scratched his chin. 'Well, it's taught us one thing.'

'What's that, my lord?'

'One never realises how necessary a necessary woman is until she vanishes.'

'I agree. I'm starting to feel bereft already.'

Sidmouth became businesslike. 'In the short term,' he said, 'Horner must be replaced. I will put that task in your capable hands.'

'Leave it with me.'

'There are eighteen of us employed in this building. Apart from ourselves and the permanent undersecretary, there's your fellow undersecretary, a chief clerk, four senior clerks and eight junior clerks. We all have our separate functions but I venture to suggest that our female colleague, Horner, is just as important as any of us.'

'I'd endorse that.'

'In having her to look after us, we've been thoroughly spoilt.'

'Where might she have gone?'

'It's a puzzle that must be solved without hesitation. I'll send word to the one man who will be able to track her down'

'And who might that be, my lord?'

'His name is Peter Skillen and I made great use of him as a spy behind enemy lines in France. Fortunately, he was fluent in the language, unlike some of the men I foolishly engaged. They paid with their lives. Now that the war is finally over – and Napoleon has been exiled – Skillen is working as a detective with his brother.'

'He sounds like the ideal man.'

'Your job is to find me the ideal woman, Grocott. I like the smell of polish when I come in here first thing in the morning. It's been sadly lacking.'

'Wherever you turn in this building, Horner's absence is evident.'

Grocott was about to leave when the Home Secretary called him back. Sidmouth snatched up a letter from his desk and brandished it in the air.

'As for that other matter we discussed,' he said, 'I've received a letter from Captain Shortland, the governor of Dartmoor.'

'What's its import?'

'Quite naturally, he's keen to speak up in his own defence.'

'Does he say how the riot began?'

'Oh, yes,' replied Sidmouth. 'The governor knows the person behind it. He's a troublemaker by the name of Thomas O'Gara, or so it appears. The fellow not only whipped the other prisoners into a frenzy of protest, he used the ensuing chaos as a means of escaping Dartmoor. Shortland discovered that

O'Gara had been hiding with a group of black prisoners, one of whom fled with him. They're still hunting the pair.'

'Can the whole episode be blamed on a single culprit?'

'No, and that's not what Shortland is doing. He freely admits that other factors need to be taken into account. Passions have been running high behind those walls for a considerable time.'

'What about the decision to open fire?'

'The governor argues that it was unavoidable.'

'How does he describe it?'

'In the same way that it will probably be described after the official inquiry,' said Sidmouth, solemnly. 'Captain Shortland insists that it was a case of justifiable homicide.'

When he left the shooting gallery, Hobday had climbed into the saddle of a bay mare and set off towards Leicester Square at a steady trot. Jem Huckvale was trailing him, close enough to keep him within sight but far enough behind to arouse no suspicion in the rider. Even when the horse was kicked into a canter, Huckvale kept pace with it, lengthening his stride and maintaining a good rhythm. Though the streets were filled with pedestrians, vendors, horse-drawn vehicles and other potential hazards, he was not hampered in any way. Huckvale glided around them all as if they were not there.

The rider zigzagged his way towards Mayfair and eventually reached Upper Brook Street. Stopping at a house on the corner, he dismounted and led the animal to the stable at the rear. Huckvale lurked in a doorway and watched from a distance. At length, the man reappeared and was let into the house through the front door. Since there was nobody else in the street,

Huckvale waited patiently. His vigil was finally rewarded. An elderly man emerged from a house several doors away. Huckvale ran across to him and raised his hat politely.

'Excuse me, sir,' he said, 'but I'm looking for Mr Hobday. I believe that he owns a house in Upper Brook Street. Do you happen to know which one it is?'

'Why, yes,' replied the man, pointing a finger. 'Hobday lives in that house on the corner.'

'Thank you for your help, sir.'

While the man went off in the opposite direction, Huckvale walked towards the house on the corner. Upper Brook Street extended from Grosvenor Square to Park Lane and contained some fine residences. Only a wealthy man could buy property there. Patently, Hobday was one of them. His identity had been confirmed and he lived in the address he'd specified. The mission was over. Huckvale felt that he'd discharged his duty and could run back to the shooting gallery with reassuring news that their new client was genuine. Before he could move, however, he heard the warning voice of Gully Ackford in his ear. It was loud and peremptory, Check everything *twice*.

It was an article of faith with his employer. Huckvale had to pay heed.

'Check everything *twice*.'

Ackford treated his assistant like a son but he could be ruthless when his orders were disobeyed. Huckvale had incurred his displeasure once before and it had been such a disagreeable experience that he had no wish to repeat it.

With a philosophical shrug, therefore, he resumed his vigil.

* * *

Peter Skillen was in the drawing room with his wife when the letter arrived. He recognised the seal at once and broke it to open to read the missive.

'It's from the Home Secretary.'

'He's not going to send you back to France again, is he?' asked Charlotte in mild alarm. 'He stole you away from me far too much when the war was on.'

'Absence makes the heart grow fonder, my love.'

'Mine didn't grow any fonder, Peter. It began to shrivel up with neglect.'

'This is nothing to do with my activities in France.'

'I'm relieved to hear it.'

'The Home Secretary wants me to find a woman for him.'

'Heavens!' exclaimed Charlotte, bringing a hand to her mouth. 'Does he expect you to become his pander? It's a revolting suggestion. Apart from anything else, he's a married man. What about his poor wife? This is a disgraceful commission, Peter. It's demeaning.' She stamped a foot for emphasis. 'However powerful he may be, I forbid you to provide him with a mistress.' Her husband laughed. 'It's not an occasion for levity.'

'Viscount Sidmouth is not searching for a mistress,' he said. 'I know him well and I can vouch for the marital harmony he enjoys. No, the woman for whom I must search is the servant who cleans the Home Office. She has inexplicably disappeared.'

'Oh, I see. I spoke too soon.'

Even when her face was puckered into an apology, Charlotte Skillen remained a beautiful young woman. Slim, shapely and of medium height, she had fair hair artfully arranged in curls. The colour of her morning dress matched her delicate complexion. Her husband kissed her gently on the forehead.

'It was my fault for phrasing the request in the way that I did.'

'You should still refuse this assignment.'

'On what grounds could I possibly do that?'

'Some paltry excuse will do for the Home Secretary,' she said, airily. 'The real reason you must turn his appeal down is that it's beneath you. It is, Peter,' she added before he could protest. 'You and Paul have just caught one of the worst criminals in the city. It was an achievement worthy of your talents. Viscount Sidmouth must have a host of minions at his beck and call. Let one of them chase after this missing cleaner.'

'Her name is Anne Horner.'

'I don't care what she is called.'

'Supposing that it had been Moll Rooke?'

Charlotte was taken aback. 'She's one of *our* servants.'

'How would you feel if Moll suddenly vanished into thin air? Would you stop me searching for her because it was too lowly a chore for me?'

'No – of course not!' she returned. 'What an absurd question! Moll is a dear woman who has served us faithfully since we were married. I'd not only urge you to find her, I'd join the hunt myself.'

'The Home Secretary obviously has equal regard for Mrs Horner. His letter talks of her loyalty and reliability. His fear is that something untoward has occurred. Not to put too fine a point on it, my love,' he went on, 'he *cares* for her safety and I find that admirable.'

She lowered her head. 'I am rightly chastised, Peter.' She looked up at him with a smile of apology. 'Do you forgive me?'

'There's nothing to forgive, Charlotte.'

'You must answer this summons. Will you ask Paul to help you?'

'No, my love,' he said, 'I fancy that I can handle this on my own. Besides, my brother will be too preoccupied. With money in his purse, he can't wait to spend it.'

The Theatre Royal in the Haymarket was packed to capacity that evening for a revival of Thomas Otway's tragedy, *Venice Preserv'd*. It was given a spirited performance by an excellent cast but few of the men in the audience noticed the finer points of the verse drama or the striking set designs and costumes. Their attention was fixed on the sublime actress who played the part of Belvidera, the daughter of a Venetian senator, caught up in political machinations over which she has no control and who dies broken-hearted at the end of the play. In the leading role, Hannah Granville wrung every ounce of pathos out of it and reduced many of the female spectators to tears. The men were equally captivated but it was her melodic voice, her lithe body, her exquisite loveliness and, above all else, her extraordinary vivacity that aroused their interest

The thunderous applause that greeted the curtain call went on for an age. Male spectators unaccompanied by wives or mistresses flocked to the stage door, ready to offer Hannah all kinds of blandishments. Because she kept them waiting, the expectation built until it almost reached bursting point. Then she appeared. Framed in the doorway, she distributed a broad smile among her admirers and lapped up their praise while pretending not to hear their competing propositions.

A man's voice suddenly rose above the hubbub.

'Stand aside, gentlemen! Miss Granville wishes to depart.'

The crowd swung round in surprise to see an elegant figure standing behind them with his hat raised in greeting. Feeling deprived and disappointed, the suitors moved reluctantly aside so that Hannah could sweep past them and receive a kiss from the newcomer. There was a collective gasp of envy.

Paul Skillen enjoyed his moment to the full before giving a dismissive wave to the throng. Then he offered his arm to the actress and spirited her off into the night.

CHAPTER FIVE

'Why didn't we head straight for Plymouth?' complained Moses Dagg.

'That would've been dangerous.'

'It's so much closer, Tom.'

'Yes, but it's also the first place they'd have gone. Soldiers on horseback can move much faster than we can on foot. They'll have warned all the ports to be on the lookout for us. That's why we had to find somewhere else.'

'I'm fed up with hiding for most of the time.'

'Then you shouldn't have been born with a black face,' said O'Gara, jocularly. 'It makes you stand out, Moses, so it's better if we move at night. Unlike me, you can't dive black into a pool and come out white.' He gave a throaty chuckle. 'After all those months cooped up, that swim we had was wonderful.'

Dagg nodded enthusiastically. 'We haven't had a treat like that for ages.'

'It helped to wash off the prison stink.'

Making their escape from Devon proved more difficult than they'd imagined. Dartmoor had deliberately been built in a remote part of moorland. The soil and the climate were unsuitable for growing crops so no extensive agriculture had developed there. Ice cold in the winter, it was also enveloped in thick blankets of fog that bewildered anyone foolish enough to travel across the bare landscape. The fugitives had the advantage of warmer weather and clearer skies but so did the mounted patrols sent out after them. Much of their days had therefore been spent concealed in various hiding places. When their food ran out, they were careful to take very little from the occasional farm. Had they stolen large quantities, the theft would have been noticed and reported. Hunger would have given their location away to those engaged in the manhunt and O'Gara knew that, if recaptured, he could expect no quarter from Captain Shortland. A reunion with the governor had to be avoided at all costs.

'When do we make our move, Tom?' asked Dagg.

'We'll wait another hour or so until they'll all have gone to bed.'

'It's dark enough now.'

'I'm taking no chances.'

'How long will it take us to get to London?'

'That depends on the weather,' said O'Gara. 'We'll hug the coast for safety.'

'It'll be good to be back at sea again.'

'That's where we belong, Moses.'

'I'd hate to be locked up again. We were like caged animals.'

'We'll be safe in London. They'll never find us there.'

They were crouched behind a hedge at the margin of a field. Having worked their way south-west, they'd found a hamlet on the coast. It was little more than a straggle of whitewashed cottages along a pebbled beach. Fewer than thirty souls lived there. When the fugitives first saw it in daylight, the sight of a couple of small boats lifted their spirits. If they could steal one, they could at last shake off the constant pursuit. While they bided their time, they took note of the tides and the jagged rocks they'd need to negotiate once afloat. A long, frustrating day had eventually yielded itself up to darkening shadows. The hamlet had gradually lost colour and definition.

Tom O'Gara was acting on instinct. When he felt that the time was ripe, he slapped his friend on the shoulder and they set off into the gloom. As they got closer to the shore, they found the aroma of the sea invigorating. A bracing wind tugged at their clothing. When it was harnessed, it could speed them away from the county. They crept warily past the little houses, reassured that no light showed in any of the windows. Reaching the boats, they dragged one of them slowly and carefully towards the water, thrilled when they felt the sea lapping at their ankles. They heaved on until the vessel began to float.

'We've done it, Moses,' said O'Gara, joyfully.

'They'll never catch us now.'

'Goodbye, Captain Shortland, you murderous bastard.'

'All aboard, Tom.'

With the boat now bobbing as each new wave rolled in, they climbed into it and felt the familiar sensation of the sea beneath them. They were just in time. Out of the darkness, a large, angry dog suddenly appeared, baring its teeth and barking furiously. Running into the water until the sand disappeared beneath its paws, it began to swim frantically towards them, as if intent on tearing them both apart. The animal gave them the impetus to hoist the sail at speed and catch the first full gust of wind. Before the dog could get within yards of it, the boat was being powered out to sea beyond its reach, as if pushed by a huge invisible hand. The last thing they heard were the plaintive howls of the dog and the outraged yells of the people who'd been roused by the barking and run out of their cottages to see what was happening. The shouting continued but the sailors ignored it. When the protests eventually faded away, they were replaced by the whistle of the wind, the flapping of the sail and the jib, the creak of the timber and the sound of the waves splashing against the hull.

They sailed on towards London.

Micah Yeomans handed over the money then raised his tankard in celebration.

'We've got them,' he said before taking a long swig of ale.

'I'll drink to that, Micah.'

Simon Medlow lifted his own tankard to his lips. The two men were seated in a quiet corner of the inn. They were beaming with pleasure.

'The trap has been baited,' said Medlow.

'You did well.'

'It was costly. I had to give a large deposit to Ackford. It was the only way to convince him that I was in earnest.'

'You've had ample recompense, Simon. There'll be more money when we finally catch the pair of them trespassing in Mayfair.'

'They'll argue that Hobday engaged them to look after the house but he's a hundred miles away. When he gets back, he'll depose that he's never seen or heard of the Skillen brothers before.'

'Meanwhile,' said Yeomans, 'the other Everett Hobday has gone back to being Simon Medlow and will have disappeared from sight altogether.' He took another sip of ale. 'I hope you asked for both of them.'

'I did, Micah. You'll nab Peter *and* Paul Skillen.'

'I've waited ages to put salt on their tails.'

'How many men will you bring?'

'I'll bring plenty,' said Yeomans. 'I know how slippery they can be.'

The Bow Street Runner was still sorely wounded by the way that the brothers had arrested Ned Greet and claimed the reward for his capture. Determined to strike back at them, he'd hatched a plot. Yeomans had been charged with the task of looking after Hobday's property in Upper Brook Street while the man and his servants were away in the country. He'd arranged for an old acquaintance, Simon Medlow, to impersonate Hobday and lure the Skillen brothers to the house. At a given signal during the night, Yeomans and his men would let themselves into the property and arrest Peter and Paul for trespass and attempted burglary. Medlow had been the ideal person to employ. He was a confidence trickster who owed the Runner a favour because the latter had turned a blind eye to his activities in the past. Medlow was not the only criminal with whom Yeomans had a mutually beneficial arrangement. In return for immunity from arrest, a number of them paid him a regular fee. Those who refused to do so had enjoyed no such indulgence from him and his colleagues. They were hunted down relentlessly until they were caught.

'Gully Ackford is a wily character,' said Yeomans. 'Only someone like you could have pulled the wool over his eyes.'

'He'll be implicated as well, of course.'

'That's the beauty of it. Ackford will have to appear in court and admit that he was taken in by the bogus Mr Hobday. It will be a humiliation for him. When word gets out that he and his detectives were so easily taken in, people will not be so keen to engage their services and the Runners will be cocks-of-the-walk again.'

'It's a clever ruse, Micah.'

Yeomans smirked. 'I swore that I'd get my revenge.'

Esther Ricks was a short, dark-haired, roly-poly woman in a plain dress that failed to conceal her spreading contours. She lived in a small terraced house off Oxford Street. When he called there that morning, Peter Skillen put her age at around forty and could see that she must have been an attractive woman when younger and slimmer. As soon as she heard that he'd been asked to investigate the disappearance of her sister, she was so pathetically grateful that she clutched his arm.

'Oh, do please find her, sir. Anne is very precious to me.'

'I'm sure that she is, Mrs Ricks.'

'We lost both of our parents and have no other family beyond each other. When Anne's husband died, we pressed her to come and live with us but she's very independent. She preferred to rent a room elsewhere. Anne said that she didn't want to impose on us. The truth of it is that she'd have felt too confined here.'

'Describe her for me,' said Peter, easing her gently away.

Given the invitation, Esther seized it with both hands, talking lovingly and at length about her younger sister. What emerged was a portrait of a hard-working woman in her thirties, turned out by the landlord on the death of her husband and forced to fend for herself. Though the menial job at the Home Office did not pay well, it gave Anne Horner an enormous sense of pride to be working, albeit in a lowly capacity, for the government. Dedicated to her role, she had never missed a day or been anything other than thorough in her duties. To the outsider, hers might seem a strange and very limited existence but it was – her sister argued – the one she chose and liked.

'That's why it's so *unusual*, Mr Skillen,' she said. 'Only something very serious could keep my sister away.'

'You say that she was in excellent health.'

'Yes, Anne was hardly ever ill. As a child, I was the family invalid, always catching some disease or other. Besides,' she went on, 'if she'd been sick or injured, she'd have sent word to the Home Office that she was unable to get there. Instead of that, she simply didn't report for work.'

'Did she have any special friends she may have visited?'

'No, no,' replied Esther, 'Anne kept herself to herself. She's always been a very private person.'

'What about enemies?' asked Peter.

'Anne didn't have any, Mr Skillen.'

'How can you be so certain?'

'She would have told me.'

'Yet, according to you, the pair of you met infrequently.

Your sister had a life that was quite separate from yours and it might contain all sorts of things and people about which you know little.'

'If she'd fallen out with someone,' Esther insisted, 'I'd have sensed it. If you're very close to someone, you don't need to see them every day to know how they're faring.'

'That's true,' conceded Peter, thinking of his brother.

'Anne just doesn't make enemies. She's such a friendly person.'

'Someone may have taken advantage of that friendliness.'

'Heaven forbid!'

Peter did his best to reassure her that her sister would be found but she remained in a state of quivering apprehension. While touched that the Home Office had procured the services of a detective to search for its humblest employee, Esther had persuaded herself that a terrible fate had befallen her sister. Something else worried her.

'If you do find Anne alive and well . . .'

'I'm confident of doing so, Mrs Ricks,' he told her.

'Will they take her job away from her?'

'Why on earth should they do that?'

'She's let them down, Mr Skillen.'

'That may be through no fault of hers. Mrs Horner will have been impeded in some way. The Home Office will surely take that into account.'

'How long will it take you to find her?'

'I can't put an exact time on it,' he said, cautiously. 'What I can promise is that I'll give the search for your sister the priority it deserves.'

Esther was simultaneously relieved and disturbed.

'What will happen until Anne returns?' she asked.

'I daresay that they'll have a temporary replacement.'

Bernard Grocott felt the absence of the necessary woman more than anyone at the Home Office. Most of his colleagues were apostles of order; punctilious men who left their desks impressively tidy at the end of the day. Grocott, on the other hand, always left papers scattered about or cupboards open, confident that the former would be stacked neatly and the latter firmly shut by the time he got there the following morning. Confidential documents were invariably locked away in drawers. It was routine paperwork that cluttered his office and made him utterly reliant on Anne Horner. Since her disappearance, his desk had been a complete mess that waited to accuse him at the start of each day. Finding someone to take over her duties was thus of prime importance to him, so he was delighted when a woman was recommended by an acquaintance.

'Have you done this kind of work before?'

'Yes, I have, sir.'

'And you know what's involved?'

'It was explained to me in full, sir.'

'When can you start?'

'Don't you wish to see my references, sir?' she asked, waving a sheaf of letters at him. 'I've had a lot of experience.'

'Someone has already spoken up on your behalf and his word is good enough for me. All that we have to decide is when you can take up your duties and what kind of remuneration you expect.'

'As to the first question, sir, I can start at once if you wish.'

Grocott let out an involuntary cry of joy. 'That's wonderful!'

'As to the second question, sir, I'll take the same wage as . . . the other woman. I'm sure it will be fair payment. I'm just glad to help you out, sir.' She looked across at his untidy desktop. 'I can see that I'm needed.'

'I am hopelessly inclined towards chaos,' he confessed.

The undersecretary could not believe his luck. He had expected to have some difficulty finding a new cleaner but he had soon stumbled on one serendipitously. While confiding his problem to a group of friends at his club, he was given the name of a possible candidate and interviewed the woman in question the next day. Ruth Levitt was older, plainer and altogether more submissive than Anne Horner. Significantly, she was eager to step into the breach. Grocott was not only delighted to engage her, he knew that he could expect congratulations from his colleagues. Viscount Sidmouth, in particular, would be pleased. In solving a thorny problem, Grocott would earn the Home Secretary's gratitude and admiration. They were factors that might one day ensure the undersecretary's promotion.

'What time would you like me to start, sir?' asked Ruth.

'As soon as we quit the building,' he replied. 'There's a lot to do, I fear.'

'I'm not afraid of hard work, sir.'

'Then I suggest that you start here in my office.'

She gave a pale smile. 'I was about to say the same thing, sir.'

When he called at her lodging, Peter Skillen was quick to realise that there were two Anne Horners. The woman's landlady described her in a way that was markedly at variance with the account given by Esther Ricks. Peter had been led to believe that the necessary woman spent most of her time alone in her rented room. Joan Claydon, the landlady, told a different story. To begin with, it transpired that Anne had disappeared for days before – though always after forewarning Joan. Where her lodger went, the landlady didn't know but she explained that Anne always fulfilled her duties at the Home Office during her periods away from the house.

'There is another thing, Mr Skillen,' added Joan.

'What was that?'

'She usually brought a small gift for me.'

'That was kind of her.'

'Anne is more of a friend than a lodger.'

'What of Mrs Ricks?' asked Peter.

'She and her sister hardly ever see each other.'

'That's not what I was told.'

'Then you was told wrong, sir,' said Joan, wagging a finger. 'Anne never really got on with her sister. When they were younger, Mrs Ricks used to bully her a lot. She was always trying to tell Anne what to do.'

'Is that why Mrs Horner refused to move in with her sister?'

'That was one of them.'

Joan Claydon was a large, expressive, motherly woman in her early fifties, surprisingly well groomed in view of her limited resources. As well as coping with two female lodgers in the modest dwelling, she had to nurse a sick husband and look after a medley of pet dogs and cats, yet she did it all without complaint. Even in repose, she seemed to be smiling and positively exuded amiability. Having met her sister, Peter could see why Anne Horner had chosen the companionship of the landlady before that of Esther Ricks. While the sister would have exerted a measure of control over Anne's life, Joan was much more understanding and tolerant. She simply wanted everyone under her roof to be contented.

'I suppose that I shouldn't say this, Mr Skillen,' she began, lowering her voice to impart a secret, 'but you might as well know the truth. When Mrs Ricks invited her sister to live there, it wasn't as a favour.'

'Why was that, Mrs Claydon?'

'She expected Anne to pay twice what I ask in rent.'

'Ah,' said Peter, 'so it wasn't simply a question of filial loyalty.'

Joan blinked. 'What does that mean, sir?'

'She wasn't merely acting out of sisterly love.'

'Oh, I think that dried up years ago.'

'Did anyone – apart from Mrs Ricks, that is – call here for Mrs Horner?'

'No, they didn't.'

'So you saw no sign of any . . . admirers?'

'I never pried into her private life, Mr Skillen. It's not my place to do that. On the other hand,' she said with a confiding glint, 'you were bound to wonder. I mean, Anne is still a lovely woman and she's kept her figure – not like Mrs Ricks, for instance. Men would look at her in a way they wouldn't look at her sister, if you follow me and I'm sure you do. But – hand on heart – I can't honestly tell you that any of them did more than look.'

After talking to her for several minutes to win her confidence,

Peter asked if he might see the missing woman's room. The landlady became very protective, saying that it would be wrong for anyone – especially a stranger – to conduct a search.

'It's something I'd never dream of doing myself,' she affirmed.

'My position is somewhat different, Mrs Claydon. My appointed task is to track down Mrs Horner and I need any assistance that I can get. It may be – and this is conjectural, of course – that there is something in her room that might give me a clue as to her whereabouts. Surely, you'd raise no objection if that clue led indirectly to her safe return.' He could see her resolve weakening. 'You're welcome to be present. I'll touch nothing that you feel is sacrosanct.'

Joan blinked again. 'That's another word I don't know, sir.'

'You can tell me where it's indelicate of me to look.'

There was a long pause, as she pursed her lips and weighed everything up in her mind.

'Are you married, Mr Skillen?' she asked at length.

'I'm very happily married, Mrs Claydon, so a lady's bedchamber is not exactly a novelty to me. I'll accord Mrs Horner's belongings the same respect that I show to those of my wife.'

Folding her arms, she studied him shrewdly. Reluctant to let anyone into rooms occupied by her lodgers, she saw that she might have to break her rule. Anne's safety was paramount and – if there was anything upstairs that might indicate where she'd gone – it ought to be available to the man searching for her. Having seen enough of Peter to gauge his sincerity, she capitulated.

'I'll show you where it is,' she said, 'but you'll have to be quiet. My husband will probably be asleep in the next room.'

'I'll tread carefully,' he promised.

She led him up the stairs, took him along the landing then opened the door of the front bedroom. Since it was the largest in the house, Peter could see that Anne Horner was the favoured lodger. As befitted a woman who worked as a cleaner, the place was spick and span. The few garments she owned were carefully hung in the wardrobe, the surface of the dressing table was glistening, the mirror shone and the whole room had a feeling of spotlessness. Snug and organised, it spoke of the quiet self-reliance of someone in straitened circumstances.

Peter felt slightly embarrassed to be intruding but necessity soon eclipsed his discomfort. Under the watchful eye of the landlady, he looked in the wardrobe and in the chest of drawers but found nothing of interest. When he lifted the cushion on the little armchair, all that appeared were a pile of out-of-date newspapers. Since Anne was highly unlikely to have bought them, he surmised that they'd been discarded by someone at the Home Office and rescued from the wastepaper basket. If she could read *The Times* and *The Morning Post*, then she obviously had an enquiring mind. What surprised Peter was that any of the clerks at the Home Office should be readers of the monthly periodical, *Lady's Magazine or Entertaining Companion for the Fair Sex*. Joan Claydon, too, was startled by the discovery that her lodger owned something so unlikely for a person of her means.

It was when Peter got down on his hands and knees that she raised a protest.

'There's no need to look under the bed, sir.'

'It will only take a second.'

'I can tell you what you'll find there.'

Before she could stop him, Peter lifted the valance and found himself staring at a mottled chamber pot. Tucked away behind it was a wooden box. He had to stretch an arm to retrieve it.

'Have you ever seen this before, Mrs Claydon?' he asked, getting up.

'No,' she replied, 'and I don't think I should be looking at it now. It belongs to Anne. We've no right to open it.'

'But it may contain letters or something else that could give the search for her some direction. I can't just leave a possible clue unexplored.'

It took time to persuade her, but eventually she consented. Peter lifted the lid and peered into the box. There were a couple of letters inside, written in a spidery hand by her late husband, but it was the rest of the contents that intrigued him. What they were both staring at was a small pile of banknotes.

He turned inquisitively to the landlady.

'How much do they pay her at the Home Office?' he wondered.

CHAPTER SIX

Whenever she stepped out onstage, Hannah Granville had an astonishing presence. It lifted her effortlessly above any of the other actors in the play. Offstage, however, she was a different person, subdued, languid and capricious. As she reclined on the bed in a flamboyant gown of Japanese silk, she snapped her fingers and pouted.

'I need you again tonight, Paul,' she said, peevishly.

'You shall have me at your command, my darling,' he assured her, 'but I'll be unable to meet you after the performance this evening.'

'Oh?'

'I have a commitment I must honour.'

'What about your commitment to *me*?'

'That's as deep and unswerving as it's been since we first met.'

'Then you must prove it. What kind of a gentleman leaves a lady at the mercy of that bellowing herd of suitors, some of whom are old enough to be my father?'

Paul laughed. 'You love every moment of their attentions, Hannah. Indeed, you float upon it like a bird on the wing. Adoration is your natural habitat.'

'Then why do you not lavish it upon me?'

'I will do so when I return.'

'From *where*?' she snapped, petulantly. 'Or should it be from *whom*?' Her voice became a growl. 'I'll not take second place to another woman.'

'None could hold a candle to you,' he said, caressing her thigh as he sat on the bed. 'All women are invisible beside you. It was the first thing I noticed at the theatre. You were the unrivalled cynosure. I couldn't take my eyes off you.'

'Yet you will happily do so this evening.'

'I do it with the utmost reluctance, my darling. And once my business has been discharged, I will get here as soon as is humanly possible.'

'How do you know I will let you in?'

'Keep me outside and I'll howl like a dog all night. Is that what you would prefer?' he teased, nestling against her. 'Would you rather have me out there in the dark or in here beside you?'

She allowed him to kiss her hand. 'I'll think about it.'

They were in the house that had been rented for her during the period when she was engaged to perform at the theatre. Hannah Granville had conquered London. Audiences had been overwhelmed by her beauty and by the irresistible talent that accompanied it. Those who'd seen her shine as Belvidera realised that any of the great female roles were within her scope. She was seen as having taken up the mantle that Sarah Siddons had put aside a few years earlier and was expected to enjoy an equally illustrious career. Paul Skillen was no mean actor himself and he'd employed his talents judiciously. Having contrived an introduction to her, he'd used his charm to secure Hannah's interest, his declaration of love to bring her within reach and his patent virility to excite her. There was also a sense of danger about him that none of her other admirers could offer.

'Where are you going this evening?' she demanded.

'I told you – I have duties to perform.'

'What kind of duties?'

He waved a hand. 'It doesn't matter.'

'It does to me, Paul. I want to know where you're going and who you are intending to see in place of me.'

'It's not in place of you, Hannah. Work, however, must come before pleasure.'

'What sort of work?'

'We have to protect a property in Mayfair.'

'We?' she echoed, sitting up. 'Who is this "we" you talk about?'

'I was referring to my brother and myself.'

'You never told me that you had a brother.'

'Well, I do,' he said. 'His name is Peter.'

'Am I to meet him?'

'There's no need for that.'

'Why not – are you ashamed of me? Are you afraid that your brother will look askance at me?'

He grinned. 'No man would ever look askance at *you*, Hannah.'

'What sort of a person is Peter?'

'He's very similar to me in some ways and the complete

opposite in others. On balance, I'm not at all sure that you'd like my brother.'

'Is he handsome?'

'Peter's as handsome as me, certainly.'

'Is he tall, manly and courteous?'

'He's all of those things, my love.'

'Then I should meet him. He sounds like a paragon of virtue.'

'That's his weakness,' said Paul with a smile. 'He's brimming with virtue. It glows inside him. He'd never meet your requirements, my darling. For a lady like you, he has one glaring defect.'

'And what's that?'

'He's irrecoverably married.'

Charlotte Skillen had seen her husband leave on a number of perilous assignments and, even though he'd always returned safely, she'd never learnt to control her fears. In the course of his work, he'd picked up a succession of cuts, gashes, bruises, grazes, sprains, dislocations and black eyes, as well as a few more serious wounds. Charlotte worried that he and his brother took unnecessary risks. Sooner or later, she felt, one or both of them would be killed. As she saw him off, she put her arms around him.

'You will be careful this evening, won't you?' she implored.

'I'm always careful.'

'That's not true, Peter. You have a rash streak in you sometimes.'

He laughed. 'I think you're confusing me with Paul.'

'I'm the one person who'd *never* make that mistake.'

'Take that worried look off your face,' he said, pulling her close. 'We'll be in no jeopardy this time. I won't even need to go armed.'

'All I want is for my husband to come home to me in one piece.'

'I can guarantee it.' He planted a kiss on her lips before detaching himself from the embrace. 'To be quite frank, what happens this evening concerns me far less than the inquiry in which I'm also engaged. It's very puzzling. A woman who is content to do all the drudgery at the Home Office unaccountably disappears. Where on earth can she be?'

'There's one obvious explanation, Peter.'

'I've discounted that one.'

'Well, I haven't,' she said, seriously. 'Mrs Horner does much of her work at night then has to walk home unattended. London is full of hazards during the day. You, of all people, know how much worse it is after dark. Trouble lurks at every corner. Evidently, the poor woman has fallen prey to a footpad or been assaulted by some drunkard. I'd wager money on it.'

'Then you must brace yourself to lose it, my sweet.'

'Why do you say that?'

'Mrs Horner has been doing this job for years,' he pointed out. 'That means she's well acquainted with the dangers that abound at night. She *knows* them and has obviously learnt to avoid them. Her landlady told me that she was no shrinking violet. Anyone who tried to harass her would get a raw reception.'

'What can a woman do when face-to-face with a desperate villain?'

'She can do what *you* did, Charlotte – and marry him.'

She burst into laughter then followed him into the hall. When she had been wooed simultaneously by both brothers, it had been a strange and heady experience for a young woman. Yet it did not take her long to make her choice. Paul Skillen was exhilarating company but it was Peter who had the qualities and attitudes she sought in a husband. Charlotte had never regretted the decision she'd made.

'I'm looking forward to meeting the mysterious Mrs Horner,' he said.

'Instinct tells me that she's already dead.'

'Then why has her body not been found?'

'Perhaps she was killed beside the river then thrown into it.'

'Corpses never stay beneath the water indefinitely. If she were hurled into the Thames, she'd have bobbed back up to the surface by now. No, she's very much alive and I fancy that her disappearance is linked in some way to that money I discovered at her lodging. How could a woman of slender means come by such an amount?'

'She might have inherited it.'

'From whom?' he asked. 'According to her sister, she had no wealthy relatives and her husband was in debt when he died.'

'Then I have no idea how she acquired that little treasure trove,' she admitted. 'What about you, Peter?'

'Oh, I can envisage three ways in which the money made its way to that box under the bed. The problem is that none of them reflects well on the character of Anne Horner.' He heard the clock strike the hour. 'I must away, my love.' He kissed her before moving towards the front door. 'Other business calls me now. The missing woman will have to take her turn in the queue.'

* * *

For a big man, Micah Yeomans had an amazing ability to shrink into insignificance in the dark. He could somehow melt into a doorway or ooze behind a pillar. The only way that Alfred Hale could detect his whereabouts was by looking for the faint glow of his pipe. When he reached the Runner, he was given a grunt of welcome.

'Well?'

'They're both inside, Micah.'

'Are you certain it was Peter *and* Paul?'

'Yes,' said Hale, 'but don't ask me which is which. They're like two peas in a pod. All I know is that Paul is the worse of the pair.'

'Peter's the more cunning. He does the thinking for them.'

'It's a pity we haven't got Gully Ackford in there as well.'

'Don't worry – he'll be hauled before the magistrate to speak his piece.' After drawing on his pipe for the last time, he tapped out the ash on the bottom of his boot. 'We've set this up well, Alfred. They'll think they're alone in the house when, all the time, Simon Medlow is tucked away up in the attic. He'll give the signal for us to move in and arrest them.' He spat into the road. 'Is everyone ready?'

'I've put men at either end of the street and others have been stationed in the adjoining streets. Quite honestly, Micah, we've got far too many people. When all is said and done,' said Hale, 'there are only two Skillens.'

'Yes, but they're like bars of soap. Just when you think you've caught one of them, he slips out of your fingers.'

'Who will actually make the arrest?'

Yeomans inflated his chest. '*I* will. The snare is all my doing. I want to see them straining to escape from it.'

'What if they suspect a trap?'

'If that were the case, they wouldn't have gone so readily into Mr Hobday's house. Have no fear, Alfred. They take their orders from Ackford and he was well and truly gulled by Medlow. So were a lot of other people, mind you,' he added with a chuckle. 'Did you know that Medlow once persuaded a wealthy simpleton to buy the River Thames?' Hale cackled. 'Then there was the time when he sold tickets to a banquet in Brighton Pavilion hosted by His Royal Highness, the Prince Regent. Those stupid enough to buy them – and there were more than a few – had a nasty shock when they turned up. Simon Medlow is a silver-tongued wizard. He cast his spell on Ackford.'

'He's a brave man to stay alone in the house with the two brothers.'

'He's perfectly safe,' said Yeomans. '*We* know he's there but they don't.'

'It's just as well.'

There was a long wait ahead of them. While Yeomans refilled and lit his pipe, Hale slipped off into a corner to urinate against a wall. He then walked around the entire area and checked that the men they'd recruited from the foot patrol were in position. Many of them were restive, wondering how long they'd have to hang about in the dark. When he suggested that they took their complaints directly to Yeomans, however, they fell silent. Nobody had the courage to tackle him.

A couple of hours drifted past before the lights in the windows of Hobday's house were snuffed out. The brothers had clearly retired to bed. It was only a matter of time before a candle would appear in the attic window to confirm that Peter and Paul Skillen were asleep. Yeomans and Hale moved in and those at either end of Upper Brook Street instinctively did the same. The net tightened inexorably.

The delay, however, was longer than they'd anticipated.

'Why doesn't Medlow give the signal?' asked Yeomans, impatiently.

'Perhaps he's trying to sell them tickets to a banquet in Brighton Pavilion,' said Hale, collecting a contemptuous glare that made him apologise at once. 'I'm sorry, Micah.'

'Shut up!'

'It was only a joke.'

'Can you hear me laughing?'

'I'm just trying to kill time,' bleated Hale.

He gasped in pain as he was elbowed in the ribs. Yeomans was watching the attic window without blinking an eyelid. When the light finally appeared, he led the charge towards the house. Using a key to open the door, he went furtively inside with Hale at his heels. A cluster of men guarded the exit. Yeomans lifted the shutter on his lantern and created a pool of light. It enabled him and his companion to search the whole of the ground floor. Confident that their quarry were slumbering upstairs, they ascended the steps as quietly as they could and went from bedroom to bedroom, opening each door wide in the hope of finding the two brothers.

But there wasn't the slightest hint that they'd even been inside the property. Something had gone wrong and Yeomans was quick to apportion blame. He rounded on Hale and hissed a demand at him.

'Are you *sure* they were here, Alfred?'

'I'd swear it on the Good Book.'

'Did you recognise the two of them?'

'Yes, Micah – they were as large as life and no more than twenty yards away.'

'That's too far in the dark.'

'I know their gait as well as my own. Peter is bolt upright when he marches along. Paul is more leisurely and has a shorter stride.' He removed his hat to scratch his head. 'Or maybe it's the other way round.'

'Be quiet.'

'It was *them*, Micah. I'm certain of it.'

'Hold your tongue, man,' said Yeomans, grabbing him by the throat. 'Just listen, will you?'

'What am I supposed to hear?' croaked Hale.

'*Listen!*'

Cocking their heads, they strained their ears. The noise was faint but insistent. It was a regular knocking sound and they soon guessed that it came from above. Charging out of the bedroom, they rushed along a corridor to the staircase that led to the attic. With Hale in his wake, Yeomans thundered up it with the lantern held high. When he turned the knob, he pushed the door wide open and shuddered at the sight that greeted them. Simon Medlow had been stripped naked then bound and gagged before being strung up naked by his feet to a thick beam. By swinging to and fro, he'd been able to hit a table with his head and summon help.

'Where in the world *are* they?' yelled Yeomans, puce with rage.

'They won't get far, Micah,' said Hale. 'We've got the place surrounded.'

But another fifty men would not have been enough to catch Peter and Paul Skillen. Having escaped over the roofs of the adjacent houses, they'd already climbed down to the ground and were calmly making their way back to those awaiting them.

Fortune favoured the sailors. Though much smaller than the vessels to which they were accustomed, it was well built and scudded through the waves. A stiff breeze helped them to maintain good speed, so they were able to watch the shore move steadily past them. Moses Dagg was concerned.

'You said we'd complain to the Prime Minister, didn't you?'

'That's right.'

'We don't even know his name.'

'I do,' said Tom O'Gara. 'I asked one of the soldiers. It's Lord Liverpool.'

'Why should a lord bother with a couple of escaped prisoners?'

'We haven't really escaped, Moses. As soon as the peace treaty was signed, it was our right to be released. They shouldn't have kept us in Dartmoor. It's a point we'll make when we write to Lord Liverpool.'

'I think we'll just be pissing in the wind.'

'Well, we've done enough of that in our time,' said O'Gara with a laugh. 'Trust me. The British have got their faults – and lots of them – but they believe in justice. That's all we're asking for. We may be free but all of our friends are still there, being punished by Captain Shortland and his men. The governor is cruel. He enjoys throwing prisoners in the Black Hole. I should know – I was one of them.'

'Jake Hendrick was another. He went mad when they locked him away in the dark for a couple of weeks. When they let him out, he was still screaming.'

'I walked out of there with a smile on my face,' boasted O'Gara. 'I wasn't going to let the governor think he'd hurt me.'

Having sailed throughout the first night, they'd kept going until they came in sight of the Isle of Wight. Since they hadn't eaten for over twenty-four hours, they looked for somewhere to land. A deserted cove allowed them to slip unseen ashore and to haul their craft onto the beach. They then climbed a rock face and took their bearings. There was a farmstead in the distance. After waiting until light began to fade, they approached stealthily and watched until their chance came. While O'Gara stole food from the kitchen with practised deftness, Dagg grabbed a bucket of water that stood beside the pump. They went hundreds of yards before they dared to fill their bellies and slake their thirst. Keeping some of the stolen rations, they made their way back to the boat and set sail once more.

Fate was less kind to them on their second night. Without warning, the wind dropped so they were forced to float for much of the time. More worryingly, dark clouds obscured the moon and stars so that they had no idea where they were or in what direction they were moving. When the wind suddenly freshened, it brought driving rain at its back and the two combined to create a storm of gathering ferocity. During their years in the navy, O'Gara and Dagg had weathered many a tempest but only in a frigate with a trained crew to battle the elements. This was a much more threatening experience altogether. Buffeted by the wind, lashed by the rain and tossed helplessly up and down by the heavy swell, they were effectively sailing blind. Neither man had the slightest idea that another vessel was bearing down on them in the inky darkness. One moment, the sailors were bravely coping with their multiple problems; the next, they were struck by something large and powerful enough to smash their boat in two.

Flung into the sea, O'Gara and Dagg were soon swimming for their lives.

They gathered at the shooting gallery to discuss the events of the previous night. When Peter Skillen explained what had happened, Gully Ackford and Jem Huckvale shook with mirth as they envisaged Medlow dangling from a beam. Charlotte, however, was less amused by the account of her husband's nocturnal exploits. She had already heard one version of it and repetition did not impress her any the more.

'You're courting danger if you take on the Bow Street Runners.'

'It was they who set up the encounter,' said Ackford. 'They sent someone here in the guise of Everett Hobday to draw Peter and Paul into that house. I had the sense to let Jem trail the impostor back to Mayfair. As it happened, the property was indeed owned by the man whose name I was given.'

'That contented me at first,' explained Huckvale, taking over, 'but I thought it best to be doubly sure. When I spoke to a second neighbour, I learnt from him that Hobday was an old man who suffered badly from gout.'

'We soon got Medlow's real name out of him,' recalled Peter. 'When you're trussed up like a turkey and hanging by your feet, you have an incentive to answer questions honestly. Before we gagged him, Simon Medlow revealed the full dimensions of the plot and enabled us to turn the tables on Micah Yeomans.'

'Bravo!' cried Ackford, slapping the desk for emphasis.

'I raise my hat to Peter and Paul!' said Jem, whipping it off his head.

'I see no cause for congratulation,' said Charlotte. 'Peter and his brother committed a crime. What will happen if this Simon Medlow sues them for assault?'

'He would first have to answer for his own crimes, Charlotte,' said Ackford, 'and there are plenty of those. In committing the latest, he posed as Hobday and entered the man's house when he had no legal right to do so. I don't think he'd *dare* recount the circumstances that led to him being given the treatment he deserved.'

'And you must consider the position of Micah Yeomans,' added Peter. 'He was the author of the conspiracy. Do you imagine for a moment that he will want anyone to know that he gave Medlow, a known swindler, two keys to the property entrusted to him by the real Mr Hobday? If it came out that Yeomans had employed a wanted man to dupe us, it would not only damage his reputation, it might well cost him his position as a Runner. In short,' he went on, 'Paul and I are in the clear.'

'More to the point,' said Ackford, holding up a purse, 'we made a profit on last night's entertainment. This was the deposit given in return for our services.' His grin broadened. 'I doubt that Yeomans will think it money well-spent.'

'He won't have the gall to ask for it back,' said Huckvale.

'No, Jem, to do that he'd have to admit that he was behind the ruse.'

'Micah Yeomans will never admit anything,' warned Peter, 'but secretly he must be fuming. He invested several pounds and all he got in return was a naked scoundrel, named Simon Medlow, whom we'll arrest the next time we clap eyes on him.'

The three men laughed afresh at the Runner's humiliation. Once again, it was Charlotte who offered a more detached appraisal of the situation.

'Two things alarm me about last night's escapade,' she said, 'so I'm unable to find any humour in it. First, we must remember that Peter and Paul escaped by clambering over the roofs of the other houses. Think how easy it would have been for one of them to fall to his death. It would have been far more sensible to stay away from that house altogether and leave them to realise that their wicked little scheme had been foiled.'

'We needed to make that point more forcefully,' said Peter.

'Did you need to risk your life in doing so? Second,' she continued, 'your triumph is only temporary. Yes, you routed Micah Yeomans last night but you forget that he has friends in high places. If you taunt him, he can make life very difficult for all of us. Savour your victory, if you must,' she said. 'Yet be prepared for serious trouble from Mr Yeomans. Of one thing we can all be certain – he'll be back.'

CHAPTER SEVEN

When he arrived at the Home Office that morning, Viscount Sidmouth inhaled the pleasing odour of fresh polish. Every desk, table and chair seemed to glow. The carpets had been straightened, windows cleaned, ornaments and picture frames dusted and the wastepaper baskets divested of their contents. It was as if a dozen necessary women had spent the night cleaning the place. Since it had fallen to Bernard Grocott to seek a replacement, Sidmouth went off to the undersecretary's office to thank him. That, too, looked as if it had been given a complete overhaul. Grocott sat behind a desk that had neat piles of letters and documents on it. When he saw the Home Secretary enter, he rose to his feet.

'Good morning, my lord.'

'I come to sing your praises.'

'That's always reassuring to hear.'

'You have excelled yourself, Grocott, and – given the impossibly high standards you maintain – that is in the nature of a phenomenon. Wherever did you find this creature?'

'Levitt came to us by recommendation.'

'Who whispered her name into your ear?'

'To be candid,' replied Grocott, 'I can't be entirely sure. I was talking to a group of friends at my club and bewailed the loss of our necessary woman. Someone – it may or may not have been Sir Roger Hollington – plucked the name of Ruth Levitt from his memory. Later that evening, a piece of paper was thrust into my hand bearing the details of how she could be contacted.' He ventured a smile. 'The result is what you see all around you.'

'Yes,' said Sidmouth, surveying the room, 'she has waved her magic wand in here and in every other part of the building. Her industry is remarkable.'

'The night watchman told me that she didn't leave the premises until four o'clock this morning.'

'What time did she start work?'

'The moment the place was empty, Levitt took over. She's much quieter as a personality than Horner but has the same urge to please. There is no better way of doing that, of course, than by creating a good first impression.'

'She has most certainly done that.'

'It's very gratifying.'

'All credit must go to you.'

'That's overstating the case, my lord,' said Grocott with a self-deprecating smile. 'I had providential help.'

Sidmouth's brow furrowed. 'Now that we are back once more in an environment conducive to thought,' he said, 'we can confront some of the dilemmas that assail us. Chief among those is this wretched business at Dartmoor.' He sucked his teeth. 'Prison mutinies are always unsettling. Escaped convicts send a shiver of fear down every spine.'

'They may have escaped but are they really convicts?'

'Can there be any doubt of that?'

'It's a legal quibble, my lord. Technically, they were not convicted of anything but holding American citizenship.'

'If one must be pedantic, they were war criminals who fought against this country. That makes them eminently worthy of confinement in my estimation. And this ringleader who was mentioned . . .' He groped in vain for the name. 'Assist me, please. Your memory is more reliable. All that I can remember is that he was of Irish extraction.'

'I believe that he was called Thomas O'Gara.'

'That's the name.'

'Have he and his accomplice been recaptured yet?'

'Unhappily, no,' said the other. 'The latest news that's reached me from Devon mentions that a small boat was stolen from somewhere on the southern coast of the county. While it may not have been taken by the fugitives, mark you, it's logical to suppose that two sailors might opt for that particular mode of transport.'

'They'd never cross the Atlantic in a vessel like that, my lord.'

'Granted, but they might make for a port where they were likely to find a ship bound for America. That would be my theory, anyway. Captain Shortland, I know, would disagree.'

'What is his opinion?'

'Well, there's clearly been some kind of personal feud between the governor and this disruptive Irishman. Shortland's letter mentions O'Gara a number of times. He believes that the fellow will endeavour to use his freedom in order to cause severe embarrassment to everyone guarding the prisoners at Dartmoor.'

'O'Gara will be wasting his breath,' said Grocott, dismissively. 'Nobody will pay the slightest heed to his voice. He is of no consequence here, my lord.'

'I concur.'

'Have you spoken with the Prime Minister?'

'He and I are of the same mind,' said Sidmouth. 'He wants an investigation into the affair to be swift and decisive. That's a view shared by the Admiralty. A joint commission is therefore being set up with a representative from the United States alongside our own. In a matter as sensitive as this, we have to be seen to be even-handed.'

'Do you still believe that the result will be a foregone conclusion?'

'Most assuredly – Captain Shortland will be exonerated and the outcry from our political opponents will gradually fade away. We can then get back to our normal day-to-day business. Thanks to Levitt,' he went on, 'we'll be able to do it in an atmosphere of bracing cleanliness.'

'Can this be true?' asked Hannah, wide-eyed.

'I would never dare to tell you a lie.'

'You and your brother escaped over the rooftops?'

'It was the best way,' explained Paul Skillen. 'There were far too many people waiting for us in the streets below. Peter and I counted well over a dozen on our way there. They lurked in every thoroughfare.'

'But you could have been killed!' she protested.

He gave her a low bow. 'Happily – as you see – I was not.'

'I'm serious, Paul! Why didn't you tell me beforehand that you were about to take such a risk?'

'I didn't say a word because you would have tried to talk me out of it. And I made no mention of it when I returned here last night because I was preoccupied with the pure joy of your company.'

'It was my right to know,' she insisted.

Paul blew her a kiss. 'And it was my right to choose the moment when I should tell you,' he said. 'That's why you first heard about it this morning.'

They had just finished breakfast at the house where Hannah was staying. After a night in each other's arms, they'd awoken in a mood of drowsy ecstasy. It had just been shattered by Paul's revelation. Though he did his best to calm her down, she remained anxious and resentful. After another triumphant performance onstage, she'd fought off her admirers, gone back to the house and waited for him. The moment he came back, they fell into bed together and everything else was put aside. It was only now that he chose to tell her the truth about his activities in Upper Brook Street.

'How often do you do this sort of thing?' she asked.

'I skip across the rooftops every night,' he joked.

'This is no laughing matter, Paul. I had no idea that you diced with death so recklessly. Did you have no concern for me at all?'

'Yes – that's why I didn't tell you beforehand. I didn't want you to worry.'

'My anxiety is all the more intense now that I know what you kept from me. I *care* for you. These past few days have been heavenly. I have felt true happiness at last.' Her tone hardened. 'Now I learn that my happiness could be snatched away any moment because you tempt Fate so wilfully.'

'Hear the full story and you'll not fret quite so much,' he told her.

'I'm not fretting, Paul – I am driven to distraction.'

Getting up from his chair, he bent down beside her and took her hand between his. He then gave her an attenuated account of the plot devised by Micah Yeomans, explaining how it had been discovered and frustrated. Paul pointed out that he and his brother were well able to perform difficult feats and had done so many times before.

'We took a coil of rope with us, you see. That later became the staircase that allowed us to descend to the ground. All that Peter and I had to do was to tie it around a chimney and climb down it.'

'What if you had fallen?'

'Then we would not be having this conversation.'

'No,' she said, tartly, 'I'd be talking to the undertaker instead.'

She got up abruptly, walked to the window, pretended to be looking through it and took out a handkerchief to dab at her eyes. Paul went after her and put both hands on her shoulders. He whispered endearments in her ear but they were met with a cold silence. He eased her around to face him.

'If you knew how many times Peter and I have done this sort of thing,' he said, airily, 'you wouldn't have a moment's disquiet. We were *born* to it, Hannah. We are natural acrobats.'

'You've frightened me.'

'I hoped that you'd be impressed, my darling.'

'What is impressive about someone falling to his death?'

He spread his arms. 'But I *didn't* fall. The evidence stands before you.'

'Stop taking this so lightly,' she reproached. 'I'm serious, Paul.'

'I know.'

When he tried to hug her, she stiffened and pushed him away. He offered her an apology but she was well beyond its reach. Hannah was fully roused.

'You told me that your brother is married,' she said.

'That's true – to a dear lady named Charlotte.'

'Did he tell *her* what he was intending to do last night?'

'Probably not,' he replied. 'Why upset her when there was no need? Peter would have told her afterwards when the danger was past and she could see that he was unharmed.'

'*You* were not unharmed by that tussle in the warehouse. I saw the marks on your body. They were hideous.'

'I explained that, Hannah. I had an accidental fall.'

'You might well have had another last night and I would have been left alone to mourn you. It's possible that Charlotte would have been mourning your brother as well. I didn't realise that the pair of you were such madcaps.'

'Some women might find that appealing,' he contended.

'Well, I am not one of them, Paul.'

When he tried to embrace her again, she stepped back out of his reach. He was perturbed. After the intimacy they'd shared, rejection was painful. Every time they'd been alone together before, she'd been warm and receptive. In the hope of winning her over, he offered a compromise.

'You are right, Hannah,' he admitted. 'I should have told you.'

'I'm glad you accept that.'

'In future, I promise, I'll be more considerate of your feelings.'

'That would not come amiss.'

'Next time,' he vowed, 'I'll warn you if I have to face danger. You have my word of honour. Will that content you?'

'No, sir,' she said with biting anger, 'it will not. You insult me by suggesting that it would. I'll not stand idly by when you tell me that you are embarking on something that might conceivably end in your death. What kind of woman do you take me to be? Because she is married to your brother, Charlotte has no choice but to suffer whenever her husband walks towards danger. I am under no such compulsion regarding you.'

Rocked by her fury, all that he could do was to gesture his remorse.

'There will never *be* a next time,' she stipulated. 'If you truly want me, you must give me proof of your love by giving up these daring adventures. I am in earnest, Paul. Put me and my needs first,' she went on, her voice acquiring a searing edge, 'or you may take yourself out of my life for ever.'

Paul felt as if he'd fallen from a rooftop and hit the pavement hard.

While her husband took a leading role in the various investigations that came their way, Charlotte Skillen was no mere bystander. Unusual as it was for a woman in her position, she, too, worked at the gallery as part of what had become a thriving detective agency. Her role was largely clerical, the main elements in it being the listing of the various clients and the upkeep of a record book of criminals with whom they came into contact. As she sat at the desk that morning, she tried to ignore the sounds of gunfire from the upstairs room where Jem Huckvale was teaching someone how to discharge a pistol with a degree of accuracy. Having listened to Gully Ackford's description of Simon Medlow, she added some details she'd gleaned from Peter. Though she had never seen the man, she was now confident of recognising him from the pen portrait she'd been given.

'Of course,' said Ackford with a chuckle, 'Peter and Paul saw rather more of him than I did. He was dressed in his finery when he came here. Stripped of that, I daresay he'd find it more difficult to cozen anybody.'

'This is an excellent description,' she said as she read it through. 'Had it been to hand when he first appeared, you'd have known him immediately.'

'He was too sure of himself, Charlotte. That's what alerted me.'

'Medlow is in our record book now – right after Ned Greet.'

'You may have to cross *him* out altogether very soon. Whether it's to the scaffold or to Australia, Ned will be going where he can't trouble any of us again.'

It had been Charlotte's idea to compile the record book. A gallery of ruffians, thieves, forgers, fraudsters, fences, cracksmen, killers, cardsharps and those who ran disorderly houses had been created over the years by her elegant calligraphy. In cases where she'd actually seen an individual, she'd even added a little sketch of the person. Inevitably, men occupied the bulk of the book but there were some women who qualified for inclusion as well.

'That collection of yours is a godsend,' observed Ackford. 'Someone walked in here last week and I *knew* I'd seen him before. Yet somehow I just couldn't put a name to a face. So I resorted to that priceless book of yours and there he was in all his glory – Will Bickerton.'

'Peter and Paul were chasing him a year ago.'

'They'll have to keep on chasing, Charlotte. When Bickerton realised I was suspicious, he vanished quicker than a rat down a drain.'

'Why did he come here?'

'He wanted someone to teach him how to shoot straight. That can often mean that someone is about to fight in an illegal duel but not in Bickerton's case. He'd never have the courage to take part in a fair contest. A sly weasel of a man like him would prefer to shoot someone in the back.'

'I'll tell Paul that Bickerton is back in London. He has an old score to settle with him. He'll have to work alone, however. Peter will be hunting for that missing woman from the Home Office.'

'That's a curious business, isn't it?'

'I'll be interested to find out what happened to her.'

Before he could speak, Ackford heard the tinkle of the front door bell. He excused himself and went off to see who had rung it. When he opened the door, he was surprised to see a handsome young woman standing there alone. Apart from female servants, the only people who came to the gallery were men so there was a novelty in her request.

'Is it true that you give instruction in archery?' she asked.

Peter Skillen had expected to wait but, when he called at the Home Office, he was shown straight into Sidmouth's office. The latter had clearly been awaiting some news about the investigation. Peter explained that he'd questioned both Esther Ricks and Joan Claydon but had learnt nothing that could point to the whereabouts of the missing servant. What he was careful not to divulge was the fact that Anne Horner had a substantial amount of money hidden beneath her bed. Since there might be a perfectly innocent reason why she'd acquired so much cash, he didn't wish to plant a seed of doubt in Sidmouth's mind about the woman. Neither did he want the Home Secretary asking the question that Peter had already asked himself. If the necessary woman had such ample funds, why did she feel the need to continue the laborious and demeaning work of cleaning offices?

'You may think it strange that we are so concerned about her,' said Sidmouth. 'Here we are, occupying a position that entitles us to answer petitions and addresses to the Prince Regent, and allows us to advise him on the exercise of royal prerogative, yet we are excessively worried about a minor employee.'

'I think that it shows genuine compassion on your part, my lord.'

'I'm impelled by a sense of duty towards her.'

'From what I've learnt about the woman,' said Peter, 'she

seems quite admirable. Though she has suffered a number of blows in her life, Mrs Horner has been undaunted. She has fashioned a life for herself that makes few, if any, demands on others. Her landlady told me how kind, helpful and unselfish her lodger is.'

'The same qualities have been noted here, Mr Skillen. Not that I've seen very much of her,' Sidmouth went on, 'because our paths almost never cross. We toil by day while she cleans up the mess here by night. There have, however, been occasions when I and my permanent secretary have worked late into the evening and left the premises as Horner was just arriving.'

'I take it that you've found a substitute.'

'I'm relieved to say that we have. Thanks to one of my undersecretaries, we now have a more than adequate replacement in the shape of Levitt. Though she has made an auspicious start, however, what we really desire is the return of her predecessor.'

'The search will be given my full attention,' said Peter.

He'd always had great respect for Sidmouth. Conscious as he was that the man was derided in some quarters for his perceived inadequacies, Peter had always found him decent, honest and considerate. In the dealings they'd had together over the years, he'd admired the Home Secretary's efficiency, doggedness and readiness to support those who worked for him. Sidmouth's years as Prime Minister at the start of the century may have been undistinguished but it could be argued that any politician would have been handicapped when operating in the long shadow of William Pitt the Younger. War had exposed Sidmouth's limitations and, though he'd negotiated peace with France, it did not last. Coping with the threat of invasion by Napoleon had put him under intolerable pressure and he'd felt a sense of relief when Pitt replaced him. Having met some of the other leading politicians, Peter Skillen had a marked preference for the Home Secretary, a man of integrity with solid achievements behind him accorded less praise than they deserved.

Sidmouth was like a distraught father enquiring about a missing daughter.

'Is there any hope that you'll find her?'

'Oh, I won't simply rely on hope, my lord. I'll most definitely track her down.'

'To survive so many dangers both here and in France,' observed the Home Secretary, 'you've had to rely on your sharp instincts. What do they tell you about Horner? Is she alive or dead?'

'She is alive, my lord.'

'How do you know?'

'I don't know – I just *feel* it.'

'That's good enough for me,' said the other, sitting back in his chair. 'I'm grateful for your reassurance, Mr Skillen. In view of the many hazardous assignments you've undertaken at my behest, you must think it rather *infra dig* to be employed on what must appear to you to be a trivial matter.'

'Not at all,' said Peter, firmly. 'I view the woman's disappearance with the consternation shown by you. I've gathered enough information about her to decide that she's a worthy individual in every way and I look forward to making her acquaintance.'

'Thank you so much for coming. Your visit has brought much comfort.' He got up to show his visitor out. 'It may sound absurd but I was beginning to think that Horner had – from motives known only to her – simply run away from us.'

Peter thought about the cache under the bed at the woman's lodging.

'On that score at least,' he said, 'I can speak with irrefutable certainty. There is no evidence to suggest flight. Whatever else she may have done, Mrs Horner has not run away from you.'

When he'd heard people talking about the luck of the Irish, Tom O'Gara had always laughed bitterly. He'd never experienced it himself. Raised in the poorest part of Dublin, he'd seen nothing but misery and deprivation around him. Like so many of his countrymen in desperate circumstances, O'Gara's father had taken his family to America in the hope of a better life for them. Instead of solving their problems, however, emigration had simply shifted them to another country. They were still poor, short of food and devoid of prospects. In a bid to lighten the load on his parents, O'Gara had run away at the age of fourteen to join the navy. There, too, he found the luck of the Irish in abysmally short supply.

Yet he'd now been forced to think that perhaps there was such a thing. Out of what could have been a fatal collision at sea had come something resembling good luck. Hurled into the water, he and Dagg had yelled out so loud for help that ropes had been thrown overboard for them. Dripping wet and still partially dazed, they were hauled up on deck to find that they were on a cargo ship sailing to London. It would get them there far quicker and safer than the small boat they'd stolen in Devon. Rum had revived them and food was pressed on them. They were among friends.

It was night when they finally docked in London and they left the vessel with a chorus of farewells from their temporary shipmates. While O'Gara was excited to be in the nation's capital, Dagg saw only the potential dangers.

'We've got no money, no food and no weapons to protect us.'

'I told you – my cousin will look after us.'

'How do we find him?'

'He lives behind Orchard Street somewhere. All we have to do is to get there and start knocking on doors.'

'It's well after midnight,' noted Dagg. 'Will your cousin be up at this hour?'

Tom O'Gara burst out laughing.

'Dermot is Irish,' he said. 'He's always up.'

CHAPTER EIGHT

Paul Skillen was in a quandary. He had to choose between the woman he loved and the life on which he thrived. There was no possibility of compromise. He was being forced to surrender something very dear to him. It was disturbing. During a series of dalliances with beautiful young women, he'd never before been scolded for taking part in daring escapades. Indeed, the others had always praised his courage and been thrilled to hear of his adventures. His intrepidity was a source of attraction for them. Hannah Granville was different. While she had, at first, been drawn by the aura of danger that surrounded him, she was disturbed by the risks he was prepared to take. The more involved she'd become with Paul, the more concerned she was for his safety. Unsettled by the injuries he'd received during the pursuit of Ned Greet, she was even more upset to learn of his antics on the rooftops of Upper Brook Street.

When he reflected upon the situation, he drew consolation from the fact that Hannah cared so deeply about him. With the exception of his sister-in-law, Charlotte, he'd never met any woman who'd left him so deliciously inebriated with love. In the talented actress, he'd at last found someone else with whom he felt he could spend the rest of his days. To lose her would be in the nature of a catastrophe, yet so would the loss of his work as a detective. Apart from anything else, the assignments he undertook gave him the income needed to court someone like Hannah. It was difficult to see how he could earn the same amount of money elsewhere. There was a more immediate concern: Paul was only one of countless suitors to Hannah Granville. When he was no longer her chosen companion, someone else would soon replace him. That thought gnawed away at him obsessively.

Much as he loved his brother, he'd never been able to discuss his private life with him. Indeed, when Peter was the successful rival for Charlotte's hand, there'd been a measure of uneasiness between the brothers that had never entirely dissipated. The one person to whom he could not turn for advice, therefore, was Peter. As a result, Paul was obliged to look elsewhere, so he went to the shooting gallery.

'Good morning, Charlotte,' he said.

'Good morning, Paul,' she answered. 'If you've come for your usual fencing lesson with Gully, you'll have to bide your time. He's teaching the rudiments of archery to a new customer.'

'The fencing can wait.'

'While you're here, I've something to show you.'

'Oh?'

'It's the description of Simon Medlow,' she said, opening the record book at the appropriate page. 'Peter thinks it's accurate but I'd like your comments as well.'

He read the entry. 'That's very good.'

'I'll be glad when I can write, "arrested and convicted" beside his name. He's evaded the law for too long. And talking of evasion,' she added, 'did you know that Will Bickerton has been seen back in London?' Paul gave a shrug of indifference. 'When he dodged you last time, you swore that you'd catch him one day.'

'And I will,' he said, impatiently, 'but I've more important things on my mind at the moment than a swindler like Bickerton.'

They were in the room at the rear of the shooting gallery. The thud of arrows into the target could be heard along with the distant grunts from pugilists trying to knock each other into oblivion. Since both Gully Ackford and Jem Huckvale were busy elsewhere in the building, Paul and Charlotte were unlikely to be interrupted. Rehearsing what he was going to say, he took the chair beside her.

'May I ask you a question?' he began.

'There's no need to be so formal – of course, you may.'

'Do you ever worry about Peter?'

'Worry?' she echoed.

'You know only too well what our work sometimes entails.'

'I try not to brood on that aspect of it, Paul.'

'Deep down, however, would you prefer it if Peter had a less hazardous occupation?'

'I'd prefer it if neither of you put your lives at risk,' she said with an affectionate smile, 'but criminals will almost invariably resist arrest and violence is therefore unavoidable. I've been compelled to accept that.'

'Have you never taxed Peter on the subject?'

'I did so regularly when we were first married and he reacted by telling me very little about his activities. When he worked as an agent in France, of course, I was at my wits' end. I didn't know where Peter was, what he was doing or whether or not he'd been killed by the enemy.'

'My brother is like me,' he said. 'We lead charmed lives. Peter's is rather more charmed than mine because he has *you* at his side but I've learnt to live with that setback, painful as it was at the time.'

Charlotte acknowledged the compliment with a nod. When she'd chosen one brother in favour of another, there'd been a passing moment of regret on her side. Paul was engaging and lively company. Given the fact that he was sought after by so many marriageable young ladies, she'd been flattered by his attentions. Nevertheless, while it would have been pleasurable to lapse into a romance with Paul, she could not see it lasting indefinitely when they were man and wife. Peter Skillen, by contrast, promised a lifelong devotion that his brother could not, in all honesty, offer.

'Why are you asking me these questions?'

'It's something I've often pondered.'

'Come now, Paul. I'll not be fobbed off with a paltry excuse like that. There's something more serious behind all this. Why not admit it?'

There was an awkward pause. 'You are right,' he said, shamefacedly.

'Who is the lady?'

'How do you know that there is one?'

'It's the only reason that could have brought you here.'

He bit his lip. 'I realise that you'll never approve of my private life.'

'It's not a question of approval or disapproval, Paul,' she said, fondly. 'I love you as my brother-in-law and respect your right to behave as you choose. You'll never have to put up with me clicking my tongue or wagging my finger at you. I've come to accept that you were never destined for a life of monastic self-denial.' He chuckled. 'So I repeat my question – who *is* the lady?'

'She must remain anonymous,' he said, firmly, 'but I will confess to the astonishing effect that she's had upon me.' He cleared his throat before speaking. 'In essence, Charlotte, the problem is this . . .'

Anne Horner's social circle was severely restricted so it didn't take long for Peter Skillen to speak to each member of it. There was unanimous praise for the cleaner as a good friend and a tireless worker. Even when her husband had been alive, she'd taken in laundry, looked after neighbours' children in return for payment and mended clothing ceaselessly. She'd also been one of the volunteer cleaners at her parish church. Everybody was shocked to hear of her disappearance and urged Peter to find her. The trouble was that he'd garnered no fresh evidence as to her likely whereabouts. He therefore adopted a different approach. Anne's stint at the Home Office ended in the small hours and was followed by a brisk walk back to her lodgings that, in his estimation, took the best part of twenty minutes. Putting himself in her position, Peter followed her footsteps so that he could see likely places where she might have been intercepted and abducted. Even at night, London was throbbing with life so it would have been no lonely trudge through the deserted streets, yet she'd made the journey for years without apparent incident. What had made her last known walk home so dangerous?

When he left the Home Office, he was in a wide thoroughfare lined with large houses. It was not long, however, before he turned down meaner streets that were narrow and winding. Dark-eyed men lounged in doorways or congregated noisily outside the occasional tavern. Children played deafening games and dogs scoured the gutters for scraps. Itinerant musicians of various kinds added to the general clamour. After less than ten minutes, Peter had counted three likely places for an ambush. It was when he turned into a long lane, however, that he found the most suitable place. Overhung by trees that cast dark shadows throughout the day, it was intersected by a series of alleys, each one affording a good hiding place for robbers intending to pounce of unwary pedestrians.

Peter soon had clear proof of that. As he walked past an alley to his left, a burly man with a cudgel in his hand suddenly leapt out to accost him.

'Your purse or your life, good sir!' he snarled.

'Take my purse,' replied Peter, pretending to shrink back in fear. 'I'll give you my watch if you spare me.'

Thinking he'd put terror into his victim's heart, the man relaxed and lowered his weapon. His other hand stretched out to receive the purse but it never reached him. Instead, he was struck on the jaw by the fearsome punch that Peter unleashed. It sent the robber staggering back against the wall. A relay of punches battered him to the ground. Grabbing the cudgel from him, Peter stood over the man.

'What's your name?' he demanded.

'I meant no harm, sir,' whimpered the other. When Peter raised the cudgel to strike, the robber cowered beneath him. 'Don't hit me, sir, I beg you. My name is Reuben Grigg and I'm a poor man. I've never done this before but my wife and children are starving and I was forced to—'

'I want none of your lies!' warned Peter, interrupting him. 'You're too ugly to be married and too selfish to give a thought for any other human being. You've done this many times and you've done it in this lane. Admit it.' Peter clipped him with the cudgel to loosen his tongue. 'Admit it, you rogue.'

Grigg rubbed his head ruefully. 'I do, sir. This is my patch.'

'Are you here night and day?'

'I work mostly at night, sir. I can see in the dark.'

'Then I need the use of your eyes. You are clearly an observant man.'

'In my trade, you have to be.'

'Were you lurking in this lane three or four nights ago?'

'Why do you ask?'

Peter kicked him. 'Answer my question.'

'Yes, yes, I was – but I had no luck. The rain kept people away.'

'Have you ever seen a woman walking this way after midnight?'

'Only if she's a lightskirt, here to sell her slit,' said Grigg with a smirk.

'This is a respectable woman of medium height and in her thirties. She'd have been walking home after cleaning some offices.'

'Then she'd have been carrying nothing worth stealing. I'd let her go.'

'Are you saying that you *did* see this woman?'

Grigg's eyelids narrowed. 'Is there money in it, if I did?'

Orchard Street ran between Portman Place and Oxford Street. Built in the early years of King George III's reign, it boasted impressive facades and sought-after town houses. Concealed behind it, however, were properties where only the destitute lived; cramped, malodorous, disease-ridden rookeries, teeming with ragged people engaged in a constant struggle simply to stay alive. Quarrelling, fighting, criminality and drunkenness were common in these slums. It was in one of these overcrowded dwellings that Tom O'Gara's cousin and family lived. At first glance, the two squalid rooms they occupied seemed little better to O'Gara than the cells at Dartmoor prison but his opinion soon changed. His cousin, Dermot Fallon, was delighted to see him again and introduced him and Moses Dagg to his pretty wife, Mary, and to the confusing litter of children that the couple had managed to produce, all of whom were short, ill-kempt, half-starved and high-spirited. The newcomers found it impossible to put them in chronological order because the children all looked exactly the same age. What they shared was their father's buck-toothed grin and his combative attitude towards their neighbours.

Though they'd arrived in the middle of the night, the sailors were given a cordial welcome and offered a part of the floor, which actually had a carpet of sorts on which to sleep. It was not until the next day that they were able to talk at length with their host. Since the ear-splitting din all around them made speech difficult, Fallon took his visitors off to a tavern where they could have a measure of privacy.

'London is the richest city in the world,' he said, expansively, 'yet they've got me and my family living like pigs. There's no justice in it, is there?'

'I'm glad you mentioned justice,' said O'Gara.

'Why's that?'

'It's what brought us here, Dermot.'

'And there was I thinking you'd crossed the sea simply to see your cousin,' teased the other. 'We can't offer you much, Tom. We can give you and Moses a place to lay your heads and might even manage a bite of food from time to time. Whatever we have, we'll share. One thing we can't get for you, though, is justice. The law is made to punish people like us.'

'We know all about punishment,' said Dagg, morosely. 'Tell him, Tom.'

'We've escaped from prison,' admitted O'Gara.

Fallon gaped. 'Is that true?'

'It's only part of the truth, Dermot.'

'Well, I want to hear the whole lot, so I do.'

O'Gara took a deep breath. 'It's difficult to know where to begin.'

'Start with Captain Shortland,' suggested Dagg.

'Was he your skipper?' asked Fallon.

'No, he was the black-hearted governor of Dartmoor.'

'He's the reason we're here,' said O'Gara.

He launched into a long and repetitive account of events since their capture. Aided and sometimes contradicted by Dagg, he talked about the foul conditions, meagre rations and inhuman punishments they'd suffered behind the high prison walls, reserving his most scathing comments for the way that the governor had ordered his men to fire on the prisoners. Fallon shared their indignation and agreed that they had to reveal the full truth to the Prime Minister.

'There's a problem,' said O'Gara. 'I can only scribble and Moses can barely write his name. If we draw up a list of our demands, nobody will even bother to read them. Our report has to look neat enough to attract attention.'

'Can you write proper, Dermot?' asked Dagg.

'No,' replied the other. 'I'm all fingers and thumbs and Mary's had even less education than me. What you need,' he went on, turning to his cousin, 'is a scrivener, someone who'll write out everything in a fine hand.'

O'Gara was worried. 'That would cost money, wouldn't it?'

'I know someone who might do it cheap.'

'Can we trust him, though? If he learns that we're on the run, he'll be tempted to turn us in and claim the reward.'

'I'll make sure that doesn't happen,' said Fallon, tapping his chest. 'If he breathes a word about the pair of you, I'll poke his eyes out and cut off his balls, so I will.' He chortled. '*That* should help to keep his gob shut.'

When he returned the keys to the owner of the house, Micah Yeomans assured him that the property had been kept under surveillance day and night and that nobody had gained entry to it. He received full payment from Everett Hobday then exchanged farewells with him before stepping out into Upper Brook Street. As soon as the Runner set off home, Alfred Hale fell in beside him.

'What did he say, Micah?'

'He congratulated us on doing our usual thorough job.'

'It wasn't thorough enough,' said Hale. 'We were made to look fools.'

'There was no need for Hobday to know that. In any case, Simon Medlow was the real fool. I'd a mind to leave him dangling there. It would have been no more than he deserved.'

'You said he was the finest confidence trickster alive.'

'I was wrong.'

'The Skillen brothers saw through him at once.'

'That was Ackford's doing, I fancy. Anyway,' said Yeomans, irritably, 'let's hear no more of our last encounter with them. We have to plan the next one.'

'Will you use Medlow a second time?'

'I'm not stupid, Alfred.'

'He might be keen to get his own back.'

'Medlow is no match for them and I've no wish to see him trussed up naked for the second time. His prick looked like a diseased turnip. The sight turned my stomach.'

Lost in contemplation, they strolled on for some while. Both were well known in criminal quarters and more than one person slunk away when he saw the Runners coming. Yeomans enjoyed the power he had to frighten people. It was a mark of his status. It also separated him from Peter and Paul Skillen. They might have their random successes but it was Yeomans and his men who represented law and order on the streets of London.

Not daring to nudge his companion out of his reverie, Hale kept pace with his long stride and waited for him to break the silence.

'I have it,' said Yeomans at length.

'I'm listening, Micah.'

'It's an idea to get back at those vile brothers.'

'The last one failed miserably.'

'We'll be more careful this time. We have to find their weak spot.'

'They don't have one,' complained Hale.

'Everyone has an Achilles heel and so must they. Yes,' said Yeomans, as he thought it through, 'we should have done this before. Find a man's weakness and we can exploit it. That's your task, Alfred.'

'What must I do?'

'Follow one of them. Learn everything you possibly can about him.'

'Which one must I go after?'

'It would be pointless to trail Peter Skillen. He's a man with no apparent vices. At the end of each day, the only thing he wishes to do is to go home to that beautiful wife of his. In his place, I'd do the same.'

'What about Paul?'

'He's your man. He's an inveterate gambler and has an eye for the ladies.'

'I wouldn't hold that against him.'

'No more would I.'

'Why should I watch him?'

'Paul is more likely to make a mistake and do something we can use to our advantage. Follow him, Alfred,' urged Yeomans. 'Cling to him like a limpet. Sooner or later, he'll give us the ammunition we need.'

* * *

The talk with Charlotte had been at once uncomfortable yet heartening. While taking care not to reveal Hannah's name, Paul had revealed the depths of his feeling for the actress. Speared on the horns of a dilemma, he could not even begin to contrive his escape. Because she knew nothing about the character of his *inamorata*, Charlotte had been careful not to give him specific advice. She had merely suggested that he should allow time to pass before he saw her again, giving the lady in question time for her ire to cool. Every close relationship, Charlotte reminded him, involved concessions on both sides and he had to be prepared to give a certain amount of ground. Paul was glad that he'd confided in her. Simply talking it through with his sister-in-law had had a calming effect on him and he was grateful for that. Once he left the shooting gallery, however, he began to doubt the value of a period apart from Hannah Granville. For both their sakes, he needed to be with her and, importantly, be seen with her in order to keep his rivals at bay.

Early that evening, he set off for the theatre with a large basket of flowers, hoping that the gift would soften her heart towards him. It was well before the time of the performance and she'd given him privileged access to her before. When he presented himself at the theatre, however, his way was blocked by the tall, angular figure of the stage doorkeeper.

'I'm sorry, sir,' he said. 'I've orders to turn everyone away.'

'Miss Granville and I are close friends.'

'A lot of gentlemen claim that honour.'

'It's true, man,' insisted Paul, 'and you know it. You've seen us both together and admitted me to her dressing room before. Now let me past at once.'

'I'd lose my job, if I did so.'

'All I wish to do is to give her these flowers.'

'Her express wish is that I'm to accept no gifts on her behalf.'

'That may be true for others but surely not for me. Miss Granville and I have an understanding. Now move aside and let me through.'

The stage doorkeeper held his ground. 'I'm afraid that I can't do that, sir.'

Paul felt a rush of anger and had to fight against the impulse to brush the man aside. He couldn't believe that Hannah would bar his entry to her dressing room. Was she acting out of spite or simply reinforcing her ultimatum? If he wanted her enough, she seemed to be saying, he had to change or he would not even be allowed near her. Paul felt sympathy for the stage doorkeeper. The man was only obeying instructions and should not be blamed for that. Taking a step backward, Paul looked down sadly at the flowers.

'Are you married?' he asked.

'I have been for twenty years or more, sir,' said the other, contentedly.

'Then take these flowers home to your wife and tell her you love her.'

After thrusting the basket into the man's hands, Paul spun on his heel and strode out of the building with his mind in turmoil.

'Where was this, Peter?'

'It was in a lane that Mrs Horner would have had to walk down on her way back to her lodging. It could have been designed for an ambush.'

'And who was this man you caught?'

'His name was Reuben Grigg, a ruffian who preyed on those passing by.'

'He chose the wrong victim when he picked on you,' said Charlotte.

'I was rather insulted that he saw me as a vulnerable target. From his point of view, I suppose,' decided Peter, 'I must have looked as if I had money about me. Also, I was evidently a stranger. He assumed I'd be off guard.'

'You are *never* off guard.'

He brushed her lips with a kiss. 'I was when I first set eyes on you, my love.'

'Less flattery and more story, please.'

'Grigg was an awkward fellow. He refused to cooperate at first.'

'What did you do?'

He smiled. 'I had to persuade him.'

They were in their house comparing notes about the day they'd each spent. Peter felt that he'd at last made headway in his search for the missing cleaner. Reuben Grigg had been a denizen of the dark corners of the lane where they'd met. Most of the people who walked down it were too poor to have anything of value on them and too aware of the dangers to be taken unawares. Grigg had first told Peter what he felt the latter wanted to hear so he had to be discouraged from telling lies. The man's own cudgel proved the ideal asset. By means of judicious blows, Peter had soon knocked the truth out of him.

'He remembered a woman who walked down that lane at night regularly,' he said, 'though he'd never accosted her. It may or not have been Anne Horner but one has to ask how many unaccompanied women would venture into such a place. On the night when we *know* she last left the Home Office, she would have taken that route home at her usual time.'

'What did this man, Grigg, actually see?'

'It's not so much what he saw as what he heard, Charlotte. There was a scuffle further down the lane, it seems, and he heard a woman scream for help. Her cries were soon muffled.'

'Why didn't he go to her assistance?'

'Grigg would be more likely to join in the assault than help her.'

'Wasn't he even curious?'

'He thought it was a lady of the night caterwauling because she hadn't been paid for her services. That's not unusual, it appears. All that Grigg was interested in was a likely victim for that cudgel of his.' Peter grinned. 'Now he knows what it's like to feel its sting.'

'Where is he now?'

'He's in custody, pending an appearance in court. As a result of my evidence, he'll get no mercy. The irony is that, in trying to rob me, he may unwittingly have helped to unearth another crime.'

'Do you really think the woman who screamed was Anne Horner?'

'It's more than possible, Charlotte. On the particular night, she would have been somewhere in that lane at that time. It was the ideal place to overpower her.'

'Why would anyone wish to do that?'

'I can only guess at their motives.'

'So where do you think she is now, Peter?'

He was decisive. 'I believe she's being held somewhere against her will.'

The dank cellar was at the rear of the house so her pleas would be unheard by any passers-by. In any case, the woman had warned her that, if she tried to call for help, she would be bound and gagged. A truckle bed occupied a corner and a stinking wooden bucket stood beside it. She had no idea why she was being held or who her gaolers were. When he brought her food, the man never spoke a word. The grating that provided ventilation let in enough light for her to see the bare stone walls covered in mildew and the undulating floor. The stench was unbearable. A small candle gave her the only illumination at night.

Having lost all track of time, she was in a state of utter bewilderment. All that she could do was to pray again and again for delivery. As she lay on the bed, she thought she heard a noise outside the cellar. She hauled herself to her feet and scurried across to the heavy oak door.

'Is anyone *there*?' she cried.

CHAPTER NINE

Jubal Nason was a sharp-featured man in his fifties with an ill-fitting grey wig, a pronounced squint and a sallow complexion. His back was hunched, his hands skeletal and his manner surly. Compared to his three visitors, he was smartly dressed but his dark suit had faded and the cuffs of his coat were threadbare. Since he'd been dismissed from his job as a lawyer's clerk, he'd fallen on hard times and iron had entered his soul. Nason was not pleased when Dermot Fallon came to his house with two strangers in tow. He looked at Moses Dagg with especial disdain.

'We've a task for you,' explained Fallon. 'It's an important one.'

'Go elsewhere,' said the other. 'I'm too busy.'

'You're never too busy to help an old friend.'

There was a dry laugh. 'I'd never call you a friend, Mr Fallon.'

'You were happy enough to shake my hand when I chanced along and saved you from being torn to pieces by that mad dog.' He turned to Tom O'Gara. 'There's gratitude 'for you! I went to his rescue and he turns his back on me.'

'That's unfair, Dermot,' said his cousin, hotly.

'It's worse than unfair. If I'd known he'd behave like this, I'd not only have let the animal eat him alive, I'd have cheered him on.'

'I don't blame you,' said Dagg, scowling. 'He doesn't look worth saving.'

Confronted by three menacing visitors, Nason decided that it was not in his interests to annoy them. He manufactured a smile of appeasement. Fallon had indeed saved him from attack by a dog. What he didn't know was that the Irishman owned the animal and had trained him to threaten people. Nason was simply the latest victim tricked into believing that Fallon had just happened to pass at a critical moment.

'I need a favour,' said Fallon, making it sound more like a command than a request. He indicated his companions in turn. 'This is my cousin, Tom O'Gara and that is Moses Dagg. They've come all the way from America to meet you.'

Nason was surly. 'What can I do for you all?'

'You can mind your manners for a start.'

'I'm not sure we can trust him, Dermot,' said O'Gara. 'He looks sly.'

'I agree with Tom,' said Dagg. 'He could double-cross us.'

'Mr Nason knows what would happen to him if he did that,' said Fallon, shooting the man a warning glance. 'I'd be back here with a whole pack of wild dogs. But don't be fooled by appearances. I know he looks like a cock-eyed back-stabber but he's a good scrivener and we need his help.' He bared ugly teeth in a grin. 'And he'll be glad to offer it, won't you, Mr Nason?'

The scrivener's eyes went from one to the other. All three were big, strong and had an edge of desperation about them. Provoking them would be a mistake. At the same time, he was determined not to offer his services for nothing.'

'I'll need payment,' he said.

'You'll get it,' Fallon promised.

'Pen, ink and paper don't come free. My time is even more expensive.'

'We'll judge what it's worth afterwards.'

'First,' said O'Gara, stepping forward so that his face was inches from that of the scrivener, 'we need your solemn vow that you'll never breathe a word of what we tell you to any living soul. Do we have it?'

'Yes, yes,' said Nason, recoiling from O'Gara's foul breath. 'You have it – on my honour.'

'Then this is what we want you to write for us.'

With frequent interpolations from Dagg, O'Gara went on to give a long, rambling account of what had happened at Dartmoor and what reparation he felt was necessary. Fallon threw in the occasional comment. Nason made a series of jottings. When the narrative came to an end, he shook his head in dismay.

'What you say may be true,' he said, 'but it would take me all day to write it out exactly as it was told to me. Your story is far too long and diffuse. It needs to be much shorter and in two parts.'

'What do you mean?' asked O'Gara.

'Well, the first section must be a description of what actually happened during this so-called mutiny. You were witnesses. That will carry weight. As for the second section,' Nason continued, 'it must list your demands in order, the first being the immediate release of all American prisoners.'

'And a pardon for me and Tom,' said Dagg.

'That will be included. Can you both sign your names?'

'Yes,' said O'Gara, 'but I want some words underneath the signatures. It must read "Thomas O'Gara and Moses Dagg, Two of the Damned." Is that clear?'

'If that's what you want,' replied Nason, 'that's what you'll get.'

'We'd better.'

'And when it's done,' said Fallon, 'it can be sent to the Prime Minister.'

'No, it can't,' advised Nason. 'He'll only pass it on to the Home Office.'

Dagg was suspicious. 'How do you know?'

'I've worked with lawyers all my life and had to contact departments of government on their behalf many times. The Admiralty has responsibility for prisons but a case like this would be referred to the Home Secretary. To save time, this plea should go directly to him.'

'I told you Mr Nason knew what he was doing,' said Fallon, appreciatively.

'Where exactly is this Home Office?' asked O'Gara.

'Mr Nason will tell you.'

'I'll deliver the document in person,' said Nason, 'some time during the night. I don't want to be arrested for acting as your accomplice. I'll just slip it through the letterbox and you can await developments.'

'We want to see what you're sending first,' said O'Gara.

'Give me a few hours and I'll have it ready for you and Mr Dagg to look over. It will be well ordered and legible. The thing that I can't promise, however, is that you'll get the desired result.'

'We must do!' argued O'Gara. 'We risked our lives to escape.'

'Tom is right,' said Dagg, angrily. 'Our friends are still locked up. We want them let out of that hellhole right away.'

'Make that clear in the document, Mr Nason.'

'Yes,' said Fallon, 'you've heard their story. They've been treated like wild beasts. Order the Home Secretary to do what's right.'

'He won't take orders from two prisoners,' reasoned Nason.

'Then he's going to be in trouble, isn't he, Tom?'

'He is,' said O'Gara. 'I don't care how high and mighty he is. If this Home Secretary doesn't release all prisoners and hang Captain Shortland by his scrawny neck, Moses and I will go after him. What's his name?'

'It's Sidmouth,' said Nason, guardedly, 'Viscount Sidmouth. But you can't threaten him. That would prejudice your claims altogether.'

'He'll do what we tell him to do.'

'And the same goes for you, Mr Nason,' said Dagg, jabbing a finger.

'Write it all out,' said O'Gara, 'and we'll come back to read it through. He's got to know we're in earnest. All we're asking for is fair treatment. If we can't get that from this man, then he needs to know his life is in grave danger.'

Peter Skillen was obliged to wait for some time before being shown into the Home Secretary's office because the latter had been holding a meeting there. When it came to an end, Sidmouth sent his colleagues away and invited his visitor in.

He could see from Peter's demeanour that he had not brought good tidings.

'You're the bearer of bad news, I fancy,' he said.

'I fear that I am, my lord.'

'Are our worst fears realised?'

'No,' replied Peter, 'Mrs Horner is not dead – at least, that's what I believe.'

'Have you made any progress in the investigation?'

'I think that I have.'

Peter explained how he'd taken the route home used by the woman and how someone had tried to rob him. Sidmouth was highly alarmed. To lose Anne Horner was an inconvenience to him. The loss of the reliable Peter Skillen, however, would be a calamity. Over the years he'd undertaken assignments that few other men would even have dared to contemplate.

'I do urge you to exercise care,' he said.

'Mrs Horner has taken the same journey on many occasions and always emerged unscathed – until now, that is.'

'I'm sorry I interrupted you. Finish your report.'

Peter went on to recount what he'd been told by Reuben Grigg and suggested that they should accept that the cleaner had been kidnapped. Sidmouth was sceptical.

'Why on earth should anyone wish to abduct her?'

'I have no answer to that, my lord.'

'Neither do I and I'm inclined to think that the woman who screamed out that night was not Horner at all.'

'That may well be true,' conceded Peter, 'but we do know that she would have been in that lane – and at that time – on the night in question. Grigg is a predator. He watches very carefully before he strikes. When I described Mrs Horner to him, he admitted that he'd seen her by day many a time but always left her alone because she was not a tempting target. What he waits for is someone with a purse worth taking.' He smiled at the memory. 'That's why his eye alighted on me.'

'The rogue got what he deserved.'

'I squeezed every ounce of information out of him that I could. Few women walk alone down that lane after dark. It is, however, a place where certain ladies transact business. Yet it's unlikely that it was a prostitute who called out for help that particular night. According to Grigg, they'll fight like wildcats and cry blue murder. This plea was quickly extinguished.'

'I pray to God that it didn't come from Horner.'

'It's a probability we have to face, my lord.'

Sidmouth was profoundly distressed. He took several minutes to absorb what he'd been told. Though he tried to persuade himself otherwise, he slowly came to see that Peter's conclusion was a valid one.

'What happens now, Mr Skillen?'

'I continue the search.'

'Where will you start?'

'In the very place where I stumbled on our first important clue,' said Peter. 'I'll go back to that lane at night and walk down it at roughly the same time that Mrs Horner did. There may be inhabitants there other than Grigg. It's a place where one wouldn't be at all surprised to find someone sleeping in a gateway. I'll search for possible witnesses who may have heard what Grigg heard on that fatal night or, hopefully, have even glimpsed something.'

'Go armed and take your brother,' counselled Sidmouth.

'Oh, I think I've removed the one real danger from that lane.'

Sidmouth shook his head. 'I remain perplexed. If we ask who would gain any advantage by kidnapping a woman like Horner, we're bereft of suspects. Nobody would demand a ransom for a cleaner earning a relative pittance. In short, there's no value in this crime.'

'Yes, there is, my lord.'

'It eludes me.'

'A motive is unclear but one must surely exist. Someone will somehow profit from this bizarre situation. That's the assumption on which they're working anyway. Meanwhile, of course, you have a competent replacement here.'

'Levitt is keeping this whole building spick and span.'

'Then her appointment was obviously prudent.'

'Forget the cleaner we now have, Mr Skillen,' said the Home Secretary. 'My overriding concern is for the one who preceded her. Where is she? What have they done to her? Will she ever be released alive?'

'I may learn more when I visit that lane tonight.'

'For your own sake, don't go alone.'

'I can manage very well without anybody else. Two of us would frighten people away. Someone on his own is sure to be approached.'

It was well after noon when Paul Skillen eventually emerged from his stupor. How he'd got back home during the night was a mystery. All that he could remember was that he'd left the theatre in a towering rage, vowed that he'd never see Hannah

Granville again then made for a gambling hell in Jermyn Street. It was a place where people who were shunned by respectable clubs could gather in order to drink their fill and risk their money on the roll of a dice or the turn of a card. Since he had so many acquaintances there, Paul was given a welcoming cheer when he appeared and several people asked him why he'd deserted them recently. It was a poignant reminder of the siren who was Hannah Granville. When he met her, Paul's leisure time had been put entirely at her disposal and he'd turned his back on gambling completely. Only her rejection of him could have sent him back to Jermyn Street.

Opening an eye, he blinked repeatedly and tried to ignore the anvil that was being pounded rhythmically inside his head. When he felt his chest, he discovered that someone had removed his coat and considerately opened the neck of his shirt. His shoes had also been taken off. It took him several minutes to realise that a servant must have carried him upstairs and eased him onto his bed. Knowing that he was safe and well, he felt the urge to drift back into a restorative slumber but a question prodded him like the prongs of a toasting fork. How much had he lost?

More often than not, he was lucky in love but unlucky when he turned to gambling and he'd often left Jermyn Street in debt, having been forced to borrow from others when his own funds ran out. To have drunk himself into such a state of paralysis, he must have been even more reckless than usual. The normal safeguards he applied when betting on something would no longer function. Instead of restricting himself to fairly modest amounts, he could easily have ventured huge bets on cards he was too blurred even to see. When they saw him so vulnerable, others wouldn't hesitate to coax every penny out of his purse. Is that what had happened? Was he going to put his hand in his coat pocket and find that he'd gambled away his house? It had happened before to others. Was Paul the latest fool to do so?

Rolling off the bed, he landed on the floor with a thud and increased the rate of strike on the anvil. It was not just the pain that tormented him; it was the fact that his body seemed to be filled with solid iron. He crawled on his hands and knees to the chair over the back of which his coat had been placed. Paul had to gather up all his strength before he was able to reach into one of the pockets. Every slight movement caused a separate agony. His head weighed a ton, putting intense pressure on his neck. Yet he eventually got his hand on something. Pausing before pulling it out, he sent up a fervent prayer that he'd not lost his house. In that eventuality, he just wouldn't know how to face Peter and Charlotte. Not for the first time, they'd be disgusted with him and so would Gully Ackford and Jem Huckvale.

Yet he had to know the truth. It took great courage to extract the contents of his pocket. Braced for the worst, however, he was instead blessed by a minor miracle. What he was holding was a fistful of banknotes, adding up to an amount that was far in excess of the money he'd had beforehand. The second pocket was equally full of unexpected plunder. The night in Jermyn Street had somehow been an unqualified success. Hannah might have spurned him but he had ample compensation for her loss. All of a sudden, he was rich. With a huge effort, he tossed the money into the air and fell asleep under a blizzard of fluttering banknotes.

* * *

When she let herself into the shooting gallery, Charlotte was in time to see a woman descending the stairs. She realised that it must be Jane Holdstock, leaving the premises after another archery lesson.

'Good day to you,' she said with a smile.

'How do you do?' said Jane, sizing her up at a glance. 'I didn't expect to find someone like you here.'

'I might say the same about you, Mrs Holdstock. That is your name, I believe.'

'Yes, it is.'

'This gallery is a male paradise. I am the exception to the rule. Ladies rarely come for instruction though one or two have learnt how to shoot a pistol here. Mr Ackford tells me that you're an archer.'

'I'm hardly that,' said Jane, modestly, 'and I'm not really here for my own benefit. I've a young nephew with a passion for stories about Robin Hood. He's been begging his parents to buy him a bow and arrow. Since his father is never there to teach him how to use it, I volunteered to do so. First, of course, I had to become proficient myself.'

'I hear that you're a dedicated pupil.'

'One likes to do things properly.'

Charlotte warmed to her immediately and wanted to continue the conversation. Surrounded by men at the shooting gallery, she found it a refreshing change to meet another woman, especially one as pleasant and well spoken as Jane Holdstock. But the visitor didn't linger. After a polite farewell, she took her leave and let herself out of the building. Standing at the open door, Charlotte was still looking after her when Gully Ackford came down the stairs.

'Hello,' he said, affably.

'I've just met Mrs Holdstock for the first time.'

'She's an interesting lady, isn't she?'

'I wish that *I'd* had an aunt who'd taught me exciting things like how to use a bow and arrow. When I was young,' said Charlotte, 'the only things my aunts taught me were how to sew a fine seam and recite nursery rhymes. Mrs Holdstock is going to turn her nephew into Robin Hood.'

'I hope that the boy has her dedication. She learns very quickly.'

'Does she have children of her own?'

'I don't know,' he said. 'She's very discreet about her private life. At a guess, I'd say that she's not a mother herself. Perhaps that's why she's lavishing her affection on her nephew.'

They went through into the room at the rear of the establishment. While Charlotte removed her hat, Ackford checked the book to see what his teaching commitments were for the rest of the day.

'Two boxers and three fencers,' he noted.

'One of the swordsmen will be Paul. He never misses a lesson.'

'Well, he's missing one today, Charlotte. He's sent word that he's not well enough to engage in a lively bout.'

She was worried. 'Has he been injured in some way?'

'No, no,' he replied. 'The servant said that his master felt sick. That's not the word I'd have used,' he added with a laugh. 'We've all seen the way that Paul has been behaving. There's a new woman in his life, Charlotte, and she seems to have made a real impact on him. That's why he's not here today. He's pining.'

She missed him. At the end of the performance on the previous evening, Hannah Granville had basked in the rapturous applause before sweeping off to her dressing room. Ordinarily, she'd have been buoyed up by the prospect of seeing Paul Skillen again. He would be waiting at the stage door to whisk her away from the melee of unwanted admirers. When she remembered how she treated him when they'd last met, and how she'd prevented him from visiting her in her dressing room, she'd realised that her lover would not be dancing attendance on her. Hannah had been compelled to leave the theatre alone, sneaking out through the usual gathering of suitors. Her bed that night seemed icily cold and uncomfortably empty.

Throughout the day, she'd reflected on the joy that Paul had brought into her life and she blamed herself for being so precipitate. With the vanity common to her profession, Hannah was not accustomed to putting herself in the position of others. Her attentions were centred wholly on herself. The rift with Paul, however, was causing her pain and regret. When she made an effort to view the situation from his perspective, she saw how cruel her ultimatum must have been to him. How would she have felt if Paul had insisted that the price of his love was her immediate retirement from the theatre? It would have been a shattering demand. Hannah was sobered. In ordering him to resign from his dangerous occupation, she was telling him to stop being the person he really was. It must have been a crushing blow to him.

As she prepared to leave for the theatre that evening, she did so without the usual exhilaration. Her performance would undoubtedly win acclaim but Hannah did not look forward to it with any relish. When it was all over, the man she loved would not be waiting for her. The bed would be even colder and more uncomfortable that night. Leaving the house, she climbed into the open carriage sent to fetch her and settled back. Rolling off to another triumph, she felt a sense of abject failure. When she died of a broken heart onstage that evening, Hannah would do so with touching verisimilitude. She would not, however, be mourning her husband, Jaffeir, stabbed to death by his own hand. Her tears would be shed for Paul Skillen, stabbed by the verbal dagger that she'd wielded.

Absorbed by rueful thoughts of him, she saw nothing of the streets through which they rattled. The stench of London for once didn't reach her nostrils. The usual pandemonium went unheard. And then, without warning, she felt an invisible hand shake her out of her daydream. It was a timely awakening. When Hannah looked around, she saw Paul walking along the pavement no more than ten yards away. Wanting to cry out his name, she was somehow struck dumb. To attract his attention therefore, she stood up and waved both arms. He looked at her as if he'd never seen her before and went on his way. Hannah felt utterly rebuffed. It was over. In making unfair demands of him, she'd driven him away for ever. Flopping back into her seat, she plucked a handkerchief from her reticule and wept silently into it.

Still wondering whom the beautiful woman in the carriage had been, Peter Skillen walked quickly on his way.

* * *

'Holy Jesus!' exclaimed Tom O'Gara. 'It's wonderful.'

'You've done a good job,' said Moses Dagg, grudgingly.

'We could never have written anything like this.'

'It's bound to make him take notice.'

'Thank you,' said the scrivener with an oily smirk.

Since neither of the sailors could read as well as him, he'd read out the document to them with ponderous slowness. They'd been amazed at the way he'd turned their angry demands into a calm and persuasive narrative. Against his will, Jubal Nason had appended a threat of what would happen if their requirements were not granted. They were thrilled at the result. Couched in educated phrases, the document was written in a practised hand by a talented scrivener. O'Gara thrust the money he'd borrowed from his cousin into the man's hand.

Nason knew that their pleas would be studiously ignored. Even though their account of the massacre at the prison had cogency, it was bedevilled by the death threat they insisted on issuing. Their word would count for little against that of the governor and his men. The fact remained that they were fugitives and there'd be a reward for their capture, especially as it would remove a potential danger to the life of the Home Secretary. Nason could feel temptation rising up inside him. Only the fear of repercussions from Dermot Fallon had held him back from informing on the two Americans.

When they'd finished poring over the document, they signed their names at the bottom of the last page. Both men had the unquenchable zeal of fanatics.

'This is one of two things,' boasted O'Gara. 'It's either a key to let all our friends out of that stinking prison or it's the Home Secretary's death warrant.'

'He *must* do what we tell him,' said Dagg, grimly.

'We know the truth of what happened. We saw it with our own eyes.'

'Captain Shortland will only tell lies.'

Nason folded the document. 'I'll deliver this tonight,' he promised.

'No,' said O'Gara, 'I'll put it through the letterbox.'

'Don't you trust me?'

'That's not the point, Mr Nason. I want you to show us where this Home Secretary can be found. We may need to go back there one day to kill him.'

Ruth Levitt was quick and methodical. When she'd cleaned one room, she took the candelabrum through to the next one. After setting it down, she worked by its light to go through a set routine. She was halfway through polishing a sideboard when she heard the click of the letterbox. Taking the candelabrum, she lit her way to the front door and noticed the letter on the carpet. When she picked it up, she saw that it was addressed to the Home Secretary so she went along to his office and put it on his desk to await his arrival.

As she returned to her chores, it never occurred to her that the missive she'd just picked up would cause so much grief and apprehension.

CHAPTER TEN

Having spoken to the night watchman at the Home Office, Peter Skillen had a clear idea of the time when Anne Horner usually left the premises. She was, it transpired, a creature of habit, cleaning the different rooms in a set order and invariably finishing with the one belonging to Viscount Sidmouth. After exchanging a few pleasantries with the night watchman, she went back to her lodging by means of her customary route. To make sure that she never took an alternative way home, Peter also talked to her landlady, Joan Claydon, who confirmed that the cleaner always came back down the long, tree-lined lane where Peter had earlier encountered trouble, and that she arrived back at the house around the same time each morning. A light sleeper, Joan usually woke up when her lodger returned.

Anne Horner had been watched. The person or persons who'd abducted her had chosen the ideal spot on her nocturnal journey home. Peter arrived at the lane that night at approximately the time when Anne would have walked down it. Unlike her, he took precautions. He had a dagger in his belt and a Manton pistol, his favourite, concealed under his coat. He also carried a lantern that could be used as an auxiliary weapon. As it happened, it was called into use soon after he'd entered the lane. A foul-smelling old man suddenly lurched drunkenly out of the shadows at him, only to be knocked back on his heels by a glancing blow from the lantern. Dazed and in pain, he fell against a wall then bounced off it. As the man bent forward to expel a stream of vomit, Peter stepped out of reach then walked away.

He did not expect any real danger. In arresting Reuben Grigg, he'd already rid the lane of its greatest threat. Criminals like him were territorial. Once they'd taken over a particular area, they were rarely challenged. Anyone tempted to operate in the lane would first have had to engage in a fight to the death. No doubt they'd decide that it was safer to respect the territory marked out by Griggs and stay well clear of it. Until his disappearance became common knowledge, nobody would try to replace him.

The lantern served its purpose. Enabling him to look in every nook and cranny, it also guided his footsteps past the accumulated refuse and human waste that littered the way. The light caught the attention of someone who withdrew into an alley and waited for him to reach it. Sensing trouble ahead, Peter slipped a hand inside his coat to hold the butt of his pistol. In the event, no weapon was needed. The person who slipped out of the alley to accost him was a young woman.

'Have you lost your way, sir?' she asked.

'No, I haven't,' he replied, holding the lantern up so that he could see her.

'You look lonely to me, sir.'

'I don't think so.'

'I've a room nearby. Would you like to come there?'

'No, thank you.'

Her voice had real pathos. 'Don't you *like* me, sir?'

Peter was no stranger to the blandishments of prostitutes. London had brothels galore and areas where whores routinely roamed the streets after dark in search of custom. In the course of his work, he'd had to pursue suspects into some of the most notorious parts of the capital so nothing surprised him. Any offers made to Peter had always been met with a polite rebuff. What upset him in this instance was that she was a game-pullet, a prostitute little more than a child. Short, skinny and wearing a ragged taffeta dress, she had a forlorn prettiness.

'Are you always here at this time?' he asked.

'I can be here whenever you wish, sir,' she said, plucking at his sleeve.

He detached her hand. 'What's your name?'

'I meant no harm, sir.'

'Where do you live?'

Hearing the authority in his voice, she drew back as if about to flee the scene.

'Have you come to arrest me, sir?' she asked, anxiously.

'No,' he told her. 'If you help me, there may be a reward for you.'

She brightened. 'I'll do anything you wish, sir. My mother taught me.'

'I'm not buying your favours. I'm after something else.'

Speaking gently in order not to frighten her away, Peter explained what he wanted.

Unfortunately, the girl was unable to tell one day from another so she could not be sure if she'd been in the lane on the night he mentioned. He got a disturbing insight into a life robbed of its childhood and brutalised by the demands of the oldest profession. Peter's instinct was somehow to save her but she was too far beyond redemption. Slow of speech and dull-witted, the girl could offer no real assistance. He was on the point of walking away when a memory stirred in her fuzzy brain.

'I don't know if I was here, sir,' she said, 'but mother was.'

'Are you sure of that?'

'She's always here.'

'Where is your mother now?'

'She's with someone.'

The girl led him down the alley until they came to a small house with perished brickwork and a broken window. As they approached, the front door opened and a middle-aged man in rough attire hurried out, pulling on his coat before disappearing in the opposite direction. Taken into the house, Peter winced as the reek of rotten food, mustiness and sheer despair hit him. The girl opened the door to the back room on the ground floor. Candles illumined a pitiful scene. A bony woman with rumpled hair and a powdered face was sitting on the edge of the bed. Completely naked, she was reaching for a filthy shift. She was amazed to see someone as respectable as Peter. Tossing the shift away, she exposed her toothless gums in a grin of welcome.

'It costs more for the two of us, sir,' she warned.

'I only wish to ask a few questions,' he said.

'Has Lily already seen to you?'

Believing that she'd been robbed of a client, she looked accusingly at her daughter. The girl shook her head violently. Peter assured the woman that he was not interested in purchasing the services either of mother and daughter. Meeting the girl had been distressing enough but the older woman's appearance was even more upsetting. Worn, undernourished and raddled, she looked old enough to be the girl's grandmother but, when he studied her face, Peter was horrified to realise that she was probably around the same age as his own wife. He couldn't bear to look at the deathly white bruised body with its sagging breasts and protruding ribs.

After dismissing her daughter with a wave, she stood up.

'How can I help you, sir?'

'It depends on how good a memory you have.'

'Oh, it's very good, sir,' she replied, treating him to another view of her bare gums. 'I forgets nothing.'

By the time that Sidmouth arrived at his desk that morning, a fair amount of correspondence had built up on his desk. He worked sedulously through it. Much of it had come from departments of government, which were passing on their problems for his consideration and making him bewail once again the fact that the Home Office was regarded as the place into which political colleagues could toss unwanted or tiresome material. It was only when he reached the bottom of the pile that he found something more arresting. It was the letter delivered at night. He read the document three times before summoning Bernard Grocott and passing it over to him. As the undersecretary worked his way slowly through it, his mobile features registered interest, astonishment, unease, alarm and outright terror in that order.

'This is extremely disconcerting, my lord.'

'It sheds a very different light on the events at Dartmoor.'

Grocott handed the letter back to him. 'I agree,' he said, 'but only if it's a true account and not some grotesque hoax.'

'The detail is too exact for it to be a hoax and it's signed by the two prisoners who are known to have escaped. Captain Shortland did warn us about Thomas O'Gara. Evidently, the fellow is determined to be the governor's nemesis.'

'However did he reach London?'

'He must be a very resourceful man.'

'I deplore the way he tries to bully you, my lord,' said Grocott, 'but there's no doubt that he can marshal an argument. This list of demands is both lucid and – dare I say it – oddly persuasive.'

'But it's rendered invalid by the threats against my life,' said Sidmouth, angrily. 'I'd never bow to coercion of this kind. If two escaped prisoners think they can scare me into introducing new legislation into the statute book, they know nothing of my character or of the way that government operates. At the same time,' he continued, moderating his tone, 'certain points are raised in the description of the mutiny that should bear close examination. If you put this document beside Captain Shortland's version of the same events, you'll see enormous discrepancies.'

'I side with the governor.'

'Let the joint commission do its work, Grocott. They need to see this deposition from Thomas O'Gara and Moses Dagg.

Though I abhor their attempt at intimidating me, I have to admit to a sneaking admiration for them.'

'Admiration?' repeated the other in surprise.

'They could so easily have ignored the American prisoners left behind and simply have taken a ship back to their homeland. In remaining here to lead what they foolishly deem to be a kind of crusade, they've placed themselves in danger. That takes courage.'

'I care nothing for *their* safety, my lord, but I am concerned about yours.'

'They've no means to carry out their threat.'

'Yet a moment ago, you were saying how resourceful they were.'

'That's true,' conceded Sidmouth, uneasily.

'You need immediate protection.'

'They'll not do anything until they know the outcome of the commission. It's clear that they're aware of its existence because they refer to it in their letter. That can only mean that they read about it in the newspapers.'

'They may not wait for the commission to pronounce its verdict,' argued Grocott. 'There's a hectoring tone in their demands and an underlying impatience. I fear that, if they don't get what they want soon, they may decide to exact revenge and you will be their target.'

'I don't *feel* in any danger.'

'Neither did our last Prime Minister.'

The reminder was so painful that it made Sidmouth twitch involuntarily. Three years earlier, Spencer Perceval, a well-respected politician with an evangelical air about him, had been shot dead in the lobby of the House of Commons by a bankrupt merchant, John James Bellingham. The fact that a Prime Minister could be murdered so easily in broad daylight had sent tremors through the political classes and every Member of Parliament became more watchful.

Sidmouth regained his composure. 'The assassin was clearly deranged.'

'Do you think that Thomas O'Gara and Moses Dagg are of sound mind?'

'Yes, I do. Palpably, they are capable of reason.'

'Yet they're driven by a dark fanaticism.'

'They have a missionary zeal, I grant you.'

'They're obsessed, my lord, and obsessions make people unpredictable. I beg of you to take precautions. Before you submit that document to the joint commission, show it to someone who can mount a guard on you. This is work for the Runners.'

'You have a point,' admitted Sidmouth, 'but the best defence is to eliminate the threat altogether. The Runners can protect me from attack but we need someone else, if we are to catch these fugitives from Dartmoor. I'm expecting a report from Peter Skillen fairly soon. He and his brother are the men for this task. They'll know how to smoke out O'Gara and Dagg.'

Though Dermot Fallon and his family had given the fugitives a warm Irish welcome, they were far less popular with the neighbours. Dagg, in particular, aroused a lot of hostility. His was the only black face in the rookery and it made him a figure of suspicion. He was blamed simply for being there and, when he gave an innocuous smile to a pretty young woman in the street, her common-law husband was inflamed with jealousy. The man lay in wait for Dagg then confronted him as he emerged out of the tenement. Short, stocky and in his twenties, the man was a chimney sweep by trade and, ironically, as black as the sailor.

'Keep away from my wife,' he warned.

Dagg bristled. 'Don't give me orders.'

'I saw the way you looked at her.'

'I don't know who your wife is and I don't care.'

'She hates niggers as much as I do.'

'Watch your tongue,' advised Tom O'Gara, standing beside his friend. 'Moses won't take insults from anybody.'

'He'll get more than insults from me. If he grins at my wife like a frigging monkey again, I'll knock him from here to Africa.'

Dagg bunched his fists. 'Who're you calling a monkey?' he demanded.

'You'd better apologise while you can,' said O'Gara to the man. 'If you call him names, he gets upset.'

'*I'm* the one who deserves an apology,' declared the chimney sweep, 'and so does Meg. This animal leered at her.'

The raised voices had brought a number of people out into the street and they formed a ring around the two fugitives. There was a sense of general resentment against the newcomers. When Dagg remained silent, the chimney sweep decided to inflict some punishment. In the belief that he could fell the man with one punch, he swung a fist with murderous intent. The blow was easily parried and so were all the succeeding attempts at hitting his opponent.

The crowd drew back as the men circled each other. O'Gara was certain of the outcome. Dagg was the veteran of dozens of tavern brawls in various ports. They'd helped him to develop teak-hard fists and an ability to throw an attacker off balance. It was exactly what he did with the chimney sweep. After dodging and weaving, he stood still to invite a punch then drew back sharply as it was delivered. All that the irate chimney sweep did was to explore fresh air. The next second, he was hit by a powerful hook that caught him on the side of the head and made him stagger. Dagg followed up with a series of solid punches to his body and head before knocking him unconscious with an uppercut that drew a gasp of fear from the crowd. While the chimney sweep slumped to the ground with blood gushing from his nose, Dagg turned to the others.

'Would anyone else like to try their luck?' he invited.

'No, Moses,' said O'Gara, 'they're too scared.'

'It was a fair fight. You all saw that.' There was a murmur of agreement. 'It's over now. You can disappear.'

The crowd slowly dispersed. Two men helped the chimney sweep to his feet and dragged him away. The fugitives traded a laugh.

'I enjoyed that,' said Dagg, flexing his hands.

'It was stupid of him to call you a nigger,' observed O'Gara with amusement. 'Did you see the colour of that idiot? He was ten shades blacker than *you*.'

Alfred Hale was still asleep when the message was delivered to his home. Dressing quickly, he set off and met up with Micah Yeomans at The Peacock Inn, the public house that was their unofficial headquarters. By way of a greeting, Hale yawned in the other man's face.

'I can't watch him twenty-four hours a day, Micah,' he protested.

'Use members of the foot patrol to take over.'

'That's what I have done. We keep an eye on him in turns.'

'Do you have anything useful to report?'

'Only that I'm half-dead because I stayed up most of the first night I watched him. I saw Skillen being taken home in a carriage from a gambling hell in Jermyn Street. He was too drunk to stand up.'

'You look as if *you're* about to fall over as well, Alfred.'

'I stood outside his house for most of yesterday and he never came out.'

'Well, I've got something more important for you to do now.'

Hale shuddered. 'Don't tell me that you want me to keep an eye on *Peter* Skillen instead. I couldn't bear that.'

'We've been engaged as bodyguards.'

He explained to the other Runner that he'd been summoned to the Home Office and asked to provide protection whenever Sidmouth needed to travel between one place and another because of a death threat that had been received. When he heard the full details, Hale was puzzled.

'Why is he afraid of a couple of escaped prisoners?'

'Does it matter? We'll be well paid. That's all I care about.'

'They won't get anywhere near him.'

'That's up to us.'

'It's an empty threat, Micah, like the ones we get every day from the foul-mouthed scum we arrest. I've been threatened with everything from beheading to being set on fire. That pickpocket we caught at the theatre last week,' Hale reminded him, 'swore that he'd tie heavy rocks to our feet and throw us alive into the Thames. It's all nonsense. Tell the Home Secretary the truth. He's not in any real danger.'

'He thinks that he is, Alfred. We're there to soothe his mind.'

'That can be done by other means.'

'I know.'

'If he's so worried about these fugitives, we'll simply track them down and throw them back into prison.'

'And we need to do it as soon as possible.'

'Why?'

'We have competition,' said Yeomans, sourly.

Hale was insulted. 'He's approached the Skillen brothers?'

'He intends to do so. *We* have to cope with the boredom of taking the Home Secretary to and fro while *they* have the excitement of a manhunt.'

'It's wrong. *We* should have been given that assignment, Micah.'

'Let's prove it. If we can arrest these men first, we'll show the Home Secretary that he should always turn to us when there's a difficult task to allot. Unlike the Skillens,' he went on, 'we have a whole army of informers we can call on. One of the fugitives is a black man and both are Americans. They'll be noticed. Spread the word, Alfred. Involve our people in the search. One of them *must* be able to point us in the direction of these two brash, benighted, would-be assassins.'

Peter Skillen arrived at the Home Office in order to report his findings with regard to the disappearance of Anne Horner. That investigation, he discovered, had been supplanted by a new development and the first thing he was asked to do was to read the disturbing letter that had been delivered under cover of darkness. What struck him was the coherence of the description of the massacre at Dartmoor, supported, as it was, by other instances of the governor's cruelty towards the prisoners. The demands were harsh but not, in Peter's opinion, altogether unreasonable. Though the document was compelling, its thrust was fatally undermined by the crude threat to murder the Home Secretary if the demands were rejected.

While Sidmouth had watched him carefully as he read the letter, he could not judge from Peter's expression how he'd reacted. As soon as the missive was handed back to him, he pressed his visitor.

'What did you think?' he asked.

'The case is well-argued, my lord.'

'I hope that you do not believe the case for my assassination is well argued, Mr Skillen. Anyone reading that vile threat against me would think that *I* was the governor of Dartmoor and that I'd been engaged systematically in the most reprehensible mistreatment of the American prisoners there. It's unjust.'

'Power brings responsibility,' said Peter. 'These men have identified you as the ultimate authority in this matter and aimed their venom at you.'

'The verdict relating to what happened at Dartmoor lies not in my hands,' said Sidmouth. 'We must await the pronouncements of a joint commission. I have no influence over it, yet I'm the one whose life is in danger.'

'What precautions have you taken?'

'I've engaged some Runners to act as bodyguards.'

'That should calm your nerves, my lord.'

'Micah Yeomans is an experienced man.'

'Yes,' said Peter, taking care not to show his rooted dislike of the Runner. 'You'll be in good hands.'

'I trust *your* hands more than anyone else's, Mr Skillen. That's why I've reserved the primary duty for you. I want these two men – Thomas O'Gara and Moses Dagg – apprehended and put immediately under lock and key so that they no longer pose a danger to me. Yeomans and his men have their uses but, in a matter like this, I turn to you and your brother.'

'That's very gratifying, my lord.'

'Do you think that you *can* find these devils?'

'Yes, I do.'

'How will you go about it?'

'Well,' said Peter, thoughtfully, 'it's clear to me that the men who put their names to that document did not actually write it. Look at their signatures. One is shaky and the other is an uneducated scrawl. The American navy no doubt has its virtues but it's not known for improving the literacy of its deckhands, and that's what these sailors were.'

'What are you telling me, Mr Skillen?'

'There's a third person involved and our search starts with him.'

'Who is he?' asked Sidmouth with concern.

'He's the man who wrote that letter. The paper is crisp and the calligraphy neat. That's the hand of a clerk or scrivener. My feeling is that he helped them to channel their understandable anger and their jumbled thoughts into an articulate whole. If they managed to escape from Dartmoor,' said Peter, 'then they are brave and able men but neither is accustomed to holding a pen. The person they employed is the crucial figure here. My brother and I will concentrate our attention on him.'

'Do you mean that I have to fear attack at the hands of *three* men?'

'No, my lord – the scrivener means you no harm. He was paid to write and not to be party to any assassination.'

'That letter *makes* him a party.'

'In legal terms, I suppose that it does.'

'He's an accessory before the fact.'

'That doesn't mean he agrees with their declared intentions.'

'Then why didn't he have the grace to warn me?' asked Sidmouth. 'When he became aware of a conspiracy to kill a member of the government, any public-spirited man would raise the alarm at once. This fellow is colluding with them.'

'I dispute that, my lord.'

'On what grounds, pray?'

'These are desperate men. They will have bought his silence by intimidation. If he reveals their whereabouts, his life will be forfeit. Under those circumstances, even the most public spirited of citizens would hesitate.'

Pausing to consider what he'd been told, Sidmouth crossed to the window, looked out of it for a few moments then withdrew sharply, as if suddenly aware that, in presenting himself as a target, he could be shot dead through the glass. He went back to his desk and sat behind it.

'Forgive me if I appear unduly anxious,' he said.

'I sympathise with you, my lord. None of us will ever forget what happened to our last Prime Minister. His eminence was no protection against an assassin.'

'Spencer Perceval was a man for whom I had the highest admiration. He may have been short in stature but he would have gone on to be a political giant in due course. Sadly, he was deprived of the plaudits he would surely have received for bringing the ship of state safely into harbour after the French and the American wars.' A smile flitted across his face. 'It's curious, isn't it? When I was Prime Minister, the whole of the French nation wished for my death and I had a number of political enemies on this side of the Channel who would have cheered at my funeral. Yet, oddly enough, I never felt the imminent danger that's been prompted by a letter from two escaped prisoners.'

'Forget about them, my lord,' said Peter. 'If they are still in London, my brother and I will find them. On the subject of searches,' he added, 'I really came here to tell you what I've learnt with regard to Mrs Horner.'

'Of course, of course,' said Sidmouth, apologetically. 'I've been so concerned for my own safety that I quite forgot the poor woman. That's unforgivable. What have you discovered?'

Peter told him about his nocturnal walk along the route home taken by Anne Horner and how he'd found someone who was nearby on the night when the necessary woman was abducted. He didn't name or describe the prostitute who'd given him the information. Peter merely said that it came from a reliable source because Lily's mother had been in the lane on the night in question.

'It was very dark,' he explained, 'but my informant does

remember seeing a woman go past her. It must have been Mrs Horner because she was the same person who went down that lane regularly. My informant had seen her many times before.'

'What happened?'

'Two people suddenly emerged from a gateway and overpowered Mrs Horner. Her scream for help was soon muffled. They dragged her back down the lane and went right my past my informant.'

'Did your informant have any idea whom they were?'

'No, my lord,' said Peter, 'but I learnt a significant fact. One of the people who kidnapped your cleaner was a woman.'

When she heard someone coming down the steps of the cellar, she got up from the bed and waited for the door to be unlocked. Expecting the man to bring her a meal, she was ready to plead with him once again for her release. But it was not her usual gaoler who came with a tray of food. It was the woman who'd helped to abduct her.

'Why are you keeping me here?' she demanded.

'That's our business,' replied the woman. 'Behave yourself and no harm will come to you. In the fullness of time, you'll be released.'

CHAPTER ELEVEN

Paul Skillen had spotted him immediately. When he realised that he was under surveillance, he'd pretended to stay in the house all day so that Alfred Hale would be forced to stare at it in vain. In fact, Paul had slipped out by the rear entrance and made his escape through the garden gate. Hale – and the man who'd later replaced him on duty – had been standing guard fruitlessly. Paul, meanwhile, had had his usual fencing lesson with Gully Ackford and spent the whole day away from home. When he'd let himself back into the house that night, the watching Runner had been none the wiser. A new day had brought a new sentry. Micah Yeomans was clearly trying to inhibit his activities by keeping a close watch on him. It was not something Paul was prepared to tolerate.

For the time being, however, he had something of more importance to ponder. Hannah Granville remained the burning issue and he felt ashamed that his immediate response to her rejection of him was to lurch off to a gambling hell and drink himself into a state of utter helplessness. It was only on the following day that he'd learnt how he'd got safely home that night. A friend had driven him there in his carriage and roused a servant to take his master in. Had Paul tried to make his own way home, he would have been easy prey for any footpad and every penny of the winnings he'd somehow accumulated at the card table would certainly have been stolen. As it was, he was now sobered in every sense and the money was intact.

On the second night away from Hannah, therefore, he'd shunned alcohol and stoutly resisted the lure of gambling. When he'd retired early to bed, he heard the rain beating on the window and savoured the thought that the hapless Runner on duty outside would be soaked to the skin. He'd awoken early and rolled over to embrace Hannah Granville, only to find that she was not there. Though their relationship had been short and a trifle tempestuous, it had quickly seemed like the norm to him. Now she was decisively absent. Reminded of her ultimatum, he spent the whole morning wondering how he could win her back and persuade her to accept him on his own terms. What he would not do, he vowed, was to court another slap in the face by trying to visit her in her dressing room before a performance.

On the other hand, the urge to see her again was so powerful that it couldn't be resisted. He therefore decided to watch her onstage from an anonymous position in the circle. If he couldn't feel the sensuous warmth of her body against his, he could at least applaud her extraordinary talents as an actress.

It was afternoon before Jem Huckvale came running towards the house. When he was let in, the first thing he did was to gabble a warning.

'Someone is watching you, Paul.'

'I know that.'

'Why is he there?'

'I suspect that he's waiting for me to slip up in some way, so that he can report my misdemeanour to Micah Yeomans. The Runners would love to hobble me and my brother but we won't give them the opportunity.'

'I've a message from Peter.'

'What is it?'

'You're to meet him at the gallery as soon as possible. He wants you to help him in a search.'

'Do you have no more details than that, Jem?'

'I'm afraid not.'

'Then I'll come at once.'

'What about that man outside?'

'It's time I made my feelings known to him,' decided Paul. 'I'll need your help, Jem. Will you do me a favour?'

'I'll do it gladly.'

'Good fellow!' said Paul, squeezing him by his shoulders. 'What a wonderful friend you are. You never let me down and you never need explanations. Now, what I want you to do is this . . .'

His name was Chevy Ruddock and he was a member of a foot patrol. Tall, gangly and with a face that boasted a veritable outcrop of warts, he was the youngest of them and thus the one most frequently put upon. Standing just around the corner, he believed that he was invisible from Paul Skillen's house. All he had to do to watch it was to take a step forward. Having been thoroughly drenched in the downpour the previous night, Ruddock was relieved to be on duty in fine weather this time but the work was onerous. His legs were aching, his feet sore and his whole body weary. He fought off boredom by counting up to a hundred then repeating the procedure. It gave him something to do.

Having seen Jem Huckvale visit the house, he'd at last got something positive to report to Alfred Hale. It made him more alert. Sensing that something was about to happen, he peered around the corner. The door of the house opened and Huckvale emerged, waving a farewell before trotting off down the street. A minute later, Paul Skillen came out of the house, put on his hat at a jaunty angle and marched off purposefully. Ruddock was on his tail at once, wishing that he didn't walk so fast or wend his way through so many streets. Paul's gaudy attire made him easy to follow, so there was no danger of being shaken off, but it was still an effort for the latter to keep up with him.

In the end, by means of Thames Street, they reached the river and Paul walked along it to a quiet stretch of the bank. When his quarry disappeared from sight for a while, Ruddock broke into a run to catch up with him. Before he reached the bank, however, he heard a loud splash as if a body had just plunged into the water. He could see no sign of Paul. Rushing to the edge, he stared intently into the river, as if fully expecting the man he'd been following to bob up to the surface. The next moment, someone shoved him hard from behind and he plunged forwards into the river, disappearing under the surface and swallowing half a pint of cold, evil-tasting, brackish water.

Before Ruddock had gathered his senses, Paul and Huckvale were two streets away, walking side by side towards the shooting gallery. The plan had worked. Paul had dropped a heavy coil of rope into the river then hidden behind an upturned rowing boat on wooden trestles. While Ruddock was distracted, Huckvale had run forwards to push him from behind before scampering gleefully away. It would be the second time in twenty-four hours that the man would have to explain to his wife why he'd come home dripping wet.

'He won't be following you for a little while,' said Huckvale, laughing.

'No, Jem, I fancy that we dampened his ardour.'

Jubal Nason was embittered. After a relatively blameless life as a lawyer's clerk, he'd made the mistake of falsifying an account in his favour, albeit involving a very modest amount. Unfortunately, he'd been caught in the act. At one stroke, he'd lost his job, his reputation and his chances of being employed elsewhere at the same wage. Though he'd escaped prosecution because of his previous good conduct, he'd been shunned by the legal profession and forced to fall back on whatever work he could get as a clerk. Jobs were few and far between, often reducing him to the role of scrivener for some illiterate client. Over a period of weeks, for instance, he'd been compelled to write meandering love letters on behalf of a middle-aged butcher trying to woo a moneyed widow who – since she, too, was illiterate – had to have the touching *billets-doux* read out to her by an obliging female friend. Nason found it galling to further someone else's romance when his had withered on the vine. The sudden decline in his income had sharpened his wife's tongue and turned her into a block of granite at night.

It had all changed. Instead of working at a desk in an office where he had status, he now operated from his own small, drab, cheerless house where he had none. Instead of wearing a smart suit, he was reduced to putting on one that had seen substantially better days. Worst of all, he was at the mercy of the acid-tongued Posy Nason, a full-bodied termagant who was unable to accept her husband's fall from grace and who dedicated her life to punishing him for it. When she came bustling into the room, he tensed instinctively.

'Do you have no work today, husband?' she demanded.

'I've a client coming in an hour.'

'That means you earned nothing at all this morning.'

'There's money owing to me, my dear,' he lied. 'And I have prospects.'

'That's more than *I* have,' she said with a vehemence born of deep resentment. 'I used to have a husband who cared for me enough to work hard at a respectable profession. All he does now is to copy out things for people too stupid to do it themselves and write letters for lovesick butchers.'

'Things will improve.'

'Why you left the position you already had, I'll never know. You had some standing there. The only thing you do here is to get under my feet.'

Keeping the truth about his dismissal from her had been difficult but he'd managed it somehow, inventing a rigmarole about the firm for which he worked deciding to reduce the number of its clerks. Nason lived in fear that one day his wife would learn the appalling truth that her husband had, as a result of his folly, been summarily thrown out of a job he did well and condemned to lead a harsher existence. The few refinements he and his family had enjoyed were now things of the past.

In her daily litany of complaints, Posy never let him forget the fact.

'When did I last have a new dress?' she asked, truculently.

'You already have a serviceable wardrobe, my dear.'

'What's fine about fading colours and ill-fitting apparel?'

'You look well in whatever you wear,' he said, trying to pay her a compliment.

'No woman is at her best in rags.'

'If your dresses are worn, repair them.'

'I've been repairing them these past six months but you've been too busy to notice. You've let me down, husband.'

'I'll atone for it in some way.'

'Well, you won't do it by keeping such strange company as you do,' she said, contemptuously. 'That coarse, pig-faced butcher was bad enough with his demand for letters to entrap a widow but the three men who came here the other day were even worse. They looked like the lowest villains. We shouldn't have such dreadful people in our home. Do you *have* to do business with a black man?'

'I'll work for anyone who'll pay me, Posy.'

'Have you really sunk so low?'

The question was like a stab through the heart and he lacked the strength to conjure up an answer. Nason had lost his self-respect and it rankled. Head on his chest and eyes closed, he waited until his wife's rant finally abated. When she stormed off to the kitchen, he was able to breathe a sigh of relief and find solace by reading the newspaper he'd borrowed from a neighbour. It took his mind temporarily off the collapse of his fortunes. After working his way nostalgically through the details of the sort of court cases in which he was once tangentially involved, he came to an item that made him quiver with interest. A reward was offered for information leading to the arrest of two American prisoners of war who'd escaped from Dartmoor and who were known to be in London. They were named as Thomas O'Gara and Moses Dagg. A brief description was given of each man.

To someone in Nason's position, the reward was a real temptation. It was large enough to pay off his debts and still leave him with an appreciable amount of money. He would even be able to worm his way back into his wife's favour by buying her the new dress she sought. There was, however, an irremovable problem and a man with his legal expertise saw it at once. In causing the arrest of O'Gara and Dagg, he'd also be putting a noose around his own neck because they were sure to disclose the fact that he'd been responsible for writing their account of the massacre at Dartmoor and for advising them how best to frame their demands. His hand had held the pen that threatened the life of the Home Secretary. Though he deprecated everything the two Americans did, Nason would be seen as a conspirator.

Having momentarily considered reporting them, he now saw that it was more important to save them from the law than deliver them up to it. If they were arrested, his name was bound to be mentioned. Two minutes with the fugitives would be enough to determine that neither was able to write legibly, reason soundly or compose a well-structured narrative. During their interrogation, someone would demand to know which scrivener they'd employed. Having no loyalty towards him, they would never dream of protecting him. He recalled what his wife had said about letting such low company into their home. O'Gara and Dagg should have been sent on their way but that would have offended Dermot Fallon and he was loath to do that. Against his will, Nason had been forced to comply with their wishes.

They needed to be warned. None of the three men was likely to read any newspaper. Until Nason had pointed it out to them, O'Gara and Dagg had not heard that a joint commission had been set up to inquire into events at Dartmoor. They would be equally ignorant of the fact that a reward had now been offered for their capture. In drawing it to their attention, Nason believed that he'd earn their thanks and, possibly, payment of sorts. He hoped that he'd also persuade them to go to ground so that they'd elude the manhunt that would be set in motion. His safety depended on theirs. He needed to make urgent contact with them.

A difficulty confronted him. He had no idea where they lived.

Instead of going home to face the strictures of his wife, Chevy Ruddock elected to report first to his superiors. He therefore squelched his way to The Peacock and found Yeomans and Hale quaffing a tankard of ale apiece. If he'd hoped for even a scintilla of sympathy, he was disappointed. The two Runners took one look at him and hooted with laughter. Their amusement was tempered by anger when they learnt that Paul Skillen had been responsible for Ruddock's dip in the River Thames.

'Did you actually *see* him push you?' asked Yeomans.

'No,' replied Ruddock, 'but I certainly felt his hands.'

'How do you know it was Skillen?'

'Who else could it have been?'

'That's for you to find out, Chevy. If he was *ahead* of you when you reached the river, how could he possibly get behind you?'

'I've been puzzling over that myself.'

'You got what you deserved,' said Hale, uncaringly. 'I told you when you first joined the foot patrol that you needed eyes in the back of your head. That advice should always be borne in mind when you're dealing with the Skillen brothers.'

'Can we arrest him for assault?'

'No,' said Yeomans, 'we have no proof that he even touched you. Were there any witnesses?' Ruddock shook his head and sprayed both of them with the water in the folds of his hat. 'You felt hands on your back but, in truth, you've no idea to whom they belonged. We can't prosecute a phantom, Chevy.'

'*Someone* should be made to pay.'

'I'll do that,' volunteered Hale, opening his purse. 'You deserve a tankard of ale for the fun you've given us by turning up like that.'

He walked off to the bar and left Ruddock alone with Micah Yeomans.

'Paul Skillen tricked me,' said the younger man, sadly.

'You obviously gave yourself away.'

'But I didn't, I swear. He couldn't possibly have seen me hiding there. How could he when he didn't stir from the house the whole day? It was only when that little friend of his from the shooting gallery called that he ventured out.'

'Jem Huckvale went to see him?'

'Yes – he was in the house for less than five minutes.'

'Then we can put a name to your attacker. It was Huckvale.'

'But he went off in the opposite direction, Mr Yeomans.'

'No, lad, he only *appeared* to do so. I daresay he agreed to a rendezvous at the river and was on hand to shove you in. Don't worry,' he went on, putting a consoling hand on the sodden sleeve of Ruddock's coat, 'far better men than you have been hoodwinked by Paul Skillen. If *he* didn't see you there, Huckvale certainly did. They worked together to get rid if you, Chevy. When you've supped your ale, go home and put on dry clothes.'

'My wife will be very upset,' confided Ruddock. 'Agnes was so proud of me when I became a member of the foot patrol. What will she think when I tell her that I was outwitted so easily and turned into a laughing stock?'

'Even you are not that foolish.'

'I don't follow.'

'Why tell her about your failure when you have a chance to boast of your success?' Ruddock was bewildered. 'Granted, you ended up in the river but it was not because some unseen hands pushed you in. You showed great bravery in wrestling with a pickpocket on the bank and the pair of you tumbled into the water.'

'Did we?'

'Use your imagination, lad. Turn a bad story into one that shows you in a good light. You never know,' said Yeomans with a chuckle. 'When she hears what a hero she married, your wife might help you off with those wet clothes.'

Hale returned with a tankard, which he handed to Ruddock. All three of them took a long swig of ale. An unpleasant experience might yet be turned into something that won praise. Ruddock smiled at the thought. Having been critical of her husband for staying out all night in the driving rain, she would mellow when she heard that he'd fought valiantly with a dangerous criminal, overpowered him in the Thames then dragged him off to gaol.

'Women are too easily unsettled,' said Yeomans, philosophically. 'My wife is a good example. She worried incessantly when I first became a Runner and had a few setbacks. So I converted them into triumphs and she was content. Tell your wife only what you want her to believe.'

'It's what *I* always do,' confessed Hale.

'Then I'll do the same,' decided Ruddock.

'Meanwhile, there's something you haven't told us.'

'What's that?'

'Where is Paul Skillen *now*?'

Face blank and eyelids fluttering, Ruddock gave a despairing shrug.

Charlotte Skillen so rarely saw the two brothers together that she relished the treat. Seated in the room at the rear of the gallery, she listened as her husband described what had happened when he visited the Home Office. Paul was intrigued by the new development. A natural rebel, he felt sympathy for the fugitives, imprisoned beyond the time when they should have been released and showing great enterprise in escaping from Dartmoor and seeking to expose the truth behind the so-called mutiny. What he could not condone, of course, was the death threat hanging over the Home Secretary. While not as close to him as his brother, he admired Sidmouth for a number of reasons. The Home Secretary might be too dry and conservative for Paul's liking but he had virtues that deserved respect. Since the man's safety depended on the arrest of O'Gara and Dagg, they had to be caught soon.

'Peter thinks that we should look for the scrivener who drew up the document for them,' said Charlotte. 'They're not educated men. They had help.'

'They're also being sheltered by someone,' Paul concluded. 'This is a foreign country to them. It's unlikely that they've ever been to a city the size of London. Anyone coming here for the first time would be completely lost, yet they've somehow found someone to look after them and find a scrivener.'

'I agree,' said Peter. 'I warrant that Thomas O'Gara is the key figure here.'

'Why is that?' asked his wife.

'He's Irish. O'Gara is one of the hundreds of thousands who fled their native country because it offered them no prospects and went to America. Many of them came here as well, of course. Irish families are large and tend to be fiercely loyal to each other. It's not beyond the bounds of possibility that O'Gara has family connections here whereas it's unlikely that Dagg has relatives in London.'

'Peter is right,' said Paul. 'We need to look at Irish communities.'

'There are so many of them, alas.'

'We'll look for a branch of the O'Gara family.'

His brother grinned. 'We'll find dozens. It's a common name.'

'Then we'll work through them one by one.'

'I still think Peter's suggestion is the better one,' said Charlotte. 'You need to track down the man who drafted that letter for them.'

'He, too, might be Irish,' argued Paul. 'They'd be taking a risk if they employed a complete stranger. As soon as he realised who they were, he'd have been likely to report them.'

'Unless he was coerced into helping them,' she suggested.

'That could be a factor, I agree.'

'We have two lines of inquiry,' summarised Peter. 'I'll search for the man who put their demands on paper. No reputable clerk would align himself with a pair of escaped prisoners, so I may be looking for someone who's either disreputable or too poor to turn any work away. Paul, meanwhile, can search through the Irish communities here.'

'Luckily, they will *be* communities,' said his brother. 'Irish immigrants stick together. I won't have to look for an isolated family. O'Gara's relatives – if indeed he has any – will be part of a much larger group.'

'What can I do?' asked Charlotte.

'Watch and pray.'

'I want to give practical assistance, Paul.'

'Then you can come searching among the Irish with me.'

'Gully needs Charlotte here to hold the fort,' said Peter, pleasantly. 'We can use Jem if need be but my wife stays put.'

She was irked. 'I always miss the excitement.'

'We can soon rectify that,' teased Paul. 'Next time Peter and I go gallivanting across the rooftops, we'll take you with us. Will that appeal to you?'

'Yes,' she said, laughing, 'it certainly would. I'd love to join the pair of you up there – as long you promise to catch me if I fall. But you haven't heard about the other search that Peter had been conducting,' she went on. 'This business with the letter from the fugitives has rather eclipsed the disappearance of Mrs Horner.'

'It hasn't eclipsed it in *my* mind,' said Peter.

'What have you learnt?' asked his brother.

Peter gave him an edited account of his investigation, ending with the assertion that the cleaner was still alive, although he was still unsure why she'd been taken in the first place. He speculated afresh on how Anne Horner had amassed so much money, yet discounted the possibility that the kidnappers knew of its existence.

'Had they done so,' he reasoned, 'they'd have already made attempts to get their hands on it yet they haven't done so. I called at her lodgings yesterday and her little treasure trove was untouched.'

'What interests me,' said Charlotte, thoughtfully, 'is that a woman took part in the abduction.'

'It's an age-old device,' Paul pointed out. 'If she'd been approached by an aggressive man, she'd probably have taken to her heels. When a woman spoke to her, however, she wouldn't have expected violence.'

'So where *is* she?'

'Waiting to be rescued by us, Charlotte,' said Peter, getting up from his chair. 'I need to speak to Gully. When I've done that, I'll start looking for the man who penned that death threat – but I won't forget Anne Horner altogether. I'm determined to plumb the mystery of her disappearance.'

Peter went out and left them alone. His brother waited until he heard him ascending the stairs before he turned to his sister-in-law.

'Have you told him?'

'No, I haven't.'

'Why not?'

'You spoke to me in confidence about your problem,' said Charlotte. 'Besides, Peter has more than enough on his plate at the moment. I'm afraid that he'd view a discussion of your private life as a distracting irrelevance.'

'That's not how I see it, Charlotte.'

'No, I'm sure.'

'It means a great deal to me.'

'I don't find it irrelevant, Paul. I can see what a profound effect it's had on you. I was touched that you felt able to confide in me.'

'I had to talk to someone or my brain would have burst like a balloon.'

'Is the situation still the same?'

'No,' he moaned, 'it's far worse. I took your advice, you see.'

'I wasn't aware that I gave you any.'

'It was indirect counsel. When you talked about marriage to Peter, you stressed the importance of each partner giving the other some leeway. Compromise was of the essence. That prompted me to . . . reach out to her by way of a concession.'

Without disclosing the name or the profession of Hannah Granville, he told her that she'd forbidden him access to her and what the consequences had been. Charlotte was dismayed to hear that he'd spent the evening gambling, yet pleased that it had turned out to be such a profitable venture. She was gratified that her brother-in-law had repented and stayed away from the card table ever since.

'Denial is good for the soul,' she reminded him.

'Then why do I feel so dejected?'

'It's because you love her.'

'I do, I do,' he said with fervour. 'Life is an arid desert without her.'

'Well,' she chided, 'that's a fine thing to say to your sister-in-law. I may not be a lush oasis but I like to feel that I was able to offer you some sustenance.'

'Oh, you did. Talking to you kept me sane. Lost love and madness are near allied. The one feeds off the other.'

'You are too ready to accept defeat. What happened to your natural optimism?'

'It's sunk without trace,' he said, gloomily.

'What about the lady?'

'She'll none of me.'

'That's not what I'm asking,' said Charlotte. 'Evidently, you've been very close. Pulling away from each other will be as painful for her as for you. There's loss on both sides. How will she cope with it? Does she have a friend to whom she can turn for comfort?'

'I've no idea,' he admitted. 'The only fact that has emerged with clarity is that I'm shackled by a cruel proviso. What I do is an expression of what I am as a man. She seems unable to accept that. As for turning elsewhere for comfort,' he went on, lugubriously, 'she has far too many people on whom she could call. That would be a case of twisting the knife in the wound, Charlotte. Unless I go crawling to her unconditionally, it's only a matter of time before I'll be forgotten. If truth be told, I'm not sure that I could cope with that eventuality.'

* * *

Hannah Granville stared unseeingly into the mirror in her dressing room. Costumed for the evening's performance, she would normally be adding the final touches to her appearance and preening. Hannah had no urge to do that now. She was still shocked at her rejection by the man she took to be Paul Skillen. When she rode past in her carriage, he'd seen her clearly yet he didn't exhibit the slightest interest, still less any affection for her. It was hurtful. A woman accustomed to having a legion of admirers had been deserted by the only one of them that she prized. Hannah had never been in that situation before and, as a result, had no idea how to deal with it.

Her dresser, a short, bosomy woman in her forties, with her face composed into an expression of deep anxiety, hovered behind her, desperate to reassure her but too frightened to speak. Over the years, she'd learnt how to read Hannah's moods and react accordingly. But she'd never seen the actress plunged into such a black and debilitating melancholy before.

Someone in the corridor outside rapped hard on the door.

'That's your call, Miss Granville,' said the dresser. 'You'll be onstage in five minutes.' She shook Hannah gently by the shoulder. 'Did you hear what I said?'

There was no reply. The actress didn't move. When she looked in the mirror, the dresser saw tears starting to trickle down Hannah's cheeks.

CHAPTER TWELVE

Since he'd not been there at the time, Dermot Fallon was intrigued to hear about the fight between Moses Dagg and the chimney sweep. When he had a drink with the fugitives at a seedy public house that evening, he pressed for details. He'd already heard a number of versions but wanted Dagg's own testimony as well as that of his cousin, Tom O'Gara. The man who'd actually taken part in the brawl was too modest to say very much about it but his shipmate was lyrical. O'Gara not only described the fight in vivid detail but also listed all the other occasions when Dagg had knocked out opponents who'd underestimated his strength and skill.

'We docked in New York harbour one time,' recalled O'Gara, 'and went ashore to slake our thirst after a long voyage. Three men began to bait Moses. He tried to ignore them but they wanted some sport. When we rolled out of there later on, the three of them were waiting for him. They called him filthy names. I was all for lambasting them but Moses pushed me aside.'

Fallon was startled. 'He took on all three of them?'

'He insisted, Dermot. I'd seen him fight many times but Moses had never been so riled before. He punched, grabbed, threw, kicked and bit until three blood-covered bodies were stretched out on the floor.' O'Gara cackled. 'Out of interest, I counted the number of teeth he'd knocked out. There were over a dozen.'

Dagg protested that his friend was exaggerating but he admitted that he'd defeated the trio of mocking sailors. Fallon clapped him on the shoulder.

'Well done, Moses!' he said. 'You're a true fighter. No wonder you got the better of Donal Kearney so easily. A word of warning,' he added, 'be on your guard. Kearney nurses grudges. Since he can't beat you with his fists, he may come after you with a weapon.'

'I'll be ready,' said Dagg, unafraid.

'If he's attacked,' said O'Gara, 'Moses will stick Kearney's brushes up his ass. He won't be able to sweep a chimney for a very long time.'

'A lot of people would be happy about that. Donal Kearney is not too popular around here. He likes to throw his weight around.'

Dagg hunched his shoulders. 'All I did was to smile at his wife.'

'Barring my Mary, she's the prettiest colleen in the tenement.'

'I noticed,' said O'Gara with a lewd grin. 'I wouldn't mind sweeping *her* chimney, I'll tell you that.' The others laughed coarsely. 'But your neighbour wasn't only upset because Moses smiled at his wife. What really set his belly on fire was that she smiled back at Moses.'

They'd deliberately chosen a table in the darkest corner so that nobody could see or hear them too well. Fallon took an additional precaution. Beckoning them closer, he lowered his voice to a hoarse whisper.

'I've a great idea to make money, so I have.'

'What is it?' asked O'Gara.

'There's a place I know where people like me go for entertainment. Sometimes it's cock fighting and other times we bet on how many rats a dog can kill in half an hour, if a hundred or more of them are tossed into the pit with him.'

O'Gara chuckled. 'It's the kind of place *we* might enjoy.'

'Where is it?' asked Dagg.

'Let me finish,' said Fallon. 'From time to time, we have a boxing match. I don't mean the sort of thing that the aristocracy and the gentry flock to see. You won't find Belcher, Cribb or Gentleman John Jackson trading punches there. They belong to a different world of pugilism. We have a *real* fight with nobody to get in the way.'

'That's the way we like it,' said O'Gara.

'Then let's see if we can find a challenger for Moses. We can say that he's the best black boxer since Tom Molineux, that other American champion. It's sure to bring a good crowd. We could sit back and watch the money roll in.'

'*We* could, Dermot, but there's no sitting back for Moses. He'll have to go toe to toe with another fighter. He'll enjoy that.'

Dagg was reluctant. 'I'm not sure that I will, Tom.'

'You can beat anybody.'

'That's not the point.'

'Then what is?' asked Fallon. 'You're not scared, are you?' When Dagg seized him by the throat, he apologised immediately. 'I didn't mean that, honestly. I take it back. I'm sorry, Moses.'

Dagg released him. 'Don't ever question my nerve again,' he warned. 'I'll take on any man. My worry is this. You're forgetting something. Tom and I are on the run. We ought to stay in hiding and not be seen in public.'

'Nobody there will give you away. Most of the people who turn up are on the wrong side of the law. Anyway, they don't know who you are or what you've done.'

'He's talking sense,' said O'Gara. 'We can't miss a chance like this, Moses. We need money to repay Dermot. It's unfair to live off him when he's got a family to feed. On the other hand,' he conceded, 'I agree that we need to be careful so we won't call you by your real name. You can fight under a different one.'

'I don't like the idea,' grunted Dagg.

'But this could be the answer to our problems. If the Home Secretary turns down our plea, we'll need to do what we threatened and kill him. There'll be a proper hue and cry then,' O'Gara emphasised. 'The only way we'll get back home to America is to bribe the skipper of a vessel that'll take us there. That will cost a lot of money. You're in a position to make it for us.' He nudged his friend. 'What do you say, Moses?'

Still uneasy, Dagg took a long time to make up his mind.

'All right,' he said at length. 'I'll fight.'

Charlotte Skillen had expected her husband back home much earlier that evening but he didn't reappear until after eight o'clock. Peter was full of apologies, explaining that he'd visited a series of lawyers in his search for the anonymous scrivener and that, having allotted so much time to one investigation, he felt guilty that he'd neglected the other. Accordingly, he'd paid a third visit to Joan Claydon in order to tell her what he'd learnt about the abduction and to assure her that he would not abandon the hunt for her missing lodger until he found her.

'I still can't see what the kidnappers stand to gain,' opined Charlotte.

'They must have a reason of sorts, my love.'

'Could someone just be trying to give her a fright?'

'Mrs Horner is not easily frightened,' he said. 'That's the impression I get of her from her sister, her landlady and the friends of hers to whom I've spoken. She's an indomitable woman. Besides, a fright is, by its very nature, a short, sharp event that achieves its effect then is over and done with. Yet she's been missing for days. That's very disturbing.'

'This case has really interested you, hasn't it?'

'Yes, it has. Having talked to a number of people about her, I feel that I know Mrs Horner. It's made me care about her. Wherever she is, the woman must be very worried about her safety. Anybody held against their will would be. She may well be as mystified by what's happened as we are.'

'What happens next?'

'I keep looking for her. As for the other business, it remains to be seen if the death threat to the Home Secretary is one that should be taken seriously. Even if it is credible,' he observed, 'nothing is going to happen to Viscount Sidmouth in the near future. The two men who signed that deposition will wait to see the effect it's had. In other words, the Home Secretary has a breathing space. Mrs Horner doesn't enjoy that luxury. She already *is* a victim of a criminal act.'

'I feel for her. She's in the most appalling position.'

'We must remember her in our prayers again, my love.'

'Yes, of course. I do sympathise with you, having two investigations to worry about. One must come first and it has to be the threat to the Home Secretary.'

'Unfortunately, the man who assisted those fugitives may be just as difficult to find as Mrs Horner. London is full of clerks and scriveners.'

'How many of them would take part in a conspiracy to commit murder?'

'Very few, I daresay,' he replied. 'But there'll always be those who will take money and ask no questions. Those are the ones I need to chase.'

'Paul may make more headway than you,' she said. 'He's looking for the men themselves.'

'I hope he finds them soon. Parts of London have large Irish communities. Life for most people is even harsher across the Channel than it is over here. Paul has a long search on his hands. I hope he's equal to it.'

Charlotte was puzzled. 'That's an odd thing to say.'

'Well, you saw him earlier, my love.'

'Not for very long.'

'You must have noticed how jaded and lacklustre he seemed. Whenever we're summoned to take on a new case, Paul is usually as excited as I am. I saw none of that excitement this time. What's wrong with him?'

'I don't know.'

'It's unlike my brother to be so distrait.'

'He may have distractions in his private life,' she said, discreetly.

'Then I'm unlikely to hear about them,' he accepted with a smile. 'Because we're twins, we're far closer to each other than most brothers – until it comes to matters of a personal nature, that is. Paul and I have never been able to converse about those. Too many things get in the way somehow. Ah, well,' he concluded. 'Let's leave him to his distractions for the rest of the evening, shall we?'

Something was wrong. Most people in the audience were unaware of it but Paul Skillen noticed it the moment that Belvidera stepped onstage for the first time. Her appearance provoked a spontaneous outburst of applause. Though he joined in the clapping, Paul was dismayed. He'd seen the play on a number of occasions and each time there was an ovation for her, Hannah Granville had floated in on it like a swan gliding elegantly across the water. That didn't happen here. She seemed mildly annoyed by the interruption and, instead of waiting for the acclaim to die slowly away, cut it short by plunging into her first speech. To someone who'd seen her scale the peaks of her art, it was as upsetting as it was disappointing. Paul couldn't understand it.

Throughout the play, Hannah gave a competent performance that flickered into life intermittently without ever rising above a certain level. Her timing was good, her movement excellent and her gestures expressive. The sheer quality of her voice was enough to enchant most onlookers. In her final scene, she did manage to summon up some real emotion before she expired from a broken heart and Paul saw a glimpse of the actress who'd captivated him when he first set eyes on her. It was not enough to convince him that she was wholly committed to her role and he was bound to wonder if she was unwell. Needing to be reassured that she was in sound health, he joined the general exodus then slipped around to the stage door and stood on the outer fringe of the predictable gathering of male admirers.

It was clear from the comments he overheard that none of the others had noticed the loss of quality in her performance and – since he recognised a number of faces – he knew that some of the spectators had seen *Venice Preserv'd* before and returned to worship at the shrine. Fortunately, none of them looked at him or he might have been singled out as Hannah Granville's former favourite and subjected to tart comments. As it was, all eyes were on the stage door. No head turned away from it for more than a moment. Every time another member of the cast emerged, there was a flurry of hope that Hannah would be on their heels but the hope quickly expired.

Paul was worried that there was something wrong with her yet determined not to let Hannah see that he was there because she might be tempted to spurn him in public. His greatest fear, of course, was that she'd already elected his deputy and would depart on the arm of one of the baying admirers. Most were older than him but there was a clutch of younger men, handsome, debonair and patently wealthy. Hannah would have a free choice.

It was an hour before they learnt the devastating truth

about Belvidera. Coming out to confront them and raising his voice, the stage doorkeeper delivered the news for which they'd patiently waited.

'Miss Granville has already left, gentlemen,' he said with a twinkle in his eye. 'She went off through the front entrance some time ago.'

There was a concerted groan of disapproval and annoyance. Unlike the rest of them, Paul was not hurt or fractious. Because he knew how much she relished male attention, he was concerned that she'd gone out of her way to evade it. Something was definitely amiss with Hannah Granville. He spent the whole of the long walk alone wondering what on earth it could be.

Nights were the worst. Though the bed was relatively comfortable, Anne Horner rarely slept for any length of time. She lay in the gloom with only the guttering candle to stave off complete darkness. During the day, she was at least able to see a small patch of sky through the grating. When that disappeared, she felt horribly alone and vulnerable. The worst thing about her imprisonment was that she had no idea what had prompted it or how long her incarceration would last. The woman who'd brought her food would answer no questions and stayed for less than a minute. She merely told Anne that she wouldn't be harmed then locked the door again.

Yet, in her view, Anne had already been harmed. She'd been frightened by the attack on her, roughly handled, threatened with punishment, taken to a house, dragged down to the cellar and forced to endure dreadful conditions. Every day brought a succession of harmful assaults on her mind, body and emotions.

The appearance of the woman had momentarily lifted her expectations but they'd been instantly crushed. It was the man who came next time, remaining silent, bringing her food and – to her intense embarrassment – taking out the bucket to empty and wash it out before returning it for further use. The stink might have lessened temporarily but she felt that her privacy had been invaded.

There were a few improvements. To while away the time, she was given some old newspapers to read and, because she obeyed orders not to yell for help, she was given freedom of movement in the cellar and allowed bigger meals. Unable to eat a morsel at first, she now devoured all the food put in front of her, if only as a way to break the soul-destroying boredom of her situation. For the rest, she was left completely alone. Early fears that the man would molest her in some way had now faded away. Like the female accomplice, he was not interested in Anne Horner as a person. They had kidnapped her for a purpose yet she still had no inkling of what that purpose might be.

One thing was certain. Nobody would come to rescue her. If she wanted to get out of her prison cell, she would have to take matters into her own hands.

It was time to plan her escape.

Donal Kearney was still throbbing with anger. When he'd been badly beaten in the fight with Moses Dagg, he'd lost some of his old authority. Instead of being able to swagger around the tenement, he now tended to skulk. Neighbours, who'd hitherto been afraid of him, actually dared to mock him, albeit from a safe distance. Kearney blamed Dermot Fallon for letting the two strangers stay with him. As long as Dagg and O'Gara were there, the chimney sweep was in danger. He had to find a means of getting rid of them. Since he was not on speaking terms with Fallon or his wife, Kearney had to move stealthily.

'What did he say?'

'Thar you was knocked out by the black 'un.'

'What did he say about those two men?'

'Thar the black 'un was stronger than you.'

'That's not what I asked you to find out.'

'Isn't it?'

'No, you fool.'

'Oh . . . I'm sorry.'

'I wanted to know why they're there.'

The boy let out a howl of pain as his father smacked him hard across the face, leaving a black palm print on his cheek. Niall Kearney was the youngest of the brood, a skinny, wide-eyed urchin of five years or so. He'd been ordered by his father to play with one of the Fallon children in the hope that he'd learn something about the two men who'd moved in with them. Grabbing his son by his shoulders, Kearney shook him until the boy cried out for mercy.

'Tell me *everything* he said,' he growled.

'I told you.'

'There must be more.'

'I arsked 'im 'bout the nigger,' said the boy, snivelling, 'and 'e said he saw 'im fight you and knock you to the ground.'

'But why is he *there*?'

'Wouldn't tell me.'

'He must have said something.'

'Yeah but . . . I forgot what it was.'

In an attempt to jog his memory, Kearney slapped him again. His son wailed.

'Do I have to knock it out of you?' asked the father, looming over him.

'No, no,' begged his son. 'I remember now.'

'Go on.'

'I arsked 'im why they was there and 'e told me 'e couldn't say.'

'Why not?'

'Farver warned 'im to keep 'is gob shut. But . . .'

'Well? Spit it out, lad.'

'Listened at the door one night and . . .'eard them talk.'

'What did they say?'

'It was . . . somethink about prison.'

Kearney's eyes ignited. 'They've *escaped*?'

'Told all I knows.'

'Good boy!' said his father, hugging him. 'Well done!'

Accustomed only to routine violence from his father, Niall Kearney didn't know how to react to this unparalleled display of affection. He flinched, as if in readiness for the next blow, then laughed wildly when it didn't actually come.

In the course of his work as a detective, Peter Skillen had become acquainted with a large number of lawyers. Most were conscientious men who abided by the strict rules of their profession and served their clients as best they could at all times. Trust was their watchword. Some, however, were less honourable, often tempted to fleece those who fell unguardedly into their hands instead of representing them in a proper manner.

A significant few – and Peter knew them by reputation – were arrant, unprincipled rogues who would stop at nothing to win a case, discredit any opposition they met and make a tidy profit. He didn't waste energy on speaking to anyone in this last category. Peter spent the whole morning going from office to office of lawyers who would give him time without trying to charge him for it and who would provide him with honest answers. Yet after a couple of hours of tramping the streets, he'd learnt nothing that got him any closer to the mystery scrivener.

It was when he called at the offices of Rendcombe and Spiller that he had more luck. Martin Rendcombe was an apparently benign old man with a weak handshake and bloodshot eyes but, having once engaged him to act on his behalf, Peter knew how steely and effective he could be once involved in a case. Steeped in the arcane practices of the law, the man was a walking anthology of precedents and procedural niceties. After he'd invited his visitor to sit down in the book-lined office, Rendcombe peered at him over his spectacles.

'It is *Peter* Skillen, isn't it?' he checked.

'Yes, it is,' replied the other.

'I did act for your brother, Paul, on one occasion. It was very confusing.'

'I don't see why, Mr Rendcombe. It's easy to tell us apart. *I'm* the handsome brother and Paul is not.' The lawyer smiled good-naturedly. 'Your time is precious so I'll take up as little of it as I may.'

Peter explained the purpose of his visit and how important it was for him to track down the man who'd written the document submitted to the Home Secretary. Shocked to hear of the death threat, Rendcombe was quick to remove any suspicion from his own staff.

'Our clerks are, without exception, men of the highest probity,' he said. 'They would never be party to anything of this kind.'

'I'm sure that they wouldn't, Mr Rendcombe.'

'Do you have this obnoxious letter with you?'

'Unfortunately,' said Peter, 'I do not. The Home Secretary insisted on sending it to the joint commission looking into events at Dartmoor. Besides, I'm not sure that you could have told anything from the calligraphy beyond the fact that it was the work of an educated hand. Every lawyer to whom I've already spoken has said the same thing – nobody in their employ would dare to become embroiled with two escaped prisoners. Had such an approach been made to their clerks, the two fugitives would have been reported immediately.'

'Quite so, Mr Skillen.'

'And it may be that the man I'm after has never worked for a lawyer.'

'Clerks exist in many other professions.'

'What guided me to you and your legal colleagues was the way in which the document was framed. It was written by someone well versed in setting out an argument. The two Americans, O'Gara and Dagg, supplied the facts but they could never have presented them to such impressive effect.'

'Then it's plainly not the work of a bank clerk.'

'I'm convinced that the fellow makes his living from the law,' said Peter, 'or, at least, he's done so in the past. Either he's retired or been dismissed and forced to scratch around for money elsewhere.'

'Ah,' said Rendcombe, 'that opens up possibilities.'

'You can help me?'

'I didn't say that, Mr Skillen. I make no promises.'

Getting up from his chair, he crossed to a large oak cupboard. Rendcombe pulled out a bunch of keys, selected one and inserted it into the lock. When the door opened, Peter saw piles of documents and correspondence neatly stacked on the shelves. The lawyer's hand went unerringly to a thin pile of papers. He took them out, came back to his desk and leafed through each sheet.

'My esteemed partner, Mr Spiller, doesn't believe in harbouring such things but I am an unredeemed hoarder. I operate on the principle that even the most minor item that passes before my eyes might one day prove to be of value.' He held up the papers. 'These are letters from people seeking employment here. In two cases, we were able to take the gentlemen on and they've given good service. In the other three cases, however, there was no question of even interviewing the people in question.'

'Why is that, Mr Rendcombe?'

'We'd already been forewarned by the lawyers who'd engaged them in the past. When someone is dismissed for reprehensible conduct, one doesn't want them going elsewhere and continuing to pollute the profession.'

'What offences did these three individuals commit?'

'They are not specified,' said Rendcombe. 'Apart from anything else, no lawyer wishes to admit details of any criminal activity that took place under his aegis in case it makes him look foolish. All that he will do is to affirm that such-and-such a person is unfit for employment. That's all we need to know.'

'Who are the three men you rejected?'

'One can be eliminated from your enquiries at once, Mr Skillen, because he is presently in prison for debt. The man who told me that – with some satisfaction, I may say – was his former employer.'

'What of the other two?' asked Peter, sensing that he'd made some progress.

'Both were clerks and both were hounded out of their jobs.'

'Yet they were not prosecuted.'

'Instant dismissal was felt to be punishment enough – that and the guarantee that they'd never again be permitted to soil the good name of the legal profession.'

'May I know who these two men are?'

'You can do more than that, dear fellow,' said Rendcombe, passing the letters to him. 'You can read their correspondence.'

'Thank you.'

'Provided that you return it, of course, so that it can take its rightful place among my cherished records. Lawyers are archivists of personal disasters. You are about to be introduced to two of them.'

Seven Dials was a misnomer. It comprised seven streets that went out like spokes of a wheel from a majestic Doric column. At the hub of a wheel was a clock with seven faces but it had been removed over forty years earlier in the erroneous belief that a large sum of money had been concealed in its base. While the seven streets remained, therefore, the dials were nowhere to be seen. Conceived as a fashionable residential area cheek by jowl with Soho and Covent Garden, it had instead become a labyrinth of streets, lanes, courts and alleys that were the haunt of petty thieves, the poorer sort of street vendors and itinerant street musicians. Shops were dark and uninviting. Stray animals loitered. Poverty and danger went hand in hand in Seven Dials. Few strangers went there alone. Fewer still made the mistake of venturing there on their own at night.

Being smartly dressed in public was an article of faith with Paul Skillen and he'd sometimes been accused of being a dandy. On his walk into Seven Dials, however, there was no call for his expensive blue coat with its high collar, broad lapels and cutaway tails. Nor was there a place for his frilled shirt, striped vest and breeches. From his wardrobe, he instead chose a selection of ragged garments that turned him into a costermonger. By rubbing dirt into his hands and cheeks, he completed the disguise. Paul even summoned up a passable version of an Irish accent.

He knew that a lot of Irish families inhabited the tenements there and it was not long before he heard the sound of Dublin voices raised to full pitch.

'Y'are a filthy 'ussy, Lena Madigan!' yelled one woman.

'Wh're you callin' filthy, you old cow?' retorted the other, a mountainous creature with wobbling breasts and a red face. 'Sure, every man in Seven Dials 'as seen everythin' you 'ave to offer and you don't even 'ave the sense to charge for the priv'lege.'

'Y'are a slut, a dirty, stinkin', slovenly trollop who was born with 'er legs apart. Yes,' added the first woman, waving a fist, 'and thar swivel-eyed sister of yours is no better. The pair of you give the Irish a bad name, so you do.'

The argument quickly degenerated into a fierce fight that Paul had no wish to watch. As the women began to grapple with each other and a crowd formed to urge them on, he walked quickly past them and turned a corner, finding himself in a narrow court inhabited by screaming children, random filth and unwholesome vapours. A one-armed man of uncertain age was selling fruit from his barrow. Paul mingled with the knot of customers who were fingering the apples in search of some that were edible. When he heard the brogue of a young man beside him, he tried to sound casual.

'D'you live hereabouts, my friend?' he asked.

'Why, so I do.'

'Then p'raps you can help me.'

'That depends.'

Tall, hollow-cheeked and hirsute, the man eyed him suspiciously.

'Who're you?'

'My name is Paul Kilbride and I'm looking for someone.'

'You sound like a Wicklow man.'

'You've a good ear, my friend.'

'I've a good nose, too,' said the other with contempt, 'and I can always smell a Wicklow man.'

'What about an American?'

'What about him?'

'That's the fella I'm looking for, so it is,' explained Paul. 'He'd be around my age. When I heard he'd come to London,

I just had to seek him out. I remembered him telling me once that he'd family in Seven Dials so this is where he'd make for.'

'Does he have a name?'

'It's Tom O'Gara.'

'And when would he have come to the city?'

'Oh, it would be within the last week.'

The man snapped his fingers. 'Then I might be able to help you,' he said. 'There's a newcomer called O'Gara who turned up out of nowhere the other day. As to his being American, I couldn't say for I've not spoken to him.'

'He'd be travelling with someone else, a black man.'

'Then it *has* to be him. I've seen them both together. O'Gara and his friend are staying in the back room on the first floor. If you don't believe me, go and see.'

The man turned away and began picking up the fruit to test its ripeness. Unsure whether he was being helped or misled, Paul glanced at the grimy tenement. If the missing sailors *were* inside, they'd not be the only criminals using the Seven Dials as their refuge. He walked to the front door and waited as a mangy dog came hurtling out and shot past him. Paul then climbed the steps to the first floor, shoes echoing on the wooden steps. The walls were bare and glistening with damp. The stench was ghastly. When he reached the room at the rear, he knocked hard on a door that was covered in stains and had the name of O'Gara carved inexpertly into the timber.

Paul waited for a full minute. There was the sound of commotion from inside then the door swung open and a massive, bearded man in his fifties stood there with his hands on his hips. He gave Paul a truculent welcome.

'Who the devil are you?' he snarled.

'I'm looking for Tom O'Gara.'

'That's what he claims,' said a voice behind Paul, 'but I think he's lying.'

Paul turned round to see the man to whom he'd talked beside the barrow. Before he could move, he was grabbed from behind in a bear hug and held by the bearded man who exerted steady pressure with his strong arms.

'What's your friggin' game?' he demanded.

CHAPTER THIRTEEN

Paul was trapped. His only hope of escape lay in taking immediate action against both of them. Otherwise, he'd be held by the bearded man, robbed by his accomplice then assaulted by the pair of them. He therefore responded quickly, kicking the young man in the stomach and making him double up in pain. Struggling against his captor, he flung his head back sharply so that he broke the man's nose and elicited a howl of fury. At the same time, he rammed both elbows into his ribs then brought his heel down with full force on his toe. The bearded man had so many sources of anguish that he didn't know which one to attend to first. He released Paul and put a hand to the blood dribbling from his nose. The young man started to flail away but it was a fleeting tussle. Paul pushed him backwards down the stairs and he rolled to the bottom where he lay in agony. As he fled from the building, Paul made a point of stepping on the man's chest.

Before the two men could recover enough to pursue him and

wreak their revenge, Paul trotted off through the narrow lanes and didn't stop until he reached Covent Garden. The fruit was more enticing there and he felt much safer. Somehow he'd given himself away in Seven Dials and learnt a valuable lesson. He could at least cross the district off the list of places he intended to visit. Tom O'Gara and Moses Dagg were not there. Two such unusual visitors would not go unnoticed by the sharp-eyed young man he'd met beside the wheelbarrow. If they were there, Paul decided, the man would have sought money for offering his assistance. As it was, he'd chosen to take it by force with the aid of his bearded friend. The two men were criminals who worked hand in glove. It gave Paul great amusement to think that they were now comparing their injuries and bemoaning their bad luck.

The Irishmen were soon displaced from his mind by Hannah Granville. He could imagine the look of horror on her face, if she'd seen him tussle with the two men. The fact that he'd escaped with comparative ease would not have reassured her. What would trouble her was that he'd gone into the volatile area of Seven Dials on his own, taking unnecessary risks as a matter of course. The moment it was all over, Paul had shrugged off the memory of the assault on him. Hannah would dwell on it at length. He racked his brains to find a way to win her back. One obvious way was to plead with her, promising to comply with her wishes while in fact having no intention of doing so. But that would mean their romance would be based on a resounding lie. Sooner or later it would become evident and she would consider the deception to be unforgivable.

Instead of thinking about his own predicament, Paul was

moved to consider hers. Hannah was patently troubled. It may have been as a result of their acrimonious parting or it might be that she was ailing in some way. What was depressingly clear to him during the performance the previous night was that she was merely walking through a part she'd hitherto played to the hilt. Was she pining for him or was she ill? Had the former been the case, she'd surely have accepted the flowers as a token of his love so he ruled out that explanation. Hannah must be unwell. That was why she'd struggled onstage. Paul felt impelled to express his sympathy in some way. Yet even as he wondered how, he saw that there was a drawback. To be aware of her sickness, he'd have to admit that he'd been in the audience watching her and he drew back from that. He certainly didn't wish her to know that he'd joined the others at the stage door and waited for a glimpse of her because it revealed his desperation.

His other dalliances had always come to a natural end, leaving both partners with pleasant memories rather than injured feelings. Paul had never had to cope with an abrupt separation before, hence his confusion over how best to proceed. Hannah Granville was a woman so used to getting her own way that she expected instant obedience to her demands. Whenever someone tried to exert control over his life, Paul responded with defiance. He and Hannah had reached an *impasse.* His fierce pride was matched by her vanity, his need of independence by her need to control. On balance, therefore, he thought it best to do nothing. To approach Hannah directly would be seen as a sign of weakness and Paul wanted to maintain a position of strength. Fears about her health could be allayed by discreet enquiries. She need never know that he was asking about her.

Meanwhile, he had plenty to keep him occupied. O'Gara and Dagg might not be hiding in Seven Dials but they were certainly somewhere in London and his job was to find them. Dismissing Hannah from his thoughts, Paul set off to renew his search elsewhere.

'*Nothing?*' cried Micah Yeomans in disbelief.

'Nothing at all, I'm afraid.'

'Is everyone blind?'

'They can't help us, Micah.'

'What's the point of paying informers, if they can't give us the information we need? How many have you spoken to, Alfred?'

'I've talked to dozens of them,' said Hale.

'Did you tell them how important it is to find these fugitives?'

'I did my best to do so.'

'So why have you come back empty handed?'

'They've let us down.'

'Then it's time to bang heads together.'

'I tried that, Micah.'

'They're idiots – every damn one of them!'

'They've helped us in the past.'

'We need their assistance *now*.'

The Runners had met at The Peacock. Any hopes that Yeomans had held of good news had been dashed. None of the informers they kept throughout London knew of the whereabouts of the two American prisoners who'd escaped from Dartmoor. Since most of them inhabited the rougher areas of the city, Yeomans had expected that at least one of them would have caught wind of the new arrivals and been able to point the Runners in the right direction.

He drained his tankard of ale and belched loudly. A thought surfaced.

'Someone is lying, Alfred.'

'They swore that they'd seen nothing.'

'What they've seen is what the newspapers have told them – there's a reward for the capture of Tom O'Gara and Moses Dagg and it's a tempting one. Instead of helping us to find the two Americans, they'll try to do it on their own account so that they can claim the money for themselves.'

'I warned them against doing that, Micah.'

'Then they might do something even worse.'

'What's that?'

'They could *sell* the information to Peter and Paul Skillen.'

'God forbid!'

'That's the last thing we want.'

'Yes,' agreed Hale, 'though we must remember that the Home Secretary did call on the Skillen brothers instead of us.'

'I don't need reminding of that,' said Yeomans with asperity. 'It's one of the many mistakes made by the Doctor.'

It was the nickname of Henry Addington, 1st Viscount Sidmouth, and it was not a flattering one. The son of a physician, he'd spent his entire career at the mercy of his critics. His ill-fated reign as Prime Minister came in the wake of William Pitt's administration and the two men were compared in a cruel epigram devised by George Canning. 'Pitt is to Addington, as London is to Paddington.' Though the judgement hung thereafter around Sidmouth's neck like an invisible albatross, he bore it with great fortitude. The Runners were well aware of the low esteem in which the Doctor was held by his political enemies and by some wicked cartoonists. Whenever the Home Secretary exasperated them, as now, they joined the ranks of his detractors.

'The Doctor is a blockhead,' said Yeomans, irritably.

'He never takes our advice.'

'No, Alfred, he'd rather listen to those abominable twins.'

'What do they have that we lack?'

'Nothing,' said the other, 'except good fortune.'

'Maybe they pay their informers more than we do.'

'Gully Ackford holds the purse strings. He knows who and where to bribe.'

'There was a time when *you* did, Micah.'

'Hold your tongue,' snapped Yeomans, thrusting the tankard at him, 'and refill this for me. Anger makes me thirsty and I am furious.'

Glad to escape his companion's rage, Hale went across to the bar. Yeomans was left to brood on the situation. It was vital to convince the Home Secretary that the Runners were far more competent than two brothers with no sanctioned position in law enforcement. Yeomans saw it as a battle between hardened professionals like himself and rank amateurs like the Skillens. While he was wholly committed to the task of policing London, they were mere dabblers.

When he felt a touch on his arm, he thought that Hale had returned with the tankard of ale. Instead, he saw that he was standing next to a chimney sweep whose sooty hand was on the Runner's sleeve. Yeomans shook it off at once.

'Don't you dare touch me!' he said, scowling.

'I'm sorry, sir.'

'Stand off before some of your filth gets on me.'

'I'm told I could find Mr Yeomans here.'

'Well, you've found him and I don't want my chimney swept so you can get out of here before I kick you out.'

Donal Kearney took a precautionary step backwards and held up black palms.

'I mean you no harm. Mr Yeomans. I've come to help you.'

'And who says that I need help?'

'They should be arrested, sir.'

'What are you babbling about?' asked Yeomans with a sneer. 'I've got better things to do than to listen to the tittle-tattle of a chimney sweep.'

'My youngest son told me, you see.'

'I don't care a fiddler's fuck what the little runt told you.'

'I set him on to one of Fallon's brats,' said Kearney with a sly grin, 'and he got the truth out of him. It's *them*, Mr Yeomans.'

The Runner glowered. 'You're asking for trouble, aren't you?'

'It's them two Americans what escaped from prison.'

Having raised his fist to strike, Yeomans froze in position.

'Could you say that again?' he asked.

'Those prisoners who escaped – I know where they are, sir.'

'*How* do you know?'

'I live in the same tenement.'

Yeomans lowered his arm. 'And where's that?'

'It's behind Orchard Street, sir. There's lots of us Irish there.'

'And you're telling me that Tom O'Gara and Moses Dagg are hiding there?'

'I'd swear it on the eyes of my children!' vowed Kearney.

Yeomans looked at him more closely and decided that he was in earnest. At that moment, Hale came back with a full tankard in his hand.

'Go back and buy another one, Alfred,' said Yeomans, taking the drink from him. 'I'm sure that our friend here would like a sup of ale as well. Unless I'm very much mistaken, he's just brought us the intelligence we sorely need.'

When he left the offices of Rendcombe and Spiller, he was in high spirits. Peter Skillen had the names of two likely suspects, both of whom had worked for respected lawyers and been unable to find the same level of employment elsewhere. When he called at the first of the two addresses he'd been given, he was distressed to learn that he'd come to a house of mourning. A neighbour explained that Peter would be unable to speak to Adam Tate because the man had died a few days earlier.

'The rumour is he died by his own hand,' confided the neighbour.

'Is there any likelihood of that?' asked Peter.

'Mr Tate was very upset when he lost his job.'

'How did he live?'

'He struggled, sir. He was too proud to borrow money so he did without. If you want my opinion, I think he starved himself to death. The last time I saw him he was skin and bone. It's a shame, sir.'

The neighbour was clearly ready to hold forth on the decline in the fortunes of Adam Tate but they had no interest for Peter. If the man had died, by whatever means, a few days ago then he couldn't have been the scrivener who drew up the document for the American prisoners. That had been dated after Tate's death. Peter had to look elsewhere. As he set off in search of the second address, his erstwhile high spirits had shrunk into a distant hope. Realistically, he couldn't expect to locate the person he was after so easily. It might well be that neither of the names he'd been given would be of any practical use. When he eventually found the house he wanted, he used the knocker without any real conviction. There was a long wait before the door was unbolted and thrown open by a podgy woman in a dowdy dress. Her resentful frown vanished when she saw a gentleman on her doorstep.

'Can I help you, sir?' she asked, politely.

'I'm looking for Mr Nason.'

'That's my husband, sir.'

'Is he in at the moment?'

'I'm afraid that he isn't,' replied Posy. 'He's out on business. Is there a message I can take for him? My husband is excellent at his job. Whatever it is that you want, I'm sure that he can oblige.'

Peter took his cue from her because it suited him to act as a prospective client. It would remove any suspicion from the woman's mind and allow him to probe into the character of Jubal Nason and the nature of the services he provided.

'Am I right in thinking that your husband works from home?'

'Yes, he does, sir. We've a room he uses as an office.'

'I believe that he once worked for a lawyer in Portland Place.'

She became defensive. 'He left because of a misunderstanding.'

'It couldn't have been because of any deficiency in the quality of his work,' said Peter, trying to put her at ease. 'The person who recommended him to me was full of praise for him.'

'Oh,' she said, relaxing. 'That's good to hear.'

'What I really need is for some documents to be copied.'

'Then you've no cause to look any further, sir. My husband is an experienced scrivener. He'll copy out whatever you wish.'

'That's reassuring.'

'His charges are very reasonable.'

'I'm always ready to pay well for work of quality,' said Peter. 'When do you expect Mr Nason to return?'

'He told me that he'd be no more than an hour or so.'

'Then I'll call back.'

'You don't have to do that, sir,' she said, afraid that he might take his custom elsewhere. 'My husband will be very upset that he missed you. He may only be half an hour, even less. Why don't you step inside and wait?'

'Thank you, Mrs Nason.'

She stood aside so that he could walk into the house. A compound of noisome odours invaded his nostrils and made him cough. She conducted him upstairs to a small room converted into an office by her husband. It was a dark, poky and unwelcoming lair. Dog-eared law books leant against each other for support. The desk was a gravy-stained kitchen table littered with papers. There was a whiff of misery in the air. It was all a far cry from the order, comfort and cleanliness of Martin Rendcombe's office. Both men might make their living from the law but Jubal Nason belonged to a decidedly lower of order of creation.

'It's not usually as untidy as this,' said Posy, shuffling papers into a pile.

'Fear not, Mrs Nason. My own study is even more chaotic.' The lie seemed to settle her nerves and she stopped hovering. 'Apart from copying documents, what else does your husband do?'

'I can't rightly say but, whatever it is, he does it well.'

Peter was hoping that she'd leave him alone so that he could sift through the papers to see if any of them linked Jubal Nason to the two fugitives but Posy was determined to stay between him and door, beaming inanely at Peter and barring his way so that her husband didn't lose a client.

'Do you happen to know where your husband went, Mrs Nason?'

'No,' she replied, 'but he left some time ago so he must be there by now.'

Jubal Nason hobbled into the court and looked nervously at the tenements around him. They were teeming with noisy life. Various heads popped out of windows to take stock of the stranger. People came and went through the main doors. Children fought battles over territory. A knife grinder sat on a stool and plied his trade with ear-splitting effect. When he tried to speak to people who went past him, Nason was studiously ignored. He was perceived as an intruder and, as such, was shunned. One person, however, did not ignore him. Nason was grabbed from behind, pushed up against a wall and held there immovably.

'What, in the name of all that's holy, are *you* doing here?'

'I was looking for you, Mr Fallon.'

'Well, I don't *like* being looked for.'

'You're hurting me,' bleated Nason.

'How did you find out where I lived?'

'It was a guess.'

'Tell the truth,' ordered Dermot Fallon, pressing him harder against the wall.

'It *is* the truth. When that dog attacked me, it was no more than forty yards from here so I guessed that you didn't live far away. I knew there were Irish people living behind Orchard Street so I thought I'd try here first.' He was unable to stop himself from being turned swiftly around and slammed against the brickwork. 'I had to see you, Mr Fallon.'

'Why – what's happened?'

'If you let me go,' spluttered Nason, 'I'll explain.'

Fallon released him and stood back to appraise him. Jubal Nason looked as dishevelled and miserable as ever. Smiling nervously, he took a newspaper from his pocket and unfolded it.

'Have you seen this?' he asked.

'Where would I get the money to buy newspapers,' said Fallon, 'and how would I find the time to read them?' He pushed Nason. 'What does it say?'

'There's a reward for the capture of your friends.'

Fallon seized him again. 'Is that why you're here, you scheming piece of shite?' he demanded. 'Have you come to rat on us?'

'No, no,' shouted Nason. 'I'm here to *warn* Mr O'Gara and Mr Dagg.'

'Are you sure you came alone?'

'Yes, I did. But if *I* can find you, someone else can so you'd better tell your friends to hide somewhere else. I'm only trying to *help*, Mr Fallon.'

'I don't like being spied on.'

'People are out looking for your friends. Their names are in the newspaper.'

'Then they'll have to be moved,' said Fallon, letting go of him again. 'And I suppose I'll have to thank you. I'd have been caught with Tom and Moses.'

'The same goes for me. Because I prepared that document, I'll be seen as a conspirator.'

'You're in the clear – we wouldn't name you.'

'Tell your friends to get out as soon as possible.'

'I will. And I'm sorry I had to hurt you a bit.'

Nason shrunk way from him. 'I wasn't spying. I needed to raise the alarm.' A dog came trotting across the court. 'That's the wild dog that attacked me in Oxford Street. What's it doing here?'

'I caught it and trained it,' said Fallon with a grin. 'I've a way with dogs and women, Mr Nason. He won't bite you again.'

The truth slowly dawned on Nason. 'It's *your* dog, isn't it?'

'It is now.'

'You made it attack me then pretended to save me.'

'Oh, what an evil mind you have,' said Fallon with mock reproach. 'There was I, saving you from being bitten through to the bone, and all you can do is to accuse me of trickery. Now shift your carcase before I tell him to take a piece out of your arse.'

'Don't do that,' said Nason, backing away. 'I'm going.'

'Good riddance!'

'You will pass the warning on to your friends, won't you?'

'No,' joked Fallon, 'I'll turn the pair of them in and collect the reward.' He shoved Nason in the chest. 'Tom is family, you Godforsaken numbskull. Of course, I'll warn them. Now – go!'

One eye on the dog, Nason scuttled off. As soon as they were out of sight, Fallon raced into the tenement and went up the stairs in bounds. He'd hated being run to ground by Nason but he could see that the man might just have rescued them from the shadow of the gallows.

There were days when Sidmouth found his work excessively tiresome and another one was added to the list when he arrived to find his desk covered in dross and trivia. Tempted to sweep it aside or delegate it, he instead applied himself with his usual vigour and gradually thinned out the pile of documents and seemingly unending correspondence on issues in which he had no interest. At least, he consoled himself, there were no inordinate demands about Dartmoor this time accompanied by threats against his life. All was calm, tedious and monstrously unexciting. It was only when Bernard Grocott came into the room that the Home Secretary found something that aroused his interest at last.

'They're back,' he declared.

'To whom do you refer, my lord?'

'I speak of those unspeakable Luddites.'

'They no longer exist,' said Grocott. 'Thanks to our prompt action, they were suppressed a couple of years ago. Those that were neither hanged nor imprisoned were transported to Australia. They can't smash machinery to pieces from Botany Bay. It's a geographical impossibility.'

'Then who attacked this factory in Nottinghamshire?'

'It was not the Luddites.'

'Find me another culprit.'

He handed the report to Grocott who studied it before passing it back to him.

'The machinery was not destroyed, my lord,' he noted. 'The whole factory was burnt down.'

'In the course of the blaze, the machinery was badly damaged. That's the hallmark of the Luddites. Fearing that they'd be put out of work by machines, they sought to destroy them.'

'It's much easier to light a fire than to smash heavy machinery to pieces. This is probably the work of some jealous rival or of an operative dismissed from his post. We are not facing a revolution in Nottinghamshire, my lord.'

'The county is nevertheless simmering. It's the same with Lancashire and Yorkshire. Opposition to the *status quo* is mounting all the time. It's inevitable that it will break out into something more dangerous and concerted.'

'Then it will be suppressed without mercy,' said Grocott.

'That's my worry. Brutal suppression creates more enemies for us and we have enough of those already.' He put the report aside. 'Well, distressing as that incident was, it did have the virtue of waking me up again. What you see on my desk, Grocott, is the most stultifying rubbish. Most of it will go straight into the wastepaper basket where it belongs.'

'It will vanish without trace before morning, my lord. Levitt will see to that. I'm eternally gratefully to the person who guided her into my hands.'

'The only problem is that having her here reminds us inescapably of Horner's disappearance. That still baffles me.'

'I had hoped that the Skillen brothers would have found her by now.'

'They will – you may bank on it. They will.'

'I thought you'd diverted their energies to the search for the two American fugitives.'

'Yes, I did, but Horner will not be abandoned. Peter Skillen, in particular, will not let that matter rest. He's a resolute man which is why I employ him so much.'

'In this instance, my lord,' said Grocott, 'you may have over-employed him.'

'I don't believe that it's possible to do that.'

The undersecretary drew up a chair beside that of the Home Secretary and worked through the remaining correspondence with him. It was largely of a routine nature and there were no other reports of violence in the shires. Both men were all too aware of the problems caused by the ending of the long war with France. Discharged soldiers had found no employment waiting for them and had become fractious. Clubs of working men and of dissident members of the middle class had been formed to foment trouble. Agitators had popped up in the major cities and there were even voices in parliament calling for radical reform. To a dyed-in-the-wool reactionary like Sidmouth, it was all very disturbing. Grocott, too, was troubled, well aware of what was bubbling away beneath the apparently placid surface of English life.

A tap on the door interrupted them. A clerk entered with the news that they had a visitor who insisted on seeing them urgently on an important manner. When he heard that the visitor was Micah Yeomans, the Home Secretary asked for him to be admitted at once. The Bow Street Runner was soon standing before him with a smile as broad as the Thames on his face. Greetings were exchanged.

'Thank you for seeing me at such short notice, my lord,' said Yeomans.

'You are not given to overstatement, Mr Yeomans. When you talk of urgency, something of significance has invariably happened.'

'It has certainly done so in this case.'

'May we know what it is?' asked Grocott.

'First, let *me* ask a question. Have Peter and Paul Skillen managed to complete their most recent assignment?'

'Why do you wish to know that?'

'All will become clear in a moment.'

'Then the answer is that the twin brothers have yet to meet with success.'

'I thought so,' said Yeomans, grinning complacently.

'Why do you find that so amusing?' wondered Sidmouth. 'Their investigation is related to my safety. Is a threat to my life something which has a comical appeal to you, Mr Yeomans?'

'No, no,' insisted the Runner, adjusting his features into an expression of deep solemnity. 'Your safety is of paramount concern to me and my men.'

'Peter and Paul Skillen subscribe to that feeling as well.'

'We felt that they needed some help, my lord.'

'Did they ask for it?'

'No, but we have provided it *gratis*.'

'That's very kind of you, Mr Yeomans,' said Grocott with light sarcasm. 'It's a pity that you didn't offer the same assistance to them when they arrested Ned Greet. You'd been after the rogue for several months. He'd never have been caught, if the Skillen brothers had not stepped in.'

Yeomans was needled. 'That's a matter of opinion, Mr Grocott.'

'I've just given you mine.'

'It accords with my own view,' added Sidmouth, 'but we digress. At the risk of seeming to jog your elbow, I must ask why exactly you are here.'

'We've found them, sir,' said Yeomans, thrusting out his chest.

'You've found whom?'

'We've located the American fugitives.'

'That's very heartening,' said Sidmouth. 'Have they been apprehended?'

'Not as yet but they soon will be. It's taking time to round up enough men. The place where O'Gara and Dagg are being hidden is a haunt for Irishmen. They can be obstreperous, my lord. We need to go in force.'

'I approve of that.'

'I just wanted to be able to put your mind at rest.'

'You've certainly done so, Mr Yeomans. I thank you.'

'I add my thanks,' said Grocott, 'though it might have been more sensible to arrest these villains before you boasted about it to the Home Secretary. We don't doubt your ability to catch them and we congratulate you on finding out where they've been concealed all this time. How did you contrive that?'

'We have our methods,' said Yeomans with a cryptic smile.

'Since you need plenty of support,' said Sidmouth, 'I take it that you'll be calling on the Skillen brothers to lend a hand.'

Micah Yeomans swelled up with righteous indignation.

'We don't need them, my lord,' he asserted. 'They had their chance and they failed to take it. While the Skillens are still searching in vain, we will catch the fugitives and put them behind bars.'

CHAPTER FOURTEEN

On the walk back home, Jubal Nason hoped that the fugitives would heed his warning and flee the tenement instantly. If they were caught, his chances of survival were slim. O'Gara and Dagg might not name him but Dermot Fallon certainly would. He had a spiteful streak and he would want to drag Nason down with them. It was the former clerk's own fault. That's what made it so sickening. He was the unwitting architect of his own downfall. It grieved him that he'd been so gullible. When Nason was attacked in Oxford Street, by what he thought was a mad dog, Fallon's appearance had not been fortuitous. It was carefully timed. In driving the dog away, he'd ingratiated himself with Nason who, apart from thanking him profusely, had actually pressed some money into his hand. The Irishman had seen him as the unwary pedestrian that he was and pounced on him, a memory that now scalded his brain. Nason chastised himself for being so easily taken in by a clever trickster and for making himself vulnerable to a second approach by Fallon.

No comfort awaited him at home. He would have to invent a story to tell his flint-hearted wife, who was bound to ask what fee he'd earned while he was away. If he told her the truth about the situation in which he'd become embroiled, he'd get no sympathy. Posy Nason was far more likely to admonish him in the most hostile terms and maintain a ceaseless rant about his grave shortcomings as a husband and provider. When he turned into his street, therefore, his pace immediately slackened to a trudge. Reluctant to return home, he was tempted to walk past the house and enjoy another hour or so of freedom from the domestic desolation that lay within its walls. In the event, his courage failed him. Drawn ineluctably back to the house, he began to rehearse his excuses.

When he let himself in, his wife came bustling down the stairs with her statutory frown replaced by the kind of benign smile he'd not seen on her face since their wedding day. Nason backed away in confusion.

'A gentleman has called to see you, Jubal.'

'Who is he?'

'He's come to engage your services.'

'What does he want?'

'He's ready to pay well.'

'How long has he been here?'

'He's been waiting far too long,' she said, pushing him towards the stairs. 'Go on up there and do business with him.'

Nason mounted the steps with trepidation. Gentlemen were not in the habit of seeking his expertise. He dealt mostly with the lower orders, ignorant people who wanted him to write letters on their behalf or advise them about minor points of law. Educated clients were rare.

'How do you do?' he said, entering the room.

'I'm pleased to meet you, Mr Nason,' said the visitor, rising from the chair. 'My name is Peter Skillen and I believe that you can help me.'

There was no handshake. Nason was too nervous to offer one and Peter kept his hands clasped behind his back. After they'd weighed each other up, Peter sat down again. Nason shuffled his feet.

'What can I do for you, Mr Skillen?'

'I need information about some of your clients.'

'Then you've come to the wrong place,' said Nason, stuffily. 'I regret to say that I'm unable to help you. Good day to you, sir.'

'This is an exceptional case.'

'To my mind, there is no such thing. I will not break a bond.'

'Then you must prepare to end your days on the scaffold, Mr Nason,' said Peter, coldly. 'When you get there, you can renew your acquaintance with Thomas O'Gara and Moses Dagg.'

Nason was stunned. Eyes glassy and legs unsteady, he collapsed onto the stool in the corner of the room. Beads of sweat broke out on his brow and his breathing became laboured. Having tried to save his skin by warning the fugitives to hide elsewhere, he'd come back home only to face arrest. His upper lip began to twitch ungovernably.

'Who are you?' he croaked.

'I'm not sure,' replied Peter. 'I could be friend or foe.'

'What brought you here?'

'I saw the document that you drafted, Mr Nason.'

'You must be mistaken, sir.'

'Oh, I think not. You have a very distinctive hand. Your wife was kind enough to show me other examples of it. When I studied the document sent to Viscount Sidmouth, I noted its idiosyncrasies. They are present in everything you write. I know that you must have delivered it to the Home Office yourself because O'Gara and Dagg are strangers to London and would have no idea where the building was. You, on the other hand, most definitely would.' He smiled. 'Am I right, sir?'

'They made me do it, sir,' wailed Nason. 'I was forced into it.'

'Why did O'Gara and Dagg turn to you?'

'They didn't, Mr Skillen. Dermot Fallon brought them here. He's O'Gara's cousin and as villainous a man as you could wish to meet.'

'You'd better tell me the whole story.'

Mastering his nerves, Nason tried to compose his thoughts. There was no hope of deceiving his visitor with a plausible tale. The man knew too much. Also, there was a steely authority in his gaze that made Nason uneasy. Only the full truth would suffice. He began slowly and gathered pace as he went along. Nothing was omitted. He explained why he'd been dismissed by the lawyer for whom he'd worked and how difficult it was to earn a regular income now that his reputation had been stained. He also described how he'd been gulled by Fallon when apparently at the mercy of a mad dog. That incident had led to the Irishman's second appearance in his life.

'I rue the day that I met that silver-tongued rogue,' he said, vehemently.

'I don't blame you, Mr Nason.'

'If he hadn't singled me out as a victim, I wouldn't have been involved in any way with escaped prisoners from Dartmoor. They were three desperate men, sir. I was too frightened to turn them down.'

'I can understand that,' said Peter. 'What puzzles me is why – having done their bidding – you didn't report them so that they could be arrested.'

'I was threatened with repercussions.'

'What manner did they take?'

'Fallon said that, if I dared to betray them, his friends would hang me up naked to skin me alive and do vile things to my wife that I couldn't, in the name of decency, repeat. It was no idle threat, Mr Skillen. I was terrified.' He eyed Peter anxiously. 'You know it all now, sir.'

'Then the first thing I must do is to congratulate you.'

Nason was astonished. 'Congratulate me?'

'Yes,' said Peter, 'what you produced was an extraordinary document, far better than anything the fugitives could have managed by themselves. The narrative was crystal clear, the demands were supported by evidence and the whole thing was couched in your inimitable handwriting. Only one thing besmirched it and that was the threat against the life of the Home Secretary.'

'I begged them to leave that out, sir, but they refused.'

'O'Gara and Dagg were too naive. In trying to get recompense for what they allege is one appalling crime, they offered to commit another. We do not live in the Old Testament. A life for a life is not an acceptable dictum in a civilised society. And, of course, they chose the wrong target. Viscount Sidmouth is not the governor of Dartmoor, nor can he be held responsible for the things that happened there. You should have advised them as much.'

'The Home Secretary is the symbol of law and order in this country,' said Nason. 'That was enough for them. Fallon was all for threatening the Prime Minister as well, but I put a stop to that.'

'What of the allegations put by O'Gara and Dagg?'

'I believed them wholeheartedly.'

'That comes through in the document.'

'I sympathised with their plight but – hand on heart – I can assure you that I do not condone what they plan to do if their demands are not met.'

'Where are they now?'

'I couldn't tell you.'

'Concealing the whereabouts of escaped prisoners is a heinous crime.'

'They were living with Fallon in a tenement behind Orchard Street but I've not long returned from there, having warned them that the newspaper was carrying a description of them and offering a reward for their capture. As a result,' said Nason, 'they may well have fled to another refuge. Where that might be, I have no idea.'

'What drove you to warn them – concern for *their* safety or for your own?'

'Unhappily, the one is fettered to the other.'

Peter sat back and studied him shrewdly. Nason was a despicable man in many ways: weak, untrustworthy and sly. Being alone with him in such a small space was an unpleasant experience. He reeked of failure. Yet he was plainly no conspirator. What he'd done for O'Gara and Dagg had been done under duress. That being the case, Peter wondered if the man really deserved to be broken on the wheels of justice.

For his part, Nason was thinking of his wife. The gentleman she'd let so enthusiastically into the house might be about to take her husband out of it forever. He could imagine only too clearly how Posy would react when she learnt that a clerk who'd made his living out of the law could now face its ultimate sanction.

Peter's face was inscrutable. Nason knelt before him and grabbed his hands.

'What's to become of me, sir?'

'I'm still grappling with another question,' said Peter, thoughtfully. 'Should I be your friend or your foe?'

Anne Horner had worked out her plan. The woman was her means of escape. There was no point in even talking to the man. He ignored her completely but his accomplice had at least spoken to their prisoner. That showed a measure of sympathy. The man usually delivered the meals and the food was surprisingly good. On some evenings, she was even given the treat of a glass of wine, something she never had in the normal course of her life. The problem with the meals was that they were irregular. Gaps of varying lengths appeared between them. On one occasion she'd been left for seven hours without food. By way of compensation, they'd given her an additional meal late the same evening.

The dungeon was not just holding her against her will. It was depressing her spirit. Anne had been forced to wear the same clothing every day and to make use of the bucket. She felt dirty, embarrassed and debased. Action simply had to be taken. It was the man who brought her breakfast and who emptied the slops in the bucket. A long interval then followed. When it came to an end, Anne heard daintier footsteps coming down the cellar steps. The woman was there at last. Opportunity beckoned.

'Stand back from the door!' ordered the woman.

'That's what I have done,' said Anne.

The bolt was drawn back and the door creaked open. Holding a tray, the woman made sure that Anne was standing against the far wall before she came in.

'There may be some more wine this evening,' she promised.

'Thank you.'

'We've no reason to make this any more unpleasant than it has to be.'

'Why are you keeping me here?'

The woman clicked her tongue. 'You know better than to ask that.'

She put the tray down on the table. During the seconds when her back was turned, Anne shot across the cellar, dived through the door, slammed it shut and pushed home the bolt. Ignoring the cries of rage from the woman, she crept up the steps, gingerly opened the door at the top and peered out. There was nobody about. She went into the kitchen, opened the rear door and ran out into the garden. The sense of freedom was invigorating.

Anne had decided exactly what she was going to say. Pulling her head back, she opened her mouth wide and tried to call for help. But the words simply would not come. Deprived of speech for so long, she struggled to find the words and to give them full volume. Instead of an ear-splitting yell, all that she could produce was a pathetic squeak and even that was soon muffled as a hand closed over her mouth and a man's arm tightened around her neck.

Struggling wildly to get free, Anne was dragged back downstairs.

Charlotte Skillen was seated at the desk in the shooting gallery and leafing through the book in which appointments were listed. She looked up when Gully Ackford came into the room. Though he'd be sparring for the past half an hour, he was breathing easily and completely unruffled. There was nothing whatsoever to suggest he'd been engaged in physical activity.

'Did you have a good lesson with Mr Stryder?' she asked.

'I had a lot of pleasure, I know that.'

'Is there any improvement?'

'None at all,' he said with a chuckle. 'Benedict Stryder is the worst pupil I've ever had. When I teach him a new aspect to the noble art, I discover that he's forgotten all the other ones. That's a sad reflection on me, I suppose. I try my best but he defeats me. In the ring, however,' he added, 'I always defeat *him*. In thirty minutes, he didn't land a telling punch.'

'Suggest that he takes up shooting instead.'

'He's as blind as a bat, Charlotte.'

'What about fencing, then, or even archery?'

'If Mr Stryder has a weapon in his hands, I don't want to be anywhere close to him. He'd probably poke his own eye out with a sword and I wouldn't let him near a bow and arrow. I prefer teaching someone like Mrs Holdstock. She learns fast and, more to the point, she *remembers* it the next time she turns up here.'

'She seems too ladylike to be Robin Hood.'

'If people come here for lessons, I'm not going to turn them away.'

'We're blessed with many regular clients at the moment, Gully,' she said, glancing at the list. 'There are bookings for several weeks ahead. It's so much better than the old days when it was either a feast or a famine.'

'We're enjoying a season of feasts now, Charlotte. We must remember to get in a stock of fatted calves.' He took a seat beside her. 'By the way, have you spoken to Paul recently?'

'Why do you ask?'

'It's in the interests of self-preservation,' he replied with a grin. 'I don't know what's got into him. When I gave him a fencing lesson yesterday, he came at me in a towering rage. It was almost as if he wanted to *punish* me for some reason.'

'Oh, I'm sure that wasn't the case, Gully.'

'I wondered if he was having trouble in his private life. It can get turbulent at times. We've all seen that.'

'Speak for yourself.'

'You're the only person he confides in. Has he said anything to you?'

'He talks to me now and then,' she replied with a meaningful smile, 'because he knows he can trust me.'

'I'm justly rebuked,' he said, raising apologetic palms. 'I shouldn't have asked. What he does when he's not working on an investigation is his own business.'

'I endorse that feeling. As for the bout you had with him yesterday, Paul does have these upsurges of energy. He loves to flex his muscles.'

'He did a lot more than flex them yesterday, Charlotte. His energy was surging like a waterfall. I pity anyone who takes him on when he's as angry as that.'

It was the second time that Paul Skillen had been caught off guard. When he went to explore another Irish enclave in the city, he made the mistake of taking Hannah Granville with him. She occupied his mind so fully that he forgot where he was and why he'd come there. It was only when someone bumped into him that his reverie was shattered.

'A thousand apologies, sir,' said an Irish voice. 'It was an accident.'

Paul was stirred. 'You did that on purpose, you liar.'

The man laughed. 'Me? No, sir, I'm the gentlest of beings.'

It was an incongruous description of a middle-aged ruffian with a squat body topped by a large head that featured deep-set green eyes and a bulging forehead. His grin exposed blackened teeth.

'Give it back to me,' demanded Paul.

'What do you mean?'

'You took my purse, you lice-ridden pickpocket.'

'I did nothing of the kind,' said the other with injured innocence.

'Give it back or I'll *take* it back.'

The man cackled. 'You'll have to catch me first.'

Intending to scamper off, he only managed a few steps before

Paul tripped him up then pummelled him into submission. Paul held him down with a foot on his chest.

'Hand it over.'

'I don't know what you're talking about,' whined the other.

'I'm talking about this,' said Paul, reaching inside the man's coat to retrieve a purse. 'I regard pickpockets as vermin.'

'I only did it in fun, sir.'

'And I only hit you in fun. Try to move and I'll do it in fun again. Now then,' he added, 'I have a little task for you. How long have you lived here?'

'I've been here for five years or more.'

'Then you can save me a lot of time,' said Paul. 'I'm looking for someone and, since you inhabit this rat-hole, you can tell me whether or not they're here.'

Viscount Sidmouth was a copious correspondent, forever answering letters, sending reports or suggesting ideas for consideration at cabinet meetings. He was in the process of penning a long missive to the Prime Minister when he was interrupted by one of his clerks. Sidmouth was interested to hear that Captain Shortland, governor of Dartmoor, had called on him. He asked that the man be admitted at once. When the visitor stepped into the room, Sidmouth rose to greet him.

'You come upon your hour,' he said, using a Shakespearean quotation that went unrecognised by the other. 'I'd not expected you to be in London.'

'I felt that I should speak to you in person, my lord.'

'You've already been to the Admiralty, I presume.'

'I've just come from there.'

Sidmouth waved him to a chair then resumed his own seat. Never having met the man, he was glad of the opportunity to do so. Stern, smart, erect and humourless, the governor looked as if he'd been born in a uniform. Sidmouth knew that it was no casual visit. Shortland was there to advance his own interests.

'I felt it was a courtesy to call on you, my lord,' he began.

'I appreciate your consideration.'

'Ideally, I would have liked a moment with the Prime Minister but I learnt that his diary was too full.'

'It's one of the perils of being what is sometimes called *primus inter pares*,' said Sidmouth. 'The first among equals is the repository of every single problem that afflicts this nation of ours. I discovered that during my tenure of the role. The present holder of it, Lord Liverpool, was my foreign secretary at the time.'

Sidmouth felt that it would do no harm to remind the governor of his eminence in political circles. Shortland had the determined look of a man who'd come to badger him and needed to be warned that the Home Secretary would not allow any pressure to be put on him.

'I thought you ought to know that everything at Dartmoor is now under strict control,' said Shortland, gruffly. 'The riot has been suppressed.'

'That nomenclature has been questioned, Captain.'

'It was a blatant act of mutiny, my lord.'

'Some have suggested an alternative description.'

Shortland was brusque. 'Then it should be disregarded.'

'So you would not describe it as a massacre, then?'

'There were incidental casualties that could not be avoided.'

'Well,' said Sidmouth, 'that's for the joint commission to decide. You'll no doubt be appearing before them very soon.'

'It's one of the reasons I came to London.'

'I passed on to them the letter which you sent me.'

'I felt that you needed to know the full details,' said Shortland. 'The mutiny was led by Thomas O'Gara who, as I explained, was a constant thorn in our flesh. He whipped the prisoners up into a frenzy of protest and the riot broke out. O'Gara took advantage of the confusion to escape.'

'Where was he beforehand?'

'O'Gara?'

'In which part of the prison was he being held?'

'That's the maddening thing, my lord. We don't know. He had vanished from the cell in which he was being kept and somehow stayed out of sight until the day of the riot. Behind the scenes, he'd been agitating for all he was worth. After he'd fled, his friends told us that he'd boasted of escaping one day. In other words,' said Shortland, as if making an unanswerable debating point, 'he led the mutiny from purely selfish reasons. That's the kind of rogue O'Gara is.'

'What about Moses Dagg?'

'He and O'Gara were old shipmates.'

'Has Dagg been a thorn in your flesh as well?'

'No,' conceded the other, 'he has not. To be honest, he's never come to our attention before.'

'Then your supervision of the prisoners has been lax, Captain Shortland. It may interest you to know that Dagg was instrumental in shielding O'Gara when they were both in Dartmoor. The reason you failed to find the Irishman was that he was living in disguise among the black sailors.'

Shortland gasped. 'Can that be true?'

'We have O'Gara's own word for it,' said Sidmouth. 'He was considerate enough to send a long report of what he calls a massacre and to explain why he feels the regime at Dartmoor is appalling in every way.'

'Would you take the word of a mere prisoner over *mine*?' asked Shortland, close to apoplexy.

'The final judgement will be taken by the joint commission. It's not for me to influence it one way or another. But since a deposition from the fugitives exists, it must be seen and weighed in the balance.'

'It's wholly irrelevant, my lord. Need I tell you what would happen if this mutiny had occurred aboard a ship? The ringleaders would have been executed and that should be so in the case of O'Gara and his accomplice.'

'Both men are wanted for an associated crime, Captain Shortland. As it happens,' said Sidmouth, 'I have a personal reason for wanting them recaptured. You'll be reassured to know that their whereabouts have been established and that O'Gara and Dagg will very soon be in custody.'

'Thank God for that!'

Micah Yeomans knew that it would be a difficult operation. That was the reason he had to deploy so many men. Irish communities, such as the one housed behind Orchard Street, were disinclined to assist Bow Street Runners and their foot patrols. Among the majority of hard-working, law-abiding people who lived in the tenements was a solid core of criminals who used the protection of the crowd. Winkling them out was problematical because they not only had lookouts on patrol but also escape routes they could use in an emergency. The big advantage that Yeomans had in this instance was the advice given by Donal Kearney. The chimney sweep knew the tenements intimately and was able to alert the Runners to potential dangers. As a result of his advice, men were stationed in various places to block off the likely escape routes. Everyone involved was armed. Yeomans insisted that the fugitives should be captured dead or alive.

'It doesn't matter which,' he said to Hale. 'Personally, I'd prefer to deliver their corpses and claim the reward.'

'Do I get a share?' asked Kearney, greedily.

'No, you don't.'

'But I told you where Fallon is hiding them.'

'We're grateful for your help.'

'The reward is for the arrest and conviction of O'Gara and Dagg,' Hale pointed out. 'You are in no position to arrest them, Mr Kearney. All that you did was to tell us where they were.'

'That's not fair!' complained the sweep.

'Then there's the danger we'll encounter,' said Yeomans. 'While you're cowering in some dark corner, my men and I will be trying to overpower some desperate criminals. There's a big risk involved.'

'I know all about risk, Mr Yeomans.'

'Stop bleating and stand aside.'

'What do you think would happen to me if anyone discovered that I was the one who told you where to find those American sailors? My life wouldn't be worth living.'

'Then it's in your interests to stay well clear,' said Hale. 'We guarantee that your name won't be mentioned.'

'Give me a share of the reward money as well.'

'Your reward lies in knowing that you did your civic duty.'

'I don't give a fart about civic duty.'

'You're holding us up,' said Yeomans, impatiently. 'Now get out of our way or we'll arrest you for impeding us in the execution of our duties.'

'I deserve payment.'

'*This* is all you deserve.'

Grabbing him by the shoulders, Yeomans pushed him away with such force that he travelled several yards before his back hit a wall. Kearney's roar of disgust went unheard. What they were all listening for was the signal and it soon came. Yeomans blew hard on the pipe and the high-pitched squeal rose above the sound of passing carts and clip-clopping horses. Everyone moved in swiftly. Urgent and long striding, Yeomans led the way with Hale doing his best to stay beside him.

'This could be a great day for us, Micah,' he said. 'We're not simply capturing escaped prisoners, we'll be saving the Doctor's life.'

'We're not doing this for the Doctor's sake,' Yeomans told him. 'We have a bigger ambition altogether, Alfred.'

'What is it?'

'For once in our lives, we can outfox the Skillen brothers.'

'I'll say "Amen" to that.'

Supported by a dozen men, they hurried down a lane that led to the tenements behind Orchard Street. Other members of the foot patrol came into the court from various directions to seal off the area. Yeomans headed for the building where Dermot Fallon lived and where the American sailors were hiding. They met with resistance at once. Alerted by lookouts, dozens of people opened windows and hurled missiles at the newcomers. Several emptied chamber pots over the raiders. Dogs came out of nowhere in a pack to bark and harass. The noise was deafening. Kicking aside a yapping hound, Yeomans reached the front door and used his shoulder to force it open. With others at his heels, he charged up the stairs until he reached the floor on which the family lived. Ready to smash his way into the rooms, he was taken aback to find the door wide open as if in welcome. Yeomans gestured for his men to scatter and draw their weapons. Then he approached with a mingled care and excitement, conscious that he was about to make some of the most significant arrests of his career.

Pistol held out before him, he plunged confidently into the room.

'Let nobody move!' he shouted. 'You're all under arrest.'

But there was no sign of the Fallon family or of the fugitives they'd been sheltering. Clear indications of a hasty departure were, however, visible. More galling for Yeomans and Hale was the fact that someone was there to greet them. Seated on rickety chairs, Peter and Paul Skillen gave them a cheery wave.

'You're too late yet again,' they said in unison.

CHAPTER FIFTEEN

Hannah Granville was keenly aware of the irony of her situation. An actress whose gifts fitted her for the performance of tragedies was herself trapped in a personal tragedy. She had lost the one man who'd brought comedy into her life because Paul Skillen had made her laugh with joy whenever they were together. He embodied all the elements she admired in a man with the exception of his urge to invite danger. Even that had had a surface appeal at the start. The more she grew to love him, the less that appeal became. Danger implied the possibility of loss and Hannah could not bear that. Even if he was not killed, he might be maimed or blinded and she could never bring herself to be a nursemaid to any man. At the time when she forced him to choose between her and his work as a detective, she'd expected her attraction to outweigh anything else in his life. She was demonstrably wrong.

There was a cruel paradox. In trying to control *his* career, Hannah had damaged her own. Since she'd parted company with Paul, she'd been unable to commit herself wholly to her role. The manager of the theatre had noticed it and so had her dresser. It was only a matter of time before the audience began to discern it as well and wonder why they were paying a high price for a muted performance instead of one verging on greatness. Lines in the play took on a new meaning for her and the suffering of Belvidera mirrored her own. The difference was that she could enjoy an ovation at the end of the play and be rewarded for her display of anguish. For the real anguish she endured, however, there was neither applause nor succour.

Paul would not bow to her demands. That much was now glaringly evident. And though he'd sworn undying love to her, he would not lack for temptation. Other women would be delighted to have such a dashing companion and they'd impose no restraints or conditions on him. They'd allow him the freedom of choice that Hannah denied him. Conscious of her folly, she felt unable to repair it. The moment that desire prompted her to go to him, pride stepped in to prevent her. She was held in a cleft stick: unable to move, unable to think, unable to compromise, unable to communicate with him in any way. It was agonising.

She could at least allow herself one treat and that was to be driven past his house in the hope that she might get a momentary sight of him. On her way to the theatre that evening, therefore, she asked the driver of her carriage to make a detour so that she could go down the street where Paul lived. From her elevated position, she might be able to see in through the front window. Hannah prayed that he might be there. A brief glimpse was all that she wanted but she was to get much more than that. As the carriage rolled past the house, the front door opened and Paul Skillen emerged with a beautiful young woman on his arm.

Hannah was mortified. She'd not simply been discarded but been replaced. In a short space of time, Paul had clearly forgotten the promises he'd made to her and found someone else. There would never be a reunion with him now.

Peter Skillen walked home with his wife at his side. In the wake of the raid on the tenement, the brothers had gone back to Paul's house and Charlotte had met them there. They'd enjoyed reminiscing about the look of utter consternation on the faces of the Runners. Micah Yeomans had once again discovered that he could not outwit them. Charlotte reminded her husband of a salient fact.

'The prisoners are still at liberty, Peter.'

'Yes, I know.'

'Doesn't that worry you?'

'In one way, it does,' he confessed, 'but another part of me is glad.'

'How can you be glad when these men are planning to murder the Home Secretary? I'm shocked.'

He grinned. 'I'm touched that I still have the power to shock, my love. After all the time we've been together, I feared that my powers would have waned somewhat.'

'I'm being serious,' she said with a hint of reprimand.

'And so am I. You asked me a question and I'm striving to give you an honest answer. When I got to the tenement earlier on, I fully expected to do my duty by arresting O'Gara and Dagg. Since I met Paul as I arrived, I was certain that, between us, we could surprise both the Americans and the man sheltering them. As it was, they surprised *us* by disappearing before we even got there.'

'Did you see that as a cause for celebration?'

'To some extent, I did. I have a sneaking admiration for them.'

'They're criminals, Peter.'

'They're prisoners of war who should have been released and who've been under the heel of a governor who revels in being a martinet. Friends of theirs were shot in cold blood. In my view, it's estimable that these two men are campaigning on behalf of all the others.'

'But they're doing it by means of a threat.'

'That, I agree, was not an act of diplomacy.'

'You should want them locked up again.'

'I certainly don't want them returned to the tender mercies of this Captain Shortland,' he said with passion. 'Even allowing for exaggeration, their portrayal of him is worrying. He's ruthless and singles out men he believes are troublemakers. O'Gara was one of them. I'd hate you to see the description of the Black Hole into which O'Gara was flung. The treatment of him was inhuman.'

'This is not your battle, Peter,' she argued. 'Viscount Sidmouth employed you to catch these men not to sympathise with their demands. Paul doesn't share your views. His attitude is simple. He wants to lock them up so that the pair of you can collect the reward.'

'Paul was maddened when he realised that they'd evaded us. That court behind Orchard Street was the third place on his list and he felt sure that they'd be there. What he didn't know, of course, was their precise location in that rabbit warren. After my chat with Jubal Nason,' recalled Peter, 'I did. He told me which building they lived in.'

'Where will they have gone?'

'Someone like this Dermot Fallon will have friends all over the place.'

'What about his family?'

'They're still there, Charlotte.'

'Why didn't you arrest them and question them about the whereabouts of the others?' He laughed. 'Is it such a ludicrous suggestion?'

'We couldn't arrest them because we didn't know where to find them. They just blended in with another family. Fallon would have made sure his wife and children were safe before he left with the others. I'll wager that Mrs Fallon doesn't have any idea of his whereabouts,' said Peter. 'He'd have deliberately kept her in the dark so that she couldn't inadvertently give them away.'

'Someone gave them away, Peter.'

'I agree.'

'The Runners must have been helped by an informer.'

'Yes, and it has to be someone who lived in the same tenement. Yeomans and his men knew exactly which rooms to raid. Unfortunately for them, the only occupants were Paul and me. I daresay they're still wondering how we got there.'

'What about the informer?' she asked.

'Fallon will find him.'

'How?'

'Men like that have eyes everywhere, Charlotte.'

'What will he do when he finds out who it was?'

'Well, I don't think he'll be paying Jubal Nason to write a letter of thanks on his behalf,' said Peter with a wry smile. 'He'll be eager to have a confrontation with the man. Frankly, I'd hate to be in the informer's shoes.'

Tom O'Gara and Moses Dagg had no complaints about being told to leave the building at short notice. They'd been expecting a sudden departure at some point. Disguised as beggars, they slipped out of the tenement and followed Dermot Fallon on a tortuous route to the river. They were now hiding in a rotting hulk that bobbed gently on the Thames. As before, they were delighted to be back on water again. The vessel was leaking and showing clear signs of its advanced age but it was the perfect haven for a couple of sailors. In a busy port with shipping from all corners of the world, Dagg's black face was no longer so conspicuous. The waterfront was a polyglot community. Men of many nations, creeds and colours met there.

Since they were the only people aboard, they had far more freedom than they had when sharing two cramped rooms with Fallon and his family. They were able to strut around on deck and watch a wide variety of craft sailing on a river that not only defined London geographically, it provided countless of its citizens with a livelihood. All sorts of people fed off the Thames, whether as wealthy merchants sending cargoes abroad, humble mudlarks scouring the banks for items of value or those in one of a hundred other river-based occupations.

'I don't like it, Tom,' said Dagg.

'We need the money.'

'Then we'll find another way to get it.'

'But this is the easiest way of all,' urged O'Gara. 'You climb into a ring and knock some misguided fool so hard that it will be a week before he wakes up again. Think how many times I've seen you do that over the years.'

'All it needs is one person in the audience who's seen the reward notice.'

'Most of them can't read, Moses. They couldn't care less who or what you are. Dermot told you the sort of people who'd be there. They come to see blood spurting and bones being broken.'

'I'm still worried.'

'You do the fighting,' said O'Gara. 'Leave the worrying to me.'

They were in the remains of what had once been the captain's cabin, a small, cramped place with damaged timberwork and cracked glass. Through the gap in the window, they could smell the rising stench of the river and hear the cries of the gulls as they rose and dipped. Among the large Irish community, O'Gara had felt at home while Dagg had been the obvious outsider. Back on board, both now felt equally comfortable and safe from the attentions of the Runners.

'I want to know who ratted on us,' said O'Gara.

'It must have been that scrivener.'

'No, he wasn't to blame.'

'He looked crafty to me, Tom. I wouldn't trust him.'

'He was the one who saved us, Moses. If he hadn't warned Dermot, the three of us would have been caught napping. I agree that Nason is a sly bastard but he's thinking about his own neck. If we hang,' said O'Gara, 'he'll be shitting his breeches beside us. Dermot will find out who tried to turn us in.'

'Where is he? I expected him back by now.'

'Be patient. He'll be here soon.'

'What if the police arrest his wife?'

'Mary's too clever for that. She'll have changed her name and taken the children to stay with friends. And you're forgetting what Dermot said. He won't even tell Mary where we are so she couldn't lead anyone here.'

'I feel guilty causing them so much trouble,' said Dagg.

'Sure, they thrive on it. My cousin will tell you the same,' said O'Gara, looking through the window. 'There he is, on his way back here.'

In fact, the river bank was thronged with people coming, going or working in some way, yet O'Gara had picked Fallon out in the crowd. It took Dagg a little longer to espy him. When he did so, he was able to relax a little. They went up on deck to lower the gangplank so that Fallon could come aboard with his dog. As soon as he'd joined them, they hauled the gangplank into position again so that nobody else could get onto the vessel. The dog immediately went below deck in search of rats.

'What took you so long?' asked Dagg.

'I had some shopping to do,' said Fallon, opening his coat to reveal a loaf of bread and a large pie. 'Hold these, Tom.'

While his cousin took charge of the provender, Fallon emptied his pockets of the fruit he'd kept there. He explained that he'd come through a market and used his dog to distract stallholders so that he could help himself to their goods. Other items of food came out of his pockets.

'You've done well, Dermot,' said O'Gara. 'This will keep us well fed for a couple of days. Did you manage to see Mary?'

'She was waiting for me with the tale of what happened after we left.'

'How many men were there?'

'Oh, they came in strength, Tom, so they offered us plenty of targets.'

The sailors laughed as he went on to describe how everyone in the tenements did their best to repel the intruders with missiles and offerings from their chamber pots. The tumult they'd created had caused great confusion. When they failed to catch any of us wanted men, the Runners left and had to endure another pelting.

'They were led by Micah Yeomans,' said Fallon.

O'Gara shrugged. 'That name means nothing to us.'

'It would if you lived in London. He's the most famous thief-taker in the city and also the most crooked. Greasing his palm is the best way to stay out of prison.'

'How did he know where we were, Dermot?'

'Who tried to stab us in the back?' asked Dagg.

'That's the man we want.'

'We'll cut his tongue out for a start.'

'Mary has a good idea who it might be,' said Fallon. 'She watched the Runners leave and got within a few yards of Yeomans. My wife has keen eyesight. She saw something that will guide us to the informer.'

'What was it?' asked O'Gara.

'Yeomans is a big man and as ugly as they come but he likes to dress well. Mary was surprised to see that he had black hands and specks of soot all over him. That can only mean one thing.'

'The informer was that chimney sweep,' said Dagg, malevolently.

'That's right, Moses. He'll get more than a beating next time.' Fallon made a vivid gesture with both hands. 'That filthy traitor, Kearney, will wish that he never left Ireland.'

Donal Kearney was still hurt, resentful and embittered. In delivering the escaped prisoners to the Runners, he'd expected thanks and financial reward. As it was, both were denied him. He was livid. Without his help, they would have had no idea where to look. Kearney had told Yeomans where they were hiding and who was sheltering them. The bonus for the sweep was that Moses Dagg, the black man who'd beaten and humiliated him, would be dragged off to prison. That thought gave him great consolation. When the raid on the tenements began, Kearney made sure that he went off quickly in the other direction. He had chimneys to sweep and his work kept him busy for hours. While he was away, he assumed, the American sailors would have been arrested along with Dermot Fallon, a man with whom Kearney had clashed in the past.

It was well into the evening before he returned home. Ready to feign surprise at the news of the raid, Kearney walked into the court and waited for someone to tell him what had happened. But everyone turned their backs on him. Dozens of people were milling around but, the moment he appeared, they fell silent and moved away from him. Even the children shunned him.

'What's going on?' he shouted.

But there was no reply. Instead of going through his usual

routine and washing off the worst of the soot at the pump, he ran up the stairs then stopped in sheer disgust outside his door. Nailed to the timber was a dead rat. Grabbing hold of it, he flung it away and opened the door. His whole family were there, huddled in a corner. His wife, a pale, thin, nervous woman with her waif-like prettiness obliterated by a mask of fear, rushed across to him.

'Thank God you've come!' she exclaimed.

'What's happened?'

'We were raided by the police.'

'Were you?' he said, pretending to be shocked. 'Why?'

'They came for the two men staying with Dermot Fallon.'

'They're criminals, Maureen. They *should* be arrested. So should Fallon.'

'But they weren't there, Donal.'

He shuddered. 'What did you say?'

'They escaped before the raid.'

'They can't have done,' he said with rising alarm. 'When I left earlier on, they were all still here. I checked.'

'People are saying it was you,' she warned.

'That's a lie.'

'Nobody will talk to us. Nobody will play with the children.'

'I did nothing, Meg, I swear it.'

'You did say you'd get even with that black man.'

'Don't you dare tell that to anybody!' he yelled, shaking her hard.

'You're hurting me, Donal.'

He shoved her away. 'You're to keep your mouth shut. Is that clear?' He glared at the children. 'And the same goes for you.'

All four of them nodded. Meg went to stand protectively between them and their father. Fear of her husband had long since displaced the love she'd first felt but she still had a bruised loyalty. Whatever he'd done, she would stand by him.

'I'll tell them,' he decided. 'I'll tell them the truth.'

Going to the window, he flung it open. Down below was the usual commotion amplified by the sound of children's squeals, shouts and laughter. Kearney's voice reverberated around the court.

'It wasn't me!' he yelled. 'As God's my witness, it wasn't me!'

He was met by an accusatory silence.

It was not until the following morning that Micah Yeomans was able to deliver his report to the Home Secretary. Since he and Alfred Hale were his bodyguards, they picked Sidmouth up from his house and set off with him in the carriage. Yeomans broke the bad tidings that the raid had been a failure.

'This is old news, Mr Yeomans,' said the Home Secretary. 'I heard it first from Peter Skillen who had the courtesy to call on me last evening. It's something that you might also have done.'

'I had no wish to disturb you, my lord.'

'When my safety is at stake, you can disturb me all you wish.'

'It was not our fault, my lord,' said Hale. 'Our informer let us down.'

'Yes,' added Yeomans, 'the fellow lives in the same tenement and has actually seen the escaped prisoners. It seems that they've been walking abroad brazenly as if they're above the law.'

'Nobody is above the law,' said Sidmouth, crisply, 'and that includes me.'

'The raid itself went well.'

'It's true,' said Hale, eager to win some praise. 'Micah deployed his men like a general in the field. We always get resistance in places like that but we swooped on them before they knew what was happening. I think we deserve recognition for that.'

'I recognise it willingly, Mr Hale,' said Sidmouth, dryly, 'but I don't feel that celebration is in order. The facts are damning. You raided a tenement in search of people who were not there. That was bound to cause unnecessary upset. You claim that you caught the residents unawares, yet I'm told that that's simply untrue. They were not only expecting you, they fought back.'

'There was some minor trouble, my lord, that's all.'

'We had control of the situation from start to finish,' said Yeomans.

'Then why were some of your men beaten back?' asked Sidmouth. 'Why did one of them have to be carried away because he was hit by a flagon hurled from an upper window? You forget that I have an alternative version of events, gentlemen. Peter and Paul Skillen were first inside the tenement. Both had the sense to dress in rougher garb so that they wouldn't look out of place whereas you and your men were instantly seen for what you are by the residents.'

'Don't believe everything that the Skillen brothers tell you, my lord.'

'They always try to portray us in a poor light,' complained Hale.

'We had sound intelligence and they did not.'

'Then how come they managed to get into the building

before you?' asked Sidmouth. The Runners traded an uneasy glance. 'There are some things you do very well, Yeomans, and there are some things best left to others. This is a case in point. I assigned Peter and Paul Skillen the task of finding those men because they have a gift for tracking down missing people. You and Hale were charged with ensuring my safety. In future, you will concentrate all your energies on that.'

'Yes, my lord,' said Yeomans, sourly.

'Yes, my lord,' repeated Hale.

'When we reach the Home Office, I want the pair of you to come in with me. It's not long before we have the celebrations for our victory at Waterloo. With your help, I want to review the arrangements. If these men are still at liberty,' said Sidmouth, 'then I may well need you beside me throughout the event.'

'We'll catch them well before that,' argued Yeomans.

'You tried and failed, Mr Yeomans.'

'And so did the Skillen brothers.'

'They didn't boast about an early arrest in the way that you did. Nor did they claim to have inside knowledge of the tenement in question. Yet they got there before you and witnessed what you must admit was your *dégringolade*.'

Hale was baffled. 'What does that mean, my lord?'

'It means that you had a bad fall.'

'Give us the chance to vindicate our reputation,' said Yeomans.

'You'll do that by keeping me alive and well. Leave the pursuit and capture of O'Gara and Dagg to the Skillen brothers. They'll succeed in the end.'

They drove on in silence until they reached the Home Office.

The Runners got out first to check that nobody was about then helped Sidmouth to alight from the carriage. As they walked towards the building, Yeomans got in a sly dig at his rivals.

'If the Skillen brothers are such experts at finding missing persons,' he asked, 'why do they still have no idea of the whereabouts of Mrs Horner?'

Everything had changed. When she was first abducted, Anne Horner was encouraged to believe that, for the convenience of her captors, she was being held for a limited amount of time before release. Her status was now very much that of a prisoner in need of punishment. Because of her failed attempt at escape, she had been bound, gagged and left in excruciating discomfort. Her bonds were only removed when she agreed that she would not try to raise the alarm again. In place of the ropes, however, she was now chained by one leg to an iron ring in the wall. Freedom to move about the cellar was a privilege taken away from her. The meals were fewer in number and less appetising. Wine had disappeared altogether. All that she was given to drink was cloudy water.

Why was she being held? Hour by hour, the question hammered into her brain like a peg into a hole. Anne had no illusions about her station in society. In social terms, she was a person of no consequence, a faceless member of the lower classes who was doomed to spend the rest of the life there. Yet there had been an unexpected glimpse of a different world. It was so unexpected that she still couldn't believe that it had actually happened. Was her kidnapping in some way related to that? It was an idea that she'd fought off for days but it was now strengthening its hold. If it was true, then it was a very painful truth. Anne was no stray captive, after all. It could well be that what was happening to her was entirely her own fault. All of a sudden, she had a new companion – remorse.

The sense of guilt was overwhelming. She had coped with it before by putting it at the back of her mind and by losing herself in her work. Anne had also been more regular in her attendance at church, popping in at odd times to kneel and to pray for forgiveness. How could they possibly *know*? How could this strange, silent man and his female companion be aware of something so intensely private? It was almost as if the pair of them had watched her relieving herself in the bucket. Nothing could be hidden from them. It was frightening. Feeling the need for fresh air, Anne tried to move across to the grating but she'd forgotten that she was chained and she yelped as the iron bit into her ankle. Wanting to cry, she wondered instead if she deserved the ordeal she was suffering. That made the pain even more searing.

Chevy Ruddock was back on duty outside Paul Skillen's house. On the previous day, he'd been one of the many men rounded up for the raid on the tenement behind Orchard Street. In prospect, it had been an exciting operation. Thanks to help from an informer, they would be capturing dangerous criminals who represented a threat to the Home Secretary. It was something about which he could boast to his wife. In retrospect, however, it had been an unmitigated disaster. Having returned home in wet clothing before, he'd been compelled to do so again because someone had emptied a chamber pot over him before pelting him with stones. Ruddock could not present himself as a hero this time. He had to admit that the raid had failed.

Keeping someone like Paul Skillen under surveillance was akin to catching a wild boar. His movements were sudden and unpredictable. Ruddock had been tricked by him once and was determined that it would never happen again. He had, therefore, changed his vantage point so that he could remain concealed behind a tree. Completely invisible from the house, he was able to see the front door clearly and watch the comings and goings. There had been no sighting of Paul Skillen but Ruddock, relying on instinct, was certain that he was still inside the house. It occurred to him that he should have been allowed to stay there the previous day and thereby be in a position to follow the man to the area designated for the raid. He might have found out how Skillen had got there first. He would certainly have been able to alert Yeomans to the fact that one of the brothers was ahead of him and that would have made the raid pointless. If the fugitives had indeed been there, they'd have been arrested before the Runners got anywhere near the court.

Surveillance was tiring. It was not long before he was shifting his weight from one foot to the other and wishing that he'd used the privy before leaving home. When the door of the house finally opened, Ruddock tensed but it was only a servant who came out. He was resigning himself to another stint of elongated boredom when something broke the monotony. Feeling a tap on his shoulder, he turned to see Paul Skillen standing behind him with a smile.

'I thought you were inside the house,' he said, gaping.

'You must have missed me leaving,' said the other, pleasantly.

'Next time I'm about to have a stroll, I'll send a servant out with a message for you.'

Ruddock's confidence was rudely shattered once again.

Bernard Grocott was still enjoying a considerable measure of appreciation from his colleagues for finding and employing Ruth Levitt. She'd been such an effective replacement for Anne Horner that many of them were starting to forget the woman who'd cleaned their offices so well for years. On his way to a meeting with Sidmouth, the undersecretary collected another plaudit.

'When it comes to choosing the right person,' said a clerk, 'you have a gift.'

'Thank you,' said Grocott.

'It's a pity you can't choose the cabinet.'

They shared a mischievous cackle before Grocott knocked on the door in front of him. Bidden to enter, he walked in to find Sidmouth pacing the room.

'Am I interrupting you, my lord?' he asked.

'No, no, come on in, Grocott. I find that locomotion stimulates thought on occasion and I have rather a lot to think about just now. Chief among my present preoccupations is Captain Shortland.'

'He seemed to depart from here in a huff.'

'That was because he couldn't persuade me to lend my weight to his cause at the joint commission. I told him that impartiality was vital. He came here expecting congratulations and left feeling slighted.'

'He misjudged you badly.'

'I, too, am capable of misjudgement,' admitted Sidmouth. 'When Yeomans told me that he had information that was bound to lead to the capture of O'Gara and Dagg, I took him at his word. Foolishly, I assured the captain that the prisoner, who, in his opinion, had engendered this so-called mutiny at Dartmoor, would soon be behind bars. I misjudged Yeomans.'

'There are distinct limits to his competence.'

'I realise that now.'

'Nobody can deny his former triumphs, mind you, but they are tending to recede into the near-distant past.'

'Protection is his forte. I always feel safe when he and Hale are beside me. With these prisoners still at large,' said Sidmouth, 'I need the Runners at hand whenever I travel. Then, of course, there are the celebrations to consider . . .'

'These men will surely have been recaptured by then,' said Grocott.

'One hopes so. London, however, offers any fugitive a million or more hiding places. It will be like searching for a needle in a bottle of hay.'

'That's a feat beyond the Runners.'

'It's precisely why I've engaged the Skillen brothers. They are true conjurers. Yeomans and his men are diligent foot soldiers but they lack imagination. If you wish for someone with magic in their fingers, look no further than Peter and Paul Skillen.'

'He thought I was *you*, Paul,' said his brother, 'and he all but fainted when I tapped him on the shoulder. It was almost as if Yeomans had failed to warn the poor oaf that there were two of us.'

'What he hopes to gain by standing out there is beyond me,' said Paul. 'I led him a merry dance the other day, then Jem dipped him in the river for his pains.'

'Leave him to his own devices. We have more important things to discuss than a lame-brained Runner.'

They were seated opposite each other, enjoying a cup of coffee. Paul was unusually subdued but Peter was animated. After another sip, he jabbed a finger.

'My mind keeps coming back to that money,' he said.

'What money?'

'The banknotes I found under Anne Horner's bed.'

'If I'm in a woman's boudoir,' said Paul with a grin, 'then the real treasure is in the bed itself. I'd never waste time looking underneath it. Flesh and blood is much more enticing than paper money.'

'How did it get there?' asked Peter, ignoring the digression.

'Perhaps she stole it.'

'There's no question of that, Paul. The woman has a spotless reputation.'

'Some people have secret lives.'

'Mrs Horner is not one of them. She's no thief so you can dismiss that explanation. Nor did she obtain the money by blackmail,' Peter went on, 'or by selling her favours. Both hypotheses are wildly out of character. It would be like you becoming Pope or me flying to the moon and back on a broomstick.'

'Strangely enough,' teased Paul, 'I've always had leanings towards the Old Religion. And there's something curiously appealing about the papacy. Being serious, however,' he said,

'I think you should forget Mrs Horner until these men are caught.'

'They take priority – and rightly so – but I can't just flush the woman from my mind. Her abduction is in some way linked to the Home Office and I want to find out how. She needs rescuing.'

'Let's turn to the fugitives first. I still feel that Nason might lead us to them. That's why I sent Jem to that address you gave me. If the scrivener goes to see those men, Jem will follow him like a bloodhound.'

'He's wasting his time,' said Peter, 'just like that fellow watching you. Nason is too frightened to go anywhere near O'Gara and Dagg and they certainly wouldn't tell him where they're hiding. He's served his purpose and they've cast him aside.'

'Then we should arrest him.'

'What's the point?'

'He helped them frame their demands, Peter. He's an accomplice.'

'Nason helped them against his will. He's a miserable little man with nothing to recommend him but I don't think he deserves to hang for his part in the business.'

'Hand him over and we'd get a reward.'

'Spare him and we'll feel we showed generosity of spirit.'

Paul laughed. 'Since when do we let *that* get between us and our job as detectives?'

'Nason is irrelevant now,' said Peter. 'He told me where to find them and that's the last we'll hear of him. Let the poor wretch slip back into obscurity.'

'What do we do in the meanwhile?'

'We keep looking for them and we count the days.'

'Why should we do that?'

'It's not all that long before we have the celebrations to mark the victory at the Battle of Waterloo. Every politician of note will be there, Paul. If you had a grudge against the Home Secretary, what would *you* do?'

Paul grinned. 'I'd wait until he came out in the open and I'd kill him.'

'That's why we must count the days until the event takes place.'

After his latest foray into the city, Dermot Fallon came back to the ship with two presents for them. The first was the news that a fight had been arranged later that week but that one of the contestants had been forced to withdraw because of illness. By using all his charm, Fallon had persuaded the stakeholder that Moses Dagg – rechristened the Black Assassin – would be the perfect substitute. Having found out all he could about the other boxer, Fallon was confident that the American would have no difficulty in beating him. Tom O'Gara was delighted with the news but Dagg still had reservations about appearing in public. It took a long time for them to persuade him that there would be no risk of being identified as a wanted man.

'You said that you had two gifts for us, Dermot,' recalled his cousin.

'That's right, Tom.'

'What's the other one?'

'It's here in my pocket,' said Fallon, extracting a scrap of newspaper. 'I tore this out when I saw it. It's a gift from the gods.'

'Show me,' said O'Gara, taking it from him to read.

'What does it say?' asked Dagg.

'Let me finish it first.'

'Is it about us?'

'No,' said O'Gara, waving the paper in the air, 'it isn't directly about us but it's just what we need. The Battle of Waterloo is going to be celebrated in Hyde Park with huge crowds milling around. The Home Secretary is bound to be there. Can you guess what I'm thinking, Moses?'

'Yes, I can,' said Dagg, chuckling. 'It's our chance.'

'Take it,' urged Fallon.

'We will.'

O'Gara tapped the piece of paper. 'Let's make a note of this date because it could well be the day when he dies. If Viscount Sidmouth hasn't answered our demands by then,' he vowed, 'we'll assassinate him as we promised and show this whole damn country that we mean to get our way.'

CHAPTER SIXTEEN

Like his brother, Peter Skillen was punctilious about keeping himself extremely fit and maintaining his proficiency with various weapons. Adept at fencing, he could always match Gully Ackford without ever quite being able to win a bout against him. When they finished their practice that afternoon, both were perspiring slightly but it was Peter who was breathing more heavily.

'You always make me work so hard, Gully,' he complained.

'Attack is the best form of defence. You fought me off very well. When I last crossed swords with Paul, *he* was the one launching attack after attack. It was all I could do to cope with him.'

'Paul likes to spice his swordsmanship with aggression.'

'He was almost demented.'

'I think I can see what's coming,' said Peter with an understanding smile. 'You want an explanation of my brother's fiery temper but I simply don't have one. Charlotte is the person to ask.'

'I approached her,' said Ackford, ruefully, 'and I was rightly slapped down for being so nosy. Charlotte doesn't break confidences.'

Peter beamed. 'I'd entrust her with any secrets.'

'I didn't know that you had any. Paul, however, is a different kettle of fish. He's a man of many secrets.'

'Ladies seem to find that a source of attraction.'

'Perhaps that's why I have little appeal to the gentler sex,' said Ackford with a world-weary sigh. 'I lack any whiff of secrecy. I'm an open book.'

Peter patted him affectionately on the back. 'It's one that's always profitable to read, Gully.'

Charlotte came into the room with the news that a visitor was asking to speak to him as a matter of urgency. Her husband showed immediate interest.

'Did he give his name?'

'He refused to do so,' she replied.

'Did he say what it concerned?'

'It is for your ears only, apparently.'

'I think I smell secrecy in the air,' said Ackford.

'What manner of man is he?' asked Peter.

'He's well spoken and well dressed. But he's rather furtive. He was shocked when he saw me and realised that a woman was employed here. I thought for a moment that he was on the point of leaving.'

'Then I'd better grab him before he goes,' said Peter, slipping on his coat. 'Thank you again, Gully.'

'It was my pleasure,' said Ackford.

Leaving them together, Peter went downstairs and went into

the room used as an office. The stranger was hovering beside the desk, and seemed unsure whether to stay or go. He was a tall, slim, fidgety man in his early forties with side whiskers covering both cheeks and heavy eyebrows beneath which a pair of darting eyes could be seen. Peter had the feeling that he'd seen the man before but he couldn't remember where. He'd certainly never been introduced to him and was not about to learn his name now.

'If you wish for instruction,' said Peter, 'the person to talk to is Mr Ackford. He owns and runs the gallery.'

'I only wish to speak to you, Mr Skillen.'

'May I know your name, sir?'

'I first have to establish if you're able to help me. Only then can I disclose more detail about myself.'

'Why did you seek me out?'

'You were highly recommended.'

'Can I at least know the identity of the person who spoke up for me?'

'It will become clear in due course,' said the man, appraising him shrewdly. 'If, that is, I decide to engage your services.'

'I am already at full stretch, sir,' said Peter, 'and am unable to take on new assignments. If you've come in search of a detective, I am not the only one here. Mr Ackford taught me all I know and Jem Huckvale, his assistant, is equally astute in matters of detection. Either of them would render you good service. Then, of course, there is my brother, Paul.'

The visitor was categorical. 'I am only interested in *Peter Skillen*.'

'I am not available, I fear.'

'When you hear what I have to say, you may change your mind.'

Heavy footsteps went past in the corridor outside and startled the man. Peter led him across the room and indicated a chair. When they sat down, Peter spent a few minutes trying to calm him and stop him looking over his shoulder all the time. He looked at the man's hands. They were clenched tight and his whole body was tense. Evidently, it had taken a supreme effort for him to come forward. Peter had to draw the answers out of him.

'I can see that you are in some kind of trouble,' he said.

'It's true,' admitted the man.

'And you'll only give me the details if absolute discretion is guaranteed.'

'I was told that was what you'd provide, Mr Skillen.'

'Then your mystery informant did not mislead you.' Peter waited for him to speak but the man was tongue-tied by shame and embarrassment. 'Are in you any danger, sir?'

The visitor's head drooped. 'Yes, I am.'

'Have you received a death threat?'

'That's what it amounts to,' said the other with a flash of anger. 'If I don't comply, they'll destroy me. I'll lose my family, my friends and my position.' He reached out to grab Peter's wrist. 'You must help me, Mr Skillen!' He released his hold as if he'd just touched red-hot metal. 'Oh, I do beg your pardon. I've no right to impose on you like this.'

'You've every right,' said Peter. 'When I first came in here, I had an idea that I might have seen you before and I've now remembered where.' The man was aghast. 'Don't be afraid. I won't reveal the fact that you sought my help to anybody. A lot has already been explained to me. I know, for instance, who recommended me.'

'He must *never* know of this conversation,' pleaded the man.

'He will not do so from me.'

'Do I have your word?'

'You may have it in writing, if you so wish.'

The man subjected him to a long, searching stare then chewed his lip before speaking. He told his story in the third person as if it had happened to someone else altogether. Peter heard of a man of good education and unflagging industry who'd worked his way up to a respectable position as a result of his service to the state. He'd married, been a devoted spouse and helped to raise two children. His wife was then struck down with a wasting disease and he nursed her lovingly until the point when he could no longer cope on his own so he'd brought a woman into the house to provide care.

Peter guessed rightly that this paragon would have a weakness. And so it proved. The man was under such unbearable pressure that he needed some support and he found it in drink. At home and at work, he began to rely on a regular nip of brandy. While it gave him the strength to carry on, it also befuddled him slightly. When he'd had too much to drink on one occasion, temptation had crossed his path.

The man pressed on, confessing his sin yet absolving himself at the same time. What he'd done was, in his opinion, at once appalling yet forgivable, a betrayal that should arouse condemnation while at the same time being an act of redemption.

It did not take Peter long to put a name to one of the central characters in the story. He finally understood why there'd been so much money under her bed.

Anne Horner was now so consumed by guilt that she barely thought about anything else. Instead of seeing herself as a victim, she came round to the view that she was serving a sentence that had been rightly imposed on her. It was a form of penance. She no longer complained or dreamt of escape. Even though it had diminished in quality and quantity, she accepted the food with gratitude. Her gaolers noted the difference in her. When she brought in a meal that day, the woman was curious.

'Something has happened, hasn't it?' she said.

'Yes, it has. I've been thinking.'

'And what have you decided?'

'I know why I'm here.'

'Oh, I wouldn't be too sure of that.'

'This is my punishment, isn't it? Someone put me in here deliberately.'

'Yes,' said the woman, 'we did but it was not to punish *you*. Our intention is to punish someone else.'

Anne was bewildered. 'What do you mean?'

'All will become clear one day.'

'Who are you and why does that man never speak to me?'

'That's the way it has to be.'

'Why pick on me?'

'It's quite simple,' said the woman, smiling. 'You're an asset.'

* * *

Peter Skillen listened to the long narrative attentively, even though he'd worked out the *denouement* well before it was reached. In his story, the visitor stressed that nothing improper had actually taken place between the man and the woman. Temptation had flickered but been resisted. What had grown up was a deep and loving friendship that in no way threatened the man's marriage or the solemn vows by which it was protected. Throughout his tale, the visitor made much of the concept of respectability. He did everything in his power to convince his listener that he had in no way deviated from it.

'Perhaps we could abandon this charade,' said Peter, pointedly. 'We both know that you're a clerk at the Home Office. I remember passing you on the stairs one day. The unnamed woman in your story is Mrs Horner and she's enduring great suffering because of you. All that you have to contend with is a ransom demand. Her problems are far more serious.'

'Do you think I don't realise that, Mr Skillen?'

'You claim that nothing untoward occurred between the two of you.'

'On my honour, it didn't.'

'Then you have nothing to worry about. Tell your wife what you've told me and the problem disappears. If they are in no position to cause you embarrassment, the kidnappers will lose their bargaining position.'

'But Anne – Mrs Horner, that is – might be hurt as a result.'

'That's a separate matter. I first want you to look me in the eye and tell me that you'd have no qualms about repeating what you told me to your wife.' The man's eyelids fluttered like butterflies. Peter was blunt. 'I think that you're being less than truthful, sir, and on that basis I must turn down your request.'

'No, no, I beg you to help me.'

'I am already hired to find Mrs Horner. She *deserves* my help.'

'So do I,' cried the man. 'Look, I apologise if I've been overly mysterious. My work means everything to me, you must appreciate that. If I were dismissed, untold misery would alight on me and my family.'

'What is your damn name?' demanded Peter. 'There's no point in hiding it from me now. I can easily find it out by enquiries at the Home Office.'

The man nodded in defeat. 'It's Beyton.'

'Then please stop trying to arouse pity in me, Mr Beyton. You may as well know that I value Mrs Horner's safety at a far higher price than I do your domestic harmony. If she'd not been led astray by you, she wouldn't now be in such danger.'

'I didn't exactly lead her astray, Mr Skillen.'

'Let's not quibble about phrases, shall we? Suffice to say that something of significance took place between you and this is the outcome. Mrs Horner is being held somewhere and you've had a ransom demand. May I see it, please?'

'Of course,' said Beyton, pulling a letter from his pocket and handing it over. 'As you can see, if the money is not paid, Mrs Horner may be harmed.'

'And your wife will learn some unpalatable truths about her loving husband,' said Peter, sharply.

He read the ransom demand. It was short but explicit, asking for a certain amount of money and threatening repercussions if it were not paid. Beyton had been given a short time in which to collect the ransom. Details of when it was to be handed over would be sent to him before too long.

Peter handed the letter back. 'This is very troubling.'

'Yes,' groaned Beyton, 'and the worst thing is that it's entirely my fault.'

Burying his head in his hands, he began to sob quietly. Peter felt no sympathy for him. What he saw was a snivelling clerk who had taken advantage of a servant then insisted that nothing inappropriate had taken place. There was a yawning social gap between them. Peter refused to believe that Anne Horner had either the skill or the inclination to seduce him. The initiative must have come from him and – whether out of pity for the man or from fear that she might lose her job if she refused – she had complied. In trying to introduce elements of romance into his account of the relationship, Beyton had gone too far for Peter. The cleaner had been set on simply because she was there. Frustrated by an arid domestic life and inebriated with brandy, Beyton had lusted after a woman. The clerk finally admitted it.

'I had a power over her,' he murmured, 'and I used it. But it was only once or twice,' he went on, gesticulating with both hands. 'I was so driven by desperation that I couldn't help myself. Mrs Horner didn't dare to resist but she didn't welcome my advances either. It was shameful, I know. When it was all over, I was disgusted. I *forced* myself on the poor woman.'

'Then you paid her to keep her mouth shut afterwards.'

'No, no, she refused to take a penny.'

'Then how did the money get into her hands?'

Beyton was staggered. 'You *know* about that?'

'I was allowed to search Mrs Horner's lodging. It was under her bed.'

'I posted the money to her,' he explained. 'She tried to give it back to me a couple of times but I rejected it. I thought I owed it to her, Mr Skillen.'

'You owe her a lot more than that,' said Peter, flatly.

Beyton was distraught. 'What must I do?' he asked. 'How can I get out of this deep pit I have dug for myself?'

'The first thing you must do is to stop feeling sorry for yourself, Mr Beyton. That will advantage nobody.'

'I agree, I agree.'

'You must regain some composure, sir. If you behave like this at the Home Office, you will soon give yourself away. You have many perceptive colleagues, Mr Grocott among them. Let him see you in this state and you are doomed.'

'You are right. I must exercise care.'

'Discharge your duties in the normal way.'

'What about the ransom?'

'You must pay it.'

'But my savings will disappear completely, Mr Skillen.'

'Borrow money. You're the kind of man who will have wealthy friends.'

'I'd never afford to pay a loan back,' protested Beyton.

'You won't have to pay it back,' said Peter, confidently, 'because you won't lose it in the first place. When the exchange is made, I'll be there to make sure that the kidnapper is caught. The money will be safe, Mrs Horner will be released and you, Mr Beyton, can go home to an ailing wife who will never know how false her husband really is.' He gave a cold smile. 'How does that sound, sir?'

Beyton cringed before him.

Moses Dagg was not impressed by the venue for the boxing match. It was a disused warehouse by the river with narrow gaps in the walls and even bigger ones in the roof. Sunlight and draughts came in from all directions. Dust hung in the air like a cloud. The ring in which Dagg was to fight was no more than a square of sawdust with four boards around it to hold back the crowd. When he kicked the sawdust in disgust, a bone surfaced with feathers attached to it.

'There was a cock fight here last night,' explained Fallon. 'The sawdust soaks up the blood.'

Dagg inhaled. 'It stinks in here.'

'It's no worse than some of the ships we've sailed in,' said O'Gara, cheerily. 'And it's a lot better than our cells at Dartmoor.' He turned to his cousin. 'Tell us a bit more about the other man.'

'Donkey Johnson is the champion here,' said Fallon. 'He's never been beaten. In fact, I can't ever remember seeing him knocked down. But then, he's never had any real competition. He does now. Having watched the way that Moses licked Donal Kearney, he'll have no trouble winning against Donkey.'

'I want to fight a man,' said Dagg, 'not a frigging donkey.'

'If I had a punch like yours, I'd take on a whole herd of donkeys.'

'What about the stake money?' asked O'Gara.

'Forget about that.'

'It's a lot of cash to put up, Dermot.'

'I raised it somehow,' said Fallon, evasively. 'Everyone will get their money back with interest when Moses wins the fight.'

'We'll need money to bet on him as well.'

'Leave that to me, Tom. I know men of quality.'

'Then they wouldn't come here,' said Dagg, wrinkling his nose. 'This is a place for drunken riffraff and the lowest scum of the city.'

'Their money is just as good as anything you'd get from the gentry.'

'I still don't like it here.'

'What I'd really like to see,' said O'Gara, grinning, 'is another fight between Moses and Kearney.'

'Donal Kearney is *mine*,' declared Fallon. 'When I have the chance, I'm going to do the whole tenement a favour and rip his ugly head off.'

'Does anyone else know that he was the informer?'

'The word will have got round by now, Tom. Kearney will be treated like a leper. I just hope they leave him alone until I can get *my* hands on him.'

He showed them around the warehouse and told them about some of the entertainment he'd seen there. It often ended in the death of an animal or in the serious injuries of a human being. The crowd would be drawn there by blood-lust. It was up to Dagg to supply their needs. The three men were just about to leave when someone appeared in the doorway to block their exit. He was a huge, hideous man in his thirties with a bald head, which was tattooed with battle scars. One of his eyes was higher than the other. Both of them gleamed with pleasure.

'So this is the Black Assassin, is it?' he sneered.

'Yes,' retorted Fallon, going up to him. 'You're finally going to meet a man who can beat you, Donkey. Make your will before you step into the ring.'

Donkey Johnson's laugh was an extended bray and the big teeth that had given him his nickname were exposed for all to see. Dagg was shorter by several inches and looked small beside the man he was about to fight. Dermot Fallon had misled him. Even for someone of Dagg's ability, beating a man of such size and obvious strength would be an immense challenge. Whoever won the fight, blood would be spilt freely in the sawdust.

'I *hate* Americans,' said Johnson, nastily.

When the three of them walked past him, a mocking bray pursued them.

Anne Horner was more confused than ever. For the first time since she'd been abducted, she'd had a conversation of sorts with the woman. It had been very puzzling. Though Anne had been described as an asset, she could not understand why. She had no intrinsic value as a person. In fact, the hours of recrimination had left her feeling completely worthless. What did they intend to do with her? Why were they treating her so badly? How long would she be held?

New questions flooded into her mind. Having spent so much time with introspection, Anne turned her attention to other people. How would her sister be coping with the news of the abduction? What would her landlady do? When would the Home Office decide that she'd just vanished of her own accord and replace her, as if she'd never been there? What of her friends and acquaintances, people she saw in the normal course of a day? How soon would they forget to miss her? Was anyone actually *looking* for her? Was she important enough to merit a search?

Anne was then assailed by another question, one that she'd fought off for days because it was so distasteful. How would *he* react? Since he worked at the Home Office, he'd have been among the first to notice her absence. What had he done about it? Would he really care? Or would he be glad that she'd disappeared out of his life? Could it be that he was in some way responsible for it? Had he wanted her out of the way? Was he paying for her imprisonment? He'd made it clear that it might be better if she gave up her job at the Home Office. The money he'd given her was intended to be ample recompense for the wages she'd forfeit over a lengthy period. But Anne had refused to be paid off and moved out for his benefit. Apart from what had happened between her and David Beyton, she liked every aspect of her work and was determined to continue doing it. Had he decided to remove her by other means?

The question was unanswerable and, in any case, she was diverted by a sound she'd heard before without quite knowing what it was. She pricked her ears and got as close to the grating as the chain permitted. A minute later, she heard it again.

It was the same dull thud.

Once it had started, the persecution of Donal Kearney began to escalate. All sorts of things were left outside his door, including a blood-covered pig's head. Neighbours refused to acknowledge him and even those to whom he was distantly related severed all links with him. In the middle of a seething mass of humanity, he and his family were outcasts. Because of his treachery, his wife and children suffered as well. It began with insults before moving on to blows. Kearney first of all tried to bully people into letting them alone but there were far too many enemies for intimidation to have any effect. As a last resort, he adopted a different approach, calling on people in the hope of convincing them that he was being unjustly maligned. Most of the time, he had doors slammed in his face but one old man, Hector Lynch, at least allowed him to state his case before coming to a decision.

'I'm here to explain things, Hector.'

'I'm listening.'

'It wasn't me, Hector,' said Kearney, earnestly.

'Then who *was* the rotten bugger?'

'I don't know. It could've been anybody. When the raid took place, I was miles away, doing my job.'

'That's not what people are saying.'

'Don't listen to them.'

'They blame you.'

'I wasn't the informer.'

'We don't like the sight of a Runner at the best of times,' said the old man, 'and we won't stand for an invasion by the bastards. Someone told them that those two men were here and all the fingers are pointing at you.'

'Dermot Fallon was a friend. I'd never rat on him.'

'That's two lies for a start. Dermot was never your friend and you'd rat on your own grandmother if you'd a mind to. We know you too well, Donal. If you can't beat someone in a fair fight, you'll get your revenge another way, however dirty it has to be. That's what you did with the black man.'

'It's not true!' shouted Kearney. 'How can I persuade you of that?'

'Ask *them*.'

The chimney sweeper blinked. 'Who?'

'Ask the lads behind you.'

Kearney swung round to see four brawny young men standing there with menacing expressions. One carried a cudgel but the other three relied on their fists. Before he could even start to reason with them, Kearney was under attack. Punches rained in from all directions and the cudgel delivered a series of hammer blows. Though he tried to fight back, Kearney was soon overpowered and beaten to the ground where he was kicked unmercifully until he was covered in blood and whimpering for mercy.

The man with the cudgel lifted it to strike again.

'No,' said the old man, intervening. 'That's enough. The person he has to answer to is Dermot Fallon. Let him stay alive until then.'

Jem Huckvale was delighted to be called back to the shooting gallery. Watching the house belonging to Jubal Nason had been tedious and unrewarding. The man had not emerged at any point and there'd been no visitors. All that Huckvale had to report was that he'd heard sounds of an argument from inside the house with the strident voice of a woman dominating the exchange.

'Thank you for bringing me back, Peter,' he said. 'If I'd

stayed there any longer, I'd have fallen asleep out of boredom.'

'Paul told me he'd sent you there,' said Peter, 'but it served no purpose. To all intents and purposes, we may forget that Nason ever existed. Your sharp eyes are needed elsewhere, Jem.'

Huckvale grinned hopefully. 'You have other work for me?'

'I will have in due course. Meanwhile, go back to helping Gully.'

'Anything is better than what I have been doing. Where's Paul?'

'He's doing exactly what he did before,' said Peter, 'and that's trying to find those men by trawling through Irish communities. Since they're being led by Dermot Fallon, it's more than likely that they'll find refuge with some of his countrymen so Paul will have an opportunity to try out his Irish accent again.'

'It worked,' said Huckvale. 'That's how he tracked Fallon down the first time. *You* had to rely on evidence given by Nason to get you to that tenement behind Orchard Street but Paul sniffed his way there first.'

'He has a knack of doing things like that, Jem. While he's taking one route, I'll be exploring others because I think we're dealing with a shrewd man in Dermot Fallon. He might actually avoid Irish communities now,' argued Peter, 'because he fears that those are the very places that the Runners will start to look. I fancy that he'll take the two Americans somewhere else altogether.'

'How will you find them, Peter?'

'As ever, it will be by a combination of luck and instinct.'

'What about the search for that missing woman? Has that been forgotten?'

'On the contrary,' said Peter. 'While you were away, I made some progress on that front. At least I now have some understanding of why she was abducted.'

'And why was that?'

Peter was frugal with the details. Having assured David Beyton that he would act with discretion, he kept the man's name and position out of the account he gave to Huckvale. He merely told him that Anne Horner was being held by people who were demanding a ransom for her release.

Huckvale was amazed. 'But the woman is only a cleaner.'

'She fulfils a vital function, Jem.'

'I thought ransoms were only demanded for people of importance.'

'Mrs Horner is clearly of great importance to someone.'

'Will the money be paid?'

'It would appear so,' said Peter, enigmatically.

The sound of gunfire from above made Huckvale look upwards.

'Gully is giving instruction to someone,' he said. 'He's going to be angry with me because I didn't have time to whiten the target.'

'Tell him that Paul sent you off on an errand.'

'I will. Oh, I meant to tell you that, on my way back here, I came past Paul's house and that man outside has gone.'

Peter laughed. 'I must have frightened him when I crept up behind him. He thought I was Paul and I didn't disillusion him.'

'That's two of us who've been taken off a tedious duty. You have to give the fellow some credit, though,' said Huckvale.

'When you get pushed into the Thames for watching someone's house, you've got a good reason to stay well away from it.'

Chevy Ruddock was delighted by the message to report to The Peacock. Any break in routine was welcome and he hoped he'd be assigned to other duties. When he got to the inn, however, he was kept waiting a long time because Micah Yeomans was deep in conversation with Alfred Hale and clearly didn't wish to be disturbed. Ruddock hovered in their vicinity. When he was finally noticed, he came in for a rebuke.

'I expected you earlier,' complained Yeomans.

'I've been here all of twenty minutes.'

'Why didn't you say so?'

'You and Mr Hale seemed to be busy.'

'You should have made your presence felt, man.'

'What do you have to report?' asked Hale.

'Very little,' replied Ruddock. 'I spent hours watching the house in the certain knowledge that Paul Skillen was inside it then he turned up behind me.'

'How do you know it was him?'

'Who else could it have been, Mr Hale?'

'It might have been his brother, Peter.'

'But he gave me the impression that he was Paul Skillen.'

'Then I'll wager that he was playing tricks on you,' said Yeomans, irritably. 'You're being taken off that particular duty, Ruddock.'

'Thank you, sir.'

'It hasn't exactly been a task at which you've shone, has it? The fact is that Paul Skillen somehow got to that tenement before we raided it. If you'd shadowed him properly, you could have followed him there then warned us.'

'You told me that I was needed for the raid.'

'Why didn't you use your initiative?' scolded Hale.

'I'd never disobey orders.'

'You threw away a golden opportunity to stay on Paul Skillen's tail.'

'That's water under the bridge, Alfred,' said Yeomans, dismissively. 'And while we're on the subject of water, I'm transferring you to a different area. From now on, you'll patrol the Thames.' Ruddock blanched. 'What's the problem?'

'If it's all the same to you, sir, I'd prefer somewhere else.'

'You just said that you'd never disobey an order.'

'I know,' said Ruddock, 'but the river holds bitter memories for me. As you know, I was pushed into it the other day and I can't swim.'

'You lived to tell the tale,' said Hale, briskly.

'There'll be two of you,' explained Yeomans. 'We've been having a lot of complaints about the rowdiness at an old warehouse where the sweepings of London gather to drink themselves into a stupor. They sometimes have a boxing match there and, when that happens, the place turns into Bedlam.'

'What am I supposed to do?' asked Ruddock in alarm.

'Impose law and order.'

'What – all on my own?'

'You'll have a man with you,' said Yeomans. 'I just told you that.'

'Two of us can't control a howling mob, sir.'

'Use your common sense, man.'

'Yes,' said Hale, 'and console yourself with this thought. Patrolling that area will be a lot more interesting than standing outside Paul Skillen's house and getting shoved into the river!'

Though he fought hard against the impulse, Paul Skillen was drawn back to the theatre once again, as if by an unseen magnet. Shedding the disguise he'd worn among the Irish, he dressed in his finery before going out. He was soon part of a noisy crowd that streamed into the theatre with high expectations. Paul wondered if their hopes were going to be fulfilled or shattered by Hannah Granville's performance that evening. All around him, he heard extravagant praise of her talents.

'She's a genius,' said one man, 'a second Sarah Siddons.'

'Nobody can rival *her*,' countered his wife.

'Miss Granville can,' interjected someone nearby. 'I've seen her and she is peerless. Mrs Siddons couldn't hold a candle to her.'

'I remain to be persuaded,' said the woman, resolutely.

'My wife is a lady of discernment,' explained her husband.

'Then she is about to discern a true marvel, sir,' said the other man. Before moving away, he touched the brim of his hat. 'I bid you both good evening.'

Paul tried to shut out the sound of the continuous eulogies because they only served to remind him of what he'd thrown away. Hannah was indeed unique, as much as a person as an actress. Her individuality was remarkable. He knew things about her that none of those around him could even imagine. They were, for the most part, endearing things that made him smile as he recalled them. Less pleasant aspects of her character and behaviour remained dormant in his mind.

When Paul took his seat in the stalls, the elderly man beside him gave a nudge.

'Have you seen this play before, sir?'

'No,' replied Paul, 'I have not. This is my first time.'

'Then you are about to view the eighth Wonder of the World.'

'I take it that you are no stranger to *Venice Preserv'd*.'

The man chortled. 'I am a true veteran,' he said, giving another nudge. 'This will be my fifth visit. You'll soon see why.'

Like Paul, the man was on his own. If he'd seen the play on the first occasion in the company of his wife, he'd made sure that she didn't return with him. Paul sensed that the woman fondly imagined that he was at his club or dining with friends. Indirectly, Hannah Granville had generated a lot of deception in some families as husbands rediscovered the lure of bachelorhood.

When the play began, the hubbub slowly died away. Belvidera began to cast her spell. Hannah's performance was markedly better. Paul was ready to concede that. While it fell short of the heights he'd seen her attain, it was more than enough to dazzle and move the audience. Resounding applause greeted the end of the play and she seemed able to enjoy it this time. Having put more effort into her performance, she reclined on the ovation, as if it were a collection of soft feather pillows. When it was all over, Paul collected another nudge from his neighbour.

'What did you think?' asked the man.

'It was a memorable performance,' said Paul.

'It certainly stirred memories for me!'

The man chortled merrily all the way to the exit. Paul hung back, wrestling against the temptation to stand at the stage door again. Hannah had disappointed all of her admirers on the previous occasion by sneaking out of the front door and Paul toyed with the notion of standing on the opposite side of the road in case she reverted to that stratagem. In the end, he was at the mercy of another unseen magnet and it pulled him round to the stage door. Staying well back, so that he couldn't overhear some of the coarser comments of the waiting suitors, Paul seemed to wait an age for her to appear, each minute charged with remorse and regret. When Hannah finally came, there was a spontaneous burst of applause and the men clustered around her before parting like the Red Sea.

Hannah Granville sailed away from the theatre with a sense of triumph but it was not the actress who caught Paul's eye. It was the handsome young man on whose arm she swept past him. He basked in the envy he was creating and raised his hat to them all in farewell. Paul was both wounded and shocked that it had taken such a short time to replace him. He felt giddy at what he saw as her betrayal. She was no longer his. The last shreds of hope had vanished.

As so often when he was in a state of despair, Jermyn Street beckoned.

CHAPTER SEVENTEEN

Bernard Grocott was among the first to arrive at the Home Office that morning. He was so used to stepping into a room that was spectacularly tidy that he was beginning to take the new servant for granted. Though he was still deeply concerned about Anne Horner's disappearance, he was more than satisfied with the woman who'd replaced her and, on balance, found Ruth Levitt preferable. Grocott hoped that she might turn out to be a permanent fixture. It was a hope that was shared by David Beyton, though for somewhat different reasons. To spare him embarrassment, he'd wanted Ruth's predecessor to leave the Home Office altogether. It never crossed his mind that Anne Horner would be forcibly removed and that he would be to blame.

'Good morning, Mr Grocott,' he said.

'Ah, there you are, Beyton.'

'You asked me to report to you first thing.'

'I did, indeed,' said Grocott. 'The Home Secretary is

spending the morning with the Prime Minister and he's asked me to review the security arrangements for the celebrations in Hyde Park. Mr Yeomans has already seen them and given them his blessing but one can never be too careful about such things.'

'I agree, sir.'

'What I need is a sounding board and you have always taken on that role with distinction. That's why I sent for you.'

'I'm very flattered.'

In fact, Beyton was feeling rather flustered, struggling to maintain a calm exterior. Ordinarily, he would have felt grateful to be singled out from the other clerks in order to have privileged access to important information concerning the safety of the royal family and the senior members of government. It would be something he could tell his ailing wife to cheer her up. As it was, he was worried about being under Grocott's scrutiny for some length of time. With so much pain and anguish churning inside him, Beyton was afraid that some of it might show in his face and manner.

'Our major concern, of course,' said the undersecretary, 'is the weather.'

'One can't control that, sir.'

'Alas, no, that feat is beyond even the Duke of Wellington, though you'd never get him to admit it.'

Beyton rose to a smile. 'His self-belief is legendary.'

'Battles are never won by doubters.'

'How true, sir!'

'Let us begin, shall we?'

Grocott shuffled the sheaf of papers on his desk. Page by page, he went through the projected arrangements for the celebrations of the victory at Waterloo. As well as the great and good of England, foreign dignitaries would also be present and their absolute safety had to be guaranteed. Beyton was only half-listening to the endless recital of names and the disposition of the soldiers. All that he was required to do was to give a series of affirmative nods and an occasional word of approval, yet Grocott seemed to feel that his colleague was being very helpful.

Sitting back in his chair, he studied the clerk for some time.

'Is anything wrong, Beyton?'

'Not that I know of, sir.'

'You have a faint air of distraction.'

'My mind has been wholly concentrated on the task in hand,' said Beyton. 'It's been an honour to assist you on such an important matter.'

'I chose you with care,' said Grocott. 'Of all the senior clerks, you're the most industrious and reliable. Every one of the others has his strengths, mind you, but you stand out. In fact,' he went on, 'I'm able to confide something that will show you how much I value the quality of your work.'

'What is it, sir?'

'My esteemed colleague, Mr Ryecart, has indicated that he wishes to retire from his post as undersecretary here. We will need to find a suitable substitute and I believe that we should look no further than your good self.'

'Heavens!' cried Beyton, overcome with surprise.

'It's no more than you deserve.'

'I'm lost for words, sir.'

'The post is not in my gift, of course, but I do have influence with the permanent secretary and I've persuaded him that you are the ideal choice. Between the two of us, we should be able to convince Viscount Sidmouth that you should be promoted.' A warning finger went up. 'This must remain a well-guarded secret,' he warned. 'As and when Mr Ryecart leaves, there's bound to be fevered speculation among the other clerks. Take no part in it, Beyton.' Grocott glanced at the clock on the wall. 'Good gracious!' he said. 'We've been here for hours. Thank you so much for your help.' Rising to his feet, he extended a hand. 'And while we're still alone, allow me to offer you my congratulations.'

'Thank you, sir,' said Beyton, getting up for the handshake.

At a time when he should have been delighted, however, the clerk felt only a sense of foreboding. If the undersecretary had known about Beyton's clandestine dealings, he would have recommended dismissal rather than promotion. That might still be the clerk's fate. When he left the room, he stood with his back to the door and thought about what had just happened. Out of four senior clerks, he had been chosen, even leapfrogging over the chief clerk. He was entitled to feel pleasure. As he went back to the room he shared with the other senior clerks, he even permitted himself a quiet smile. As soon as he sat down at his desk, however, he was brought back to reality with a bump.

Staring up at him was a letter in a hand he'd seen once before.

Paul Skillen stripped off his shift and lowered himself into the hip bath of cold water that he'd asked a servant to prepare. Ignoring the chill and the discomfort, he told himself that they were the least that he deserved after a night of recklessness at his favourite gambling hell. He scooped up handfuls of water and let them drop over his head as a penance while he bemoaned his loss of willpower the previous evening. Hannah Granville was a woman with multiple attractions. It was inevitable that she should cope with the loss of one suitor by finding another one to dance attendance on her. When he thought about the new beau, Peter was forced to admit that he had charm, fine apparel and striking good looks. In addition, he had youth on his side. It rankled that Hannah had chosen someone who was five or six years younger. The memory made him wet his head a second time.

Having woken up very late, he'd been too groggy even to contemplate breakfast. His mouth was dry, his head pounding and his stomach mutinous. All that the bath had done was to bring him fully awake and allow him to see the folly of his actions. Paul had not only drunk too much in the convivial atmosphere in Jermyn Street, he'd contrived to gamble away nearly all the money he'd won when he was last there. It was a tale of unrelieved loss. He'd lost Hannah, he'd lost face, he'd lost resistance to the siren call of the gambling hell, he'd lost all his self-control through excessive drink and he'd lost a sizeable amount of money. Worst of all, however, was the fact that his self-respect had once again withered.

Wanting to suffer in privacy, he was dismayed when told that his brother had called to see him. Paul was minded to tell his servant to send Peter away with an excuse but he knew that he'd only call on urgent business. He therefore made an effort to repair some of the visible damage inflicted on him at the card table. When he finally staggered downstairs, he felt marginally better. Peter was characteristically frank.

'You look perfectly dreadful, Paul.'

'That is an optical illusion, dear brother.'

'I recognise the cloven hooves of Jermyn Street when I see them stamped all over your face. How much did you lose?'

'Let's not discuss that,' said Paul, sinking into a chair. 'How are you?'

'I suspect that I'm in a far better condition than you.'

'What of my revered sister-in-law?'

'Charlotte sends her love,' said Peter, 'but I'm not here solely as my wife's emissary. There's been an interesting development.'

Paul showed interest for the first time. 'You know where the fugitives are?'

'Not yet, I fear. The development relates to the disappearance of Mrs Horner. I now know the motive that lies behind it.'

'Where is she?'

'I'm hoping to find out before too long.'

Speaking slowly so that his brother could follow what was being said, Peter told him about the ransom demand. He revealed neither the name nor the status of David Beyton and made no mention of his relationship to the missing woman. The pertinent fact was that money was going to be handed over and Peter was determined to be there to retrieve it and to arrest the kidnapper. Though he appeared to be still in a daze, Paul had obviously listened with care.

'There's something you're not telling me, Peter.'

'I've told you all that you need to know.'

'It's absurd,' said Paul. 'Who would pay money for the release of a servant?'

'This person would.'

'Then he must be a close relative or a dear friend. Or is

it conceivable that he might actually be her lover?'

'He is not her lover,' said Peter, unwilling to dignify what had happened between Beyton and Anne Horner as an act of love. 'For some reason, he feels a deep obligation to her.'

'But you're not going to disclose what that obligation is.'

'I'd be breaking a confidence, Paul.'

'Then I'll harass you no more. Do you wish me to be involved?'

'No,' said Peter. 'One of us must continue the search for O'Gara and Dagg. You are best placed to do that. You can mingle with the Irish far more easily than I could ever manage. If I need assistance, I'll call on Jem.'

'Do you have any clues as to who sent that ransom note?'

'I'm not well versed in calligraphy but I have the feeling that it was written by a woman. I say that because it was oddly reminiscent of Charlotte's handwriting.'

Paul guffawed. 'Since when has Charlotte been penning ransom demands?' He put a hand to his forehead. 'I wish I hadn't done that,' he moaned. 'My skull is splitting apart.'

Peter was unsympathetic. 'If you're going to spend so much time among the Irish,' he warned, 'you'd better learn to hold your drink. And if you must play cards for money, at least stay sober while you do so. That way you'd be more aware of your losses and quit before they became too punitive.'

'Forget about *my* financial problems. Let's turn to Mr Anonymous. A tidy sum is being demanded by way of ransom. Can he afford it?'

'He'll *have* to afford it somehow, Paul.'

* * *

During an afternoon lull, David Beyton asked for a little time off to visit his bank. He'd already managed to send details of the second letter to Peter Skillen but he had to raise the money himself. On the walk to the bank, he debated how that might best be done. As well as his salary as a senior clerk, Beyton had a comfortable private income. Thrifty to the point of being parsimonious, he'd built up substantial savings at the bank. The only time he'd drawn on those savings was when he'd had a crisis of conscience over his treatment of Anne Horner. The money was in no way payment for services rendered. That would have insulted her. Beyton had been at pains to explain that it was a means of assuaging his guilt and providing enough money for her to retire from her job at the Home Office. To his chagrin, she'd insisted on staying there, as an immovable reminder to him of what he'd done to her when in his cups. Every time she saw him, she offered the money back but he steadfastly refused it and it remained with her.

Beyton could not understand her mentality. According to Peter Skillen, she kept the money under her bed instead of using it to pay for better lodging and giving up work altogether. His relationship with the necessary woman, he now realised, had been doomed. They'd been watched and that thought was unnerving in itself. Someone had become aware of what was going on between them. Even though Beyton had tried his best to be secretive, a pair of eyes had somehow seen what was happening. The clerk had blatantly lied to Peter Skillen, telling him that sexual intercourse had only occurred once or twice. He'd justified the deceit by arguing to himself that there had only been two occasions inside the Home Office. Other meetings had taken place in what he'd believed to be discreet hotels. Evidently, they were followed to one of them and the purpose of their visit there discovered.

That was not something he would ever divulge to his bank manager, a God-fearing family man who would need another explanation for the sudden withdrawal of funds. By the time he'd reached the bank, Beyton had worked out his excuse.

'I wish to take my beloved wife abroad,' he said, uxoriously.

'Is she able to travel?'

'Oh, yes, Mr Holland. Her physician recommends it. Because the sea air is so good for her, we go to the coast whenever possible but a complete change of scene might act as a tonic for her. Now that hostilities have at last ceased, of course, France is a possibility but my mind veers towards Switzerland.'

'I've heard good reports of the country, Mr Beyton.'

'I want nothing but the best for my wife.'

Ebenezer Holland was a rotund man in his fifties with the appearance and manner of a prince of the church. Beyton had often envisaged him with a mitre on his head and a cope around his shoulders. He'd even persuaded himself that there was the faintest aroma of frankincense in the manager's office.

'Why do you need the money at such short notice?' asked Holland.

'I've promised to hand it over to the man who will organise our travels for us. It's in the nature of a large deposit, you see. Other clients of his have allowed him to make expensive arrangements then changed their mind about going on holiday and left him out of pocket. I believe in fair dealing,' Beyton went on. 'It's a principle of which I'm sure you'll approve.'

'I do so wholeheartedly.'

'Thank you.'

'In dealings with me, you've acted with the utmost integrity.'

But the manager was not yet ready to give his episcopal blessing and release the money. He probed away gently for several minutes and Beyton had to embroider his story about some non-existent foreign travel. While his client was talking, Holland consulted a ledger.

'You and Mrs Beyton have been exemplary clients of mine,' he said. 'In other words, you've both remained solvent and made no undue demands on the bank. The largest deposit, I see, is still in the name of your wife. It has been with us for several years and accrued an appreciable amount of interest.'

'I would never touch my wife's money,' said Beyton, piously.

'Marriage to the dear lady puts it within your reach.'

'That's irrelevant, Mr Holland.'

'If you say so,' returned the other. 'As to the money, I will have it ready for collection tomorrow morning.'

Beyton was disappointed. 'I'd hoped to take it away with me.'

'Another night will make no difference, surely.'

'You are right,' said the clerk, pretending to be was happy with the arrangement. 'I'll call here tomorrow.'

'How *is* life in the higher echelons of government?'

'It has its drawbacks, Mr Holland.'

'Public service must bring rewards of the heart.'

Beyton smiled but he was squirming inside.

Even in daylight, the ramshackle warehouse had an aura of danger about it. Since he'd been told to be wary of it, Chevy

Ruddock made a point of locating it when he went on patrol. Surrounded by litter, it stood beside the river like a ghost of its former self. Ruddock eyed it with suspicion.

'That's the place, Bill,' he said.

'You don't need to tell me that, Chevy. I've been here before.'

'Have you seen any trouble?'

'I've seen nothing else. Whenever there's a dog fight, a cock fight or something else on there, the place is in uproar and we can't do anything about it.'

'Mr Yeomans told me to impose law and order.'

'Then he's talking out of his you-know-what.'

William Filbert gave a throaty laugh. He was a tubby man in his fifties with ruddy cheeks and a drooping moustache. Having been a member of the foot patrol for many years, he'd learnt how to cope with difficult situations.

'The trick is to wait,' he explained. 'If you see two villains knocking lumps out of each other, never try to arrest them because, if you do, as sure as the sun rises, they'll both turn on you. No, Chevy, you wait quietly until one has battered the other senseless and is puffing like a grampus himself, then you move in. Let a man tire himself out before you arrest him.'

'That's not always possible, Bill.'

'It's not possible here, I grant you,' said Filbert. 'That warehouse is like the seventh circle of hell some nights. When people spill out of there, there'll be a dozen brawls at the same time. That's when you use your common sense and walk past as quickly as you can. Impose law and order? Yeomans must be joking. It'd be nothing short of suicide.'

'What about the rest of the river bank?'

'You have to watch your back, Chevy. Water rats are everywhere and I mean the two-legged ones as tall as you and me. They come out at night to sniff and nibble.'

Ruddock didn't like what he was hearing. He'd been on patrol before in the sort of residential areas where there was comparatively little trouble. The Thames was very different. It was at once the city's lifeline with the world and its cesspool. Inns and ordinaries lined its banks. Brothels and gaming houses offered entertainment and false promise. Vibrant by day, it was even more hazardous at night. The dilapidated warehouse was a symbol of the dark underbelly of the capital.

As they strolled on side by side, they were met by what looked at first like a small child. A man's deep voice came from its throat and they realised that they were talking to a dwarf in ragged attire and with a cap pulled down over his forehead.

'Good day to ya, gintlemin,' he said, obsequiously. 'I've good news for ya.'

'What is it?' asked Ruddock.

'Be rand 'ere termorra noight.'

'Why?'

'There's a big fight on.'

'There's always fights along the river,' said Filbert.

'This one is spishul,' said the dwarf. 'Be at the ware'ause termorra.'

'What's happening?'

'Donkey Johns'n is goin' to beat the Black Assassin.'

'I've heard of Johnson before,' said Filbert. 'He beats everyone.'

The dwarf extended a palm. 'I'm tekkin' bets that 'e'll eat the man alive. Want to 'ave a wager, gints?'

'No, we don't.'

'It'd be easy money for ya.'

'It'd be even easier money for you, you scoundrel,' said Filbert, pushing him rudely aside. 'If we were stupid enough to place a bet, we'd never see a penny of our winnings. Be off, before we arrest you for trying to defraud us.'

'I'm as 'onest as the day is long,' protested the dwarf. 'I've been tekkin' bets for years and I allus pays art. Come on, gints. I'll give ya good odds.'

'And I'll give you a good kick up the arse if you keep bothering us. You're a public nuisance. Crawl back into whichever hole in the ground you sneaked out of.'

Filbert walked off with Ruddock at his side. Neither of them saw the repertoire of crude gestures being made behind their backs by the angry dwarf.

'You were very harsh with him, Bill,' observed Ruddock.

'It's the only language they understand.'

'Who is this Donkey Johnson?'

'He's a bloodthirsty bruiser who'll take on any man for money and knock his brains out to please the crowd. I've been past here before when Johnson is fighting. The noise from that warehouse is deafening.'

'Is he going to win tomorrow's fight, then?'

'Yes,' said Filbert. 'I don't know who this Black Assassin is but, when it's all over, his friends will be collecting money for his funeral.'

* * *

Moses Dagg had two valuable attributes as a boxer. He had a punch that could knock most men unconscious if it landed in the right place and he was extremely nimble. As they sparred in the sawdust-strewn area in the warehouse, Tom O'Gara was made all too aware of his friend's skills. Dagg was so light on his feet that he was able to dodge any punches that O'Gara threw at him. In fact, the latter spent most of the time hitting fresh air. His frustration made him try even harder but Dagg was equal to anything that came at him, ducking and weaving and, when he had to take a blow, fending it off expertly with his forearms. When O'Gara was panting for breath, his friend brought an end to his opponent's misery by delivering an uppercut that caught him on the chin. O'Gara sank to the floor as if he'd been poleaxed.

'That was wonderful!' said Fallon, clapping his hands.

'I don't think Tom would agree,' said Dagg, stooping over his friend. 'Give me a hand to get him up again.'

They hauled him to his feet then lowered him into a chair. Fallon had a bucket of cold water standing by and he laughed as he poured it over the loser's head. O'Gara slowly recovered.

'What happened?' he said, rubbing his chin.

'Moses put you to sleep.'

'It was like being kicked by a horse.'

'Horses are stronger than donkeys,' said Fallon, 'as Johnson will find out tomorrow. He'll have the surprise of his life.'

'He looked slow to me,' said Dagg.

'Yes, Moses, he is. While you prance on your toes, Donkey Johnson lumbers. The trouble is that you're not only fighting him. If he starts to struggle – and I've seen him in difficulties before – he forces his opponent up against the boards so that his friends can get in some sly punches from behind. Remember that. Don't let him pin you to the boards.'

'Point out who these friends are,' said O'Gara, grimly, 'and I'll make sure they don't interfere. I'm not having Moses attacked from behind. Anything else he should know, Dermot?'

'Johnson spits and bites.'

'I've met plenty who've done both,' said Dagg, 'so I'm used to it.'

'And there's no holds barred so he'll try to wrestle you to the ground and use his feet on you. Watch out for his heavy boots.'

'They'll slow him down.'

'Moses will dance rings round him,' said O'Gara.

'Johnson'll come charging out at the bell,' predicted Fallon, 'and try to finish you off very quickly because he'll soon be short of breath. Tire him out by moving him around then go in and finish him off.'

'Thanks for the advice,' said Dagg.

'One last thing – we go to the fight with weapons. If things get out of control, we'll have trouble. I'll bring daggers and shillelaghs for both of you.'

'We couldn't do this without you, Dermot.'

'No,' said Dagg, 'we owe you thanks.'

Fallon grinned. 'I'm the one who should be thanking *you*. Moses. I'll not only get a share of the prize money, there'll be winnings to collect from the wagers I place. The pair of you will have more than enough money to pay for your passage back to America.'

'We're not going until we've finished our business here.'

'That's right,' said O'Gara, 'our friends are still locked up in Dartmoor. We want justice for them and for us. And you should remember that *you* want justice as well, Dermot. You have to collect a huge debt from someone.'

'Oh, I haven't forgotten Donal Kearney,' Fallon promised him. 'I've a couple of lads keeping an eye on him for me. I'm just letting him stew a little first.'

Kearney had been so badly beaten that he was unable to work. Tended by his wife, he lay on the bed with his hands held against his cracked ribs. Having cleaned the blood from his face, his wife gently dabbed at his bruises with a wet cloth then mopped his brow. His two black eyes made him look as if he'd just cleaned a sooty chimney. He was more beleaguered than ever. His neighbours let him know what they felt about him by banging on the door as they went past or by shouting abuse at him. Out of concern for their safety, he'd forbidden his family to venture out. Kearney scrabbled around for a means of escape from his ordeal. Indelibly marked as a police informer, he could not move freely around the tenement any more. His one hope lay in getting someone on his side that might keep the others away from him.

Groaning at the effort, he got up from his bed and rose to his feet. His wife begged him to stay with them but Kearney was purposeful. Letting himself out of the room, he collected some cruel jibes from children playing on the stairs. He tried to ignore their ridicule and went to some rooms along the corridor, slapping the door with the flat of his hand because his knuckles were too raw to use. When the door opened a few inches, the face of Mary Fallon came into view.

'What do *you* want?' she asked in surprise.

'I just want someone to listen.'

'Dermot said that I wasn't to speak to you.'

'I want you to take a message to him, Mrs Fallon. It's very urgent. Tell him that it wasn't *me* who told the Runners that you were hiding fugitives here. I'd never lift a finger to help them. Everyone knows that. I despise the Runners. They're like vermin to me.'

She tried to close the door. 'I have to go, Mr Kearney.'

'No, no,' he said, putting a foot in the gap to keep the door open. 'All I ask is that you give me a fair hearing.'

'My husband's made up his mind. He'll never change it.'

'He might if you tell him the truth. Explain to him that it was someone else who was behind that raid. I was miles away and I can prove it.'

'Go away, please. It's dangerous for you to be seen here.'

'Don't *you* turn your back on me as well.'

Mary was resolute. 'It's what you deserve, Mr Kearney.'

'Oh, it is, is it?' he asked, letting his anger take over. 'Very well, if you won't help me then I won't help you.'

She was disturbed. 'What are you going to do?'

'You'll soon see.'

Determined to get his own back on the Fallon family, he lumbered towards the staircase, intent on telling Micah Yeomans where they could find Fallon's wife and force her to disclose the whereabouts of O'Gara, Dagg and her husband. He didn't realise that Mary Fallon didn't actually know where the men were hiding. In his rage, he simply wanted Fallon, the man most likely to kill him, to be arrested and locked up. Kearney and his family could then flee the tenement and live elsewhere.

After lurching down the steps, he realised that he couldn't even leave the building. Two of the young men who'd beaten him earlier were lounging either side of the doorway. They stiffened as he approached.

'Go back to your hutch, Kearney!' snarled one of them.

'You're going nowhere,' said the other.

'Our orders are to keep you here until Dermot Fallon comes for you. Now take yourself off or we'll kick the daylights out of you again.'

It was no use. All that Kearney could do was to creep upstairs again.

Charlotte Skillen liked to think that she made a useful contribution both to the running of the gallery and to the disparate assignments that came their way. She was therefore thrilled when her husband wanted her more directly involved. Instead of being cooped up in an office, she would be working beside him for once. When they were getting ready to go out that evening, he outlined his plans, though he didn't disclose Beyton's name or his reason for wanting the necessary woman liberated.

'The exchange will take place tomorrow in Hyde Park,' he explained. 'It will be in the middle of the afternoon.'

'But there'll be crowds about, Peter.'

'That's why they've deliberately chosen that time and place. The more people who are about, the better it is. They'll act as a kind of screen. With so many bodies there, it will be more difficult to see what's going on.'

'What am I to do?'

'Keep your eyes peeled, my love,' he said. 'I'll watch from one direction and you'll do so from the other.'

'Does the gentleman have the money?'

'He assures me that he'll pick it up from the bank in the morning.'

'What have you told him?'

'I've said that he must follow my instructions to the letter. I don't want him looking over his shoulder to see where I am. That will ruin everything.'

'It's a lot of money to hand over,' she said. 'He must care for Mrs Horner a great deal if he's prepared to part with that amount.' She nudged him. 'Would you pay a large ransom if I was being held somewhere?'

'I'd pay every penny I owned, Charlotte, but I'd also make sure that I got it back very quickly once you were safe. Your price is above rubies. As for this gentleman,' he went on, 'this will be a supreme test of his nerve.'

'I thought you told him that he'd get the money back.'

'He will,' said Peter, 'if you and I are as alert as we should be.'

'I'll do my best.'

Charlotte looked at herself in the mirror then turned to him for approval.

'You look as gorgeous as ever, my love.'

'Thank you, a night at the theatre is a rare luxury for us.'

'Work must always come first.'

'We're entitled to some pleasure, Peter.'

'What's the play called?'

'*Venice Preserv'd*. The talk is that Hannah Granville is nothing short of magnificent.'

'Is it a comedy or a tragedy?'

'Oh, I don't believe she'd act in a comedy. Her gift is for tragedy.'

'That's a pity,' he moaned. 'We have enough of that in our daily lives. When I go to the theatre, I expect to enjoy a good laugh.'

'Well, don't you dare laugh in *Venice Preserv'd*.'

Reaching for his hat, he put it on then offered his arm to his wife. They left the house and walked together along the pavement. His mind veered back to the clerk.

'This fellow is a lucky man,' he said. 'He can just walk into a bank and secure the ransom without undue difficulty. Most people would struggle to raise that amount. They'd either turn to their friends or fall into the hands of gullgropers.'

'Paul did that once, didn't he?'

'Yes, he ran up debts at the card table and couldn't afford to clear them. I was able to give him a loan but it was insufficient so he went to a gullgroper. They do business with unlucky gamblers all the time. The interest rate was exorbitant. Fortunately,' said Peter, 'my brother had a good win soon afterwards so was able to pay off the loan. Since then, he's been much more careful with money.'

'Paul has too many expensive tastes.'

'It makes him work all the harder.'

'Why aren't you calling on him for assistance tomorrow?'

'A woman is less likely to arouse suspicion, Charlotte. If you're walking in the park, the kidnappers are unlikely to give you a second look.'

'How many of them are there?'

'Oh, I think we're only talking about two people,' he said. 'It will be the man and the woman who abducted the cleaner. They'll know exactly what the gentleman looks like because they followed him at an earlier stage.'

'What will happen afterwards, Peter?'

'Afterwards?'

'Yes, when it's all over and Mrs Horner is released. Do you think she'll go back to work at the Home Office? How will she react if she comes face to face with this gentleman who's in a position to buy her freedom?' she wondered. 'She must be undergoing the most harrowing experience.'

Anne Horner clung to the belief that she would one day get out of her cell and put the pain and the accumulated humiliation behind her. When she could move around the cellar, she'd had a degree of freedom but now, chained like a dog, she was unable to stray beyond its length. She was close enough to the grating to feel the air coming in but too far away to see out of it properly. How someone in her position could be described as an asset was beyond her. The deprivation she'd suffered day after day had dulled her brain. Hope and prayer were her only allies and she was beginning to lose faith in both of them. When they went, the descent into black despair was inevitable.

There it was again – the unexplained thud. She leant in the direction of the grating to see if she could identify the sound at last. Thirty seconds later, she heard it again but she still couldn't understand what the noise was. On the other hand, she could just pick out the sound of voices in the garden. A man and a woman were talking. The odd word and occasional phrase drifted into her ears but she had no idea what the conversation was about. What she heard clearly was their laughter.

It was followed by another thud.

'You never miss,' he said, clapping his hands.

'Mr Ackford taught me well,' she explained. 'Practice makes perfect.'

'I'm glad that he didn't know *why* you wanted lessons.'

'He still thinks that I wanted to turn my nephew into Robin Hood.'

'I'm a little old to be your nephew, Jane,' he said with a smile, 'and since you're younger than me, you are a very peculiar aunt.'

'How many aunts can hit a target with a bow and arrow?'

'None can do it as well as you.'

Slipping an arm around her waist, he kissed her and she responded with passion. He was a tall, slim, dark-haired man in his early thirties who radiated a quiet charm. Jane Holdstock was besotted with him. It was for his benefit that she'd taken archery lessons at the shooting gallery. They shared the same objectives and, for his sake, she was prepared to do anything that he wished. When he pulled away from her, he took the bow from her hands and laid it on the ground beside the quiver of arrows.

'That's enough practice, I think,' he said. 'You are a real Robin Hood.'

'I'd rather be a Maid Marian.'

'Then you shall have your wish.'

Taking her by the hand, he led her into the house and up the stairs. When they reached the landing, Jane remembered something.

'What about Mrs Horner?' she asked. 'It's time for her meal.'

'Let her wait. We come first.'

CHAPTER EIGHTEEN

As usual, Hannah Granville arrived early at the theatre. She always gave herself plenty of time to get into her costume, apply her make-up and prepare herself fully for the performance by thinking herself into the role. As she powdered the actress that evening, the dresser paid her a fulsome compliment.

'The manager thought that you were superb last night, Miss Granville,' she said, respectfully, 'but, then, you always are.'

'Thank you.'

'Everyone is talking about you. They long to see you as Lady Macbeth.'

'They will do so one day.'

'It was the role in which Mrs Siddons excelled but I think you would shine even brighter. When do rehearsals begin?'

'I have not yet signed the contract.'

'But I thought that you were eager to take on the part.'

'I need a long rest from the theatre,' said Hannah, 'so I'm not able to commit myself at this moment.'

She raised a hand to indicate that she'd been powdered enough then she scrutinised herself in the mirror. Satisfied with her appearance, she gave a nod and the dresser removed the cloth put around her to protect her costume from the cosmetics. Hannah rose to her feet, walked up and down to make sure that the costume hung properly when she moved then she began to mouth speeches from the play. The dresser melted into invisibility. Nothing was allowed to interfere with the actress's routine before performance.

After a long while, Hannah became aware of the other woman's presence.

'What sort of house do we have?'

'Every seat has been sold, Miss Granville.'

'People have a great appetite for tragedy on the stage,' mused Hannah, 'whereas they hate it in their own lives.'

'That's true. But it's the great tragic roles that allow an actress like you to soar. Audiences will remember a Belvidera or a Lady Macbeth long after they've forgotten a Viola or a Rosalind.'

'Comedy is for those of lesser emotional scope.'

'That is what Mr Dalrymple said,' recalled the dresser.

Hannah smiled. 'I was quoting him, actually.'

'He was transported by your performance last night, Miss Granville.'

'So he told me.'

'Will Mr Dalrymple be in the audience this evening?'

'Yes,' said Hannah, 'and he'll be escorting me out of the theatre afterwards. I do so hate being besieged at the stage door.'

'It's the price of fame.'

It was not long before the call came for Hannah to take up

her position in the wings. She could hear the excited buzz of the audience and it lifted her spirits. When the curtain rose, the commotion gradually faded away and, from the opening line, the play began to exert its grip. By the time that Belvidera swept into view, the audience was entranced. A burst of applause marked the sight of the tragic heroine but it died away as she began to speak. Hannah's voice was clear and melodious, a musical instrument with an almost unlimited range; it was complemented by her graceful movement and command of gesture. She dominated the stage effortlessly once again.

Hannah waited until her eyes had adjusted to the glare of candlelight before she let her gaze wander over the audience. She scanned the stalls in the hope of seeing the friendly face she'd been told would be there but she was instead given a sharp jolt. Seated only a few rows away from where she stood was Paul Skillen. Beside him was the attractive woman Hannah had seen with him before. It was like a physical blow. In daring to attend the theatre with someone else, she felt that he was deliberately taunting her and she was so shaken at first that she forgot her lines and was forced to take a prompt. Recovering quickly, she lost herself in her role.

Peter and Charlotte Skillen, meanwhile, looked on in sheer wonder.

Micah Yeomans and Alfred Hale began their day by acting as bodyguards to Viscount Sidmouth as he travelled by carriage to the Home Office. Talk turned at once to the security arrangements for the forthcoming celebrations.

'I'm glad that everything is now settled,' said Sidmouth,

'and that you are happy with what's been proposed.'

'If anything,' opined Yeomans, 'you will be too well-protected, my lord.'

'That pleases me and it will please my wife even more.'

'Nobody will be allowed to spoil what should be a memorable occasion.'

'On the principle that a second opinion is always valuable,' said Sidmouth, 'I asked one of my undersecretaries to look at our preparations. He, in turn, discussed them with one of my senior clerks. Both were duly impressed.'

'So were we, my lord,' said Hale.

'There is, however, one threat on the horizon.'

'Our patrols are still searching for the fugitives.'

'We hope to have them in custody before long,' said Yeomans. 'You have no need to fear them, my lord. They threatened to kill you if their demands are not met, yet the joint committee will probably not have reached its verdict by the time we celebrate our victory at Waterloo.'

'It may have done so,' warned Sidmouth. 'Evidence has been taken from all quarters. A swift conclusion may be reached and reported in the newspapers. And something else might incite them to violence.'

'What's that, my lord?'

'The whole nation will be celebrating our victory over the French, obliterating the fact that we actually lost our war against America or, at least, that's how it appeared after our disastrous defeat at the Battle of New Orleans. That fact will not be ignored by these patriotic sailors. I do hope the Skillen brothers catch them in time.'

'*We* are more likely to do that,' said Yeomans, staunchly.

When they reached the Home Office, the two Runners walked him to the front door and waited until he was safely inside. They then went off on their usual rounds. It was mid-morning before Yeomans and Hale stopped off at The Peacock to rest their legs and have a refreshing tankard of ale. Someone was waiting for them.

'What are you doing here?' demanded Yeomans.

'I need to see you.'

'We're thirsty. Buy us a drink.'

'Yes,' said Hale, 'we can't think straight until we've had our first taste of ale. Make yourself useful for once.'

Chevy Ruddock was abashed. Keen to divulge what he felt might be valuable intelligence, he was being compelled to part with some of his modest wages in order to satisfy the thirst of the senior Runners. He walked disconsolately to the bar. It was only after they'd quaffed their ale, that the others took any notice of him.

'Why have you come bothering us here?' asked Yeomans.

'Bill Filbert and I were on patrol by the river,' said Ruddock.

'We know that.'

'Someone told us about a fight in that old warehouse tonight.'

'So?'

'It's between someone called Donkey Johnson and another man.'

'Boxing matches usually *are* between two people,' said Hale, sarcastically. 'Why should we be interested by this one?'

'The other fighter is called the Black Assassin because he really is black.'

'Lots of them are bare-knuckle fighters. I remember seeing one called the Black Pearl and there was a Black Demon as well. He gave the Game Chicken a real scare at a fight in Portsmouth. The Game Chicken was Hen Pearce. I bet on him once and he earned me a pretty penny.'

'The man wanted us to place a wager,' said Ruddock, 'but Bill got rid of him. Later on, we met someone else who was taking bets. He told us a lot more about the two boxers.'

'You're starting to bore me, Ruddock,' said Yeomans, yawning.

'Donkey Johnson used to be a waterman. He got that strength by rowing people across the Thames. All the money will be on him.'

'Fights mean trouble. I hate them.'

'You haven't let me tell you about the Black Assassin yet.'

'What is there to tell us? He's a nigger and that's that.'

'He's an *American,* sir.'

Yeomans was in the act of sipping his ale. The information made him splutter. Lowering the tankard, he looked across at Hale then both of them turned to Ruddock. They were listening at last.

'It made me think, you see,' said Ruddock. 'This man didn't know what his real name was but he's never fought at the warehouse before so he must be a newcomer. If he's a sailor, he'll know how to use his fists. They're always brawling. It could just be – I'm only guessing, mind – that the Black Assassin is the very man that we've been looking for.'

'He could, indeed. Well done, Ruddock!'

'Thank you, Mr Yeomans.'

'You kept your wits about you for once,' said Hale.

'Bill Filbert thought I was dreaming,' said Ruddock. 'He reckoned that we should stay well away from that warehouse but not if he really is our man. I want to be there to find out the truth.'

'We'll come with you.'

'Yes,' said Yeomans, 'we certainly will. If the Black Assassin really *is* Moses Dagg, his friend will be there as well. We can nab the pair of them and claim the reward. Apart from Filbert, who else have you told?'

'Nobody at all,' replied Ruddock.

'Keep it that way. This must be our secret.'

'We mustn't let the Skillen brothers know about this,' said Hale. 'They'll be green with jealousy if we do their job for them.'

'I could be wrong,' said Ruddock. 'We've had black boxers from America coming here before. They get hauled off a plantation and brought to London to be a rich man's butler or something. Their master also acts as their patron and arranges fights for them. The Black Assassin could be one of those.'

'He could also be Moses Dagg,' said Yeomans.

'What am I to do?'

'Go back to that warehouse and see if you can find out any more details about the fight. We'll meet up with you here later on. In the meantime, keep your mouth shut and tell Filbert to do the same. We don't want this intelligence to leak out.'

'No,' said Hale, smirking. 'We want to be the ones to arrest O'Gara and Dagg. They're *ours*.'

'There's someone else we need to arrest, Alfred,' said Yeomans.

'Who's that?'

'We want to capture that elusive Irishman who's been shielding the two fugitives – Dermot Fallon.'

They met by prior arrangement in a quiet lane off Charing Cross. The first thing that Fallon did was to hug his wife. Mary was relieved to see him still at liberty. She assured him that the children were well but that they were short of money. Fallon slipped some coins into her hand and promised that there would be a lot more money to come very soon, explaining that, since they'd last met, much had happened. He told her about the fight and about his expectation of certain victory for Moses Dagg.

'What will happen then, Dermot?' she asked, worriedly. 'Will they be going home to America?'

'They've got something important to do first.'

'Are they still bent on killing someone?'

'They don't make idle threats, Mary.'

'Oh, I do hope that you won't be involved. You're in enough trouble as it is.'

'Tom is family. If he needs me, I'll be there.'

'Please don't take any risks,' she pleaded.

'I was born to take risks,' he said with a laugh. 'You knew that when you married me. And I'm still here. Nothing can touch me, darling, so don't you fret.' Embracing her again, he kissed her tenderly on the forehead. 'You go back home and tell the children I love them and that I expect to see them very soon.' He released her. 'Has there been any sight of the Runners?'

'No, Dermot, they've left us alone.'

'That means I can move back in with you before too long.'

'What about Tom and Moses?' she asked. 'Will they be coming back with you? It will only put us in danger again.'

'What did I say a moment ago? Don't you fret. Everything will be all right. Tom and Moses won't be coming back. As soon as they've done what needs to be done, they'll be on a ship to America.' He kissed her again. 'I thought you'd be pleased to see me and all you've done is to worry yourself sick.'

Mary smiled. 'I'm sorry, Dermot. Being with you again is a joy. I hate not having you with us.' Her frown reappeared. 'I had an unwelcome visitor.'

'Who was it?'

'Donal Kearney.'

'What did that traitor want?' he asked, muscles tightening.

'He tried to persuade me that he wasn't the informer,' she said. 'Everyone else has shunned him so he tried to win me over. I told him that you'd made up your mind and that nothing would change it.'

'He *dared* to bother you?'

'He was in a terrible state, Dermot. They beat him up badly.'

'I'm not standing for that, Mary.'

'What are you going to do?'

'Nobody is allowed to bother you, least of all that two-faced chimney sweep. Where is he now?'

'He's trapped in the tenement with his family.'

'Then I'll pay him a visit this afternoon,' said Fallon, anger building. 'It's high time that Kearney was wiped off the face of the earth.'

* * *

After a fruitless morning asking questions in yet another Irish community, Paul Skillen returned to the shooting gallery for refreshment. When he joined her in the office, Charlotte gave him a cordial welcome.

'I'd never take you for a costermonger, Paul,' she said. 'You may look the part but there's a kind of nobility about you that always pokes through.'

'Luckily, nobody else noticed it. The Irish took me as one of their own.'

'Have you found any trace of the fugitives?'

'No, Charlotte, I met dozens by the name of O'Gara but none of them had a relative in the American navy. I came back here for a rest.'

'Then you can join us in a meal when the others finish work. Gully is teaching a young boxer and Jem is fencing someone. He may be small but Jem is a match for most people with a sword in his hand.'

'Where's Peter?'

'He'll be schooling someone in how to hand over money to the kidnappers. Peter wants me there when the exchange takes place. I'll take Moll Rooke.'

'Is she that pretty servant of yours?'

'Yes, we'll appear to be in Hyde Park for a stroll whereas I'll really be there to keep watch on what takes place.'

'Do be careful,' he said with concern. 'The kidnappers may be dangerous. Make sure that you don't get too close to them.'

'One of them is a woman, apparently.'

'Women can be just as deadly with a pistol in their hands.'

Thinking of Hannah Granville, he decided that a woman

could be equally deadly without a weapon. She had certainly injured him severely. Paul was tempted to talk about his private life to Charlotte again but he drew back as Jem Huckvale came into the room. There was a friendly exchange of greetings.

'Some people never learn,' said Huckvale. 'I do believe that I could still beat Mr Ridley if he was the only one with a sword in his hand.'

'I'd like a bout with you some time,' said Paul.

'That can be arranged. Whenever I take you on, I'm the pupil and you're the teacher. The only swordsman better than you is Gully.'

'One day I may even surpass him.'

'I doubt it,' warned Charlotte. 'A sword is like a fifth limb to Gully.' She studied her brother-in-law. 'I must say that you're looking in your prime, Paul. When he saw you yesterday, Peter said that you were far from your best.'

'That was the result of overindulgence, I fear,' admitted Paul. 'I'd had a chastening experience in Jermyn Street. I feel my old self today.'

'You ought to seek entertainment away from the card table.'

'I've told myself that many times, Charlotte.'

'There was a time when you loved the theatre.'

'Yes,' said Huckvale, 'it used to be your passion.'

'Peter and I went to see *Venice Preserv'd* yesterday,' she said. 'We were spellbound from start to finish. Hannah Granville is the most extraordinary actress. You really ought to see her, Paul. She's giving a performance that left the pair of us dazzled. Peter is not as fond of the theatre as I am but Miss Granville enthralled him. You'd love her as well.'

Paul made no comment. He was doing his best to cope with the sudden pain he felt. Without realising it, Charlotte had just opened a wound and poured in a liberal amount of salt.

After he'd collected the money from the bank, David Beyton was in a continuous panic. The purse in which he'd put the banknotes seemed to be red hot and to weigh a ton. He was terrified that someone would rob him and reproached himself for not taking Peter Skillen with him by way of protection. Having got safely back to the Home Office, he locked the purse in a drawer and applied himself to his duties. In the afternoon, he excused himself to go off to an unspecified appointment. When he held the purse once more in his hands, it seemed even heavier.

He met Peter at an inn close to Hyde Park.

'Thank God you've come!' he said.

'I always honour a promise, Mr Beyton.'

'I've been in agony. It's a miracle that I was able to keep a straight face at the bank and at work. I've had a fire raging inside me since I got up.'

'What you're doing is a means to an end,' Peter reminded him, 'and none of it would have been necessary had you not put yourself – and Mrs Horner, of course – in such a vulnerable position.'

'Don't pour scorn on me, Mr Skillen,' begged the other. 'I can do that for myself. I just want to know what I must do.'

'It's quite simple, Mr Beyton. Follow the path designated in the ransom demand and wait until someone relieves you of the money. Your work is then done. Leave everything else to us.'

'You've brought assistance?'

'My wife and one of our servants will be hovering nearby,' said Peter. 'What I fail to see, my wife certainly will. You, meanwhile, can go back to the Home Office.'

'But I want to know the consequences.'

'You'll have to be patient.'

'And I *must* have the money back,' insisted Beyton.

'You have a disturbing habit of forgetting the plight of Mrs Horner. She is the victim here and not you. Bear that in mind as you walk through the park.' He glanced at the man's ashen complexion. 'Do you need a drink to stiffen your spirit?'

'I couldn't hold a thing down.'

'Then let's go,' said Peter, getting up. 'You lead the way and I'll follow on behind. Listen out for the clock chiming the hour. That's your cue. If you're not there at the exact time they stipulated, they'll walk away and implement their threat.'

Donal Kearney knew that he'd come. Dermot Fallon was not a man given to acts of mercy. Once he'd identified an enemy, he'd take action against him. Kearney was the latest victim. His attempt to talk his way out of his dilemma had not only failed, it had gained him a terrible beating. He could barely see through one eye and the whole of his body was throbbing with pain. Kearney spent all the time at the window, staring down at the court below and fearing the return of Fallon. To his alarm, the man finally appeared with his dog, striding into the court with a sense of purpose before stopping to talk to one of his neighbours. Kearney couldn't hear what was being said but he quailed when Fallon pointed up to the window out of which he was looking. Pulling away, the chimney sweep rounded on his wife.

'Take the children into the other room,' he snapped.

'Why? What's happened, Donal?'

He raised a hand. 'I won't tell you twice.'

'We're going,' she said, ushering the three small children out of the room. 'But I'd still like to know why.'

Kearney slammed the door shut behind them then returned to the window. Fallon was still talking animatedly to the neighbour. Kearney opened the window and leant out defiantly.

'You'll never get me, Fallon!' he roared.

'Come down here, you rat!' demanded the other, 'or I'll come up there and fetch you. This tenement has been infected by you for too long.'

Fallon was about to head for the door when he heard a maniacal laugh from above. Looking up, he saw that Kearney was clambering out of the window. The chimney sweep had decided that the one way to escape death at Fallon's hands was to kill himself. With a cry of triumph, he flung himself into the air and hurtled down from the top floor of the tenement, hitting the paved surface of the court with a bone-crunching thud that brought an instant crowd. Within seconds, the broken body was an island in a sea of blood.

Cheated out of his revenge, Fallon went over and spat on the corpse.

Peter Skillen stayed well behind him. As he entered Hyde Park, David Beyton followed the prescribed route at the gentle pace Peter had recommended. The clerk was soon walking past the scores of other people enjoying a stroll in the afternoon sun. There were some trees ahead and – having reconnoitred the park earlier – Peter had told his wife to loiter there. Accompanied by their servant, Charlotte would be largely concealed from view yet would be able to see clearly the path that the clerk was taking. Once he was mingling with the crowd, Peter was able to lengthen his stride so that he could get closer to Beyton.

He was no more than thirty yards away when the exchange took place. It happened so quickly that it would have been easy to miss the incident altogether. A young woman seemed to bump into Beyton. After she'd said something to him, she walked swiftly away. Peter knew at once that she'd taken the ransom money. The woman cut across the grass and went past a knot of people. When she came out the other side, Peter was waiting to intercept her.

'Excuse me,' he said, blocking her path. 'I'd like a word.'

'What do you want of me?' she asked in surprise.

'The first thing you can do is to return the money you just took from Mr Beyton. After that, you can tell me your name and that of your accomplice.'

'I don't know what you're talking about, sir. I have no accomplice.'

'Do you deny that you took charge of a purse?'

'No, I don't.'

He extended a palm. 'Then hand it over.'

'I don't have it any more, sir.'

'Where is it?'

'I gave it to the lady who asked me to take it from her brother,' explained the woman. 'That's all I did. I have no idea what was in the purse. I simply passed it on to the lady as she requested.'

'Which lady?'

'She didn't tell me her name.'

Peter was livid. He'd been duped. Patently, the woman in front of him was not one of the kidnappers. She'd been told a plausible tale and had agreed to take a purse from a man who was walking towards her. Unseen by Peter, she'd slipped it to one of the people he was really after. Though she'd taken part unwittingly in a criminal act, he could not blame her. After apologising, he sent her on her way.

David Beyton came panting up to him in despair.

'Why did you let her go?'

'She was not the woman we're after, Mr Beyton.'

'But she took the money from me.'

'That's all she was paid to do. She was an intermediary who passed on the purse to the woman who actually hired her.'

'So where is the money now?' wailed the other.

Peter shrugged an apology. 'I don't know.'

'I thought that you were going to arrest someone.'

'So did I.'

'Instead of that, I've lost all that money and have no guarantee that they'll stick to their side of the bargain. What's going to happen now?'

'In my opinion,' said Peter, 'there may be grave repercussions.'

When they got back to the house, they counted out the money and found that it was the correct amount but that didn't soften Diamond's annoyance.

'He disobeyed his orders.'

'I had a feeling that he might do so,' said Jane Holdstock. 'I hoped that we'd frightened him enough but I was mistaken. What exactly happened?'

'As soon as that woman had given you the purse, a man came out of the crowd and accosted her. He was clearly there in support of Beyton. Had you taken the purse on your own, you'd have been arrested.'

'It's just as well that you were there.'

'I saw everything from my hiding place among the trees.'

'Mr Beyton is very foolish.'

'Agreed,' he said, 'but he's a clever fool. If we hadn't been careful, one of us could now be cooling our heels behind bars. He hired someone to follow him and you almost got caught.'

'What would you have done in that instance?'

He drew a pistol from his belt. 'I'd have used this.'

'Be careful, Vincent.'

'I'll kill anyone who gets in our way,' he asserted. 'That includes Beyton or anyone else he's stupid enough to bring along. We've come too far to worry about the occasional death.'

'What do you think we should do?'

'We should make Beyton *suffer* for trying to trick us. I'd really like to send his wife an account of how he and Mrs Horner spent their time together but that can wait. Now that we've had one ransom from him, we should ask for another and bleed him dry. It's the least that he deserves.'

'How long are we going to keep her locked up?'

'She's not going anywhere until we're ready, Jane.'

'I'm beginning to feel sorry for her,' she confessed.

'Then you ought to remember the way she pushed you aside and locked you in the cellar. If I hadn't heard the noise of the door slamming, she might have got away completely. Think what would have happened then.'

'All our plans would have been in shreds.'

'Mrs Horner stays where she is.'

'What about her meals?'

'Reduce the portions even more,' he decreed. 'If she complains, tell her that it's all Beyton's fault. That will give her something to think about.'

Tom O'Gara and Moses Dagg were enjoying a meal on the ship. Since he was due to fight that evening, Dagg took care to eat sparingly. He knew that he had both the skill and the punch to defeat his opponent but he also realised that it would have to be early on in the bout. Even on their brief acquaintance, he'd seen that Donkey Johnson was a powerful man. If the fight dragged on, it would become a test of endurance and Johnson might wear him down. Dagg resolved that he wouldn't let that happen. It would lose Dermot Fallon a lot of money and leave Dagg himself in a battered condition. Remaining at liberty depended on his being able to move quickly and defend himself against arrest.

They were in the captain's cabin when a stone hit the window and caused it to crack even more. It was the signal that Dermot Fallon had returned. They went up on deck and lowered the gangplank to let him and his dog aboard then drew it up again.

'What happened?' asked O'Gara. 'Did you see Kearney?'

'Were you able to strangle the rogue?' added Dagg.

'No,' said Fallon, sulkily.

'Don't tell me that he escaped.'

'There was no chance of that, Moses. It would be easier to escape from Dartmoor than from the tenement. *Everybody* was on guard.'

'So why didn't you kill him?'

'I was too late. Kearney jumped out of his window and landed dead at my feet. He made a terrible mess on the paving.'

'I don't like the sound of that,' said O'Gara.

'Some of the blood went over me,' complained Fallon, showing the specks on his sleeve and trousers. 'I wanted to make him die slowly. He chose a quicker way.'

'I'm worried, Dermot. A suicide will be investigated. That might bring the Runners back to the tenement. Someone may say something out of turn.'

'They won't do that, Tom. Besides, what can they say? Nobody knows that we're here, not even Mary. It's only a question of time before it's safe for me to move back in with my family.'

'I've got a family back in New York,' said Dagg, nostalgically. 'Tom has got a child or two along the east coast. He believes in spreading his love about.'

O'Gara grinned. 'I can't help it if women like me.'

'If their husbands ever catch up with you, expect a lot of trouble.'

'That's the beauty of being in the navy, Moses. You can take your pleasure where you find it then sail away before their husbands catch up with you.' He glanced at his cousin. 'Is everything ready for tonight?'

'Yes,' said Fallon, 'the place will be packed.'

'There you are, Moses. You've achieved fame as the Black Assassin.'

'I don't want to be remembered as the man who beat Donkey Johnson,' said Dagg, bitterly. 'If our demands are not met by the Home Office, I want to be known as the black assassin of Viscount Sidmouth.'

On the walk back to their house, Peter and Charlotte Skillen had their servant in tow so it was not possible to have a proper conversation about the misadventure. When they got home, however, and when Moll Rooke had returned to her domestic duties, they were able to tell their respective stories.

'I failed,' admitted Peter. 'I thought that I'd caught one of the kidnappers in the act but all I'd done was to apprehend an innocent woman who'd been offered money for receiving and passing on a purse.'

'So you didn't see the purse being given to someone else.'

'No, Charlotte. The park was too crowded.'

'Yes, my view was often obscured.'

'The gentleman is hopping mad and blames me for ruining everything. We're no closer to identifying the people who abducted Mrs Horner.'

'That's not exactly true, Peter.'

'What do you mean?'

'Unlike you, I did see the exchange – or at least, I think I did. As soon as that woman took the purse from him, she walked straight towards a second woman and seemed to brush past her. *That's* when the purse would have changed hands.'

'I'm sure that you're right.'

'The second woman headed for the trees and walked within yards of me. She was joined by a man who came out of hiding and escorted her quickly towards the exit. I only had a glimpse of him but I did see the woman's face.'

Peter was excited. 'And you recognised her?'

'Oh, yes, I knew her at once.'

'Who was she?'

'Her name is Jane Holdstock and she took archery lessons from Gully. I spoke to her on one occasion. She's the last person you'd expect of being a kidnapper. On the other hand,' she added, thoughtfully, 'she's equally unlikely to want instruction in the use of a bow and arrow.'

David Beyton was so confused that he walked straight past the Home Office. It was only when he crossed a road that he saw what he'd done. Turning around, he decided that he needed time to recover before facing his colleagues again. Otherwise, one of them was bound to notice his obvious distress and the fact that his hands were trembling uncontrollably. Peter Skillen had let him down badly. That was how he viewed the situation. In seeking the help of the detective, he'd relied on comments made about him by the Home Secretary and decided that, if Sidmouth saw fit to employ Skillen, there was no better man in London. Beyton's assessment of him was different. He believed that the detective was solely responsible for the loss of the money. Having someone to blame was a form of consolation.

It was several minutes before he felt able to return to his work at the Home Office. Letting himself back into the building, he exchanged a few words with one of the junior clerks then had a short conversation with Bernard Grocott as the latter emerged from Sidmouth's room. In spite of his misgivings, Beyton didn't attract any undue attention or awkward questions. What everyone else saw was the quiet, sober, dedicated senior clerk. Having missed so much of the day, he tried to make amends by staying at his desk when his colleagues began to drift out of the building. When he looked through the window, he could see Micah Yeomans and Alfred Hale coming to collect the Home Secretary. Once the three of them had departed, Beyton knew that he was the only person in the building.

Instead of being able to relax, however, he was assailed by demons yet again so he found work to occupy his mind: writing a series of letters then reading all the documents put on his desk for consideration. Hours raced past. When he checked his watch and saw how late it was, he decided to go home. It was only when he reached the front door that he noticed the letter laying on the mat. The familiar handwriting made his stomach lurch and his heart pound. Snatching it up, he opened the letter and read the new demand that it contained.

Then he slumped to the floor in a dead faint.

CHAPTER NINETEEN

When they escorted Viscount Sidmouth back to his house, they said nothing about the intelligence that had fallen into their lap for fear that he would insist on passing it on to Peter and Paul Skillen. Instead of helping the brothers, Yeomans and Hale were bent on displacing them and regaining their status. Once they'd done their duty as bodyguards, they repaired to The Peacock. When he saw that Chevy Ruddock was already there, Yeomans ordered Hale to buy a drink for the younger man. All three of them then adjourned to a table in the corner and nursed their tankards.

'What else did you find out?' asked Yeomans.

'I discovered that the fight is usually a bloodbath,' said Ruddock with a shiver. 'The boxers don't abide by Broughton Rules. They make their own up as they go along.'

'Who did you talk to?'

'There was a man sweeping up in the warehouse and he'd heard all the gossip. The Black Assassin *is* an American sailor and he's replaced a boxer who had to drop out at the last moment. Nobody knows what the newcomer is like but they all know Johnson and think it would take a Cribb or a Belcher to beat him.'

'It's a bit late for Jem Belcher,' noted Hale. 'He died a few years ago. I once saw him beat Jack Bartholomew. When he lost an eye, Jem became a publican and served good beer. It's a shame he didn't last longer.'

'Spare us your reminiscences, Alfred,' said Yeomans, 'Let him speak.'

'The place is very rough inside,' explained Ruddock, 'and it stinks to high heaven. They've got chairs and benches but most people prefer to stand, especially when things get exciting. I made a point of measuring it out so that I could do a drawing.' He produced a rough sketch from his pocket and unfolded the paper before using a stubby finger to jab away at it. 'This square is where the fight takes place. There's sawdust on the floor. Over here is the main entrance but there are two other ways in and out – here and here. We'll have to keep all three covered to stop either of the fugitives getting out.'

Yeomans was impressed. 'You're a clever lad, Ruddock.'

'Thank you, sir.'

'And you're sure that this Black Assassin *is* Moses Dagg?'

'I'd put money on it, Mr Yeomans.'

'That means Thomas O'Gara will be there as well.'

'And Dermot Fallon,' said Ruddock. 'He often goes to the warehouse. The man I talked to says that Fallon is well known there.'

'We're home and dry!' cried Hale, slapping his thigh.

'Don't count your chickens, Alfred,' cautioned Yeomans.

'All we have to do is to deploy our men properly.'

'We did that when we raided the tenement behind Orchard Street and it was an ignominious failure.'

'That's because somebody knew we were coming.'

'The same thing could happen tonight.'

'It could be even worse,' said Ruddock, artlessly. 'The Skillen brothers could get there before us once again.' He recoiled from the barbed looks they directed at him. 'I'm sorry. I didn't mean to say that.'

'Then don't ever say it again,' ordered Yeomans.

'I won't, sir, I promise.'

'Forget that you've ever heard of Peter and Paul Skillen. *We* are the true police here in London and tonight will show us at our best.'

'I'll take care of O'Gara,' volunteered Hale. 'I can manage him. If the nigger is good enough to get into a boxing ring, I'd rather leave him to you, Micah.'

'What about me?' asked Ruddock. 'Can I arrest Dermot Fallon?'

'You can do what you're told,' said Yeomans. 'What time *is* the fight?'

'It won't start for hours yet.'

'Then you can round up some other members of the foot patrol for us. We need to go there in force.' After downing the rest of his ale in one gulp, he gave a loud belch. 'I can't wait to see the Home Secretary's face when we deliver O'Gara, Dagg and Fallon up to him.' He straightened his shoulders. 'There ought to be a knighthood in this for me.'

* * *

It took a long time for David Beyton to stop gibbering and to speak coherently. Peter Skillen waited until his visitor eventually thrust the letter into his hands. He read it calmly then looked up.

'It's impossible!' cried Beyton. 'I can't get that amount of money so soon.'

'We have to lure them into the open somehow, sir.'

'They're demanding *twice* what I paid them before.'

'Yes,' said Peter, handing the letter back to him, 'but the interesting thing is that the nature of the threat has changed dramatically. What you were facing the first time was the possibility that your wife might be informed of your infidelity. Yet there is no mention at all of Mrs Beyton in the letter you received today. They've shifted attention to their captive. If you don't comply with their demand, Mrs Horner will be killed.'

Beyton groaned. 'I can't have her death on my conscience, Mr Skillen.'

'It's good to know that you've rediscovered a conscience, sir. Had you possessed one earlier, the relationship that landed you in this situation would never have taken place and you would now be sitting at home with your wife, untroubled by any peccadilloes in your past.'

'I know that. I've said it to myself a thousand times.'

'Then I won't labour the point,' said Peter. 'We need to decide on a means of dealing with this new crisis. Let's take the first demand in that letter. Are you able to raise that amount of money?'

'I can't just conjure it out of the air, Mr Skillen.'

'The kidnappers seem to think that you can. My guess is that you were followed home at some point so that they could see where you lived. Do you have a large house, sir?'

'It's very large, as it happens. I inherited it from my father.'

'Then they'd assume that you could borrow money against the property.'

'That would take time and they don't really give me any.'

'They clearly think you are wealthier than perhaps you are.'

'I'm not impoverished, Mr Skillen,' said the other with a touch of indignation. 'I managed to provide the full amount of the first demand from my savings. I was assured by you that I wouldn't lose any of it because you would intervene. And what happened?' he asked, fixing Peter with a stare. 'I forfeited the whole amount and am now asked to pay twice as much.'

'I've apologised for my misjudgement,' said Peter, earnestly, 'and will make amends next time.'

'But that's a stipulation made in the letter. I am to go alone. If they see any sign of a confederate, Mrs Horner will suffer as a result.'

'She already *is* suffering, sir.'

'Then how do we rescue her?'

'I have a plan to do that, Mr Beyton,' said Peter, 'but I can't put it into effect until we know the details of the exchange. Last time, they chose a busy park. The chances are that they'll select somewhere less crowded next time so that anyone who comes in support of you will be spotted easily.'

'Or to put it another way,' said Beyton, dolefully, 'they'll get away scot free with the money and I'll be financially ruined.'

'That won't happen, sir.'

'There's no way to prevent it.'

'I believe that there is. We've had a setback and we must put it aside. Granted, we lost the ransom but the episode was not without a positive gain.'

'We gained absolutely *nothing*.'

'Then I must contradict you, sir. Involving my dear wife during the exchange has delivered a bonus for us. She recognised one of the kidnappers.'

Beyton sat up. 'She did? Who *is* the man?'

'It was the woman, sir, the one who walked away with your money.'

'Do you know her name?'

'We know the one that she gave at the shooting gallery,' said Peter, 'but it may have been an alias, of course. She took instruction there from Mr Ackford. I've never met the woman but my wife did so and has given me a description of her. I'm hoping that Mr Ackford may be able to tell us a little more about Jane Holdstock, as she was called. Shortly before you arrived, I sent a servant to the gallery with an urgent message.'

Paul Skillen was at the gallery when his brother's message was delivered. He discussed it with Gully Ackford and Jem Huckvale.

'Do you remember this woman?' he asked.

'I remember her very well,' replied Ackford.

Paul chuckled. 'I didn't know that you trained people in abduction, Gully.'

'All she learnt from me was how to use a bow and arrow.'

'She became a useful archer very quickly,' said Huckvale. 'When I whitened the target she'd been using, I could see how many of her arrows had hit the mark. Mrs Holdstock was only aiming over a short distance, mind you, but she had real skill.'

'I can endorse that,' said Ackford. 'As soon as she learnt to hold the bow properly, she got better and better. Each time she came, it was obvious that she'd been practising at home.'

'Why did she come in the first place?' asked Paul.

'She said that she wanted to teach her nephew how to be like Robin Hood.'

'Did you believe her?'

'I did at the time. In view of what Peter says in his letter, however, I've become doubtful. This nephew could well be a figment of her imagination.'

'So why did she bother to pay for lessons?'

'I used to wonder that,' said Huckvale. 'What use is a bow and arrow to her? You would have thought that a respectable woman like that would have better things to do with their time.'

'Perhaps she intends to murder her husband,' joked Paul.

'Then she should have learnt how to shoot a pistol. That would have been much easier and more effective.'

'We can rule out her husband,' said Ackford, reflectively. 'She called herself Mrs Holdstock but I didn't get the impression that she was married. I saw her left hand when she took off her gloves. There was no wedding ring.'

'I wish that I'd met her,' said Paul. 'She sounds like an intriguing lady. What sort of a person was she, Gully?'

'She was very pleasant but single-minded. Mrs Holdstock had no time at all for conversation. She never told me where she lived or what her husband – if he ever existed, that is – thought of her coming here. Charlotte met her one day and even she couldn't get much information out of the woman. Mrs Holdstock let none of us know about her private life.'

'Did you get the feeling that she was hiding something?'

'Oh, yes – there's no question of that.'

'I saw her leaving on one occasion,' recalled Jem. 'As I was coming down the street, Mrs Holdstock left the gallery and walked to the corner where she was met by a tall, dark gentleman who raised his hat to her then offered his arm. So perhaps there *is* a Mr Holdstock, after all.'

'He might also be her accomplice,' said Paul, interest rising. 'Mrs Horner was abducted by a man and a woman. You might have been looking at *both* of them, Jem. Describe this fellow.'

His first attempt was a disaster. The arrow missed the tree altogether and bounced off the stone wall at the end of the garden. Jane Holdstock laughed. She showed him how to hold the bow before fitting the arrow into place. Then she helped him to draw back the bowstring. When he released it, the arrow hit the outer edge of the target that hung from the tree.

'That was a definite improvement, Vincent,' she said, encouragingly.

'It was only because you were helping me.'

'I struggled at first then, all at once, I got the knack of it.'

'I'll leave it to you from now on.'

After retrieving the arrows, Vincent Diamond led the way back into the house. Though pleased to have received the ransom money, they were still annoyed that their instructions had been disobeyed.

'I was afraid that Beyton might do something silly like that,' he said. 'It was just as well you hired someone to take the purse from him. Otherwise, you'd have been grabbed by that man and I'd have been obliged to shoot.'

'I'm glad that it never came to that.'

'So am I. There were too many witnesses.'

'Do you think that Beyton will be able to raise the money in time?'

'That's his problem, Jane,' he said. 'We've given him two days and it should be enough. That beautiful house of his is well beyond the reach of most clerks at the Home Office. Beyton must have private wealth.'

She smiled. 'Then we'll help to spend it wisely for him.'

'A fool and his money are soon parted.'

'What about Mrs Horner?'

'She stays where she is until he pays up for the second time.'

'Being locked up down there is really telling on her, Vincent,' she said with a vestigial sympathy. 'Whenever I go to the cellar, she's weeping.'

'Stop looking at her as a human being. She's just a pawn in a game.'

'Suppose that Mr Beyton refuses to obey our demand?'

'Then his wife is going to have a very nasty surprise,' he said. 'But I doubt very much that we'll be in that position. Beyton frightens easily. If he thinks that he'll be responsible for Mrs Horner's death, I'm sure that he'll do as he's told.'

Before they got within fifty yards of the old warehouse, they could hear the raucous noise from within. Hundreds of patrons were enjoying the spectacle of a terrier killing rats with methodical brutality in the ring. Bets were being laid about how many he'd dispatch in a certain length of time. Money changed hands briskly. When the corpses began to pile up, a man tipped another sack of live rats onto the sawdust. Most of them scurried to the corners of the ring and some even tried to run up the boards. When they saw the dog, a few even made the mistake of attacking him and were snapped in half by his gleaming teeth. Spectators urged the animal on and its owner shouted commands. The crowd surged to and fro around the ring.

It was into this maelstrom that Moses Dagg stepped. A place full of foul-mouthed ruffians, drunken sailors and a smattering of prostitutes was familiar territory for him. He'd been in similar establishments in ports around the world. As a regular visitor, Dermot Fallon felt completely at home, waving to people he knew and collecting a series of greetings. The only person who had reservations was Tom O'Gara. He'd seen the complacent grin on the face of Donkey Johnson, who was lounging in a corner with a tankard in his hand and a couple of burly friends beside him. For the first time, O'Gara realised the scale of the challenge that Dagg was taking on. In the mounting delirium, and with the vast majority of people cheering him on, Johnson would be a formidable opponent.

The sight of Fallon's dog diverted the newcomers, burrowing madly through the legs of the spectators to get to the ring. Hearing the terrier's bark, the dog was eager to join in the entertainment. He leapt over the board, saw the rats darting around and pounced on one straight away. Pleased to have competition, the terrier increased the speed with which he crushed the vermin between his teeth. Fallon's dog followed suit and people were soon placing wagers on which one was the better rat-killer. Fallon was quick to bet on his own animal.

O'Gara and Dagg, meanwhile, were approached by a tall, emaciated man in his sixties with a beer-stained cap perched on his straggly white hair and a moulting beard that fell to his chest. He introduced himself as Nathan Egerton, the referee for the fight. The first thing he did was to feel Dagg all over, finding two hard lumps under his coat. He pulled out a dagger and a shillelagh.

'No weapons allowed,' he announced.

'I'll take care of those,' said O'Gara, seizing them from Egerton and slipping them under his coat. 'I hope you'll search Johnson for weapons as well.'

'With fists as big as his, he doesn't need any.'

'What are the rules?' asked Dagg.

'No gouging of eyes, no biting below the belt, no throwing sawdust into each other's faces. For the rest,' said Egerton, 'anything goes. There's one last thing to remember, Mr Dagg. I'm the referee. My decision is final.'

'Make sure that it's an *honest* decision.'

The old man was hurt. 'You'll get nothing else from me.'

An ear-splitting cheer suddenly went up and they turned towards the ring. The contest was over. Two ragamuffins jumped into the ring and began to load the dead rats into their sacks. Well over a hundred were gathered up. Another urchin climbed over the board with a large bucket and scattered fresh sawdust over the blood-covered morass. Panting for more action, the animals had been reunited with their owners.

Fallon pushed a way through the crowd with his dog under his arm.

'Did you see that?' he asked. 'He just won me two pounds!'

It was a good omen.

When they gathered at the appointed spot, darkness was falling and there was a persistent drizzle. Micah Yeomans looked around the wet faces and gave his men their orders. Hale was beside him, tossing in the occasional comment. Filbert was a reluctant member of the foot patrol but Ruddock was in the front line, chest out and eyes glinting. From where they stood, they could hear the surging tumult inside the warehouse. It made some of them move back in alarm but Ruddock displayed no fear. However big and boisterous the crowd, he was ready to wade into it. Yeomans, however, advised patience.

'The fight has only just started by the sound of it,' he said. 'Let's give them plenty of time to burn off their energy. Ruddock?'

'Yes, sir?'

'You can be our lookout.'

'Thank you, Mr Yeomans.'

'It's a reward for what you did. Can you all hear that?' he went on. 'It was this man who learnt there was a nigger fighting and who wondered whether it was the one who escaped from Dartmoor. Ruddock used his brains.'

'Well done, Chevy,' said someone, setting off a general murmur of praise.

'Why didn't you do the same thing, Filbert?'

'I was going to,' claimed Filbert.

'Ruddock had to do it alone.'

'It was my idea really. Chevy will admit that.'

'You said it was a waste of time, Bill,' argued Ruddock.

'No, I didn't. You need to wash your ears out.'

'And you need to start telling the truth,' warned Yeomans. 'I'd always believe Ruddock before you. He can stand by the door of the warehouse and watch the fight while you stay within hailing distance.'

'I'll get soaked in this drizzle,' protested Filbert.

'It will help to keep you awake. When Ruddock gives you the signal, run and fetch the rest of us.'

'Where will you be?'

'We'll be sheltering in The Jolly Sailor. I'm told that there's a barmaid in there with the biggest tits in England. While we're feasting our eyes on them, you can stay out in the rain. Call us when it's time to move in, Filbert.' A thunderous roar suddenly went up inside the warehouse. Yeomans rubbed his hands together. 'The fight is warming up,' he said. 'Let's go and drink to a night of triumph, gentlemen.'

The preliminaries had been inaudible. Nathan Egerton had done his best to call the spectators to order but excitement was running too high and drink was flowing too freely. O'Gara and Fallon were acting as Dagg's seconds. Johnson seemed to have everyone in the warehouse firmly in his corner. When stripped to the waist, he was a fearsome sight with bulging muscles and a carpet of coarse hair from neck to midriff. However, Dagg had noticed a potential weakness. His opponent had a sizeable paunch whereas the American had no superfluous flesh.

His naked torso glistened in the candlelight and drew many grudging compliments. Spectators close enough could see the livid scars on Dagg's body, souvenirs of brawls in which knives and broken bottles had been freely used. One thing was immediately evident about the Black Assassin. He was a survivor.

The fight had started as Dagg had expected. Donkey Johnson came rushing at him with teeth bared in a mocking grin, hoping to fell him with a first murderous blow. He swung his arm wildly but Dagg ducked beneath it and hit him with a vicious hook that stung the bigger man's ear. Johnson needed a moment to clear his head before hurling himself into the fray once more, flailing away with both fists. Dagg used his feet this time, swaying out of reach then replying with some fierce counter punches that jolted his opponent. While he could hurt Johnson, however, it was obvious that he could not yet stop him in his tracks. The man was too big, strong and wily.

After another failed attempt to land a meaningful punch on the Black Assassin, Johnson changed tactics. He lowered both arms to his sides and taunted Dagg with outright abuse. The crowd took up the chant, demanding that the American get on with the fight instead of dancing around their champion. Dagg responded by doing something he'd planned in advance, flinging himself at Johnson and delivering a relay of swift punches, saving the heaviest of them for his opponent's mouth. Three of his front teeth, which had given him the appearance of a donkey, were knocked out and blood was sprayed everywhere. Shocked by the bravado of it all, the crowd fell eerily silent. Something unheard of was happening in front of them. Their unbeaten champion was losing a fight.

Johnson was not finished yet. Enraged by the loss of his teeth, he went back on the attack, throwing punches so rapidly that Dagg was unable to elude them all. Instead, he took them on his forearms, protecting his body from any damage. The occasional counter punch rocked Johnson back on his heels but he soon recovered to swing his fists once more. Since he was at last inflicting punishment, the onlookers found their voices and egged him on, offering all kinds of obscene advice about what he should do to his challenger.

O'Gara and Fallon were exhorting their friend to finish his opponent off but their voices were drowned out by the mob. In any case, Johnson was not going to be defeated without a colossal and sustained effort. Seeing his chance, Johnson grappled with Dagg then shoved him hard against the board where a friend was waiting to lend his help. The man began to pummel Dagg from behind but his involvement in the fight was only momentary because the American jerked his elbow back so hard that it knocked the breath out of him and made him double up in agony. When he tried to raise his head again, the man was grabbed from behind by Fallon and dragged clear of the crowd. One crack with the shillelagh was all it took to knock Johnson's friend unconscious.

Dagg had been rescued from his unseen attacker but he still had to contend with an infuriated Donkey Johnson with blood streaming from his mouth. The bigger man was starting to pant stertorously, but the power of his fists was not diminished in any way. What was clear was the fact that he was slowing down. After punching himself free from the board, Dagg got back to the middle of the ring and began weaving so cleverly that Johnson's fists were missing him by inches. Diving forwards out of frustration, Johnson got hold of his shoulders and pulled his head back with the intention of smashing it down on the bridge of Dagg's nose but the American took immediate action to counter the tactic. He lowered his own head immediately so that Johnson's forehead smashed into the top of the Black Assassin's skull and did little more than give him a headache. The clash of heads, however, had dazed Johnson and he reeled back. Dagg was on him at once, battering away at the paunch with both hands until the bigger man retreated a few paces in sheer agony.

Dagg pursued him relentlessly; switching his attack to Johnson's face and opening a deep gash over one eye. Blood gushed out and there was a roar of protest from the crowd. Having bet on their champion, they were watching him being beaten by a faster and more cunning opponent. Advice poured in from all sides.

'Hit him in the bone-box, Donkey!'

'Draw his cork!'

'Smash his face in!'

'Break his arms!'

'Bite his black balls off!'

'Kill him!'

Blind in one eye and with his energy sapping away, Johnson resorted to foul play, lashing out with a foot and catching Dagg on the thigh. As his opponent went down on one knee, Johnson lunged forward and grabbed him by the throat, squeezing hard and making Dagg's eyes bulge. Verging on hysteria, the crowd pushed forwards and shouted their champion on with partisan vigour. At long last, Donkey Johnson seemed to have the advantage.

Chevy Ruddock could see nothing whatsoever of the fight. Standing just inside the main door, his view was blocked by solid ranks of bodies. The only indication he had of what was happening in the boxing ring came from the crowd. The clamour rose in volume, subsided, rose again to a higher pitch then dissolved into a collective groan of disappointment. A sense of outrage filled the warehouse and a volley of expletives was fired. When brawls broke out among the spectators, Ruddock decided that the fight was over. Running out of the door, he waved to Filbert who was standing dejectedly in the rain with a lantern in his hand. When he saw the signal, Filbert turned on his heel and trotted forty yards along the river bank to The Jolly Sailor. When he pushed his way into the bar, he found his colleagues drinking happily out of the rain. There was no time for Filbert to join them. His only reward for being on sentry duty outside was to feel the sensuous brush of the barmaid's enormous breasts as she went past him with tankards in both hands. For a second, he was bemused.

'What's happened?' demanded Yeomans.

'The fight's over,' said Filbert.

Even his friends could not believe that Dagg had won the fight. When he was down on one knee and being throttled, it looked as if he was going to lose but the Black Assassin had reserves of power. As the grip tightened on his throat, he hit the side of

Johnson's head with a punch of such ferocity that it made his opponent release him and stagger back. Dagg leapt to his feet and hit him from all angles, exploring his paunch, flattening his nose, opening up another gash on his face and attacking him with such bewildering speed that he was unable to defend himself. After pinning Johnson to one of the boards, Dagg completed his assault with an uppercut that caught him on the chin and sent him sprawling into the sawdust. The champion had been defeated. It was a highly unpopular victory and some of the patrons tried to get at the winner in order to vent their anger on him. While O'Gara defended his friend, Fallon went off to collect his winnings. Johnson remained unconscious on the ground.

The warehouse was a scene of utter pandemonium. When Yeomans arrived with his men, it was impossible to pick out the fugitives at first. Dagg's colour eventually gave him away. It was Ruddock who spotted the Black Assassin and pointed him out to Yeomans. The Runners pushed their way through the crowd to get at him and his friends. O'Gara and Dagg were still fighting people off when Fallon came charging over to them.

'We're leaving,' he yelled. 'The Runners are here.'

'Moses is exhausted,' said O'Gara. 'He needs a rest.'

'Then you'll have to carry him out, Tom, or he'll be resting in prison.'

'I'll be fine,' said Dagg, looking at his bruised knuckles. 'I'm used to pain.'

'Let's go,' ordered Fallon. 'They've probably got men at the doors but I know another way out. Follow me.'

He made his way towards a staircase in the corner of the

building, throwing anybody brutally aside if they got in his way. The Americans went after him, O'Gara helping Dagg along. Though he'd won the fight, the Black Assassin had taken a fair amount of punishment and was aching all over. His body was awash with sweat and covered with the blood of his opponent. Ruddock came out of the swirling mass and grabbed him around the neck, only to be lifted bodily by Dagg and hurled away like a rag doll. Filbert got even shorter shrift from O'Gara. When he tried to arrest him, he was felled instantly with a punch between the eyes.

The person in real difficulty was Fallon. Yeomans had him in a firm hold. Having had the Irishman pointed out to him by Nathan Egerton, he'd caught him at the bottom of the stairs. Fallon fought back but Hale arrived to help his colleague. Between them, the Runners overpowered him. When O'Gara and Dagg reached the stairs, they saw that he was unable to escape. Ready to attack the Runners, their intervention proved unnecessary because Fallon's dog came to the aid of its master, biting Yeomans and Hale in turn and forcing them to release their grip. While the animal kept the Runners at bay, the three men went up the stairs and ran along a landing until they came to a window. Though it was a long drop to the ground, they jumped out fearlessly and rolled over as they hit the flagstones below.

'Meet me back at the ship,' ordered Fallon.

'Where are you going?' asked O'Gara.

'I'll lead the Runners astray.'

'Thanks, Dermot.'

O'Gara fled into the darkness with Dagg. The dog had now

appeared at the window and was yapping away. Fallon gave the command and the animal hurled itself out, landing safely in his master's arms. After hugging the dog, Fallon patted the full purse at his belt. It had been a very profitable night.

There was considerably less profit for the Runners. Though they scoured the river bank for the three men, they were unable to catch any of them. All that Yeomans and Hale had to show for their efforts were some shredded clothing and some nasty bites on their legs. Ruddock's coat still bore the marks of Dagg's sweat and Johnson's blood. All three of them paid a second visit to The Jolly Sailor. Ruddock was ordered to pay for the drinks. While they were quaffing them, Yeomans issued an edict.

'Nobody must ever know about this,' he said.

'We ought to tell the Home Secretary,' suggested Ruddock.

'He's the last person to be told.'

'I don't see why, Mr Yeomans. After all, we did track the three of them down to that warehouse and we did tackle them. We showed intelligence and courage.'

'What use are they for a dog bite?' said Hale, sourly.

'We *almost* caught them, Mr Hale. You had Fallon in your grasp.'

'Don't remind me.'

'And don't you dare tell anyone,' added Yeomans.

Ruddock nodded and sipped his drink. When the barmaid tripped past them, none of them even spared her surging bosom a glance. They were too preoccupied with the failure of the night's enterprise. A Stygian gloom descended on the trio. Only when they'd emptied their tankards did Ruddock dare to offer consolation.

'It could have been worse,' he said, innocently. 'Peter and

Paul Skillen could have been waiting outside the warehouse to arrest all three of them as they came out.'

Yeomans hit him first.

David Beyton's first visit to the bank had been uncomfortable enough and he'd felt as if he were walking on eggshells in bare feet. The second conversation with Ebenezer Holland was even more excruciating because – unbeknown to his wife – he was about to raid her account and needed a convincing excuse to do so. Having rehearsed his story until he felt he was word-perfect, he put on a mask of compassion and spoke in a voice laden with sympathy. The bank manager listened impassively.

'It's very irregular, Mr Beyton,' he observed.

'Necessity is a hard taskmaster, Mr Holland.'

'It was only yesterday that you drew heavily on your own savings. Within twenty-four hours, you're back here to inform me that your travel plans have been abandoned and that you need funds for building work on the property.'

'It was on medical advice,' said Beyton, solemnly. 'My wife's condition has deteriorated so much that the doctor felt it inadvisable for her to go abroad. The effort would be too much for her and, he pointed out, medical facilities in other countries fall short of what we've come to expect here. Imagine how I'd feel if she contracted some terrible disease and we had no recourse to treatment.'

'There was no mention of the possible danger when you last came here,' said Holland, sharply. 'Mrs Beyton's health must obviously stay at the forefront of your mind but it was certainly not there yesterday.'

'I confess that I was being too hasty then.'

'You are even hastier today, sir. Before I can sanction the withdrawal of such a large sum, I need to be persuaded that it is absolutely essential.'

'Oh, it is,' said Beyton. 'Even though we have a nurse in the house, carrying my wife up and down the stairs every day is proving to be an onerous undertaking. What we need is an additional set of apartments built onto the back of the house with a bathroom attached. We will also knock down an old stable block and build a large rockery in its place so that my wife can look out on the beauty of nature and – in warmer weather – sit on the terrace outside.' There was a stony silence. 'It's Mrs Beyton's dearest wish,' he went on, risking a smile that somehow degenerated into a glare. 'And while she's still with us, I am always responsive to her desires.'

The bank manager pinched his lower lip between his thumb and forefinger and regarded him with mingled surprise and suspicion. Beyton had been his client for many years and never caused him the slightest trouble. He'd been consistently solvent and invariably cautious when making any decisions affecting his finances. Yet he was now taking what Holland believed was immoderate action.

'Being responsive to the desires of one's marital partner,' he said, measuring his words carefully, 'is a sensible path for any husband to follow but there are limits. Two days ago, it was Mrs Beyton's wish to go to Switzerland. This morning, it seems, her inclination is to have extensive work done on the property. These sound less like real desires than caprices that arise on the spur of the moment. What will Mrs Beyton be requiring finance for tomorrow – a whaling expedition, perhaps?'

Beyton was stung. 'Your sarcasm is misplaced, Mr Holland.'

'Then I apologise wholeheartedly,' said the other, coldly. 'I just want to know if this is your last demand or simply the latest one.'

'Clients are permitted to change their minds, you know.'

'I agree, sir, and they do so all the time. But I've never had anyone perform the kind of financial manoeuvre that you and your wife have just done.'

'When may I collect the money?'

'If you want my advice, sir . . .'

'Then I'll ask for it,' said Beyton, interrupting him. 'At the moment, it's of no consequence. The decision has been made by my wife and is endorsed by me. We wish to withdraw the specified amount as soon as is possible.' Seeing that the manager had qualms, Beyton rose to his feet. 'Damnation!' he exclaimed. 'Whose money is it?'

'Calm down, sir,' said the other, both hands aloft. 'You are perfectly entitled to dispose of your capital as you wish. I accept that. But there's really no need to hector me. Anybody would think that this was a matter of life and death.'

It was all that Beyton could do to retain his self-control.

CHAPTER TWENTY

One of the most enjoyable ways in which Hannah Granville could pass the day was to embark on a shopping expedition. She always spent more time examining items than actually buying them but that, too, could be pleasurable. Since she was now well known by sight to any theatregoers, she needed the protection of a man and had the company that morning of Felix Dalrymple. As they strolled down Piccadilly, past Fortnum and Mason, the grocers, and past John Hatchard, the celebrated bookshop, they looked a handsome pair. There was no need for Hannah to carry any money because her fame was enough to command instant credit and she'd already run up a large bill at a milliner's in Conduit Street and a dressmaker's in Bruton Street. To be able to say that they served such a fine actress was a persuasive advertisement for both shops. While she revelled in her morning promenade, she was conscious that her companion might not get the same satisfaction from the endless perusal of dresses, hats, and the multiple accessories that went with him.

After spending the best part of half an hour choosing a new purse, she turned to Dalrymple.

'Have I bored you enough, Felix?'

'You could never bore me,' he said, gallantly.

'Perhaps you wish to do some shopping on your own account.'

'There's nothing of which I have immediate need, Hannah, so I am content to watch you bringing joy into the mundane lives of shopkeepers.'

She laughed. 'I don't flatter myself that I do that.'

'While you are inspecting their wares, I am watching those who serve you and they are invariably excited by your presence in their establishments. The longer you stay, the more thrilled they are.'

'I like to dress well and making the right choices takes time.'

'The result is always exquisite.'

She squeezed his arm by way of thanks for his compliment. Strolling on, they came to a shop with bolts of fabric in the window. The bright colours and the subtle sheens caught Hannah's eye.

'Could you bear to indulge me yet again, Felix?'

'I'll do so willingly.'

'You're too kind.'

'Not at all,' he said, complacently, 'I relish my position as a figure of constant male envy. You turn heads wherever you go, Hannah, and, as a result, I reap a harvest of jealousy. Step inside the shop and it will happen yet again.'

His prophecy was fulfilled the moment she entered the emporium. Ignoring their wives or female companions, every man in there gazed at her with undisguised interest before shooting an envious glance at Dalrymple. The manager abandoned the customer to whom he was talking and scuttled across to her, bowing as if in the presence of royalty and rubbing his hands together.

'You are most welcome, Miss Granville,' he said. 'How may I help you?'

'We've come only to look.'

He stood out of her way. 'Then please do so as long as you wish.'

'Thank you.'

She began to examine the various fabrics on display, feeling their quality as she did so. Dalrymple waited patiently, offering a smile to the men still staring at them. A few people walked past and offered her compliments on her performance. Hannah thanked them graciously but took care never to engage in conversation with any of her admirers. As she moved further into the establishment, she was suddenly confronted by Charlotte Skillen, who let out a cry of delight.

'Good morning, Miss Granville,' she said, 'what a happy encounter this is! I never thought I'd have such good fortune. Allow me to say what a wonderful performance you gave as Belvidera.'

'Thank you,' said Hannah, enjoying the praise

'We thought you were truly magnificent.'

'It's kind of you to say so.'

'In fact, my husband has not stopped talking about you.'

Hannah was rocked. 'Your *husband*?'

Having looked at her properly for the first time, she

recognised the woman she thought she'd seen with Paul Skillen. During his time with the actress, Paul had always insisted that he was a bachelor. She felt horribly betrayed. Instead of being involved in what she believed was an untrammelled love affair, Hannah had simply been a diversion for a married philanderer. The idea that she'd been a hapless victim of his charm made her erupt with anger.

'Take me out of here, Felix,' she snapped.

Dalrymple was concerned. 'You look unwell, Hannah. What's amiss?'

'Take me out of here *now*.'

Viscount Sidmouth was working his way through the morning's correspondence when Bernard Grocott came to see him with some documents that required the Home Secretary's signature. After dipping his quill in the inkwell, Sidmouth appended his name before handing the documents back.

'It seems as if we may get a decision from the joint commission earlier than I expected,' he said.

'Have they considered all the evidence available?'

'It appears so. They were anxious to deliver a prompt verdict so that the matter could be put aside and normal life could resume at Dartmoor.'

'Life in any prison is far from normal,' remarked Grocott. 'Indeed, it's the very departure from normality that causes so much distress among the prisoners. I'm not speaking up on their behalf,' he added, hastily. 'If they commit a crime, they deserve to lose their freedom. I'm just trying to understand how they must feel when wrenched away from everything they hold dear.'

'What most of the prisoners in Dartmoor hold dear is this immature nation of theirs and, as we know to our cost, it engaged precipitately in a war against us. We are dealing with enemies, Grocott. The joint commission will recognise that.'

'Yet the peace treaty has now been ratified, my lord.'

'They remain prisoners of war until released.'

'Or until they're recaptured,' said Grocott, thinking of the fugitives. 'Has there been any news of the search for O'Gara and Dagg?'

'Peter and Paul Skillen continue their work with the usual diligence.'

'I'd value some positive results.'

'Be fair to them,' said Sidmouth. 'They did track the men to their lair in that Irish community and got there ahead of Yeomans and his men.'

'Yet the Americans remain at liberty, my lord, and it now seems that a verdict on the riot will be delivered *before* the celebrations in Hyde Park. If that is the case, and if O'Gara and Dagg become aware of it, you will become a marked man.'

'I am well protected.'

'These men are hotheads. They may resort to extreme measures.'

'I'm satisfied with the arrangements made for my safety,' said Sidmouth, easily, 'and for that of others. As I often reflect, when *I* was steering the ship of state, I was a target for every member of the French nation yet I survived without a scratch.'

'This is a different matter.'

'I agree. During the war against Napoleon, millions of people wanted me dead. That number has now reduced to a mere two.'

'They have an accomplice in Dermot Fallon.'

Sidmouth was untroubled. 'That simply raises the total to three.'

'You're unwise to ignore this threat, my lord.'

'On the contrary, I take it very seriously. It's the reason I asked for Yeomans and Hale to act as my bodyguards. They impart confidence and make me feel secure. As for Dermot Fallon,' he continued, reaching for a letter, 'I had some interesting news about the tenement in which he hid O'Gara and Dagg.'

'What is it?'

'A man committed suicide there by jumping from an upstairs window. He was a chimney sweep by the name of Donal Kearney. Do you spy a connection?'

'Ah,' said Grocott, recalling the raid. 'Yeomans and his men were given help by an informant living in that slum behind Orchard Street. Could this be the man?'

'I'll get Yeomans to confirm it.'

'If he *did* betray the fugitives,' said Grocott, 'and if the other residents became aware of it, Kearney's life would not have been worth living.'

After another secret meeting with her husband, Mary Fallon returned to the tenement with some much-needed money and with a message for all the other residents. It was the express wish of Fallon that the persecution of the Kearney family should cease. In losing her husband, his wife and their children had suffered enough. They were no longer to be treated as despised outcasts. Mary spread the word and, though some people complained about the change of attitude, they all abided by

Fallon's decision. It was left to Mary to pass on the news to the widow.

When she knocked on the door, there was no answer even though she knew that the Kearney family were inside, mourning their loss and hiding from their enemies. She banged the door with her fist and raised her voice.

'Could I speak to you, please, Mrs Kearney?' she asked. 'It's Mary Fallon. I've got something for you.'

'Go away,' said Meg.

'Nobody is blaming you for what happened. It was your husband who was the informer. People's anger died with him, Mrs Kearney. We mean you no harm.'

'Leave us alone. *Your* husband helped to kill mine.'

'Mr Kearney took his own life.'

'He was driven to it by people like that vile man of yours.'

'I can't deny that,' said Mary, sadly. 'You need time to mourn and I'll trouble you no longer. But you're free to leave the tenement now. Nobody will harm you.'

'They've already done that,' said the other, bitterly.

'I'm sorry that it came to that.'

'You might be, Mrs Fallon, but that murderous husband of yours isn't sorry.'

'Dermot is the one who wants you and the children to be treated more kindly from now on.' There was an ironic laugh from the other side of the door. 'Yes, it may be no comfort now but in time you may become more grateful.'

The door was flung open and Mary found herself facing a woman who was brimming with anger and haggard with grief. Fallon had told his wife to give her some money but it was the wrong gesture at what was patently the wrong time. All that Mary could do was to mouth an apology and walk away. She felt as if the woman's blazing eyes were burning holes in her back.

When he left the bank after his awkward interview with the bank manager, the first place that Beyton went to was Peter Skillen's house. A manservant took him into the drawing room. Peter soon joined him and noticed his visitor's hunted look. He offered him refreshment but it was declined.

'What happened, Mr Beyton?'

'I've just had the most embarrassing conversation in my entire life,' said the other, shifting nervously in his seat. 'Though I'd concocted a story for my bank manager, it was clearly not plausible enough. He came within an inch of mocking me, Mr Skillen. At a time like this, I need sympathetic understanding.'

'Your bank manager can't offer you sympathy, if he doesn't really understand why you need it, sir. But have no qualms about the fictitious excuse you employed. Bank managers are accustomed to hearing unbelievable claims. They judge a client on his character and not on the tale he tells. You, I suspect, are held in high regard.'

'I was until this disaster struck me,' moaned Beyton.

'Did you secure the money?'

'Yes, I did, but only after a long battle. Mr Holland was very suspicious of my motives. He'll never look at me in quite the same way again.'

'He might do so,' said Peter, 'if you put the money back into the account.'

Beyton sighed. 'There's little chance of that happening.'

'There's every chance.'

'They got away with the entire amount the first time.'

'That was because of a miscalculation,' admitted Peter, 'but we learnt two important things. First, we discovered that we are dealing solely with a man and woman and, second, that the latter's name is Mrs Jane Holdstock. I'm told that when she left the shooting gallery one day, she was met by a gentleman who may well be the accomplice who assisted her in Hyde Park.'

'It's a pity that nobody assisted *me*.'

Peter was brusque. 'If you'd rather find someone else to hold your hand in this enterprise,' he declared, 'then you are more than welcome to do so. It will, of course, oblige you to reveal details of your private life to a stranger who may not guard them as closely as I do. For my own part, Mr Beyton, I will continue my search for Mrs Horner independently of you and – one way or another – I will find her.'

Beyton was taken aback by the outburst and alarmed at the thought of losing Peter's guidance. He apologised for his sarcastic remark, explaining that it arose from desperation. Beyton promised to do exactly what Peter advised.

'When can you collect the money?'

'Not until tomorrow morning,' said Beyton with disappointment. 'I was hoping that I could withdraw the amount today.'

'That would have been unwise, sir,' warned Peter, 'so you should be thankful to your bank manager for looking after the money overnight. It's perfectly safe in the bank. Would you really like to have as large as a sum as that under your own roof?'

Beyton pondered. 'I suppose not,' he said. 'Now that I think about it, I'd feel very uneasy. Knowing what the money was for, I'd hate it to be held in such close proximity to my wife. It would be a source of great discomfort to me. I'll pick it up tomorrow instead.'

'Between now and then, you will receive details of the exchange. Since earlier missives were delivered to the Home Office, then the latest should arrive there as well. I'll need to know what your orders are.'

'Don't come with me this time, Mr Skillen.'

'I'll not be seen, I warrant you.'

'Then how can you arrest the kidnappers?'

'They'll be followed to the place where they're holding Mrs Horner. Their arrest will take place immediately and she will be released. Your troubles will be over, sir. They won't be able to communicate with Mrs Beyton while they're in custody and Mrs Horner will finally be safe.'

'Make sure that you get my money back from them.'

Peter was firm. 'I will do things in order of importance, sir. Replenishing your bank account is something that will have to wait.'

Annoyed at the rebuff, Beyton nevertheless accepted it.

'There's something else I'd like you to ensure, Mr Skillen.'

'What is it?'

'Persuade Mrs Horner that she mustn't return to the Home Office.'

'She may well not wish to do so. The ordeal she's undergone, as a result of her work there, may deter her from ever going near the place. If, however, she did decide to go back, I would do nothing to dissuade her from that course of action.'

'But you must see how awkward it would be for me.'

'That's immaterial, sir.'

'I'll *pay* you to keep her away.'

Peter was appalled. 'Then I'll respond in the same way as Mrs Horner. I'll return the money along with a dusty answer. When I accepted this commission,' he said, 'it was not in order to safeguard your sensibilities. A woman's life is at stake. I will not remind you why. Rescuing her is all that matters in the first instance.'

'There's something you don't know,' said Beyton, drawing himself up. 'I am on the verge of promotion. I've been told in confidence that I have been singled out as a future undersecretary. That's a position of some significance, Mr Skillen. I'll not have it compromised by the presence of an unwanted cleaner.'

'The lady was not always unwanted.'

'Get rid of her somehow, that's all I ask.'

'Then you are asking the wrong person,' said Peter, resolutely. 'Mrs Horner is able to make decisions without any advice from me. If she *does* choose to return to her old job at the Home Office, she will have my full support.'

It was not until the afternoon that Dermot Fallon joined them on the vessel. He came aboard with his dog and a large leather bag. While the three men went off to the cabin, the dog ran below deck in the hopes of repeating its success by killing rats at speed. Fallon put the bag on the table and opened it, taking out enough food and drink to keep them supplied for days. The last two items he produced were wrapped in pieces of cloth.

'What have you got there?' asked O'Gara.

'There's one for you, Tom, and one for Moses.' He took off the cloth. 'There you are – a pair of duelling pistols.'

'I don't want to shoot Moses.'

'I know that but you'll want to defend yourself in a tight corner.'

'That's true.'

O'Gara picked up one of the weapons and examined it. Dagg was less interested in the pistols. His major concern was with the injuries he'd picked up in the fight. He had cuts and bruises all over his body and both his hands were swollen. His knuckles were raw. Every time he moved, he felt a shooting pain.

'This is a fine pistol,' said O'Gara, approvingly. 'It's well balanced.'

'I bought plenty of ammunition.'

'What kept you away so long?' asked Dagg.

'I had a lot to do,' replied Fallon. 'It's not often that I have so much money to spend so I enjoyed it. Mary and I shared a pie together then I gave her enough money to last a week or more. Things have gone quiet in the court since Kearney killed himself. Before too long, I may be able to move back in there.'

'We'll stay here. It suits us.'

'We belong on the water,' said O'Gara. 'I'm looking forward to a voyage across the Atlantic – when we've done all that's needful here, that is.'

'When that time comes, you'll need this,' said Fallon, slapping a pile of banknotes down on the table. 'That will buy you both a passage and leave you with money to spend.'

'Thanks, Dermot.'

'Moses earned it.'

'How much did you pay for these duelling pistols?'

Fallon laughed. 'I didn't exactly pay for them, Tom. They sort of jumped into my bag, the little rascals, and just wouldn't get out.' He thrust his hand into the bag again and drew out a battered newspaper. 'I also helped myself to this in case there was any news of that committee looking into the massacre.'

'They *must* listen to our demands.'

'Captain Shortland deserves to be hanged,' said Dagg.

'If there's nothing in today's edition,' promised Fallon, 'I'll steal another one each morning. We don't want to miss the verdict, do we?'

'No, Dermot, we don't.' Dagg picked up the other pistol. 'If it's the *wrong* verdict, of course, I'll be arranging a little duel with the Home Secretary.'

'You won't get the chance,' boasted O'Gara. 'I'll have shot him dead.'

Though he'd intended to return to the gallery by a different route, Paul Skillen nevertheless walked past the theatre and awakened his demons. He reminded himself that their estrangement arose from her concern for his safety. His response emanated from a deep-seated refusal to let anyone else take decisions about his life. The result was a stalemate. From his point of view, it was poisoned by the fact that Hannah, in such an unconscionably short time, had found a substitute for him. While she still occupied *his* mind, Paul had been consigned to her past without a second thought.

When he reached the gallery, he was still simmering with regret. Charlotte was talking to Gully Ackford as he entered the room. Their greeting earned only a grunt by way of acknowledgement.

'Have you been living the life of an Irishman again?' she asked.

'No, thank you,' said Paul, grimacing. 'Most of them are almost destitute. Conditions in Ireland must be truly terrible if they're driven to come here and live in the rookeries. They're like so many ants in a giant anthill.'

'So where have you been today?'

'I've been doing your husband's bidding, Charlotte, and it's your fault. You were the one who identified Jane Holdstock. Since she was that interested in archery, she would need a bow.'

'That's right,' said Ackford, taking over. 'She'd asked me where she could buy one and I suggested a few places. Paul got the same names off me.'

'I hadn't realised how many people spend their leisure time in the butts,' said Paul. 'Now that we have so many firearms, I thought that bows and arrows were things of the past but there are clubs for archers keeping an ancient sport very much alive. Thanks to Gully, I found the shop where Mrs Holdstock went and she did indeed buy a small bow, suitable for a child, and a quiver of arrows.'

'So she *does* have a nephew,' said Charlotte in surprise.

'I wonder if the lad realises that his aunt is also a kidnapper.'

'What did you find out about the lady, Paul?' asked Ackford.

'I merely confirmed everything that you said about her, Gully.

She was a handsome woman with a quiet confidence and a determination to say very little about herself. I'd love to know why.'

'So would we all,' added Charlotte.

They were interrupted by a knock on the door. Jem Huckvale popped his head into the room to tell Ackford that one of his pupils had arrived for a lesson in the boxing ring. The older man went out immediately, leaving Paul alone with Charlotte.

'This all began when a cleaner was abducted from the Home Office,' she said.

'Yes, it did and the maddening thing is that we still don't know why.'

'Peter may do so but he's keeping the information to himself.'

'That means he's bound by a solemn promise, Charlotte.'

She smiled inwardly. 'He made several of those to me at the altar.'

'Sometimes it's dangerous to know too much.'

'That's why I never press him, Paul. He won't break a confidence.' She looked up at him. 'By the way, you'll have to be quick if you wish to see that play I recommended. *Venice Preserv'd* ends its run next week.'

'I'll . . . let it pass, I think.'

'You'll be missing a theatrical triumph.'

'So it appears.'

'Peter is going to be so cross when he hears what happened to me this morning,' she said, gaily. 'He fell madly in love with Hannah Granville. Wait until I tell him that I actually met her.'

Paul tensed. 'Where was this?'

'It was in a shop in Piccadilly. I went in to look at some fabrics and Miss Granville came in with this fine-looking young man. I couldn't resist going over and telling her how much we enjoyed her performance.'

'How did she react?'

'Rather strangely, as it happens.'

'Oh – in what way?'

'Well, I wasn't the only person to offer a compliment. Others did so as well and she accepted their comments with obvious pleasure.'

'What happened when *you* spoke to her?'

'She was very pleasant at first then she made it very clear that she didn't wish to talk to me.'

'Why was that?'

'I really don't know,' said Charlotte. 'To be honest, she was extremely rude. In anyone else, it would have been unforgivable but I suppose that we must make allowances for someone in her profession. And her odd behaviour doesn't obscure the fact that she's still giving the most remarkable performance in that play.'

Paul could take no more. Excusing himself, he left the room.

It had been a bruising encounter for the Bow Street Runners. When they'd tried to make some arrests at the old warehouse, they'd met stern resistance and been bitten by a dog. Their high hopes had foundered. As they made their way to the Home Office late that afternoon, Yeomans and Hale both walked with a limp.

'It pains me to say this,' Hale began, 'but Ruddock may be right.'

'Don't mention that idiot's name to me.'

'You didn't think he was an idiot when he told us about the fight.'

'No,' admitted Yeomans, 'that's true. We only learnt of the event because of his quick thinking. Perhaps I was too hard on the lad.'

'Looking back, I think we both were, Micah. What Ruddock suggested may be a good idea, after all. The fact is that we *did* track down the wanted men and that's more than the Skillen brothers managed to do.'

'What's the point of tracking them down if we don't arrest them?'

'We deserve credit for trying,' argued Hale. 'There were hundreds packed into that warehouse and we were hopelessly outnumbered. The Doctor needs to be told that. It might convince him that we need to increase the size of the foot patrols. There's some advantage in this for us, Micah.'

'Possibly,' said the other, mulling it over. 'We certainly acted bravely last night, Ruddock included. He tackled the nigger. You and I were both injured in the execution of our duties, so that might be brought to the attention of the Doctor. We may have failed in our objective but we got within inches of the fugitives and deserve plaudits for that.'

'You agree, then?'

'I do, Alfred.'

'And we must put in a word for Chevy Ruddock.'

'Why?' asked Yeomans. 'We don't want anyone else to share our glory. All that he did was to stumble upon the fact that the Black Assassin might be one of the men we were after. It was left to us to organise the raid. Keep his name out of it.'

When they reached the Home Office, they saw that the carriage was there to take Sidmouth home. They were let into the building and only had to wait a few minutes before he came out to them, putting on his hat in readiness for departure. Yeomans seized his moment and told him about the raid on the warehouse and the attempted arrest of O'Gara, Dagg and Fallon. He made much of the wounds inflicted on them by the dog and insisted that they needed more men at their disposal in future. Sidmouth listened to it all with an interest edged with slight suspicion. He had the feeling that he was being given a highly edited account of what happened.

'Who first realised that these men would be there?' he asked.

'We did, my lord,' said Yeomans, boldly.

'You must have had good intelligence.'

'We always do.'

'Then why didn't you communicate it to Peter and Paul Skillen? They have been retained to arrest these men.'

'There was no time to involve them, my lord,' said Hale, quickly. 'We either had to take prompt action on our own or allow the fugitives to escape.'

'So we did what you would have expected of us,' said Yeomans, 'even though we acquired some wounds in the process.'

Keeping his reservations to himself, Sidmouth congratulated them on showing initiative and courage. All three of them left the building and climbed into the waiting carriage. As it rolled away from the kerb, Sidmouth broached a new topic.

'You'll no doubt recall your raid on that tenement behind Orchard Street.'

Yeomans nodded. 'It remains fresh in our minds, my lord.'

'A man killed himself there yesterday by jumping from a

high window. A verdict of suicide will be returned but that may not explain what really happened.'

'Do you know the fellow's name, my lord?'

'It was Donal Kearney, a chimney sweep.'

Since he was seated opposite them, Sidmouth could see their startled reaction. Kearney had obviously been the informer who'd helped them. As a result, his position in the tenement had become hazardous. The chimney sweep, Sidmouth reasoned, had chosen to die before he was killed by his vengeful neighbours.

'It's no use having spies,' he warned the Runners, 'unless you take adequate steps to protect them.'

Even though he was expecting the letter to come, David Beyton was still jolted when it actually arrived. He had to wait until all his colleagues had left the building before he was able to read it. The instructions were terse and peremptory. He was reminded that he had to go to the appointed place alone or there would be dire consequences, both for him and for Anne Horner. Thrusting the letter into his pocket, Beyton left the Home Office guiltily and made his way to Peter Skillen's house. He was invited in and taken to the drawing room. Shown the instructions, Peter noted that they were in the same handwriting as the earlier missives and felt once again that it was the work of a woman who was presumably Jane Holdstock. Evidently, she had no compunction about issuing a death threat. Without saying a word, Peter left the room and was away for several minutes. When he returned, he unfurled a map of London and placed it on the table. Both men crouched over it.

'You are to walk around Grosvenor Square,' said Peter, indicating the place on the map. 'You'll be watched every inch of the way. If anyone else appears to be with you – or lurking nearby – they will do exactly what they threaten.'

'It will be the end of my career!' groaned Beyton before correcting himself quickly. 'Mrs Horner's predicament is far worse than mine, of course, and that should never be forgotten.'

'Do exactly what you're told, sir.'

'Where will you be, Mr Skillen?'

'It's best if you don't know.'

'Why not?'

'You won't be tempted to look in my direction.'

'That makes sense.'

'Obey your orders, sir.'

Beyton was anxious. 'But you will be nearby, won't you?'

'I won't abandon you.'

'And you still remain optimistic?'

'Having seen the location they've chosen, I'm more than optimistic,' said Peter with conviction. 'It's a part of London that I know extremely well. I'll be at hand, I assure you and I'll have assistance.'

'From whom, may I ask?'

The question went unanswered.

Vincent Diamond and Jane Holstock rode along Park Lane in a trap and took note of the preparations being made in Hyde Park. Fences were being put up, platforms were being erected and hundreds of chairs were being unloaded from wagons. Tents and canopies were going up everywhere. Men were working into the evening to get everything ready for the forthcoming celebrations to mark the victory against Napoleon at the Battle of Waterloo.

'We'll take a stroll through the park tomorrow to get a closer look,' said Diamond. 'Everything seems well advanced.'

'The Prince Regent will be pleased.'

'He enjoys showing off and where better to flaunt than on an occasion like this when the eyes of London will be upon him?'

'The Duke of Wellington will have pride of place, however.'

'He'll insist upon it, Jane. He, after all, is the conquering hero. That's not what *I'd* call him, mark you,' he said, darkly, 'but it is how he's perceived in England and, as we both know, perception is everything.'

'I couldn't agree more.'

He flicked the reins to draw a faster pace from the horse then turned to her.

'What do you think Beyton will do?' he asked.

'I think we've brought him to heel this time, Vincent. We'll get the money.'

'We'll ruin him if we don't. Why on earth did he set his sights on someone like Mrs Horner?' he asked in tones of disbelief. 'It's such a grotesque dalliance. Can you imagine the two of them together?'

'I can't imagine Beyton with *any* woman. He's so unappealing.'

'There's a cruder word for it.'

'I'd like to be there when they meet again,' she said with relish. 'If I'd had to undergo the privations that she's suffering,

I'd have a few choice words to say to Mr Beyton, even if it meant that I'd lose my job.'

'That's not an issue, is it?'

'I think that it might be.'

'After all that's happened,' he said, 'she won't even consider going back to the Home Office, surely.'

'Oh, I think that she will.'

'Why do you say that?'

'Well, a vacancy is about to occur, isn't it?'

He went off into a peal of laughter and put an arm around her.

Ruth Levitt worked at twice her normal speed; cleaning each of the rooms in the order she'd set herself. The night watchman let himself into the Home Office at regular intervals to check that all was well before continuing his round of the other buildings in the vicinity. It meant that she knew exactly how much time she had at her disposal. When she'd dusted the last desk and emptied the last wastepaper basket, she hurried downstairs and went into the Home Secretary's office. Placing the candelabrum on the desk, she took out a skeleton key and inserted it into the drawer. When it failed to engage with the lock, she jiggled it about as instructed and heard a satisfying click. The drawer now opened without resistance.

She knew exactly what she was looking for and did so as swiftly as she was able, sifting through a pile of documents until she came to one that had especial interest. Ruth had come prepared. Taking some paper from her bag, she put it on the desk then picked up the quill. She proceeded to copy something out in a neat hand. When that task was done, another remained and it required a second search through the documents. She soon found what she was after. There was far too much for her to copy out this time so she made a series of notes instead, making sure that she included the pertinent details. She worked swiftly and with a sense of mounting excitement. Once her notes were finished, she put all the documents back in their original order and slipped them into the drawer before shutting it. The skeleton key worked instantly this time. She took the candelabrum into the hall, extinguished all but one candle then waited for the night watchman to arrive. Minutes later, he let himself in.

'Have you finished, Mrs Levitt?' he asked.

'Yes, thank you. Mr Doggett.'

'No problems to report?'

'There are none at all.'

'Then I bid you good night.'

'Good night, Mr Doggett.'

He stood aside so that she could walk past him and out through the open door.

'I'll see you tomorrow,' he called after her.

But she made no reply and, as she was swallowed up by the darkness, he could not see that she was smiling quietly to herself.

CHAPTER TWENTY-ONE

Anne Horner had gone through a whole range of emotions. The naked fear she'd felt during the abduction had changed to anger, moved on to indignation, settled briefly into a mood of defiance then declined slowly into a sense of hopelessness. She no longer even thought of release, still less of escape or even survival. There was simply no future to contemplate outside the narrow confines of the cellar. It was as if her mind had shrunk to the same dimensions as her little world. Except for the variation in the times of her meals, each day was the same. She ate, she moved about awkwardly, she sat in a state of utter boredom and she slept. She had even come to accept the basic sanitary arrangements as being the norm. Anne lacked the strength to protest and the pride to feel humiliation at her treatment.

It was Jane Holdstock who brought the meal that morning, setting down the tray in front of the prisoner. Her buoyancy came in sharp relief to the despair of the older woman.

'Cheer up, Anne,' she said. 'Today might be a special one for you.'

'Don't taunt me.'

'I am perfectly serious. If your friend behaves himself, you might see the last of this place.'

'You said that before.'

'He tried to deceive us,' explained Jane, 'and that was very silly. We've given him a second chance that is also his *last* chance.' Anne gave no reaction. 'There's something that intrigues us. What attracted you to a man like that?'

'Leave me alone.'

'Or were you given no choice in the matter?'

Anne turned her head away. 'I don't want to talk about it.'

'In effect, *he* put you in here and only he can get you out.'

'Why do you have to hurt me so much?' pleaded Anne. 'Isn't it enough to chain me up and keep me down here?'

'It's only for a certain length of time.'

'You're taunting me again.'

'That's not true.'

'How would *you* like to be locked up?' She rattled the chain. 'How would you like to have this around your leg?'

Jane was annoyed. 'I'm trying to help you,' she said, irritably, 'but you just don't want to be helped, do you?' She went back to the door. 'Enjoy the meal. It may be your last in here.'

She walked out and slammed the bolt home. Anne sagged back into despair.

Tom O'Gara stood beside the bulwark and waited for his friend to surface. Moses Dagg had been for what he hoped would be a refreshing swim in the river but he was still weakened by the fight and not able to stay in there for long. Breaking the surface, he tossed his head then made for the ship. O'Gara threw the rope overboard and slowly hauled him back on deck. When he'd finally come aboard, Dagg flopped down on his back. He was breathing heavily.

'How do you feel, Moses?'

'Half-dead.'

'I hope you didn't swallow any water. The Thames is an open sewer.'

'I needed a swim, Tom. You should have come in with me.'

'I'd rather stay here.'

Dagg could feel the warmth of the sun on his naked body slowly drying him off. After a couple of minutes, he made an effort to sit up and left a wet patch on the deck where his back had been. Having wallowed in the Thames, he'd been both cleansed and wearied. Though the injuries sustained during the fight still smarted a little, he felt less pain than before.

'I want to go home, Tom,' he said.

'We both do.'

'London is not the place for me. I could never settle here.'

'We're sailors. We can't settle anywhere. We're born to roam.'

'How much longer must we stay?'

'We're here until we get satisfaction one way or the other,' said O'Gara.

'They're still out looking for us. We've escaped from them twice now. We might not be so lucky the third time.'

'It's not luck, Moses; it's a blend of skill and courage. We escaped from Dartmoor during a massacre. If the soldiers had been able to shoot straight, we'd have been killed. Dodging a few Runners is child's play compared to that. Besides, we have Dermot on our side. He'll look out for us.'

'Why is he being so helpful?'

'I'm his cousin.'

'I think there's more to it than that.'

'There is,' said O'Gara. 'His father died in an English prison so Dermot knows what it's like to be caged. He only visited his father once. When he went there the second time, the prison doctor said that he'd died of smallpox. Dermot didn't believe him. His father – my Uncle Harry, that is – was like you and me. He wouldn't let anyone push him around. He'd have been a troublemaker in prison. It might have got him killed. That's why my cousin has sympathy for us,' he said. 'We're like my Uncle Harry. Now go and put some clothes on. Dermot will be here any moment.'

Hauling himself up, Dagg padded off towards the cabin, leaving his friend on deck. O'Gara looked down the river at a three-masted vessel that was making its way upstream towards him. The sight revived memories of his time in the navy and he longed to resume his life as a sailor. It was, however, an ambition that had to be set aside for the moment. The persistent yapping of a dog sent him to the other side of the deck and he looked down to see Fallon waiting to come aboard. He lowered the gangplank then stood aside as the dog raced past him. As soon as his cousin had stepped on deck, O'Gara pulled up the gangplank.

'I've got bad news, Tom,' said Fallon, waving a newspaper. 'They've not delivered a verdict yet but it looks as if the commission has made up their mind.'

'Did they read that account we sent them?'

'I don't know.'

'That's what actually happened, Dermot, word for word.'

'It's what you and Moses told them but you're only two voices against a lot of others. The most important one is the governor's. They were always likely to believe him instead of you.'

'So what's the decision?'

Fallon opened the newspaper. 'This only says what they *think* will happen.'

'And what's that?'

'Well, to start with, they call it a riot and not a massacre. Your name is mentioned as the person who started it.'

'That's a lie!' shouted O'Gara, seizing the paper from him and reading it. 'Justifiable homicide! Is that what they call it? Captain Shortland orders his men to fire on unarmed prisoners and it's justifiable homicide?'

'They've closed ranks against you, Tom.'

'Didn't they listen to *anything* we said?'

'There's worse to come,' Fallon pointed out. 'If you read to the end, you'll see that the governor is not only cleared of any blame, he's likely to win promotion.'

O'Gara was furious. 'They're going to reward him for inciting murder?'

Scrunching up the newspaper, he flung it to the deck and stamped on it in disgust, ridding himself of a torrent of bad language as he did so. Fallon waited until his cousin's rage had cooled slightly.

'You ought to read something else in there, Tom,' he

suggested. 'It's the details about those celebrations in Hyde Park. Viscount Sidmouth will be there.'

'Then there'll be another case of justifiable homicide!' vowed O'Gara.

While he now had the money in his possession, David Beyton had had to endure another difficult meeting with the bank manager. The latter's disapproval was put in forceful terms. Striking an episcopal pose, Holland had looked as if he was about to excommunicate his client. Beyton closed his ears to the criticism. All that he could think about was what lay ahead. Grosvenor Square was within walking distance of the bank but, when he set out, he suddenly felt vulnerable. Peter Skillen had accompanied him to the first exchange and given him a sense of security. That no longer existed. Carrying a large amount of money in a leather pouch, he felt that the eyes of every thief in London were upon him and that he might be robbed before he even reached his destination. The consequences would be momentous. Anne Horner's life would be imperilled, Beyton's adultery would be made known to his wife and nearly all of their capital would disappear. His brisk walk suddenly became an undignified trot.

When he got to Grosvenor Square, he slowed down and tried to regain some poise. His instructions were to walk around the perimeter of the square until someone intercepted him. His head darted in all directions, searching for Peter Skillen as well as for the person who'd relieve him of the ransom. After walking around all four sides of the square, he began to wonder if he'd mistaken the instructions. Nobody came and there was no sense that anybody was watching him. A few pedestrians strolled past him and there was the occasional carriage and rumbling wagon. Beyton started a second peregrination but this, too, yielded no result. Losing his nerve, he stopped and glanced over his shoulder. The long wait was agonising. Were they deliberately making him suffer?

It happened so fast that he was left in a state of confusion. A gig came round a corner at speed then the horse slid to a halt beside him. The driver leapt out to seize the bag from him then jumped back into the gig, snapping the reins to set the animal in motion again. When the vehicle disappeared around a corner, all that Beyton could hear was the rasping echo of its wheels.

It was over as quickly as that.

With the aid of a telescope, Peter Skillen had watched it all from the window of a house on a corner. Running into the square, he waved his arms and the signal brought another gig into view. It was driven by Jem Huckvale with Charlotte Skillen by his side. Peter indicated the direction in which the first vehicle had gone and the other one went in pursuit. Beyton ran across the square to Peter.

'Why didn't you stop him?' he demanded.

'We want to catch both of them, sir, and we needed the man to think that you'd obeyed his orders. My wife is following him.'

'With respect to Mrs Skillen, what use is a woman in this situation?'

'She's there to allay suspicion, sir. Had *I* been trailing the kidnapper, he'd know that I was after him because he's seen me before. If he looks over his shoulder now, he'll think he sees a lady being driven by a servant. But you must excuse me,' he went on. 'We don't want them to get too far ahead.'

At that moment, Paul Skillen rode into the square with another horse in tow. When the two animals clattered to a halt, Peter was in the saddle at once. He and his brother set off together at a steady canter, leaving an open-mouthed Beyton staring after the twins in wonderment.

Huckvale was a skilful driver. Keeping the other gig in sight, he stayed well behind it so that he didn't attract attention. When other vehicles got between him and the gig he was pursuing, however, his vision was obscured and he was forced to reduce speed. He thought he saw the vehicle turn into a side street but he couldn't be sure. When he drove down the same narrow thoroughfare, he saw that the street was empty. Annoyed with himself, he pulled the horse to a halt.

'We've lost them,' he sighed.

'They definitely came into this street,' said Charlotte. 'Perhaps they turned left at the far end. Go on slowly, Jem.'

Before he could drive on, Huckvale heard the sound of horses behind him. Peter and Paul trotted up to the trap.

'Where are they?' asked Peter.

'We don't know,' admitted Huckvale.

'They must have turned left off this street,' said Charlotte.

'Then we're in luck,' said Paul.

'Why?'

'I know it. It's a cul-de-sac.' He dismounted. 'Let's go on foot. Jem can look after the horses. If we go galloping up the street, we'll give the game away.'

The first thing that Vincent Diamond did as he entered the house was to hold up the bag like a trophy. Jane Holdstock threw her arms around him and kissed him. Then the money was emptied onto the table and they gloated, each picking up a handful of banknotes and letting them cascade down again.

'This will make our work much easier,' said Diamond. 'With this amount of money at our disposal, we can bribe almost anyone.'

'Beyton obviously did as we instructed.'

'There was no sign of anyone else in Grosvenor Square. When we've moved to the other house, we'll send him word of where the prisoner is being held then he can come and release her.'

She laughed. 'That will be a touching reunion. I'll be sorry to miss it.'

'What I'll miss is seeing Beyton's face when he realises that his indiscretions led to far more than a mere demand for money. In fact . . .'

He broke off. Standing beside the front window, he'd seen movement on the opposite side of the street. When he peered through the glass, he tensed.

'We've got to go,' he said, decisively.

'Why?'

'I was followed, after all. The man out there is the one we

saw with Beyton in Hyde Park. That fool has double-crossed us. Quick – out through the back door.'

'But we can't just leave everything, Vincent.'

'Run, woman!'

Gathering up handfuls of money, he stuffed them into the bag then led the way to the back of the house. A few seconds later, Peter Skillen crossed the street and looked in through the front window.

Paul Skillen, meanwhile, had worked his way round to the gate at the rear of the garden. When he tried to open it, he found that it was locked. The next moment, he heard hurried footsteps coming down the garden and stood back in readiness. The door was unbolted then opened and two figures appeared. Paul accosted them and told them that they were under arrest. The man was startled; unable to believe that the person he'd just seen in the street was now in the lane at the rear of the house. It seemed impossible. He recovered quickly. When he tried to push past, Paul grappled with him, knocking the bag from his arms and sending banknotes all over the ground. The fight was short-lived because Jane was armed. Taking a pistol from inside her coat, she knocked off Paul's hat then used the butt of the weapon to strike the back of his skull. The blow was enough to daze him. Diamond threw him against the garden wall and Paul's head struck the hard stone, knocking him unconscious at once.

Jane bent down to gather up the money but Diamond pulled her away.

'Forget that,' he snarled. 'Just run!'

* * *

He knew that it was the right house because the gig he'd seen earlier was standing outside. After knocking on the door for the best part of a minute, Peter decided on a different mode of entry. Taking out his pistol, he smashed the window then knocked the remaining shards out of the way before climbing gingerly into the house. After a quick search of the rooms on the ground floor, he went upstairs with the pistol cocked but the place was empty. Through a window in the back bedroom, he saw his brother stagger in through the garden gate with one hand to his head. Peter hared down the steps and out into the garden, rushing across to support him.

'What happened, Paul?'

'I was struggling with the man when the woman – Mrs Holdstock, I suppose it must have been – hit me from behind with something. I went out like a snuffed candle. By the time I'd regained consciousness, they'd disappeared.' He managed a weak grin. 'But I managed to save the money,' he continued. 'It's scattered all over the place.' He glanced at the house. 'How did you get in, Peter?'

'I had to smash the window.'

'What did you find?'

'I haven't had time to do a proper search. But you need a wet cloth on that bruise of yours,' he said, looking at the back of his brother's head. 'There's no blood but the lump is already coming up.'

'I know. I can feel it. To be honest . . .'

'Be quiet!' said Peter, cutting him short. 'And *listen*.'

'What am I listening for?'

'I thought I heard a voice.'

They fell silent and looked around. The sound was very faint but they both heard it. Peter sensed that it came from the grating above the cellar. Crossing over to it, he knelt down and peered in.

'Is anyone there?' he called.

The reply was more audible. 'Yes, I am.'

'Is that you, Mrs Horner?'

Charlotte had not been included in her husband's plan simply to assist in the pursuit of one of the kidnappers. Peter had rightly assumed that, if they were led to the house in which the two of them were staying, their hostage would be there as well. He wanted his wife at hand to comfort a woman who'd been through a frightening ordeal and that's exactly what Charlotte did. When she was released from the cellar, Anne Horner was almost delirious with relief but she was also weakened by her ordeal and largely incomprehensible. Charlotte made her lie down in one of the bedrooms and went to get a drink to revive her. But the luxury of a feather bed was too seductive and Anne fell into a deep and restful sleep.

The brothers, meanwhile, gathered up all the banknotes in the garden and put them back into the leather bag. They then conducted a search of the whole house and put everything they found on the table in the dining room. There were so many surprises that Paul forgot all about the thudding ache at the back of his skull. He picked up the bow and arrow.

'I suppose that I was lucky,' he said. 'If she'd had this, she'd have fired an arrow at me instead of simply knocking me unconscious.'

'It wouldn't have been an ordinary arrow, Paul,' said his brother. 'That might wound but it wouldn't necessarily kill you. This, however, would.'

Holding a small bottle he'd just uncorked, he sniffed it and passed it over.

'What is it?' asked Paul, smelling the liquid in turn.

'I'd say it was poison.'

'Do you think it was going to be used on the arrow head?'

'It's very likely. That's why it was attached to the quiver. I want an apothecary to test it first. He'll tell us how lethal it might be.'

'For whom was a poisoned arrow intended?'

'They had someone in mind.'

They sorted their way through the other items, which included the purse that was handed over by Beyton in Hyde Park. As promised by Peter, all of his money had now been retrieved but he'd failed to arrest the kidnappers. Paul picked up some sheets of paper and scanned them. His eye was immediately caught by something.

'*Your* name is on here, Peter,' he said in surprise.

His brother took the sheet of paper from him. 'Where?'

'It's near the top.'

'So it is – and so are one or two other names I recognise. I worked with this man in France,' said Peter, pointing someone out. Thinking it through, he was very disturbed. 'Do you know what this might be?'

'What?'

'It's a list of names and addresses of agents who worked or still are working for the British government. This is highly

confidential and could only have come from the Home Office.'
He put it down. 'How could Mrs Holdstock and her accomplice
possibly have got their hands on it?'

'You might ask the same question of this,' said Paul, reading
another sheet of paper. 'It's the seating plan for His Royal
Highness and other dignitaries at the celebrations in Hyde
Park.'

Peter looked over his shoulder. 'Heavens!' he exclaimed as
he studied the notes. 'This is what they're really interested in.
They didn't abduct Mrs Horner simply in order to hold her to
ransom. They wanted her out of the way so that they could
get someone into the Home Office in place of her. This whole
business is a plot devised by French patriots who refuse to accept
our victory at Waterloo. They mean to strike back.' He took the
seating plan from his brother and inspected it. 'Somebody on
here was destined to have a poisoned arrow in his back.'

Anne Horner could not believe the kindness that was being
shown to her. After the horrors of her imprisonment, she
was treated with excessive care and respect. When she'd had
a restorative sleep for an hour or so, she came awake to see
Charlotte seated beside her. Anne was pathetically grateful for
her rescue.

'Who are you and how did you find me?'

There seemed no point in distressing her with details of the
ransom demand and a reminder of her ill-fated relationship
with a clerk at the Home Office. Charlotte simply told her that
she belonged to a detective agency and that they'd managed
to track the kidnappers to that address. While Anne had been

sleeping, Huckvale had made some enquiries of the neighbours. It transpired that the house had been rented on a short-term lease that was about to expire. Little had been seen of the man and woman who lived there and no servant had been spotted at all. One neighbour talked of hearing strange noises from the cellar of the house but had not connected them with a kidnap victim.

'All we know is that the woman called herself Mrs Holdstock,' explained Charlotte. 'She came to our shooting gallery and took lessons in archery.'

'*That* must have been the noise that I heard,' said Anne. 'It was a sort of thud.' Her eyes filled with tears. 'I can't tell you how I feel, Mrs Skillen. It's been a nightmare. I thought I'd never escape from that cellar.'

'You're free now, Mrs Horner. As soon as you feel well enough, we'll take you back to our house and send for a doctor to examine you. While you're recovering, you'll be a guest under our roof.'

'But you don't even *know* me.'

'We know enough to make you very welcome.'

Anne reached out to squeeze her hand in gratitude then burst into tears.

David Beyton had been on tenterhooks. He'd made a provisional arrangement to meet Peter Skillen at a tavern but had to wait a couple of hours before the latter eventually turned up. Beyton leapt up from his chair.

'I thought you'd never come,' he said, anxiously.

'We had a lot to do, Mr Beyton.'

'What happened? Did you catch them? Is Mrs Horner safe? Where's my money?' Peter put the leather bag on the table. 'Thank goodness!' exclaimed the other, grabbing it. 'I thought I'd lost it for ever.'

'It's all there, sir, including the first amount that you handed over.'

'My bank manager will be thrilled to see it back in the account.'

'Are you going to tell him the truth this time?' Beyton sat down guiltily and Peter took the seat opposite him. 'As for your other questions, I'm pleased to tell you that Mrs Horner is safe and apparently unharmed.'

'Where have you taken the kidnappers?'

'They got away, I fear,' confessed Peter.

'You mean that they're still at liberty?' cried the other, eyes protruding in fear. 'If they know that I tricked them, they'll do what they threatened.'

'We've no way of stopping them, Mr Beyton.'

'You were meant to arrest them.'

'We did our best,' said Peter, levelly. 'We followed them to the house where they were staying and recovered some valuable evidence but Mrs Holdstock and her accomplice escaped through the garden.'

'This is dreadful. They're bound to tell my wife now.'

'Then I suggest that you go straight home and tell her yourself first. We've saved Mrs Horner's life and restored your money to you. We've also learnt that the ransom demand was only part of a much wider conspiracy. In view of that,' said Peter, 'we feel that we've achieved something important. There's danger ahead but at least we know in what form it's going to come.' He looked with disgust at Beyton, clutching his money to his chest. 'Count your money, sir,' he advised, 'then do what you should have done already and have a long, honest conversation with your wife.'

When she took Anne Horner back to the house, Charlotte had a hip bath filled with cans of hot water so that the woman could feel clean again. Since her own clothing was badly sullied, Anne was given the loan of various items. After she'd had refreshment, she asked if she could lie down. Charlotte conducted her to a bedroom and made sure that she was comfortable. When she came downstairs, she found that Paul had arrived.

'How is she?' he asked.

'She's very tired and still very confused.'

'Has she been seen by a doctor?'

'I've sent for one but I don't think there's any physical harm. It's her mind that's been damaged, Paul. She still can't believe that she's free at last.'

'They had her chained up in that cellar.'

'I know,' said Charlotte, sadly. 'She told me about it. Compared to hers, my life is so privileged. While she was being treated like an animal, I was free and living in comfort, enjoying a night at the theatre, shopping in Piccadilly, visiting friends, working at the gallery and doing all the things that I love to do. I was in heaven while she was in hell.'

'Poor woman,' said Paul. 'I do sympathise. But I'm glad that you mentioned your trip to Piccadilly. I've been thinking about the way that you were spurned by that actress.' He feigned ignorance. 'What was her name again?'

'Miss Granville – Miss Hannah Granville.'

'In my experience, thespians usually lap up praise of all kinds.'

'That's what she did at first,' recalled Charlotte. 'When I congratulated her on her performance, she was all smiles. But as soon as I told her that Peter and I had thoroughly enjoyed the play, she took offence and stormed off.'

Paul was roused. 'Were those your actual words?'

'No, I merely said that my husband and I were entranced by her.' She looked at him shrewdly. 'Are you all right, Paul? Did I upset you in some way?'

There was a long pause while his brain whirred. He then became aware that she was still eyeing him with consternation.

'No, no,' he replied, kissing her on the cheek by way of apology. 'You haven't upset me at all, Charlotte. I'm sorry. My mind strayed for a moment. Let's think about Mrs Horner,' he said, pretending to do so. 'She has first call on our attention.'

Peter Skillen showed the papers to the Home Secretary and explained how he believed they'd come into the hands of the attackers. Sidmouth was flabbergasted. Torn between gratitude and alarm, he didn't know whether to thank Peter for uncovering a conspiracy or to contemplate the horror of what had occurred. In the event, he unlocked his desk and took out a pile of documents. They were in the precise order in which they'd always been.

'Somebody gained access to them, my lord,' said Peter.

'But everyone on my staff is entirely trustworthy. That's why I appointed them. I've known them for years.'

'You haven't known your necessary woman for years.'

'Levitt? No, I can't believe that it was her.'

'She was alone in here during the night, my lord. If she were in league with the conspirators, they'd have provided her with a means of opening that drawer. If they can rent a fine house like the one we saw, they obviously have funds. Mrs Levitt will have been offered far more than she could earn doing menial chores here.'

'No, no,' said Sidmouth. 'She came with the highest recommendation and she arrived at a time when we most needed her.'

'Isn't that enough in itself to arouse suspicion?' asked Peter. 'She may have done good service while she was here but I'll wager than you never set eyes on her again.' He indicated the papers. '*That's* what she came for, my lord.' Sidmouth reeled. 'May I suggest that you keep all documents of real importance in a safe? Having had the honour of serving as an agent in France, I was pleased to see my name recorded in the list but it was very unwise to add my address. That should have been kept separately by you alone.'

'You are right, Mr Skillen,' admitted the other. 'I've been too lax. It won't happen again. As for Levitt, if she really *is* involved in this conspiracy, I will hang my head in shame. It never crossed my mind for a second that we'd allowed a French spy to work here.'

'Who recruited her, my lord?'

'It was one of my undersecretaries. And before you accuse

him,' he went on, 'let me tell you that Grocott is a man of unimpeachable character. Levitt was, I seem to recall, recommended by a friend at his club.'

'Then you need to know who that friend was, my lord, because the chances are that he, too, is implicated in some way.'

'Dear me!' exclaimed Sidmouth. 'We have enemies all around us, it seems.'

'Victory on a battlefield is never a final event,' said Peter. 'There will always be those who yearn for revenge, alas, so the conflict continues in other ways.'

'It's not only vengeful Frenchmen we must fear.'

'Who else, my lord?'

Sidmouth picked up the copy of *The Times* on his desk and waved it.

'This contains an article about the deliberations of the joint commission on the massacre at Dartmoor prison. Someone has leaked their verdict in advance.'

'What is it?'

'It's one of justifiable homicide,' said Sidmouth. 'How will Thomas O'Gara and Moses Dagg react to that, do you think?'

Dermot Fallon hired a horse and cart so that all three of them could drive to a leafy suburb where they'd be unlikely to be disturbed. When they'd found a wood that suited their purpose, O'Gara used a dagger to carve something into the trunk of a tree. As he stepped back, the others saw that it was the shape of a head.

'You go first, Moses,' said O'Gara.

Dagg had already loaded the pistol. Holding it at arm's

length, he took aim and fired. There was a loud report then O'Gara examined the tree.

'Well done!' he said. 'You blew his brains out first time.'

Hannah Granville was still in turmoil. While her career as an actress had reached a new peak, her private life was tortured with regret. She still found it difficult to believe that she'd been so comprehensively deceived by Paul Skillen. The realisation had been a severe blow to her. In an effort to shed her preoccupation with him, she went to the theatre an hour earlier than usual that evening so that she could be alone in her dressing room and concentrate on the performance that lay ahead. She was greeted by the stage doorkeeper who gave her several letters of congratulation that had been delivered by hand. Hannah looked forward to reading them. When she entered the dressing room, however, there was no chance of even opening them because she had company. Paul Skillen was seated in a chair.

'Good evening, Hannah,' he said, rising to his feet.

'How did *you* get in here?' she gasped.

'I always told you that I was resourceful.'

She turned away. 'I'll have you thrown out at once.'

'No, no,' he said, stepping between her and the door. 'Please listen to what I have to say. If you still wish me to go, I'll walk out of your life for ever.'

'You've already done that, Paul. When I saw you in the audience with your wife, I saw how cruelly I'd been misled.'

He laughed. 'So that's it! I prayed that it might be.'

'It's hardly a subject for amusement.'

'I'm laughing with relief, Hannah, don't you see? My

sister-in-law told me what happened when she met you in that shop in Piccadilly. You snubbed her.'

Hannah froze. 'Did you call her your sister-in-law?'

'Yes, her name is Charlotte.'

'She told me that she was your wife. I saw her with you *twice*.'

'What you saw was my twin brother, Peter,' he explained. 'We are often mistaken for each other.' She remained unconvinced. 'If you don't believe me, I'll take you to their house after the performance and you'll see for yourself.'

'Why didn't you tell me that you had a twin brother?'

'I wanted you all to myself, Hannah – and I still do.'

Her voice softened. 'You've given me so much anguish, Paul.'

'Then I apologise unreservedly. By the same token, however, you've given me great pain. How do you think I felt when I saw you leaving the theatre with that handsome young man?' She stifled a laugh. 'Don't deny it. By the sound of it, you were seen with him by my sister-in-law as well. He's my replacement.'

'Yes, I was seen with him,' she confessed, 'but Felix is not a replacement for you. It would be very improper, for a start. Felix Dalrymple is my half-brother. He was in London for a few days so we spent time together, that is all. I needed a man to keep my admirers at arm's length and Felix did that admirably. How strange!' she went on. 'I have been in agony over this phantom wife of yours and you thought that I'd turn to the first man who paid me a charming compliment. What a pair we are, Paul!'

The differences between them had suddenly dissolved completely. Hannah no longer wanted him to abandon the dangerous work that meant so much to him and Paul no longer bridled at the thought that someone was imposing limitations on him. In retrospect, their disagreement seemed petty. All that mattered now was that they were back together again.

Paul smiled at her. 'Why don't you lock that door?'

When they tumbled out of The Peacock that night, Micah Yeomans and Alfred Hale had drunk so much that they needed the assistance of a wall to remain upright. After staggering the best part of a hundred yards, they rested against the window of a tailor's shop. Yeomans was offended.

'The Doctor has done it again,' he complained. 'He's giving someone else undeserved credit. We had to listen to him praising the Skillen brothers for rescuing that woman when he should have been berating them for letting the villains get away to cause even worse trouble. Luckily, *we're* the ones who'll be guarding the Doctor at the celebration. We'll show Peter and Paul how it should be done.'

Hale was worried. 'We could be in danger ourselves, Micah.'

'We live with that danger every day.'

'This is different,' said the other. 'We know the streets of London. Wherever we go, we can take care of ourselves. There'll be thousands of people in Hyde Park on the great day. An attack could come from any of them. We can't possibly keep an eye on them all.' He gave a shiver. 'I don't fancy being shot in the back with a poisoned arrow.'

'That won't happen, Alfred,' said the other, contemptuously. 'That warning about a poisoned arrow was nonsensical. It was dreamt up by Peter Skillen to give the Doctor a fright.'

'But they found a bow and arrow and a bottle of poison.'

'So they say.'

'According to the apothecary who examined it, that poison would have been fatal. Just imagine that, Micah.'

'I don't believe a word of it,' said Yeomans with an extravagant gesture. 'And I certainly don't believe that Mrs Levitt is involved in the conspiracy. She's there to clean the rooms, for heaven's sake. She probably can't even read or write.'

Bernard Grocott also had doubts that Ruth Levitt was in any way responsible for the theft of secret information from the Home Office. Having found and appointed her, he felt that he knew her better than anybody. He'd also enjoyed the praise of his colleagues for replacing Anne Horner so soon and with such an efficient deputy. Grocott refused to believe that his judgement had been so fallible. When he let himself into the building early the next morning, he expected to find every room as clean as it usually was and every desk gleaming. Entering his office, however, he had a profound shock. It was exactly as he'd left it the previous evening. The place had reverted to its earlier chaos. She was gone. Ruth Levitt had not been anywhere near the Home Office.

Grocott slumped in his chair and braced himself for the collective censure of everyone with whom he worked. Admiration would very quickly turn to reproof. The woman he'd brought into the Home Office had been there as a spy. Colleagues would taunt him about that for a long time to come. The question that they – and the Home Secretary, for that matter – would ask was who had recommended her to Grocott in the first place. He searched his memory like a dog digging frantically for a bone but a name failed to appear. Grocott accepted the awful truth.

He didn't know.

Ruth Levitt was seated in the drawing room of her house with her guests. She had shed the crumpled dress she'd worn as a cleaner and was now wearing fine attire that altered her appearance completely. Her hair had been brushed and she had a dignity absent during her time at the Home Office. Having done what she was paid to do, she was distressed to hear that the information she'd gleaned had been lost. In her eyes, it meant that her time as a servant had been wasted. She was bitter.

'After all that effort, we have nothing to show for it,' she protested.

'That's not true,' said Diamond. 'Losing that list of names was a pity but I did have a chance to study the seating plan at the celebrations. I know exactly where our target will be sitting now.'

'What use is that if they're aware of your plan, Vincent? You were followed to the house by someone who'd certainly have searched it afterwards. If they're clever enough to find you, they'd have the intelligence to work out what you had in mind.'

'Then we simply amend the plan,' argued Jane. 'I know how you must feel, Ruth. It was demeaning for you to pretend to be a cleaner when you have servants at your beck and call here.'

'I did it because I believed in our cause.'

'And because you were extremely well paid,' Diamond pointed out.

'I earned my money,' she retorted. 'You didn't. Thanks to

your blunder, you lost everything that you'd extorted out of Beyton.'

'Forget about him. He betrayed us and we did as we threatened. His wife now knows all about his antics. He'd have got a frosty welcome home yesterday.'

'They'll be searching for us now,' said Jane.

'Yes,' he agreed, 'we must be very careful.'

'Well, they won't find me,' insisted Ruth, 'because the house is in my late husband's name. And they'll never work out that my maiden name was Regine Le Vite, hence the change to Levitt. Like both of you, I had a French father and an English mother.'

'My father died years ago,' he said, 'fighting against the British army.'

'Mine never lived to see France defeated,' said Jane, 'and I'm glad of it. It would have broken his heart to watch Napoleon being humbled and the royal family restored to the throne by our enemies.'

'Let's concentrate on our plan,' suggested Diamond. 'Since they found the bow and arrow, we'll have to abandon that mode of attack. It had the advantage of being unexpected but that's no longer the case.'

'What will we do?'

'It's more a question of what you and Ruth do.'

'I'll do anything I'm asked,' said Ruth, 'as long as it doesn't involve cleaning and polishing. A night at the Home Office used to leave me exhausted.'

'They've seen Jane and me,' he told her. 'They'll be on the lookout for a man and a woman. The sight of two women is unlikely to get a second look. You'll be at the celebrations together and I'll tell you exactly where to go.'

'The important thing is to have our escape planned,' said Jane.

'I'll take care of that. Within the week, we'll be back in France.'

'I'm staying here,' said Ruth. 'For the most part, I hate the British but I have to admit that life is London is very comfortable.'

'That's your decision,' said Jane.

There are still many details to work out,' said Diamond, 'but we have days to go yet so I have plenty of thinking time. I might even be able to solve the mystery that's been plaguing me ever since yesterday.'

Ruth was puzzled. 'What mystery is that?'

'How can I see a man out of the front window on the opposite side of the road then bump into him again when I run out of the garden gate? There's no way that he could have got there in time. It defies logic.'

Even if they'd stood side by side, nobody would have taken them for twins. Peter and Paul Skillen had used effective disguises. Both were dressed as gardeners with hats pulled down over their faces. Peter was wearing a false grey beard and moving at a speed commensurate with old age. Paul was pushing a wheelbarrow, stopping to pick up anything he found on the lush green sward in Hyde Park. It was two days before the celebrations and rehearsals were taking place. Marching in strict formation, the band practised one of its stirring military anthems. Peter knelt beside a flower bed and pretended to weed it.

The brothers were within a relatively short distance of the main platform. It was on that raised area, festooned with flags and bunting, that Viscount Sidmouth would be sitting with His Royal Highness, the Prince Regent, the Prime Minister and senior members of the government. Peter had reasoned that anyone with serious intentions of assassination would be certain to get the lie of the land in advance. Now that everything was finally set up, the rehearsal could be watched and the disposition of soldiers noted. Scores of people were about, drawn by curiosity and anxious to see the place where the celebrations would be held. It was impossible for Peter and Paul to pick out everyone who merited a closer inspection so they selected only the most obvious cases. All of the people who had so far been taking a more than casual interest in the main platform had turned out to be quite harmless.

Peter then spotted something of concern. A horse and cart pulled up on the road running alongside the park. Two men alighted and walked towards the main platform. There was nothing sinister about the pair. They might have been out for an afternoon stroll. It was the driver who alerted Peter. On a warm day, he was wearing a hood that all but obscured his face. What were still clearly visible, however, were the driver's black hands. Peter rose to his feet and removed his hat briefly by way of a signal to his brother. Leaving their work, they converged slowly on the platform. The two men from the cart didn't notice them at first. They were too absorbed in looking at the platform and walking around it.

Before they challenged the men, Peter and Paul made sure that they got between them and the cart, thereby cutting off their means of escape. When they got close enough, they heard Irish accents. It was the confirmation they needed.

'Good afternoon, Mr O'Gara,' said Peter.

'And the same to you, Mr Fallon,' added Paul.

The greetings had an immediate effect on the men. Their instinct was to run back to the cart but their way was blocked. They therefore tried to run around the brothers in a wide arc. Peter and Paul were far too quick for them, sprinting after a man apiece until they got within reach. Peter tackled O'Gara around the legs and brought him crashing to the ground, dazing him in the process. Paul jumped on Fallon's back and was carried a dozen yards before his weight was too much for the Irishman. A fierce fight developed between them. The advantage was very much with the detectives because they were working *with* the Bow Street Runners for once. Yeomans and his men had been lurking in some bushes in case they were needed. When they saw what was happening, they broke cover and ran towards the action.

Peter dragged O'Gara up by the scruff of his neck and handed him over to Yeomans and Hale. Intending to help his brother, he saw that Paul already had an able assistant. Ruddock had grabbed Fallon from behind and pinioned his arms. Both Irishmen had been caught. Attention now shifted to the horse and cart. Enraged by what he'd seen, Moses Dagg set out to rescue his friends. He flicked the reins and reinforced the command with a loud yell. The animal began cantering across the grass. When Dagg reached the little group, he hauled on the reins and the cartwheels threw up a series of divots as they ground to a halt.

Dagg reached inside his coat for his pistol but he was too slow. Paul had already leapt up onto the cart and seized him by the wrist so that the weapon pointed upwards. There was a ferocious struggle with O'Gara and Fallon urging on their man. Unaware of its implications, a small crowd gathered to watch the fight but it was soon over. The pistol went off, discharging its bullet harmlessly into the air, and the horse bolted. With the two men still grappling madly, the cart went careering across the grass and scattered everybody in its way. The horse was galloping towards some trees. When it got close, it suddenly veered off to the left, overturning the cart in the process and throwing its two occupants to the ground.

Releasing his hold on the other man, Paul did several impromptu somersaults before coming to a halt on the grass. He leapt up at once to continue the fight then saw that it was already over. Hurled from the cart, Dagg had fallen awkwardly and now lay motionless.

Viscount Sidmouth was so pleased with the turn of events that he walked up and down his office with barely subdued glee.

'All three of them were caught,' he said. 'O'Gara and Fallon are in custody and, since he broke his neck in the fall, Dagg will no longer be of concern us. The Skillen brothers have removed a terrible weight from my shoulders.'

'The Runners did their part,' Grocott reminded him. 'A word of praise to Yeomans and Hale will not come amiss, my lord.'

'Indeed, it won't.'

'And while one problem has been solved, another still remains.'

'I'm very cognisant of that.'

'It has caused me much soul searching,' said Grocott. 'I was unwittingly embroiled in the plot and am stricken with remorse.'

'Don't take it to heart,' advised the other.

'But I must, my lord. I should have realised that it was too great a coincidence. We lose one servant and another one drops into our hands straight away. Had I not been so unguarded at my club, a great deal of anguish would have been spared. As it is, I've finally remembered who put the name of Levitt in my ears.'

'You thought it might have been Sir Roger Hollington.'

'I checked with him,' said Grocott, 'and he denied it. The person he nominated was Joss Crowther, barely an acquaintance of mine. I've no means of furthering that acquaintance because he has withdrawn to an estate he owns in Normandy. In short, I'm ashamed to confess, he was a co-conspirator.'

'There are French spies everywhere, Grocott. That's why I employ so many agents of my own to counter their activities. Peter Skillen is the best of them.'

'Let's hope that he can frustrate the designs of these people.'

'I'm sure that he's working on a way to do just that.' Sidmouth took his seat behind the desk. 'Meanwhile, of course, we have the good news that Horner is to return to her duties. After recent events, I wouldn't have been surprised if she'd wanted to shake the dust of the Home Office from her feet for ever.'

'I'm told that she was determined to resume work.'

'She wants to put the horrors of the past behind her.'

He picked up some papers from the desk and looked through them. That was usually the signal for the undersecretary to leave so Grocott moved to the door.

'One moment,' said Sidmouth, raising his head, 'there's something I meant to ask you. Have you seen Beyton today?'

'Why do you ask, my lord?'

'I passed him on the stairs earlier on and he was completely cowed. He hardly noticed that I was there. Is he ailing in some way?'

'I really don't know, my lord. Now that you mention it, however, Beyton has been rather taciturn of late. When I told him that he was in line for a promotion, he was delighted. He should be revelling in the news.'

David Beyton was the first to arrive at the Home Office the next morning. Letting himself in, he went straight to the room that he shared with the other senior clerks. A shock awaited him. The desks of his three colleagues had been cleared of any papers and polished to a high sheen by Anne Horner. She'd not tidied away anything on Beyton's desk. Instead, she'd put a wastepaper basket on it. When he looked inside, it contained the pile of banknotes he'd once given her by way of a belated apology. In the wake of his domestic turmoil, it was a wounding blow. Removing the object from the desk, Beyton sat down, took out a sheet of paper and began to write a letter of resignation.

'The situation has changed,' said Diamond.

'I don't think so,' argued Jane.

'You read the report in the newspaper. In the light of what

happened with those fugitives from prison, security arrangements have been reviewed. That means far more guards will be around the main platform and the seating will be changed. We'll have no idea in advance where our target will be.'

'I agree with Vincent,' said Ruth. 'We must adapt our plan.'

'But we'd lose the very essence of it,' asserted Jane.

'That can't be helped.'

'The whole point of the exercise was that it would take place in public in front of a vast audience. It was to be a visible demonstration that France is not without its true patriots. We'd be sending a message that would echo around Europe.'

'We will still do that, Jane.'

'But not in the most effective way.'

'The matter is settled,' declared Diamond. 'We follow the new plan. Apart from anything else, it makes it far easier to ensure the safety of all of us. In a huge crowd in Hyde Park, we'd have had no real control. With the new plan, we do.'

'Very well,' said Jane, moodily, 'I agree to the change, but it's against my better judgement.'

He enfolded her in his arms. 'You say that now but, when it's all over, you'll want to celebrate just as much as we do. *Vive la France!*'

'*Vive la France!*' said the women in unison.

Arthur Wellesley, 1st Duke of Wellington, was a figure of towering importance. Victories achieved in India and Portugal had made him a national hero but his success at Waterloo, when outnumbered by the French, had sealed his reputation as a soldier of the highest order. Having fought off the many

English politicians who wanted to dismember and, thereby, weaken France, he was appointed Commander-in-Chief of the forces occupying Paris but was brought back to London to be at the heart of the celebrations in Hyde Park. A grateful nation was ready to acclaim their saviour.

As a man, however, he had faults. He had a brimming self-confidence that allowed him to ignore the advice of others and pursue his own objectives. Impatient, restless, occasionally irresponsible, he was too ready to pour contempt on some of the men serving under him. Iron discipline had helped him to control a turbulent coalition army and it defined the man. He was straight-backed, imperious and striking in appearance with an aquiline nose that had earned him the nickname of Old Hooky. It was his firm belief that the finger of God was upon him and he ascribed his success to the intervention of the Almighty. That did not prevent him from feeling a sense of entitlement and he luxuriated in the honours that were showered upon him. The celebrations that day were an act of homage to him and he intended to enjoy every moment of them. There would be speeches in his honour, martial music, military manoeuvres, lavish refreshments and, to cap it all, a grand firework display. It would be a memorable occasion in every way.

Massive crowds had already gathered at the venue but there was a sizeable number of well-wishers outside his house as well, waiting for a glimpse of him as he set off with his wife in the open carriage that awaited them. Wellington was the first to come into view, resplendent in his uniform and raising his hat in acknowledgement of the resounding cheers. Poised in the doorway, he turned his head in both directions so that all could see the beak-like nose.

Jane Holdstock saw him clearly. She was seated beside Ruth Levitt in a gig and she raised her whip in the air. It was a signal that brought Vincent Diamond cantering down the road on his horse with a pistol in his hand. When he got level with Wellington, he took aim and fired. From such a short distance away, he expected to score a direct hit but Wellington seemed to anticipate the shot and dived nimbly out of the way, rolling over on the ground before leaping straight up again. Diamond, meanwhile, had ridden on down the road, only to find that the gig bearing his accomplices had been stopped by a phalanx of armed soldiers and that the two women had been placed under arrest. Standing in front of the solid line was Peter Skillen, hands on hips and a challenging smile on his face. As Diamond's horse reared up on its back heels, Peter moved forwards to grab the rider but he was kicked away. Turning his mount in a semicircle, Diamond went back in the other direction but that exit was also now filled with soldiers.

Waiting in the centre of the road was the Duke of Wellington though he looked very different now. Coat and hat had been discarded and the famous nose had been halved in size. Diamond was bemused. He was looking at someone who bore an amazing resemblance to the man at the other end of the road. Paul Skillen took advantage of the rider's momentary confusion, rushing forwards to seize the bridle then reaching up to pull Diamond from the saddle.

'We fight on equal terms now,' he said, getting in the first punch.

Diamond fought back with unexpected savagery, punching,

kicking and trying to spit in Paul's face. He'd been deceived into thinking that he could shoot the Duke of Wellington when the man who'd emerged from the house had simply been his double. That realisation instilled extra venom into his blows but most of them were taken on Paul's arms and deflected. Years of practice in the boxing ring at the gallery had toughened him and taught him all the refinements of pugilism. He took the wind out of Diamond with a punch to the stomach then proceeded to deliver telling blows to his face and body. It was not long before he'd reduced his opponent to a shambling wreck. Gripping him by the collar, Paul hurled him into the arms of a waiting soldier.

'Take him away before I kill him,' he said.

The celebrations went on for hours and, as the Guest of Honour, the Duke of Wellington even took precedence over His Royal Highness, the Prince Regent. Everything went smoothly and without interruption, enabling Viscount Sidmouth to sit back and receive warm congratulations from the Prime Minister, Lord Liverpool. In every way, the event had been a signal of triumph.

Celebrations of another kind took place afterwards at the home of Peter and Charlotte Skillen. Paul was there and so were Gully Ackford and Jem Huckvale. Over a glass of wine, they talked about the way that the fugitives from Dartmoor had been thwarted and the agents from France had been arrested. Everyone was amazed at the accuracy of Paul's impersonation of the Duke of Wellington.

'Weren't you afraid?' asked Charlotte.

'I was more afraid of the Duke than of his would-be assassin.

It took an age to persuade him to let me act as his double. After all,' said Paul, 'everything depended on guesswork. We knew that someone was the target but who would it be?'

'I thought that it would be the Prince Regent,' said Ackford.

'And I was certain that it would be the Prime Minister,' admitted Huckvale.

'No,' said Peter, 'it was the Duke who symbolised the defeat of France. He was always going to be the most likely victim. Thanks to my brother, the Duke escaped the attack.' He turned to Paul. 'It was the nose that did the trick. It was so convincing. How ever did you manage that?'

'I have a dear friend, an actress,' said Paul, fondly, 'and she schooled me in the wonders of make-up. When she finishes playing Belvidera at the Theatre Royal, I intend to ask her for more instruction.'